HOMESICK

also by ESHKOL NEVO in english translation

World Cup Wishes

HOMESICK

a novel by ESHKOL NEVO

translated by SONDRA SILVERSTON

DALKEY ARCHIVE PRESS
CHAMPAIGN / LONDON

Originally published in Hebrew as *Arba'ah Batim Ve-Ga'agu'a* by
Kinneret, Zmora Bitan, Dvir Publishing House Ltd, 2004
Copyright © by Eshkol Nevo
English translation © by Eshkol Nevo
Worldwide translation copyright © The Institute for the Translation of Hebrew Literature
First U.S. edition, 2010

Library of Congress Cataloging-in-Publication Data

Nevo, Eshkol.
[Arba'ah batim ve-ga'agu'a. English]
Homesick : a novel / by Eshkol Nevo ; translated by Sondra Silverston. -- 1st U.S. ed.
p. cm.
ISBN 978-1-56478-582-4 (pbk. : alk. paper)
1. Jerusalem--Fiction. I. Silverston, Sondra. II. Title.
PJ5055.35.E92A7313 2010
892.437--dc22
2009054268

Partially funded by the University of Illinois at Urbana-Champaign
and by a grant from the Illinois Arts Council, a state agency

The Hebrew Literature Series is published in collaboration with
the Institute for the Translation of Hebrew Literature and sponsored by the
Office of Cultural Affairs, Consulate General of Israel in New York

www.dalkeyarchive.com

Cover: design and composition by Danielle Dutton
Printed on permanent/durable acid-free paper and bound in the United States of America

Prologue

In the end, he put all the remaining furniture out on the
street. A friend was supposed to come with a van and pick
it up. So he waited there. Sat down in an armchair and
nibbled on a pear. A neighbour was washing his car, a hose
in his hand. He remembered that when he was a child, he
used to watch the streams of water running off the cars to
see which would be the first to land. Now he looked at the
time. Half-past eight. His friend was fifteen minutes late.
That wasn't like him. Maybe, in the meantime, he should
arrange the furniture the way it would be in a living room.
Maybe not.

A woman whose bags he once carried from the shops
made her way between the sofas and smiled at him as if
she had something to say.

Another woman stumbled against the cabinet and grumbled: you're blocking the way.

1

Topographically, we're talking about a saddle. Two humps, and between them a shopping mall that's common ground for all. The hump where the Ashkenazim live is a well-tended town called Mevasseret. It has an air of optimism and the residents share it. The other, once a transit camp for new immigrants from Kurdistan, is a welter of shacks and villas, daisies and debris, tree-lined lanes and dirty streets. Its official name: Maoz Ziyon. Unofficially, it's called Castel, after the old army post on the top of the hill where soldiers fell during the War of Independence. Now it's a memorial site visited by their descendants. When you get there, right after the traffic lights, you'll find Doga and Sons. A small market with not much to it. But if you have a question to ask, that's where to do it.

*

A random sampling of announcements posted on the notice-board next to Doga and Sons: Course in practical Cabbala, call now and get a discount. New date set for the Boy Scout ceremony that was rained out. House calls by a certified cosmetician. Private maths lessons given by a qualified mathematician. Find your religious roots with Rabbi Itzhak Fein. The event will take place, rain or shine.

*

The man they asked at Doga made a mistake, and though they'd turned the right number of corners, Amir and Noa didn't find the apartment that was for rent, but ended up instead in a house of mourners. A large woman wept endlessly. Other women passed around trays of pastries and tea. No one noticed Noa and Amir, but they didn't feel right about leaving once they were there. Squeezed into a corner of the sofa, they listened to stories about the son killed in Lebanon and sneaked glances at their watches, wanting to be gone. Amir clasped his hands and thought: this is my chance to be really sad. Here I can stop trying to be happy and let the black squid ink of sadness flow through me freely. Noa played with her hair and thought: I have to pee. Funny how grief makes people want to eat.

An hour later, they stood up, nodded to the large weeping woman, made their way past knees and chairs to the door and went to find the apartment they'd been looking for.

But their passion in the search was gone, and they didn't feel the same urgency any more.

*

The apartment had two rooms. A living room the size of a kitchen. A kitchen the size of a bathroom. A bathroom with a squeegee to mop up the water that sprayed on to the floor from the shower. But none of that bothered them at all. And they didn't care that the landlord lived on the other side of the wall. Or that they'd lie in their bed with only an asbestos roof overhead. They'd decided to live together; nothing would stop them. Even though he was studying psychology in Tel Aviv and she photography in Jerusalem. Mevasseret is a good compromise, she said. Tel Aviv isn't so far, considering you have a car. And I love the light here, she added, it's so bright, so clear. He took her hand, led her to the window and said: We can plant a garden over there. The landlord, sensing he was about to clinch the deal, said: It's not like the city. There's parking everywhere.

*

A month earlier, when we were still trying to decide, I had

a dream. I'm pushing a heavy truck up the road to Jerusalem, pushing it from behind like Superman: from Lod to Modi'in, from Modi'in to Latrun, from Latrun onward. At first, I'm running effortlessly, the truck is flying forward and the wind is scattering my worries. But after the entrance to Sha'ar Hagai, when the road gets steeper, I suddenly start sweating and panting in an extremely un-Supermanly way. On the level section before the sheer climb up to the Castel, I can barely breathe and the truck is barely moving. Cars honk at me, children looking out of windows point at me and laugh, but still I continue, loyal to some demanding internal command, and with my last ounce of strength I manage to roll the truck to the top, to the Mevasseret bridge. And then, when I stop to catch my breath and take my hand off the truck for a minute to wipe the sweat off my forehead, it starts rolling backwards. On to me. I try to stop it, lean the entire weight of my body against it, but that doesn't help. My Supermanly strength is suddenly all gone, and now I'm just someone trying to stop a truck that weighs a hundred times more than I do. It's moving faster by the second. Shocked cars veer away from it at the last minute. A bus-stop support bends under it. And I'm running backwards, trying to slow it down by giving it small shoves and sticking a leg out in front of me, the way you do when you want to stretch your muscle. Despite my ridiculous efforts, the catastrophe – and this is clear to me in the dream too – is inevitable. And sure enough, at the bottom of the slope, a little before Abu Gosh, it happens. The truck hits a car that hits a car that hits a dividing wall. Twisted iron. Twisted limbs. A mosaic of glass and blood. The end.

When I woke up, filled with terror, I thought I understood the dream.

I called Noa and told her: Live together, yes. Closer to Jerusalem, yes. But not past Mevasseret.

*

4

Ah, yes, there's something else, the landlord said just as they were about to sign. Noa thought he was going to talk to them about the property tax or something like that. The neighbours over there, he said, lowering his voice a little and pointing to the house across the way, their son was just killed in Lebanon. So if you want to listen to music, try to keep the volume down. Of course, Amir said, no problem. We won't bother them, you'll see. And besides, Mr Zakian, Noa added, you don't know us yet, but we're a quiet couple. As quiet as can be.

*

I finally cried, but not because of what everyone thought – because my big brother, Gidi, had been killed, even though I loved him very much and my throat burned after the soldiers who came in the middle of the night left and Mum started screaming – but because all of a sudden I was sick and tired of no one paying attention to me. It all started when I cut my finger making salad for the people who came to the *shivah* and because of the onion that makes clouds around your eyes so you can't see where your finger is or where the knife is. The blood started coming out and filled the space between my nail and the pad of my finger – Mum taught me what to call that part of the finger – and Dad, who didn't do anything but fiddle with his pipe and sit next to Uncle Menashe without talking, said, can't you see I'm busy, Yotam, why are you making such a big deal out of it, it's just a little cut, where are the plasters, go and ask your mother where the plasters are. But Mum was in the middle of one of her 'Gidi, oy Gidi's and all her friends were sitting around her trying to calm her down, and to get to her I had to walk past all of them, so I stood behind a chair in a corner of the living room, not sure whether to go back to Dad or break through the circle around Mum, and in the meantime, the blood had already filled my whole hand, which is a very scary sight, even though I'm not a chicken, and all of a sudden, before I could control it and swallow the tears like I do sometimes when someone hurts my feelings in class, I started to cry, not a soft, small kind of crying, but a loud sobbing kind of crying, like a baby, and naturally all the ladies jumped right up and made a circle around me, and Mum hugged me tight and Aunt Miriam, her sister, ran to get a plaster, and they all whispered to each other, poor child, they were so close, and yelled for Miriam to hurry up, and the television guy who was outside interviewing Uncle Amiram – the family's official spokesman, not only because Mum and Dad didn't want to talk, but also because he's the head of a department in the Electric Company and knows how to express himself – the television guy must have heard that something was going on inside and he came in with his cameraman and tried to shove a microphone into Mum's mouth, but Uncle Amiram ran in after them saying, what are you doing, what are you doing, we agreed you wouldn't film inside the house, and the ladies shouted, get out, leeches, have you no shame, and started pushing the cameraman, they actually put their hands on his chest and shoved him till he was thrown outside with his huge camera, and then they went at Uncle Amiram, why did you let them in? and he said, I didn't, they just walked around me and went in, those bastards, and Aunt Miriam came back with a plaster and wrapped it around my finger gently, without hurting me, and stroked my hand and my cheek and whispered in my ear, I'll make the salad, OK?

*

When you say the word 'landlord', you think of an older, annoying man. This is not the case with Moshe Zakian. He's only a couple of years older than Amir (though he's Sima's husband and the father of two). A bus driver with a bald patch and a small potbelly hanging over his belt. He knows how to fix everything: locks, electrics, a blocked sewer. He doesn't talk much, he's more of a doer. And he's crazy about his wife. Anyone can see that. The way he always moons at her, as if she were a movie star. He does whatever she says. Nods his head yes whenever she talks. And when it comes to talking, she's one of a kind. Sharp tongue, sharp mind. You'll enjoy being here in the Castel, she says when Amir and Noa arrive with their belongings, you'll see. Everyone knows everyone else here, like a family. And it's quiet, so you can study without any noise to bother you. I wasn't always like this, she says, looking into Noa's eyes, I went to college too. Took courses in accounting. But now I stay at home because with the children, there's so much to do.

*

It took us only a day or two to set up the apartment. After all, what did we have? Not much. A sofa from my aunt, a desk from her parents, a few chairs from friends, knick-knacks and bric-à-brac we'd accumulated separately in our previous apartments, some of Noa's framed photographs on the wall, a mattress stained with our fucking, a TV with a colour button that didn't work. And that was it. The first few days, after all those communal dumps we'd lived in, fighting about bills and waiting in line for the shower, we felt as if we were in a palace. A king and queen. A man and a woman. We could talk on the phone for hours on end without a second thought. We could fill the fridge with things we liked. We could walk around the living room in our underwear or without it. We could make love anywhere in the apartment, any time we wanted to, without worrying that a room-mate might come home early. All we had to do was lower the blinds beforehand. The neighbours across the way are still in mourning and we didn't want to deliberately offend them.

*

Not enough time has gone by. This story is still bubbling away.

The only way to touch it is to dip a finger in it.

And snatch it out without delay.

*

The first picture in the album doesn't even show us, Amir and me, together. I mean together in the sense of a couple who can't keep their hands off each other. Modi took that picture, I think, at the hidden spring of the Dargot River. It was a surprise shot, no saying cheese and no posing, and that's exactly what I love about it. Even though it's over-exposed and the focus is far from perfect, it captures something real. Everybody looks wiped out, in a good way, like after a long hike. Yaniv is stretched out with his hat over his face. Yael, who was his girlfriend then, is lying with her head of curls on his stomach, and one curl has dropped to the ground. Amichai is passing an army canteen to Nir, whose red cheeks show how much he needs it. Hila, the one who asked me to come along 'not to get to know guys, just to get to know the desert', is looking for something in her bag, maybe a sweatshirt, because the tank top she's wearing is too thin for the wind that's blowing. Adi the bookworm is holding a book, something published by Am Oved, judging by the size, but she isn't reading it. Her green eyes are peering over it, smiling at Modi. She's the only one who knows he's sneaked up on us to take the picture, maybe because they were going out.

All of them – Yaniv, Yael, Ami, Nir, Hila and Adi – are more or less together, that is, close enough to each other to put them into an imaginary circle not very large in diameter, maybe three metres. Only two people are outside the circle: Amir and me.

Amir is sitting on a boulder that protrudes over the spring, hugging his knees to his chest, staring at everyone. I'm leaning against my bag on the other side of the spring, staring at everyone.

It's incredible how similar our expressions are.

Every time I look at that picture, I laugh. The two observers. It's no wonder it took us three days of mutual observation before we talked, three days of me thinking he was alternately ugly and handsome, interesting and tiresome, shy and arrogant, three days of waiting for him to hit on me and, at the same time, hoping he wouldn't. It wasn't till the fourth day, the last day of the trip, that I realised that if I kept on waiting it would end up being one of those might-have-beens, so I worked up my courage, made the most of a moment when we were far from everyone else, and asked him a stupid question: did he know why only the boulders on the right were coloured, and he said no, he didn't know, he didn't really understand that kind of stuff. He held out his hand to help me over the next boulder and the touch of his hand was soft, much softer than I'd imagined. But none of that has anything to do with the picture. I've got carried away.

*

A nice couple, I say to Moshe after the students close the door behind them.

Very nice, he says, folding the lease and putting it into his shirt pocket.

But a little strange, don't you think? I ask, pulling the lease out of his pocket and putting it into the binder we keep our documents in, where it's supposed to be.

What's strange? That they live together and aren't married? he asks and helps me put the binder back where it belongs.

No, don't be silly, that's very common nowadays, lots of couples move in together before they get married to see whether they can get along, if they're right for each other – not like you, who went and got married to your first girl-friend when you were twenty-one.

But it worked out great for me, Moshe protests, giving me a big smile.

OK, so it worked out for *you*, I smiled back at him, but I'm talking about the principle of the thing.

What principle? Moshe asks, reaching for the TV remote.

Never mind, I say, it doesn't matter.

He turns on the TV. Sports. It looks like I'll have to explain the principle to my sister Mirit. She has a lot more patience with gossip. There's no getting away from it, women are women and men are men.

Sweetie, Moshe says suddenly, his eyes still on the game, do you remember that my brothers are coming on Saturday?

Yes, I remember. How can I forget? There's so much to do before they get here. I have to make sure the dairy knives don't slip into the meat knife drawer. Check that everything in the refrigerator is glatt kosher, because regular kosher isn't good enough for them. Count the candles, and if we don't have enough, go to the store to buy some more. Turn on the hotplate before the Sabbath starts. Look for my kerchief. Wash it. And everything has to be finished by Thursday night, because they always show up early on Friday. They're afraid that a traffic jam – it doesn't matter how many times I tell them that there are no traffic jams at that hour – might make them late for the beginning of the Sabbath. And God forbid that Menachem, his oldest brother, the big rabbi from Tiberias, should think that anyone here is a slacker and doesn't come up to his standards. You don't know him, Sima, he'll make a big deal out of it, Moshe had explained to me all over again, every time Menachem came, for the past six years. And it made me mad all over again, every time. Who said it has to be like this? Why does Rabbi Menachem always have something to say about my clothes whenever we go to see them in Tiberias, and when he comes here, why do we all have to do whatever he wants?

But I don't say anything. Not a word. I know how important it is to Moshe. And Moshe is important to me. I'm willing to do a lot to keep the peace. Almost anything.

*

On the first floor of Moshe and Sima Zakian's house, which our apartment clings to like a fungus on a tree, there are three rooms, a father, a mother and two children. On the second floor, in what is left of the original Arab house, live Moshe's parents, Avram and Gina, founders of the Zakian tribe: six children and almost twenty grandchildren. And on our first Saturday in the new apartment, we get to meet the whole clan. The occasion: a seventieth birthday celebration for the taciturn old grandfather. On Friday, the family arrives in dribs and drabs for the festivities. The first to make an appearance in their multi-doored pickups, dressed in black, are the Zakian children who have become orthodox and moved to Bnei Brak and Tiberias. After them, still well before the beginning of the Sabbath, come all the rest, with and without skullcaps. They all sit on plastic chairs on the small lawn made up of rectangles of pre-grown grass, the lines separating them still visible. They send Sima to ask the students to join them. No, thank you, we decline, we have papers to write. But Sima insists and takes hold of Noa's hand: haven't you heard, all work and no play ... Noa doesn't know what to say, so she goes along with her and I follow in their wake. Moshe gets two chairs for us, we smile in thanks and after Sima introduces us, she invites us to help ourselves to the food on the table: stuffed grape leaves, *kubeh*, rice made with a spice I don't recognise, salads and all kinds of sweets. The children, with or without sidelocks, play hide-and-seek, and the conversation flows pleasantly. It turns out that Yossi, Moshe's younger brother, is a photography buff, and Noa tells him a little bit about her classes – I notice that no one takes an overt interest in psychology – and when he asks her advice about what camera to buy, she explains the pros and the cons. The sun sinks slowly to the horizon between the rising Jerusalem hills and the conversation drifts to other subjects more closely related to family – problems, solutions, childhood memories. An occasional Kurdish expression is tossed into the conversation, *kapparokh, hitlokh, ana gabinokh*, and they translate for us immediately so we won't feel out of it – sweetheart, light of my life, I love you. I make my way through the cascades of Noa's hair to her ear and whisper, *ana gabinokh, ana gabinokh*, and I think, there's an aura around us when we're together, an aura that keeps out loneliness. She grabs my hand under the table and whispers into my neck with an optimism that's rare for her, we got lucky with this place, didn't we?

*

Do you love me, Amir?

Yes.

Why?

What do you mean, why?

I mean, what do you love about me?

Lots of things.

For example?

For example, the way you walk. I really love the way you walk.

The way I walk?

Yes, quickly, like you're in a hurry to get where you're going.

What else?

Now it's your turn.

My turn? Hmm . . . I love the way you are with people. The way you know how to say something real to people that will touch them.

You're like that too.

Not really, I'm harder than you are.

No, you're not, you're very soft, here, feel this.

Yes, I really am soft there.

And in other places too.

Really? Like where?

*

I couldn't decide whether to take that picture. I was afraid that the click of the camera would wake Amir, he sleeps so lightly. And the way he looked – curled up on the grass in front of our bungalow in Amirim, like a kitten, and his long lashes and sleep-soft cheeks – that made me hesitate too. It occurred even to me, a chronic photographer, that maybe not everything should be photographed, maybe I'd just leave things as they were for once, not document them, keep them burnt only into my memory. But the light, the magical twilight and the composition, the squares of the Indian sweater inside the squares of lawn, the three oranges growing on the branches of the tree, and the forgotten, torn basketball net that was just enough to keep the scene from being too idyllic – I couldn't control myself.

And of course, he woke up.

But he didn't complain the way he usually did. We were easy with each other that weekend, and with ourselves. We were good together. Not in retrospect, not out of nostalgia. Not in anticipation. But here and now good. Very good. I remember that in the morning we made love slowly and he touched every part of my body with his finger as if he were proving to himself that I was real, and it made me laugh and then it excited me. After we came, gently, and got under the blankets again, I told him about the Advil night. I'd never told any of my old boyfriends about it, not even Ronen, and we were together for almost a year. I was afraid it would scare them off, and only with Amir did I feel for the first time that I could let go of the secret, that he'd know how to keep it, so I put my lips against his chest, as if a chest could hear, and I told him. He listened quietly, didn't get scared and didn't give advice, just stroked my head over and over again, the way you stroke a child's head. Until I fell asleep. When I woke up, he was already outside on the lawn.

After I took his picture and saw that he wasn't angry at me for waking him up, I put my camera down and joined him. I hugged him from behind, threaded my hand into the space between his chest and his sweater and whispered lovers' nonsense. From the angle of his cheek, I could see that he was smiling lazily, and he reached an arm behind him to pull me closer.

On our way back to the world, on the road that wound between the Galilee hills, we started talking about maybe moving in together next year, even though he was still going to school in Tel Aviv and I was still studying in Jerusalem. How can I sleep without you? he said, and I crossed over the valley made by the handbrake that separated us and grabbed hold of his hand. We'd talked about that possibility before, but always in very general, noncommittal terms. Neither of us wanted to suggest it in so many words, as if the one to suggest it first would be responsible for making sure it didn't fail.

*

Moments of flickering doubt in Noa:

When Amir insists on hanging that sad picture – a man who looks like Gérard Depardieu sitting on a bed in a hotel room shadowed in gloom, with something that looks like an old radio next to him, looking out at the pale moon – in the middle of the living room. 'It's the only thing in my life that's permanent, the only thing that goes with me to every apartment,' he says, checking to see that it's hanging just so. But that picture makes her feel so low.

And the way he tidies up after her drives her up the wall. Look, she tries to explain to him, without the mess I can't create anything at all. He nods and continues to follow her around and pick up shoes. Socks. White hairbands. Black hairbands.

And there's another unpleasant thing: in the two weeks they've been living together, all the projects she had started for school have stalled. When Amir is in the apartment, she can't concentrate on anything. Her mind is always wandering. It's only in the shower that her thoughts flow freely. Only in the shower do ideas come easily.

So she stays in the shower hour after hour, until the hot water is gone and her fingers are wrinkled like an old lady's or a newborn baby's.

*

Only a plaster wall separates the students from the Zakians. And Moshe put a small hole in it. Why? So the students can stick their hands through it to switch on the water heater, which is in the landlord's house but heats the tenants' water too. So every time Noa and Amir want a hot shower, they first remove the piece of wood that covers the hole in the wall. Then they stick a hand into the home and lives of the other family, and then withdraw it quickly, as if it had never been there at all. But sometimes (after all, everyone likes to shower at the same time most days), two hands reaching for the switch would graze. And once a week, usually on Thursday, the piece of wood is shoved aside and a Zakian hand drops in letters addressed to 'Amir and Noa – care of the Zakian family.' (I'll set up a mailbox for you, Moshe had told them with a smile, but it'll take a while.)

When he hears the thud of the letters hitting the floor, Amir leaves his books and notebooks and runs to see what has come that day. To see if, along with the mail from the university, there is also a letter from Modi, his best friend – who's so far away.

*

These are hopeful days. In the news, Pilot Pens publishes a picture of the peace agreement signing ceremony, with a close-up of the pen they used. Abu Dhabi is considering renewing its relations with Israel (how we've missed you, Abu Dhabi). There's talk of economic projects, joint agricultural enterprises, cucumber of the courageous. There's a building boom in Gaza. Trees are being planted in Ramallah. An Arab village is offering summer cottages to Jews. Pitta, hummus, *zata'ar*, whatever you want. And believe it or not, they're swamped.

*

Hey m-a-a-a-n, what's happening?

Before anything else, I have to describe the place I'm writing from. It's called Reconcito which, translated loosely from Spanish, means hole. And, bro, this is one hell of a hole. To get here, you have to call the owner Alfredo a day in advance from the closest city to set up transportation. Only a jeep can make it through the lousy road that leads from the city to the farm and, of course, Alfredo is the only one who has a jeep. And what does Reconcito have that makes such an operation worth while? Not a hell of a lot. A few horses. A few cows. A small hostel with eight beds. A restaurant that serves two meals a day. And then there's that elusive something that I've no idea what to call, but it's the thing that draws all the tourists to this place. What do I do here? It's like this. From the morning on, I sit on a crooked wooden chair, in the same position, and watch how the same things – the cows, the trees, the clouds – look different all the time. Because of the sun, which moves. Because of my mood. Because of the fact that I'm looking at them for the third time. Sound weird? Sorry, that's how it is when you're in 'trekness' mode. Yes, I've developed (in the course of a single day) a new theory here that says people have three basic modes of consciousness: 'soldierness', 'civilianness' and 'trekness', which spread out on this kind of axis:

Soldierness————Civilianness————Trekness

And here's the explanation: remember that feeling you get when you come home from the army and change from your uniform to your pyjamas and, all of a sudden, your body turns limp, all the air drains out of your chest and the hardness out of your shoulders, and you know that for at least the next forty-eight hours you don't have to be afraid that anyone – the platoon commander, the regiment commander, the military police – might take away your liberty? That's the difference between 'soldierness' and 'civilianness'. It's that you know no one can tell you what to do. That you and only you decide what to do. Now, pay attention. The difference between 'civilianness' and 'trekness' is the same, but it's internal. Because even after you've given back your uniform and moved on, once and for all, to 'civilianness', you still have to listen to those internal policemen of yours. Still have to act the way people who know you expect you to act. In the 'trekness' mode, through a process that isn't exactly clear to me (remember, this theory is still being developed), you get rid of all of the above, one after the other. And your consciousness, at least in theory, remains open to surprises and amenable to changes.

So what do you think, future psychologist? (Before you shoot me down, remember what Zorba the Greek said to the old head monk of the monastery who explained to him the three totally weird theories he'd spent his whole life working on – wait, I don't remember the exact words he used, let me look for it in the book. Here it is, I found it: 'Your theories can save many souls, my Old Father,' Zorba said to the head monk, and before he lied to him, he thought – and this is where the really beautiful sentence comes – 'Man has another, much greater obligation that is above and beyond the truth.'

I talked to my mother and she told me that you and Noa moved in together. To tell you the truth, I was pretty surprised. The last time we spoke before I left – remember? – after you clobbered me in tennis (you competitive bastard, couldn't you send me off with a victory?) you said you were afraid it wouldn't work, didn't you? That you had a feeling you'd met her too soon. But it looks like things have worked out for you two since then. So I'm happy for you. Where exactly is the Castel: before Hummus Abu Ghosh or after it? Anyway, I promise to come and visit when I get back (right now, that looks very far away, but who knows).

The sun is setting on Reconcito now, the clouds are painted orange and a light breeze is making the treetops dance. In a little while, when it's completely dark, the fireflies will start flickering. An amazing sight, a dance of lights. But, except for them, there are no lights here at night, and it's a little hard to keep writing this way (even though it might be interesting to write once at night without seeing what you're writing, without worrying about straight lines and spaces between letters, without thinking about whether you're being understood or not. Maybe I'll try that with my next letter. Poor you).

Meanwhile, *adios*.

Send me something to the Israeli Embassy in La Paz. People tell me they hold letters there.

Regards to Noa.

Modi.

*

Sometimes Amir sees him when he goes outside – the little brother of the soldier who died. In the deserted field between his house and theirs, the boy pets stray cats. Shepherds ants. Builds a monument to his brother, stone on top of stone.

Always alone.

He never looks up and tries to catch Amir's eye, even though he knows he's standing nearby.

*

You can hear everything through these walls, and when I say everything, I mean everything. More power to them, those students, almost every day and sometimes twice a day. And the sounds she makes, oh my God. I mean, not always, sometimes you only hear the bed creaking and the two of them laughing, but every once in a while, when it works for them, she has no shame, that Noa, she lets all the pleasure out, and the funniest thing is that Lilach, my little one, every time she hears Noa enjoying it, she gets scared and starts crying, and I have to pick her up and calm her down, and myself a little bit too, because the truth is, those noises get me all confused. I mean, sometimes it's just annoying and I feel like knocking on their door and telling them to turn down the volume if they don't mind, but sometimes, when Moshe is on the road till late and I'm alone in the house all day with the nappies and the running noses and the radio that plays piano music, then those noises give me a kind of tweak under my stomach and I start looking at the clock, come on, when will Moshe get home, and when he finally does, if the kids are in bed already, I hug him a little longer than usual, and kiss him on the chin, which is a kind of signal we have, and he starts complaining, I'm tired, dead tired, but I know him, my teddy bear, and I know what to do to wake him up: black coffee, a few steamy looks, some rubbing on the back of his neck, and in a few minutes we're in bed, without making noises, but with lots of feeling good, because we've been together for eight years, since high school, and we know what to do and what to say, except that at the end, when it's all over and we're lying on our backs, a little bit apart from each other, Moshe always mumbles, *baruch ha'shem*, thanks be to God, and that annoys me, so I say why *baruch ha'shem*, what does God have to do with it, because I hate it when he starts talking like his brothers, but no matter how many times I tell him that, he keeps on saying *baruch ha'shem* and claims it just comes out of his mouth automatically.

*

When we were sitting *shivah*, I couldn't wait for it to be over, for all the people to go back to their own houses, especially Aunt Miriam, because she was the reason they moved me into the living room. I wanted us to take the chairs and the mattresses out of the living room, and the piles of dishes, and the half-eaten pieces of *kubeh*, so there'd finally be some space and they'd let me go back to my room and play games on my computer or watch TV, which I couldn't do all week, and I'd have time to think about Gidi and all the new things they said about him last week, some of them really not true, like for instance that he loved the army and all that, but the minute the *shivah* was over and Aunt Miriam, who was the last one to leave, disappeared into the taxi that came to take her to the airport, I was already starting to miss the noise and felt sorry I'd wanted everyone to go, because all of a sudden there was a new kind of quiet in the house that was different from the Saturday morning quiet when everyone's sleeping or the quiet in my class when the teacher tells everyone to read silently from their readers.

Mum and Dad hardly ever talk to me, and if they do, then it's only to tell me what to do – brush your teeth, turn down the sound on the computer – or to ask questions like what do you want in your sandwich or what time should we pick you up after your karate class? What's even weirder is that they hardly ever talk to each other either. And if they do talk, let's say at supper, you can hear in every sentence – even if it's only 'pass me the pepper' – that they're angry.

Dad's angry because of the shrine – that's what he calls it – that Mum is setting up for Gidi in the living room. He doesn't say anything to her, but you can see what he's feeling from the way the muscle in his cheek starts twitching every time she hangs up another picture or lights another candle or frames another one of the letters we got from the army. And Mum is angry at Dad for the things he said to the newspaper. 'Why did he have to do that?' she asked Aunt Margalit on the phone when Dad was at work and I was hiding behind the cabinet, listening. 'I don't understand him. If he has to pour his heart out, let him talk to me. And besides, why does he attack other parents? Where does he get the nerve to judge them?'

This isn't the first time Mum and Dad have been mad at each other.

When Mum wanted to have another baby, two years ago, it was like this. But Gidi still lived at home then. He'd take me to his room and make me fall down laughing with his animal imitations, and then he'd sit me down on his bed and explain to me that it's normal for Mum and Dad to disagree, it doesn't mean they'll get divorced tomorrow like Roy's parents did, and chances are they'd make up in a week or two and everything would go back to the way it was.

But Gidi's gone now and when I can't take the mood in the house any more, I go straight out to the empty lot without telling anyone first. I jump out the window in my room so Mum won't ask where I'm going, land on the ground with my legs spread, like a gymnast, hop over the fence and go to collect more stones for the monument. Or I play with the cats. No one bothers me with questions. No one looks at me as if I'm a statue in a wax museum, the way the kids in my class have been doing since I went back to school.

Only that tall student who lives in the apartment across the way comes outside sometimes to hang his washing up, or look for the newspapers he thinks are in the bushes. I know that all the newspapers are on the roof, because the guy who delivers them doesn't feel like going all the way to the door, so he throws them from the road and misses, but I don't say anything. Yesterday, after he tripped over a big rock and fell while he was looking, he smiled at me because he felt stupid, and I almost smiled back, but at the last minute I sealed my lips together and pretended I didn't see. I don't need someone else to feel sorry for me.

*

Amir, there's a noise in the living room.

It's the wind.

Maybe it's a thief?

It's the wind, but if you want, I'll go and check.

I want. I love feeling that you're strong and you protect me.

Does that mean I can't be weak with you?

You can, but not too much. Come on.

I'm getting up.

Wait a sec, what do we actually have to steal?
Nothing. Wait, we do. The newspaper.
We still haven't had a single one?
No.
Did you talk to the delivery people?
Yes.
So, maybe Madmoni's workers take them? They get here at six every morning.
Great, Noa, blame the Arabs. It really figures they'd steal *Haaretz*.
Why not? Doesn't it have a property section?

*

That's the house, I'm sure. Or maybe not? For two weeks, ever since we started building the extension here for Madmoni, I've been looking at the house across the street, looking at it a lot. First thing in the morning, I look, and during the breaks, and at the end of the day too, when we're sitting on the pavement waiting for Rami the contractor to pick us up and take us back to the village. The bottom part of the house is new. *Ya'ani*, I mean renovated. Clean stones with thin lines between them. A family with two children lives there – the husband drives for Egged, I can tell from the bus – and there's a young couple living in a little apartment at the back, but all I can see of it is the roof and some aerials.

If there was only that part, at the bottom, I wouldn't think anything.

But upstairs on the second floor where the old man and the old woman come out sometimes, upstairs it's built in the old way, stone on top of stone, the way they used to build in the village. And one stone, in the corner, sticks out like it did in that building, I remember. And another stone, on the left of the door, is as black as the black stone we had, though I remember it being on the right side. And the window has a little arch, just like my parents' window did.

*

My family moved to a lot of different apartments, at least ten before I went into the army. From Jerusalem to Haifa. From Haifa to Jerusalem. From Jerusalem to Detroit. And within each city, too. But no matter how many times we moved, the worst pain I ever felt was the move we made when I was in Year 10. It was during the football World Cup, so I remember the year: '86. Mexico, '86. Belgium against the Soviet Union. Spain against Denmark. Lots of goals. Live broadcasts in the middle of the night. The time people are sleeping, but I can't fall asleep. From eleven o'clock, I'm tossing and turning in bed trying to decide whether I should finally rebel against this moving from place to place that my father forces on us every few years, whether the time has finally come to stand up and say: enough, I'm staying here. In Jerusalem. With my friends. You can all go back to Haifa. Over and over again, I picture in my mind what's going to happen in the next few weeks. How at the going-away party, the girls will kiss my cheek and all the kids will take my new phone number and promise to stay in touch, how two or three at the most will call during the summer vacation, and we'll see each other maybe once, in Jerusalem, of course, because it's hard to get from there to Haifa, and how, even if we see each other more than once, even if the incredible happens and they do come to Haifa, when school starts we'll drift apart, the letters will get shorter, the silences on the phone will get longer, and the names of all kinds of people I don't know will start coming up in their stories.

Unless – the possibility runs through my mind again – I rent myself a room. Yes. In some old lady's house. There are ads like that in the local papers sometimes. But where will I get the money to rent a room? And where will I do my laundry? And how often can I eat scrambled eggs, which is the only thing I know how to make?

Every night, as the time for the game comes closer, I get up and take my blanket into the living room to watch the game on TV, without sound, so I won't wake everybody up. When there's a goal, I choke back my shouts, and when the broadcast, including the round-up and analysis, is over, I put on my coat and go out into the Jerusalem night, still wound up with the mute suspense of the football game, and walk down to the shopping centre, to the lit-up but closed SuperPharm, where I look at the packages of nappies and toilet paper, read over and over again the posters showing all their special sales until I'm sick of it, and sit down on one of the chairs outside the neighbourhood café, which are tied together with an iron chain. I'm freezing from the cold and think that maybe I should tie myself down with a chain too, like they do in demonstrations, so I won't have to move. I look at the few passing cars and make up stories about them: that's a Mossad agent coming back from a spying mission in enemy territory, that's a prostitute coming off her shift . . . and only when the first strips of light appear and light up the park, and the rubbish trucks are creaking at the end of the street do I get up from the chair, run all the way home and lie down in bed, pretending to be a good boy. After a little while, I get up and go into the kitchen, drink my morning chocolate milk with Mum as if nothing has happened, and go to school and talk back to all my teachers because I'm too tired to behave myself and because they can't do anything to me anyway. I'm moving to Haifa.

*

There was a strong wind when I took the picture, you can tell from Amir's crest of hair, which has an impressive presence even on normal days, but here it's actually threatening to move out of the frame, and from the bushes behind him that are bent strangely towards the right. But what's really interesting about the composition is not the wind but the discrepancy between the figure and the background, between the central event and what's happening behind it. The figure, of course, is Amir, who's holding an oval wooden sign in one hand that says NOA AND AMIR'S

HOUSE – you can read it if you strain – against the door. In the other hand, he's holding a big hammer that Moshe the landlord lent him. In a minute, he'll pull some nails out of his pocket and try to hang the sign on the door. At first, the nails will bend on him, but after a few tries, he'll manage to do it. Meanwhile, he's smiling a big smile that's a combination of real happiness – it was, after all, an occasion – and a spark of scorn directed at me as if he's asking: why this posing, Noa, why does everything have to be photographed? Behind him, behind the dramatic event, you can see the neglected empty lot between our house and the house where the bereaved family lives. A crooked iron post, bushes, a small pile of rubbish topped with a huge plastic jerry can, a few boards the contractor forgot to take, small rocks, large rocks, and one mangy cat looking at the camera with glittering eyes. I'd be happy to say that I noticed all those details while I was taking the picture, that I closed the shutter so that everything would be in focus, but the truth is, I didn't. Some of the things in the field are blurred, and the ones that aren't, are dim. I forgot again what Ishai Levy, who teaches us the history of photography, told us in our first year: no frame has only one story; always look for other stories around the edges.

After we finished nailing the sign on the door and checked that it was straight, we went inside, pulled down the blinds and celebrated the event in bed. We celebrated everything between the sheets, or between the blankets, actually, because it had already started to get pretty cold. We celebrated moving the queen-size mattress into the bedroom. Buying the radiator. Even our first big purchase in the supermarket at the shopping centre (he spread honey on my nipples and then licked it off. Slowly.).

Amir always wants us to stay in bed, hugging each other for ever, but after a few minutes I always want to, have to, escape to the shower.

*

And what was strange was that even when I was standing on my own two feet, even when I had no one else to blame, I kept on moving compulsively. I've lived in seven different apartments since the army, seven times boxes, nails, butterflies. If you look at each move separately, you might say I was cursed. The landlord decided to sell the apartment on Hashmoniam Street. Maya decided to fall in love with her lecturer's assistant. My room-mate in Ramat Gan had a nervous breakdown. But the bittersweet truth is – and it took me a while to admit it – that there's something addictive about frequent changes, the anticipation, the adrenalin that surges with every new leaf you're about to turn over. I think – we learned this in our first year – that just as people get addicted to the runners' high after jogging, people can get addicted to movers' high or changers' high (the Americans will be sure to find a technical name for it).

I was addicted. Addicted to those muscles that tense up when you're about to leave something. Sometimes I thought I'd never kick it.

And sometimes, I thought that maybe I could, like yesterday, when we hung the sign on the door and then made love, and stayed in bed for hours talking and snuggling while the wind rattled the windows but not us.

*

Moments when Amir is happy that he's Noaandamir:

When they're sitting on the sofa at the end of the day, having a hot drink and telling each other, through the steam, about the hurts, the victories, the small moments of loneliness that happened in their lives apart. The conversation flows, every word spoken in its time, and again he remembers: her soul is intertwined with mine. And also: when he comes home late, walking gingerly along the path, sneaking over to the window to peek at her through the slats of the blinds, her face serious and her brow furrowed as she labours over one of her projects. Or: how her lips open slightly when she's watching TV. Or: how her glance wanders sometimes, hanging on an imaginary hook on the ceiling, and though it's clear she's daydreaming, it's not clear what she's feeling. And he also loves: when they watch *The X-Files* together on Tuesday nights. And laugh when Mulder always leaves Scully alone at the worst times. And they jump – chills slithering down their spines like a child down a water slide – when the music on the soundtrack is scary. Noa presses up against him, so he'll keep the monsters at bay. And he puts his strong, manly arm around her, knowing it's a pose, but enjoying it anyway.

*

Sometimes, on Fridays, in the middle of the main street of the Castel, two cars stop window to window and the drivers begin a short conversation. What's new, you think Beitar will come out of its slump, when's the baby due? The neighbourhood traffic behind them comes to a standstill. And what Noa likes is that no one even thinks of honking his horn.

Sometimes, on Saturdays, the air carries the sound of a *darbuka* into their house. Distant. Dim. Amir drums the rhythm on his statistics book. Noa takes her clothes off and dances for him.

And a small prophet dances with them for a while, swaying his bald head and smiling a crooked, devious smile.

*

There's a new CD in Noa and Amir's house: *I'm Your Fan*. New renditions of Leonard Cohen songs sung by many different singers. But a thread of dark magic runs through each and every one, and it lingers. Amir's favourite is 'Hallelujah', the last track. '*Love is not a victory march, it's a cold and it's a broken hallelujah.*' Noa's favourite is track number six, a French song that fills her with a kind of pleasant tension, even though the language is beyond her comprehension. Sometimes, in the morning, when they can only listen to one song because they have to get going they argue about which of the two to play. On the other side of the wall, in the Zakian home, there's not a single angry voice. Moshe is on the road and Sima is totally free to listen to the music of her choice. Her CD of the month: *Caramel, Bonbon et Chocolat*, a collection of French love songs that she listens to a lot. Sima learned French at home; her mother, may she rest in peace, taught her when she was very young. 'French is the language of beauty,' she'd say, and she made Sima practise till the words flowed off her tongue. Her mother also taught her that God is first of all in your heart, and all the rest – the interpretations, the rules, the regulations – is just window dressing. And a father who leaves his daughters has no God in his heart, even if he obeys all the commandments and recites every blessing. When Sima hears Nino Ferrer, she dreams of slim French men with well-trimmed moustaches and remembers her mother sweeping the kitchen floor in their apartment in the Ashkelon housing project, dancing with the broom, only her black hair swaying in the small room.

In the house of mourning, there is no music now. No one banned it in so many words, but, right after the funeral, the house became shrouded in silence somehow. Sometimes, when Yotam's father feels like he can't take it any more, he goes down to his car, sits inside and closes the door. Then he tunes the radio to a talk show, but not because he's interested in what people have to say. He hopes that the soothing sound of other human voices will make the pain go away. Sometimes, when Yotam's mother feels she can't take it any more, she turns on the small kitchen radio with the volume down low. She listens to a single song and turns it off right away so no one will know.

When Yotam feels he can't take it any more, he goes out to the empty lot.

*

Finally, I called the boy to come over. I asked him if he knew where our newspapers were disappearing to. He pointed to the asbestos roof. From where I was standing,

I couldn't see what was on it, so I made a questioning gesture with my hand. He signalled me to follow him. We climbed over the stones, careful of potholes, till we reached a small rise in the middle of the field between the houses. We climbed it and, from the top, we could see on to the roof. Dozens of neglected rolled-up newspapers lay on it. The delivery boy must have been too lazy to go all the way to the door and, instead, tried his luck at newspaper-throwing. Thanks, I said to the kid, and he answered politely, you're welcome, and with shoulders stooped he turned to go back to what he'd been doing. Hey, kid . . . I called. I wanted to keep him from leaving. There was something about him, about his dejected look, about those sharply creased pants, the shirt with the sleeves that were too long, the shoes with their big white tongues, the way he always stroked the cats – something that touched my heart. Besides, I didn't feel like going back to statistics. What's your name? I asked him. Yotam, he answered. Nice to meet you, my name's Amir, I said and held out my hand. He extended his small hand, gave mine a brief shake and pulled it back quickly. What now, I thought. How do we go on from here? Wanna play? I heard myself say. He gave me a quick look, checked out my height and said, play what? He was right. Play what? After all, we were fifteen years apart in age. I tried to think of something before he took off, but all the games that came into my mind were old ones that had passed their sell-by dates. Atari, Scrabble, Monopoly. Like that.

A rusty iron pole sticking up from the ground caught me eye. I remembered that when we went on trips, my father and I used to play at throwing stones at a target. Let's see who hits that pole first, I said. All right, he agreed, picked up a stone and threw it. There was a metallic sound. Bull's-eye. OK, I thought, I'm dealing with a pro here.

Let's see who hits the Coke can first, I said.

Where?

There, next to the skip.

And that's how the game developed. From the Coke can we moved on to the plastic water bottle. From the water bottle to a large rock that was further away. Till suddenly, without warning, he said, bye, I have to go, and started running back to his house. I called after him, bye Yotam, but he didn't turn around. He probably didn't like the game, I thought to myself. OK, and his partner was a little too old for him.

The next day, when Noa was at college, he showed up at my door. With a backgammon set in his hand.

*

We're on a break now. They let us have one a day. Half an hour. If we take more, Rami yells and takes it off our pay. And we get paid almost nothing anyway. Jabber takes out the pitta, Nayim takes out the *labeneh*. Najib and Amin take out some vegetables and start cutting up a salad. They don't let me do anything because I'm older. Sheikh Saddiq they call me sometimes, to make me mad, even though I'm faster and better at my work than all the younger ones. With me, there are no surprises. When it comes to measuring, I'm never even a millimetre off. When it comes to pouring cement, I check all the ties and joists ten times. Here, Nayim passes me a piece of pitta and the plastic container of *labeneh*. *Shukran* I say, thank you, and my mouth fills up with spit even before I dip the pitta into the *labeneh*. They make Nayim's *labeneh* from goat's milk in his village, and it's famous in all the other villages. There's no *labeneh* like it, not even in the most expensive restaurants – sour and soft, like it should be. I taste some and pass it to Ramzi. He's busy arguing with Samir about the difference between Jewish girls and Arab girls. Our girls are a lot more exciting, Samir says. With them, there's room for imagination, not like with the Jewish girls who walk around half naked. Amin doesn't think so. Nayim and Jabber put in their two pence. I've already heard those discussions about girls a thousand times and know all the different opinions by heart, so I move away a little bit and lean against the wall at an angle that lets me see the house. Even after a month, I still haven't made up my mind about it.

I'd forgotten about that house for years. I was four when they threw us out, or maybe five, I don't know. When we ran away, they left behind the jug my birth certificate was in. For all the years since then, I forgot everything, and it was in prison, of all places, that I remembered. I wasn't inside for a long time, only six months. I'm not an Intifada hero, not the chief of a fighting unit, all I did was 'assist in terrorist activity', and it wasn't even on purpose. I gave a lift in my car to someone who wanted to stab a soldier at the gates to the military government office, and I didn't even know he had a big knife under his coat or that the Secret Service was on to him already and waiting for him there. Not that they believed me when they questioned me. Why should they believe an Arab? They slapped me. Shook me. Twisted my arm and then every finger separately. But they didn't have any proof, and they caught him before he stabbed anyone, so they only gave me six months. I got off cheap, like they say. But those six months, *wa'alla*, like a hundred years for me – those thoughts about my wife and my sons, and the time, the time that never passes when you're in prison. Even though they have roll call in the morning and roll call in the afternoon, and even though I took two Hebrew lessons a day from the famous Mustafa A'alem, who was in for twenty years and knew Hebrew better than the Jews, even so, the time didn't pass.

You're lying there on your bed at night, you can't fall asleep because of the fleas and the snoring, and the air stinks so much you can't breathe, and because there's nothing to do, you start imagining things. You see *jinim*, *ya'ani* demons, walking around the room, you hear voices talking into your ear and when the night's over and you're sure you're *majnun*, completely crazy, and you're so scared that you feel like crying, all of a sudden you start to remember things you didn't even know you had in your head, the face of a boy who was your friend, a slap your father once gave you, and that house, the house you left. Like from inside the smoke of a *nargileh*, the rooms float up one by one, the small kitchen that was always full of pots, the bathroom with the door so low that Papa had to bend his head to go through it, the small step you had to walk down in order to go into the living room, the three mattresses on the floor, Monir's, yours and Marwan's, no, first yours, then Monir's and then Marwan's, the floor tiles that had drawings on them, the broken tile in the right-hand corner, the heavy door that creaked a little when it closed, the yard where you and your brothers used to play, and the window with the arch that looks so much like the window of the house I'm looking at now. The house that belongs to that family whose name I still don't know.

Yesterday, on my break, I went to see what the name on the door was. A young woman with eyes like a tiger came out from downstairs and asked, can I help you? I was flustered, I didn't know what to say, so I asked if I could have some water, and she asked, are you Madmoni's worker? I said yes, and she said, so why doesn't he give you water? But she went inside anyway and came out with a bottle, and I said thank you. I didn't know what to do with my eyes, so I kept them on my shoes, on the spots of plaster, then I turned around and walked towards Madmoni, and I even drank from the bottle while I walked, even though I wasn't thirsty, so she wouldn't think I lied, but I don't think she saw because I heard the door slam shut.

Yallah ya sheikh, back to work. Amin stopped the thoughts that kept spinning around in my brain like a cement mixer. He stood above me and held out his hand. I got up on my own. I'm no old man you have to help up.

*

32

She's a good person, that Noa, really, that's for sure. Yesterday, I had to go to Doga to get nappies and I didn't want to leave the children alone, so I knocked on their door and she opened it wearing white pyjamas with little sheep on them – probably so there'd be something to count at night when they can't fall asleep – and she said right away that she'd look after them, even though I saw from the open book in the living room that she was in the middle of something. All she said was, I'm warning you, Sima, I'm not too good with children, and I said, well then, sweetie, this is your chance to practise with other people's kids before you have your own, and she laughed with her whole body – all the sheep moved – and said, it'll be a long time before that happens, and I said, why, how old are you that you talk like that, and she said, twenty-six, I mean soon, my birthday's in another month, and I said isn't that funny, I'm twenty-six too, and she opened her eyes wide and said, no, you're joking, and I pretended to be insulted on purpose and said, why, do I look that old? She blushed, poor thing, and started to stammer, no, of course not, I just thought, you know, because of the children, of course not, Sima, you look terrific, even Amir says so, and I said thank you, and posed like a model. I lifted my head and pulled my hair back with that gesture Moshe likes so much, and the sheep moved again, and then it was quiet while we made our comparisons in our mind. I think she felt sorry for me, I'm not sure, but I felt a bit bad then for not putting on make-up in the morning. Anyway, I finally said, get yourself together, sweetie, I'll wait for you, and she said, I'll be there in fifteen minutes, just let me have a shower.

While I was waiting for her, I peeled an orange for Liron and thought: there's no reason to feel sorry for me. It's true that I don't go to university every day, and I don't wear beautiful skirts like she does (those legs of hers, like a model's). It's true that I don't meet any gorgeous men and I don't sit in cafés or walk around with a fancy camera that costs at least ten thousand shekels (that's what Moshe says), but none of that stuff is worth one minute with the children, like yesterday when Lilach did research on my thumb, looked at it, pulled it, put it in her mouth. Then moved over to my little finger. I had a laughing fit about how thorough she was. Or when Liron says to me a week ago, his face all serious, Mummy, you're more beautiful than all the other girls, when I grow up I want to marry you. Can anything compare to that? And besides, I will go back to college. Moshe and I have talked about it already. After they grow up a little. I'll finish my degree and work in my field like a real career woman. Where's the fire? Like they say, good things come to those who wait. That's what I was thinking while I fed Liron the peeled orange. Lilach started whining. It's always like that. Every time he gets something, she cries. Even if she doesn't really want it. I tickled the bottom of her foot to calm her down and reached out to the bowl of oranges with the other, but then I heard steps outside and thought it was Noa. I put the orange on the table and got up to open the door.

An Arab worker, one of Madmoni's, was climbing the stairs that go up to Avram and Gina. Excuse me, are you looking for someone? I asked. He started to um and ah. No, I mean yes, I mean no. I thought I'd caught him red-handed. But doing what, I didn't know. All of a sudden he asked for water. Water? Doesn't Madmoni give you water? No, he doesn't. I filled a bottle and gave it to him. Liron was peeping out from behind me, scared to death. Lilach kept on crying, want owange, want owange. The worker's eyes were glued to his shoes. His face was red. Maybe from embarrassment, maybe from the sun, I don't know. He took the bottle and said, thank you very much. And left.

When Noa came, I told her what happened. I should report it to the police, I said. Who knows who that man is and what he's up to. Calm down, Noa said, he was just thirsty. But who can guarantee that he won't come back?

I asked, and took Lilach out of the crib and held her close to my breast. Now she was really crying. Screaming. I don't like it, Noa, an Arab wandering around outside. What if he wants to kidnap my Lilach? Noa gently stroked Lilach's soft, downy hair. With two fingers. Back and forth. In Noa's honour, the little girl opened her green eyes (not from me, that amazing colour is from Moshe's side) and gradually stopped crying. See, I told you, why did you say you're not good with kids? Well, it's not hard with Lilach, she's special, Noa said, and I felt the pride swelling up inside me, even though I knew she was trying to be nice. OK, Sima, she said and put a hand on my shoulder. You can go to Doga now. But what about the . . . I started to object. It's all right, I won't open the door to anyone, she interrupted me and looked at her watch. Go on. They're closing soon.

I took my bag and went. Outside, I looked at Madmoni's workers and tried to find the one who'd asked me for water. He wasn't there. There were only two younger ones laying bricks and giving me hungry, creepy looks. I pretended to ignore them and walked a little faster.

*

They warned us about it in the first lesson of the semester. The lecturer bent over the microphone and said: There is a well-known phenomenon among students studying psychopathology. They tend to think that they are suffering from some of the mental diseases they are learning about. This happens all over the world, so don't be frightened, OK? That's what she said into the microphone, and the class responded with peals of laughter that rolled from the first rows all the way to the back of the hall. Us? Frightened?!

And now, in the morning, the house is empty. The sounds of drilling from Madmoni's direction cut through the silence in random bursts. I'm sitting in front of *Abnormal Psychology* by Rosenman and Zeligman, third edition, and it's happening to me. Just like she said. Obsessive compulsive? Of course. Yesterday I came back twice to check that I hadn't left the gas on. And once to check that I'd locked the top bolt on the door. Phobic? Absolutely. What else would you call my fear of dogs, which started after a German Shepherd bit me in Haifa when I was nine, and only gets worse with time? And anxiety, what about anxiety? A person only needs six of the ten symptoms of chronic anxiety, Rosenman and Zeligman write, to be classified as pathological. With fear and trembling, I count how many symptoms I have, trying not to cheat myself the way I did back when I answered the 'Test Yourself' questions in Maariv's *Teen Magazine*, and count three. Because my heart's pounding while I'm counting, I add 'rapid pulse'. The total: four.

Two more, just two more, and I cross the thin line. Then nothing will differentiate me from the Helping Hand Club in Ramat Chen. In another two weeks, I'm supposed to start volunteering there. They say it improves your chances of being accepted into a Master's degree programme. This isn't a hospital, Nava the co-ordinator explained to me in the preliminary conversation we had yesterday in the mouldy shelter. (Why do they put them in a shelter? I thought to myself as I walked down the stairs. To protect them from the world or to hide them from it?) This is a social club, she said. People come here after being released from psychiatric hospitals. Most of them are on medication, some live with their families and some in protected housing. Our job is not to save them or to restore them to sanity, but to help them pass their time in the club pleasantly. That's why we prefer to call them 'members' and not 'patients', even though the therapeutic value of this place is clear. While she was speaking, I thought to myself, why is it so neglected here? Her words are nice, but the walls are cracked, the steps stink of urine, and the pictures someone drew with a marker on pieces of A4 paper are all hanging crooked. What's the big deal about straightening them? You have no idea how much the members are looking forward to your coming, she interrupted my thoughts: they're actually counting the days. I nodded at her in understanding, looked bravely into her eyes, and suddenly wanted very much to get up, just to get up and run out of that shelter into the open air, into the sunlight. I actually felt my leg muscles tighten so I could stand up, but at the last minute I stopped myself and said to her: Thursdays are most convenient for me.

*

When Noa comes home, Amir tells her about Rosenman and Zeligman's anxieties, and, in the same breath, about the neighbour's son, who turned up at their door for the second time. She listens and doesn't say anything for a minute or two, then finally responds, the way only she, who knows him so well, can. Her words are unrelated to what Amir just said, but they hit the nail right on the head: Amiri – she says quietly, twirling his hair into rings and rows – you know, you amaze me. You're so hard on yourself and treat everyone else so gently.

*

He didn't ask me about Gidi the second time either. We played backgammon and draughts and backwards draughts, a funny game he taught me, where you let your opponent take all your pieces and the winner is the first one left without any, and every once in a while he got up and brought us something to eat, bread with chocolate spread, or peanut-flavoured Bamba crisps from the giant-size bag his girlfriend, Noa, who's addicted to it, buys every week, and also something to drink, pineapple juice he makes from a syrup that I didn't like very much but didn't feel comfortable about saying so. Between games, we talked, mostly about football. He's a Hapoel Tel Aviv fan and I support Beitar Jerusalem, so we played around at making each other cross. Talking like a sports announcer, he described Moshe Sinai's famous goal that destroyed Beitar's chances at the championship years ago, before I was born – Eckhouse kicks the ball high, Sinai gets into position and . . . the ball flies into the net!!! – and I put down his pathetic team,

37

which always loses, especially the important games, and we found out that there's a TV series we both like, *Star Trek – The Next Generation*, so we talked about the characters, and he said his favourite is Troy, the ship's psychologist who can read people's feelings, which makes for lots of funny situations, for instance in the episode when she knows that Riker is in love with her even before he tells her; and I said that my favourite character is Wesley, the young officer, and he asked me, why? And I said, because he's very brave, and also because he's a little bit like my brother Gidi, and he looked up from the draughtboard and asked, your brother who was killed? Then I realised that he did know about Gidi and just didn't want to make me feel bad, and all of a sudden, because he asked about Gidi as if he was asking if I wanted more Bamba, I wanted to tell him – him, not the school counsellor who's always straightening her desk when we talk, not Mum, who has it hard enough without me bugging her, and not Dad, who lives inside himself like a snail – I wanted to tell him what I feel, and my throat started to burn, my eyes filled up with tears so I couldn't see what was happening on the board, and Amir didn't say anything, didn't move from his place on the rug, just waited quietly for me to talk, but I didn't know where to start, I didn't know how to say the words, and before I could find a sentence, even an ordinary sentence, to start with, the door opened and his girlfriend walked in.

They gave each other a long, tight hug, the kind my parents haven't given each other in a long time, and she smiled at me and said, so you're Yotam! I've heard a lot about you, and she held out her hand. I didn't know what to say because I hadn't heard anything about her, except for once when someone rang in the middle of a game and Amir said, 'How is she? Same as usual, bothered and beautiful', but that didn't count because maybe he wasn't talking about her, even though, according to what I saw then, she really was beautiful, though I didn't really know much about girls.

Anyway, all I said was, yes, and she looked at the table and said, oh, I see somebody besides me likes Bamba, and again I didn't know what to say, because I couldn't tell whether she was cross that we took her Bamba or laughing, so all I said was, OK, I'm going, and Amir jumped up and said, where are you running off to? She stood next to him and said, you're welcome to stay, but I didn't want to, I suddenly felt cramped in their apartment and I didn't feel like talking any more. So I put the pieces in the board (I was going to lose in another second anyway), closed the iron hook, put the board under my arm and left.

*

Night has fallen on the Castel, Maoz Ziyon. In the Zakian home, they turn off the last light. Only the small lights that no one notices will stay lit all night. The oven clock. The clock on the VCR. The emergency night light on the kitchen counter near the cookie jar. In the next house, where the bereaved family lives, the lights were turned off quite a while ago. Only the memorial candle is burning in the living room, every little gust of wind blowing the flame to and fro. Yotam's parents are in bed, lying back to back, not sleeping and not making a sound. Each one needs to be held, but neither one turns around. The father is thinking: tomorrow's a month, we'll go to the cemetery for the unveiling of the gravestone. I hope there's no one we forgot to phone. The mother is thinking: what is going to happen to that child, he's hardly ever here. Whenever he should be doing homework, he seems to disappear. And Yotam himself is already sleeping. In his dream, there's a forest where thick tree trunks reach as high as the sky. Gidi is climbing one of them, and suddenly turns into his neighbour, Amir, who played backgammon with him. Twice.

And the neighbour, Amir, closes the book, *Research*

Methods, because he can't absorb any more, it's so late. He goes to the fridge and takes out a chocolate dessert that's past its sell-by date. Walks back to the bedroom, scratches his head, puts the book back on the shelf near his bed.

There's not a sound on the street. No people, no cars. It's time to go outside, to breathe some stars.

*

Moments when it's hard for Amir to be Noaandamir:

When she messes up the house and claims it's the only way she can breathe. Neatly organised places make her feel like she's in a prison cell, and all she wants is to leave. Don't be silly, he tells her, and picks up a damp towel that's lying on the rug, a used tissue and a cotton ball. It has nothing to do with freedom or prison. You're just lazy, that's all.

When she interrupts him during a football match, especially when he's watching his favourite team, and asks him for the millionth time: that rule, offside, exactly what does it mean?

And also: when her need for creative space turns aggressive. When all she cares about is this frame and that negative. And all of a sudden, she can't see him even when he's standing a metre away. Night or day. And her entire body is telling him: go. At those moments he swears he'll get back at her. He'll wait till she wants to be close to him again, and he'll be so cold that she'll never forget. Or he could get angry and give her a piece of his mind. But Amir's not that kind. At least not yet.

*

Enough of the album for today. On the next page, the black-and-white series starts, a series of pictures of Amir everywhere in the house, pictures with sharp, dramatic contrasts that make him look like a movie star from the 1950s. Especially the one taken in the bathroom when he was shaving, with little smidgens of lather near his ears. When I look at that picture, I can actually smell his smell.

Something between vanilla and cinnamon. And that really is too much. Enough, Noa. The past is past. Close the album now. Go to the bookcase. Hide it behind the encyclopaedias.

*

Her shift at the café is over at midnight. She's home by twelve-thirty. But I go out to the Zakian steps a little before that. She loves me to wait outside for her, it thrills her every time and, after a full day of summarising chapters of the book, with one break to play a silent game of backgammon with Yotam, I'm yearning for her. On the other hand, and there's always the other hand, a tiny desire to be alone for a little while longer is darting in and out of my consciousness.

No one is out walking on the streets of the Castel at this hour. The wind carries the faint mutterings of the Madmoni family's TV. A bluish light flickers from their first-floor window. The extension to their house is dark. Actually, it doesn't exist yet. They're building it now. The more my eyes adjust to the darkness, the more details I can see. Scaffolding, iron rods, buckets strewn all around, upside down, and a whitish something that looks like a pitta right in the middle of the roof. The workers themselves have already gone, unless one of them stayed to sleep in the little tin hut they built below the house. If there is someone there, he's probably frozen. It's only the end of October, but it's cold here in the Judean hills. I rub my hands together and then bury them in the sleeves of my sweater.

A ray of light suddenly appears, illuminating the houses at the end of the block. Something that looks like the small van that takes her home comes crawling along the street. A plan begins to take shape in my mind. I'll let her get out, let her cross the street, sunk in thought, let her come right up to the bottom of the stairs I'm sitting on, and only then will I say, in the dulcet tones of a night-time radio

41

broadcaster: hello Noa from Maoz Ziyon. No, I think, rejecting the plan out of hand, she'll be scared. Or maybe she'll be angry. Why ruin things? In another few days, it'll be a month since we moved to the Castel, and, like I wrote to Modi, touch wood, everything's OK so far. We haven't had any fights, at least not any big ones. The fucking is passionate, intense, the best we've ever had. The way she understands me, from inside, and can cut through all my defences with a single sentence straight to the truth. And the way she winds her hair up in a towel after her shower and skips-drips all over the house.

True, there's a kind of tension brewing under the surface all the time, like a shark slipping down under clear water. And even when we're closest, I feel my shadow moving away from us, taking off for somewhere else. When I drive to Tel Aviv in the morning and my Fiat bolts out of Sha'ar Hagai, I feel like I'm bolting out of some narrow space too. But maybe that's just how it is. That's how it is with couples.

The van stops. She gets out and thanks the driver. The most beautiful collarbone in the world appears when she bends. Another couple of rides and the driver will fall in love with her. She waves goodbye to him, wraps her black scarf around her and in a single movement, pulls out the hair trapped between the scarf and her neck. Then she buries her small fists in her long red coat (one night, she wore that coat with only panties under it, in my honour) and starts in my direction in that skipping walk of hers that bursts out of her coat.

*

Meanwhile, in Tel Aviv they're starting to set up the stage – pulling ropes, dragging boards, putting up lights. A Centurion tank from the armoured corps exhibition last Succoth has been left in the square. The logistics manager of the rally is on his mobile now, pleading with the army officer in charge: put it somewhere else, anywhere. But that logistics manager isn't what he seems. He has a secret dream. He wants to write a book and then sign copies during national book week. He wants to hear his name on the loudspeakers at the shopping mall: the author is signing copies of his book at the publisher's stall. And the queue of people will be immense. He even has an idea for a book, an exciting novel set during the War of Independence. And also a title: 'Burma', after the name of the road to Jerusalem paved by the fighters. But he can't find the time to write it. The wife. The kids. This job, a bottomless pit. For instance, this peace rally on Saturday night. They say that more than a hundred thousand people will come to hear Rabin and the mayor speak, and they're probably right. If even the smallest thing gets screwed up – if the loudspeakers squeak, if they don't take away that Centurion tank they were supposed to pick up this week – his boss won't hesitate to take it out on him. So it's better to get back to work now, he tells himself. To make calls, raise walls, nail boards. And for the time being, leave his dreams on the shelf.

*

Today, out of the blue, in the middle of a lecture, I really missed you.

Lucky me.

I just wanted to get up and go straight home.

So why didn't you?

You know . . .

Get up, get up, I'll meet you at the door in my under-wear.

And with a big hug too?

Sure, a big hug too. Why, did something happen at college?

Nothing special. I have days like that when Bezalel seems like one big maze and I'm the mouse, and every little conversation drains me, and I think that no one in the world loves me, no, even worse, that there's something hard inside me that doesn't let people love me.

What are you talking about?

It's like a hungry tiger has its claws around my throat and won't let go.

Yes, I know the feeling.

You do? What's going to happen to us, we're too much alike.

No we're not. You're messy and I'm organised.

How many times do I have to tell you, I'm not messy, I'm free.

Sounds like one of those soul songs, 'I'm not messy, I'm fr-e-e-e-e-e'.

With Gidi Gov and Mazi Cohen in the background.

Accompanied by the Steve Miller Band and Singers.

The Hungry Tiger Singers.

Come here for a minute. Yes. Closer. Closer. You protect me from my tiger and I'll protect you from yours, OK?

*

At the end of the month, the water heater exploded. No one knew yet that it was a metaphor. Someone, they didn't know who, forgot to flip off the switch and all of a sudden, a little after one in the morning, it blew. A big boom, like a clap of thunder, but shorter. And a one-time geyser sprayed into the night air, covering the roofs and the field below with water.

Within seconds, everyone was outside. Moshe and Sima, Amir and Noa, and Yotam and his mum. (His father stayed asleep: the sound fitted right into the war he was dreaming about, the sound of an exploding bomb.)

During the first few seconds, they thought the worst (an earthquake, a Scud missile, even a terrorist bombing), but when the water began dripping from the roof, splashing on the asbestos and raising vapour, they realised it was nothing alarming. Noa went inside to turn off the switch, and her hand brushed against Sima's, who had gone inside with the same objective in mind. Amir reassured Yotam by waving his hands and yelling: go back to sleep, kid, everything's fine! The cats organised a meowing support group next to the washing line. Moshe Zakian stood outside, twisting a non-existent sidelock with his finger, thinking about how much money he'd have to pay. And decided to take care of it the next day.

Chorus

Sometimes we're rap
Dissin' each other all the time
Words, knives, nasty cracks
Listen up, yo
We do it all in rhyme.

Sometimes we're trance
Smashin' heads, necks, eyes
Bitin' shoulders, asses, thighs
Night train! Take your seat!
'Did you come?' 'Can you get me something to eat?'

But every time I think I know
How it's supposed to be, all this you and me.
This you and me, hey,
The beat shifts, the disk warps
Love is a jittery deejay.

'Cause sometimes we're blues
Playin' in a key that's oh so sad
Did you say something? No, did you?
We'll talk about it tomorrow –
I'm tired too.

And sometimes we're an Israeli folk tune

The kind that is so nice to croon
Scratch me here, stroke me there
Oh why can't it be just this fine
All the time?

'Cause sometimes we're Iggi Pop
or A Hard Day's Night
Sometimes it's rock guitars
And distortion all night

But every time I think I know
How it's supposed to be, all this you and me
All this you and me, hey,
The beat shifts, the disk warps
Love is a jittery deejay.
The beat shifts, the disk warps
Love is a jittery deejay.

Music and lyrics: David Batsri
From the Licorice album, *Love As I Explained it to My Wife*,
Produced independently, 1996

2

The drive was actually fine. My little Lilach didn't cry too much, she just threw up a bit on the ride down to Jericho because of the turns, but I cleaned her up with the napkins I brought with me and gave her some water to drink. On the Jordan Valley Road, she went back to smiling that smile of hers that makes her look like an angel, and Liron played quietly with his Tetris. Usually, he keeps on shoving his head between the front seats and Moshe doesn't like that because it's dangerous, so they argue about it the whole way, but this time, because of the Tetris, he sat close to the window and didn't look up from the screen, not even when Moshe said, look, here's Lake Kinneret. Too bad, Liron, you're missing out, I told him, because it really was something to see: a giant blue pool glittered between the mountains like a mirror. I don't believe it, he said – and for a minute, we thought he was admiring the pool – I beat my own record! I beat it! Moshe laughed and said, that's great, kid, and my little Lilach started giving a whole speech in her own language, biddy, bodu, bu du ja. Liron, pleased with himself, finally put down the Tetris, tickled her stomach and asked, Mum, what's bigger, the Kinneret or the sea? I said, the sea, and he asked, how do you know? I said that you can't see where the sea ends, but you can see where the Kinneret ends, and he didn't say anything, but looked satisfied with the answer. The four of us drove along like that, the Kinneret on our right, a whole row of kibbutzim on our left and Greek music in the middle, Moshe singing along with Poliker singing about Aleka, the poor little Greek boy who was no Alexander. I drummed the rhythm on Moshe's knee and thought, no question about it, we have to get out of Jerusalem every once in a while, to get a breath of fresh air, especially during such a tough week when all the TV stations are talking about Rabin, may he rest in peace.

But the minute we got to Rabbi Menachem's house, my good mood was ruined. On the trip up there, I somehow managed to forget that visits to Moshe's brother are no big pleasure, which is why we only go two or three times a year, but as soon as we walked in and said, Shabbat Shalom, and Menachem said, may your Shabbat be blessed, and lifted Liron into the air and forced his face close to the *mezuzah* and said, little man, didn't you ever hear about kissing the *mezuzah*? I remembered why those Saturdays get on my nerves so much that I always leave with my hair full of electricity. But I didn't say anything. I didn't want to spoil Moshe's time with his oldest brother, who actually raised him because Avram and Gina used to work from morning to night. The two brothers hugged and kissed each other on the cheek, and Bilha, Menachem's wife, came over and helped me off with my jacket. No matter how hard I try to dress modestly, I always feel naked next to her. Bilha didn't say a word, but she didn't have to: the way she looked at my new earrings said it all. I checked that all the buttons on my blouse were buttoned. After the seder night last Passover, Moshe really let me have it about the bottom button – not the top one, mind you – of my white blouse that had been open and everyone could see – God help us – my belly button. I didn't need that again. Meanwhile, my Liron had joined the 'sidelocks unit', Menachem's four sons – I can never remember their names in the right order – and followed them out into the garden. Lilach was handed over to Hefzibah, the pretty, oldest daughter who always kept her eyes glued to her patent leather shoes. Hefzibah took her to the small room where Menachem and Bilha's new baby girl, Bat-El, the latest in the production line, was waiting.

We were invited into the living room for coffee before the meal.

Your Liron is quite a man already, Menachem said, and handed his brother a *yarmulke* and a hairpin.

Moshe nodded proudly and put on the skullcap.

And the little one, Menachem went on, looks just like you, Sima. She has such a beautiful face.

That Menachem, he knows what to say to everyone, I thought, but I still couldn't stop my mouth from spreading into a smile.

Tell me Moshe, Menachem said in a more serious tone, what's the condition of the *mezuzot* in your house?

The smile was wiped off my face. My big toe climbed over the toe next to it in my shoe.

The *mezuzot* are in order, I think, Moshe answered and, sounding afraid, he added: someone came to check not too long ago. Why do you ask?

Some people say that all the troubles we've been having recently are because the *mezuzot* are being neglected, Menachem said.

I don't understand, I broke in, are you saying that Rabin is dead because of neglected *mezuzot*? I couldn't control myself. The way I felt came out in the tone of my voice, just begging for a fight. Moshe gave me the kind of look he usually saves for drivers who cut him off on the road. Bilha stirred the coffee, which was already completely stirred. Menachem didn't say anything, thinking about how to answer me.

Everything is in God's hands, he finally said. He looked up at the ceiling, leaving me the choice of whether to take his bland remark as an invitation to go to war or as a proposal for a ceasefire.

Maybe you should go and see how Lilach is doing? Moshe suggested. I had a lot of good answers for 'everything is in God's hands', for instance, 'all is known in advance, but each may choose his way', but I didn't want to make things worse than they already were, so I did what Moshe said and went to the baby's room with my coffee cup in my hand. Lilach and Bat-El were lying there, their cots side by side, and Hefzibah was standing over them singing a lullaby I knew from somewhere. I stood next to her, looked at the babies' faces and sipped my coffee slowly. All of a sudden, I saw that they looked alike. I mean, Lilach is a little bit prettier, really, but there was something the same about the cheeks and the colour of the eyes, and that was the first time I noticed it. Just like twins, Hefzibah said, as if she'd heard what I was thinking, and I said yes, the Zakians have strong genes, and I asked her, what's that song you were singing? You have to teach it to me, I'll sing it to Lilach next time she wakes up at three in the morning, and Hefzibah said, everyone knows that song, don't you? She sang the words again, 'The angel who hath redeemed me from all evil, bless the lads,' and then I realised where I knew that melody from. Hefzibah kept on singing in a soft voice – 'And let my name be named on them, and the name of my fathers Abraham and Issac; and let them grow into a multitude in the midst of the earth' – and the memory slowly became clearer.

Ashkelon. Night time. My father comes into the room Mirit and I share and sits down on her bed. I remember thinking: why not on my bed? He already has long side-locks and a prickly black beard. He's wearing a white button-down shirt and black trousers. With one hand, he strokes my head, and with the other, Mirit's cheek, and in his nice warm voice, he sings us that same song. But he trills it a little more. He sings it to us a few times, till we fall asleep. The next morning, he disappeared with all his belongings except for a new pair of Adidas trainers my mother kept in the drawer for a few months in case he came back. He didn't come back, except in Mirit's dreams. Every morning she'd tell me, whispering as if it was a secret, so Mum wouldn't hear, that in her dream Dad carried her around on his shoulders, and in her dream he read her a story and told her he missed her. In her dream.

About a year later, my mother found out through the neighbours that Dad was going out with a rabbi's daughter in Jerusalem and at night she took the beautiful new Adidas trainers out of the drawer and put them outside next to the big rubbish bin, along with a few of their wedding pictures, and in the morning the trainers were gone, but the pictures stayed there, mixed in with all the bags of rubbish for at least another week, because the city workers were on strike.

That's enough of that song, I blurted out to Hefzibah and swallowed a sourness that rose into my throat. She stopped singing in the middle of a word and looked shocked. I must have sounded more upset than I meant to. The two babies started to cry in a perfect duet – when one stopped to take a breath, the other started crying. I took Lilach out of the cot and held her close to my breast, not only to calm her down, but to calm myself down too, until Moshe came to call us to the table. He couldn't look me in the eye. What had he been talking about with Menachem? I asked myself. Your daughter's crying, I said and held Lilach up to his face the way you hold up evidence in a court, even though I didn't know exactly what I was trying to prove. He sighed, ignored my sharp tone and asked us again, almost begged us, to come to the table, Bilha laboured long and hard to prepare the meal, it wasn't nice.

I thought, what's this 'laboured long and hard'? That didn't sound like him. It sounded like Menachem. It's always like that. A minute after they see each other, Menachem's words start coming out of his mouth.

Moshe took Lilach from me and she pressed up against the soft stomach she loved so much and stopped crying. That made me feel better – seeing them together always calmed me down – and I followed them. We sat down around a table loaded with food, and at the head was the *Shabbat challah* covered with a white cloth and two fancy candlesticks that had been handed down from generation to generation in Bilha's family, just like the stories about them. Menachem gave a sermon on the portion of the week, full of broad hints about the times we were living in, when the religious population was being unjustly attacked and we had to strengthen our faith, restore it to its former glory and respond to all the slanderers with prayers for the Almighty. When he said 'strengthen our faith', he kept his eyes on Moshe and again I had the feeling that they had come to some kind of agreement while I was with Lilach. I didn't say anything. Later, I thought that maybe my not talking gave Moshe the wrong idea, that I agreed with his brother and also with their secret pact. But all of that came later, after the silence. When it was actually happening, I said to myself, what kind of secret pact are you thinking of, Sima? They probably talked about their father's operation; calm down. I gave Liron some salad from the bowl because whenever he takes food by himself, it falls on to the table, and I smiled at pretty Hefzibah, who was sitting across from me, to make up for my being short with her before. I had some of Bilha's chicken and potatoes in orange sauce and asked her for the recipe. And I said amen.

*

First of all, bro, I want to set the record straight. I'm not writing this letter on drugs. I didn't sniff any coke, didn't drink any San Pedro, didn't eat any mushroom omelettes. They do smoke here every once in a while, mainly the Israelis, but I personally haven't rolled a single joint since I arrived in this country of mountains. The air here is too fresh and clear to dirty it with smoke. Even sweet smoke. Why am I saying all this? So that after you read this letter and think I flipped out, you'll know it's not because of chemicals. I'm high, that's true. But only on beauty.

Yesterday, on the peak of the Inhiama, it was so beautiful that for the first time in my life, I thought there might be a God.

Wait, hold on a sec before you run to the phone to tell my parents that their son has finally lost it, to organise a special rescue mission, the elite corps, the air force, an article in the weekend news magazine.

Hold your horses, like they say in English.

I can see you sitting in your small home (you didn't describe it, but I have a feeling it's small), that picture of the sad man with the radio hanging over your head (unless Noa managed to convince you to part with it, but I don't think so), stockinged feet on the table, steaming tea in your hand (it should be cold now in the hills of Jerusalem, right?), rereading the first lines of this letter and thinking: what happened to the friend I know? Where's the football nut? First he lays on me a theory about modes of consciousness that he's developing and now he thinks all of a sudden that there is a God.

Wait. I didn't say there's a God.

I said that yesterday, after three days of a long winding trek, I woke up with the sunrise. I went out of the shack (not exactly a shack, more like a tin hut) and suddenly saw that I was on the roof of the world (we'd arrived there the day before, in the dark, those lazy Australians stopped every two metres). I went and sat on a large flat rock overlooking the valley. It was freezing, so I shoved my hands under my knees. The mountains below were still covered with soft morning clouds. Some of the higher summits peeked out. The sun hadn't shown its face yet, but its rays bathed everything in a transparent, almost white light. And there was no soundtrack at all. Can you imagine it? No honking horns. No buses. No humming air conditioners. Not even birds chirping. Total silence. I don't know if you can understand, but there was something about it that made me feel reverent. All of a sudden, I felt that all my little problems, the annoying way I missed Adi, it was all so small. There's a kind of grand order of things, maybe a divine order (OK, maybe not), and I'm a dot in it, a tiny sliver of a dot, a zero, zilch. I'm about as important to the world as a fly in the Sinai.

I don't know, there was something comforting in that thought.

Then the others woke up and came to sit with me on the rock, and the magic faded a little. I wanted to share it with them, but just the thought of having to find words in English to describe what I felt made me lose the urge. So I promised myself I'd write to you when we got to the town at the foot of the mountain, and I smiled hello at Diana from Sydney, who, first thing in the morning, wearing a faded tracksuit and with her hair still messy, looked like a princess (See? You have nothing to worry about. Some things about me will never change).

So here I am. We took a good hotel, pampering ourselves after the trek, so there's even a desk I can put my writing pad on. Every once in a while, the voices of vendors in the nearby Indian market drift through the window. By the way, that market is really something. I walked around it today with Diana and thought about your Noa – I mean, ninety-nine per cent of the time I was thinking about how to seduce Diana (today she wore trousers that zipped over her ass, can you see it?) but every once in a while, a thought about Noa crept in – how she would love it here. Every few steps, a picture for *National Geographic*. Today, for example, it started raining while we were wandering outside (cats and dogs, as if the guy in charge of rain on a Hollywood film set got confused about quantity). All the vendors in the open market grabbed their merchandise and ran to the roofed section (roofed with sheets of torn plastic, just so you don't make the mistake of thinking they ran into a shopping centre), and only one old lady whose legs were probably too heavy to run stayed where she was, closed her eyes and let the rain soak her through and through. Picture it: one old Indian lady alone with vegetables spread on the mat in front of her in the middle of a large sandy area that was turning into mud. Her face was carved with lines like the sole of a shoe. Her hair was blacker than black. And the clouds overhead. And the old bus that opens into a stall in the back. Nice, right? So what are you waiting for? Grab your backpacks and come.

You wrote that sometimes you feel like there's no air in your apartment. That your souls bang into each other like the bumper cars at a fair. So come on, what are you waiting for? Come here. You'll have all the air you need, believe me. And there are no cars here at all. Yes, I know you're both bourgeois now. I read it in your letter. Apartment, work. Nappies before you know it. But maybe you could drop by for a few hours?

I promise not to go on and on about God.

Meanwhile, write to me at the Israeli Embassy in Lima.

(Your last letter was nice, but too short. Sometimes, you can wait two days for a train here. Try harder, man. Tell me a little about what's happening there. Peace, no peace. The score in the Hapoel/Maccabee game. What happened to Licorice, that group of David's. We're pretty cut off here.)

Yours,
Modi

*

On 4 November, that 4 November, I went to David's place to console him after his girlfriend dumped him. On the way, a little before the turn at Motza, they announced on the radio that Rabin had been shot. By the time I arrived, he was already dead. The spokesman's announcement and all that. We sat silently in front of the TV in David's living room. He looked terrible. Thin, his hair a mess, his eyes dead. We hadn't seen each other since I moved to the Castel. He was up to his ears in rehearsals with his band, Licorice. I was busy adjusting to the fact that I was a couple. We'd spoken on the phone and set up dates to meet, but one of us always cancelled at the last minute. I didn't know how to make him feel better. He really loved her, that Michal, from the bottom of his mixed-up soul. And I didn't know if it was right to talk about it now that the Prime Minister had been killed. We didn't say anything for another couple of minutes, just stared at the pictures coming from the square in Tel Aviv, and then the phone rang. Maybe that's her? his eyes lit up: maybe she changed her mind. He grabbed the receiver. It was Noa, who wanted me to come home right away. She's scared. She's sad. She feels all alone. And the way she said 'home', the gentleness – I'd never heard that word said with such gentleness. I got up from the sofa with an apologetic look on my face. David said, it's OK, man, it's perfectly OK, and he walked me down the steps to the car.

The street was deathly silent.

The cold Jerusalem air made us shiver. We each hugged ourselves. And said we'd talk tomorrow.

*

I search the photograph, trying to find something in it that gives an inkling about the day it was taken. The night before, we went to the Knesset to see Rabin's coffin, but the queue was enormous and we didn't get in. We tried to join the kids sitting in circles below the Rose Garden, singing sad songs, but we felt a little strange. 'Fledgling Fly Away' didn't exactly apply to us and there was a kind of innocence in the air that neither of us could connect to no matter how much we wanted to. I took a few pictures of the area, especially the stands that had been set up on the side of the road, selling corn on the cob from steaming pots, and we drove home slowly, cautiously. Everyone drove like that, with exaggerated politeness, the first few days after it happened, as if they were trying to rectify some deeper wrong by driving carefully.

It was sunny when we woke up the next day, and I said to Amir, let's go to the Sataf Springs, it's practically next door. We're always so busy studying that we don't go out, and when will we have another day when we're both free, and Amir said, OK, let's do it. He put his psych books (I have no idea when he took them out) back on the shelf and dressed in his chill-out clothes – an NBA t-shirt with long sleeves and loose trousers that 'let his balls hang free'. I put on jeans and a hat, made us cheese sandwiches and took a picnic blanket out of the cupboard.

I look at the picture again. I took it from above, from the stone rim of the small pool. Amir was just getting out of the water, leaning on his arms to lift himself up. That's when I clicked the shutter. His tennis muscles – he hasn't played since Modi went away, but he still has the muscles – were almost bursting out of his arms (an impressive sight, even though I'm not crazy about bodybuilders), the two mounds of his chest were glistening, I really felt like resting my head on it, and for some reason, his uncombed hair had fallen over to the right. He had some white hair even then, but you can't see it here because it's wet. Two large drops are dripping down his forehead. There's another on his eyelash, and he looks surprised, a tiny bit mocking, Noa, Noa, taking pictures again? The light is marvellous, the soft light of early November, the sun is dancing on the water, illuminating his face just right.

And also the face of the Arab boy sitting in his underpants on the far edge of the pool dangling his legs in the water.

Maybe this is where the inkling I am looking for is hidden, in that boy's face. Even though he's only background, seemingly random, he's looking at the camera with a pretty serious and angry expression on his face. His eyebrows are contracted, his lips are pressed together in the kind of expression older boys usually have, and if you look carefully, you can see that his right foot is half-way out of the water, getting ready for a kick that would only collide with air, but is aimed – or at least looks like it is – at the camera. Maybe what happened in the square a couple of days before had put up the wall of fear again and that boy, even if he doesn't understand the whole meaning, senses it somehow. Maybe his parents, or his grandparents, lived in the Arab village of Sataf, whose inhabitants were uprooted in '48, and during this nostalgic trip to the springs they decided to tell the boy who it was that kicked them out of here.

Hey, come on. Enough. It's obvious that you've been spending too much time in Bezalel, Noa. Are you starting to be a phoney intellectual too? Just a few minutes ago, that boy asked for a sip of your Coke, and when you handed it to him, he said thanks a lot and gave you a nice big smile. What's the connection between the assassination and the Arabs? It'd be better to admit that there are no inklings in the picture. Or maybe there are and you'll be able to see them in retrospect. That happens sometimes too: you look at a picture you've seen a thousand times before, and suddenly a new detail jumps out at you. That's how my best project last year was born. I was looking at pictures of my family, and all of a sudden, I noticed a puddle of water on the edge of one of them. That picture had been taken in the summer – you couldn't mistake the burning light of an Israeli summer – but the puddle was as large as a winter puddle. In the middle of August, I started looking for puddles in Tel Aviv and the surrounding towns. In car parks. In industrial areas. In the back yards of grocery shops. It was amazing how many I found. I took pictures of them with almost romantic lighting, as if I were photo-graphing a Norwegian fiord, and I chose an angle that made the puddle look bigger than it was. I called the project 'Summer Puddles', and the lecturer stopped the lesson in the middle, told everyone to stay in their seats and ran to get the head of the department, because 'this is something he has to see'.

On the way back from Sataf, Amir and I argued. A lively debate whose words got all tangled up and somehow turned into a bitter argument. It all started when I said I was sick and tired of living here, in this puddle that drowns its inhabitants, that it looked to me as if things would get very bad now and that I'd started thinking about doing a Master's in art abroad in New York, say. Amir said that the States wasn't such a bargain, he'd already lived in Detroit with his parents and they put too much ice in their Coke, and when you go to play basketball at the YMCA, there are ten people standing there and each one takes a shot into a separate basket, and besides, he's sick of moving; but I insisted, reminding him of Modi's letter from South America, the one he'd read to me the day before, and I said don't you feel like getting away for a little while, to sit and look at old Indian ladies all day? He snorted disdainfully and said in an all-knowing tone, bullshit, you take yourself with you everywhere you go, and he turned up the radio to signal that he wanted to end the discussion, and, slightly annoyed, I said, hey, aren't you tired of those sad songs, for example? He said, no! and turned the volume up even higher and locked himself up inside himself like a steel car lock, I could actually hear the click, but I didn't know what to say to soften him up, because I didn't really understand what had hardened him like that. The minute we got home, he escaped into his fat books, and even though I followed him and said, when we finally have a free day after so long, it's a shame we have to waste it fighting, even then he wouldn't make up, didn't even turn his head towards me. So I went into the living room and looked at the picture I hate, the one with the sad man, and prayed that Amir would argue with me, that he'd get up and shout, because I can't stand it when someone's cold to me like that, and I turned on the TV and turned it off. All of a sudden, our whole apartment seemed too small, too cramped, and my mouth filled with the taste of defeat and I felt that it wouldn't work, that the whole idea of living together would end in tears and I'd screw up my final project on the way. I went outside for some air, to calm down, but it was so cold that I ran back in, and inside, no one was waiting for me, except for the man in the picture who, just like before, kept looking outside through the window.

*

In eight years we never had a fight, Moshe and me. Not since we met. Maybe we would've kept going and broken the Guinness world record if the car with the megaphone hadn't come down the street inviting the people who lived in the neighbourhood to a rally with the great rabbi, with a performance by the singer Bennie Elbaz, in the square in front of Doga's shop.

We were sitting in the living room watching *Wheel of Fortune* with Erez Tal and Ruth Gonzales, and things were really peaceful. We hadn't voted for her in the contest, but she was adorable on that programme, with her curls and her accent. She looks good, that Gonzales, I said to Moshe, and he said, yes, but not like you, and gave me a kiss on the shoulder, and I said, you're a riot, not everyone has to compare with me, but inside, I was glad he still said that, even though I have given birth twice, and my hips have spread and my hair doesn't shine much any more, like they say in the adverts, and I even have some small wrinkles around my eyes when I laugh. I stroked the back of his neck as a reward, and I combed Liron's hair with the fingers of my other hand. He was sitting on my left and reading the letters on the screen out loud to show that he already knew the whole alphabet by heart, even though he got confused sometimes between letters that look alike. Lilach was awake, but quiet, completely hypnotised by the TV. The students weren't making noise with their music. Avram and Gina didn't come to the door with biscuits. No one called from one of those polling companies to ask what our political position is after the assassination (ever since that time I said I'd answer their questions, they never leave us alone). There was a bowl in the middle of the table with two bunches of grapes in it, black and green. Every once in a while, someone took a grape.

When you're living your everyday life, you don't think about the good things you have. You're almost always too busy thinking about what you don't have. But right then, I remember thinking: look at how beautiful this is, Sima. You have your small family. A whole family, like you dreamed you'd have when you were a girl. And then, just when an engineer from Yavneh won a refrigerator worth four thousand shekels, the sound of the megaphone broke into the victory music. What's the junkman doing here now? I muttered, still full of the pleasant feeling my thoughts were giving me, and Moshe turned down the sound on the TV and said, that's not the junkman, Sima, listen. 'All neighbourhood residents are invited! Bennie Elbaz, in the square in front of Doga!' the megaphone shouted. And Moshe filled in the rest: there's a big rally, the whole neighbourhood's going. The great rabbi will be there, and all the heads of the movement. It's going to be something special. Terrific, I said, grabbed the remote control and made the TV louder. The engineer from Yavneh also won two plane tickets to London and a chance to be in the finals. Wanna go? Moshe asked. Why, what do I want with them? I answered. We were both looking at the TV, we didn't dare look at each other. Then, all of a sudden, he got up from the sofa so fast that I couldn't believe it was him, stood in front of me and blocked the screen. I don't understand you, Sima. It wouldn't hurt us to listen to some Torah. To learn a little Judaism. It's far better than sitting here and watching this rubbish on TV. Daddy, Liron said, jumping up, I want to go to the rally with you. Absolutely not, I cut in before Moshe had time to agree. It's late and you have to go to sleep. I don't know why you don't have your pyjamas on yet. Brush your teeth, put on your pyjamas, and go to bed. Get a move on. Liron walked to his room, but didn't hide how much he didn't want to. Move please, you're blocking the screen, I told Moshe. He moved aside slowly, on purpose. The megaphone, which had already moved away from our street, was coming back. This time, not only music was coming from it. OK, I'm going anyway, Moshe said, looking at me expectantly. I didn't say anything. And when I get back, he added in that same puffed-up tone that his brother Menachem uses, I want to talk to you. And if you don't come home, my dear husband, should I go and look for you in Bnei Brak? I asked without taking my eyes off the TV. Yes, in Bnei Brak, Moshe repeated just to annoy me, and then he put on his warm jacket, went out and slammed the door.

Lilach started to cry. I picked her up. Don't worry, sweetie, it's just the wind, I lied to her. I was cross with myself for lying. So what if she doesn't understand, you don't have to get her used to lies from the time she's little. Look, I pointed to the TV, it's the finals. I took a green grape and put it in her mouth. She shoved it away with her hand and pointed to the black grapes. No problem, have a black one, you don't have to throw it on the floor, I said, and pulled some black grapes off the bunch for her. She chewed them happily, one after the other, then went back to watching *Wheel of Fortune* with me. In the finals, the engineer from Yavneh won a Mitsubishi, free petrol for a year and a music system for his car.

*

I remember the day Nasser resigned like it was yesterday – that's what Mama says when we're sitting in front of the TV watching the programmes in memory of Rabin.

Everyone knows that she's going to tell the same story we've heard already, but we still want to hear again, because she always adds new details that would be interesting even to people listening to it for the hundredth time. Sometimes, when she's in a good mood, she makes little digs at us, her children.

Everybody had gathered around the TV in Jamil's café, she starts, and I make the sound lower on our set, out of respect for her. It was an ugly brown TV with a tall aerial like a tree and terrible reception, she goes on. Every few seconds, a big white stripe would move across the screen from top to bottom, and the button for the sound was broken, but it was the only TV in the village and no one wanted to miss out. People were standing on the tables with their backs up against the wall, anything as long as they could see. The *shabab*, the boys, she says, giving me an accusing look, were standing so close to the young girls that some of them took advantage and touched places they shouldn't, may Allah show them the right path, and Jamil ran around in the crowd with plates of hummus and beans and bottles of fizzy drinks. People had big appetites before Nasser talked. *Ya'ani*, everyone knew from the rumours and Jewish newspapers that the war was lost, but no one thought he would ... just like that, out of the blue. Everybody thought another one of his great speeches was coming, like the ones he gave that made your whole body shake when you heard them. Oh God, he knew how to talk, that Nasser. Raising his voice and lowering it, choosing the words like a poet. But that day, the minute he walked on the stage, you could tell from the expressions of the people standing behind him, his advisers, that something was wrong. His face was as white as noon, and his forehead was sweating so hard that even on Jamil's poor TV, you could see the drops, and all of a sudden the café was completely quiet. It's hard to believe, but even Marwan – she looks at my brother, who's talking to his wife, Nadia – was quiet. Nasser

64

went up to the microphone and started reading from the page in a weak voice: Brothers! he said – I remember the first sentence perfectly – we always speak frankly to each other, both in victory and in hard times, when the moment is sweet and when it is bitter, only in this way can we find the right path. Then he explained how the Americans helped the Israelis in the war, how the Israeli Air Force attacked first and the Egyptian soldiers fought like heroes, and the Jordanian soldiers also fought like heroes, and finally he said that he, Jamal Abd al-Nasser, was to blame and was resigning from the presidency, and, beginning tomorrow morning, he would be placing himself at the service of the people. When he finished and picked up the pages and walked off the stage, you could see one of his advisers wiping tears from his eyes with a handkerchief, and then, all together, the men in the café wiped the salty drops from the corner of their own eyes with their little fingers, even the biggest, strongest men, Najh Hasein, *allah yerhimu*, who'd been in a Jordanian prison for ten years, and Husam Mernaiya, who was the boxing champion of Ramallah three times in a row, and even your father, the hero – and here she looks at my father, who looks down – you have nothing to be ashamed of, that's how it is, when they give a person hope and then snatch it away from him, it's harder than if they hadn't given you anything to begin with, and that Nasser, with his laughing eyes and beautiful words about the great, strong Arab people – he was like a father for us, a father who made us believe that there was light in the world, that before we went to heaven, we would go back to our village, to our land, and our heart would not be like the seed of a bean cut in half, and we would stop wandering from place to place like gypsies.

She picks up the key that she wears around her neck, the key to the old house, kisses the rusty iron, and continues.

Then the Egyptians went into the streets and lay down

on the roads and begged, and Nasser cancelled his resignation and went back to being president. But it wasn't the same any more. He was sick and weak by then, and three years later, he died. Everyone went to Jamil's café again – the prices there were in liras now, not dinars – to watch his funeral.

She takes a sip of her coffee, checks to see that everyone is listening, and continues.

And I'll tell you what's strange: now Itzhak Rabin is dead, the Rabin who finished off Nasser, the Rabin whose soldiers shot above our heads in '48, the evil Rabin, Rabin the devil, and instead of being happy, instead of dancing in the street and clapping, I'm sad. Look at his granddaughter, a pretty girl, crying. She looks like her grandfather, the way Marwan's Raoda looks like her grandfather. I can't help it, I'm sad for her. All the leaders, they always have a bad end. And what will happen now?

*

When our teacher talked about Rabin's murder, she had exactly the same expression she had when she told the class that Gidi had been killed, and right away it made me suspect that maybe that expression, the serious look in her eyes, the way she bit her lips, all that was just a mask she puts on when she thinks she has to be sad. When she finished, she sat on the edge of her desk and asked us to talk, to say what we felt. Like it always is in those situations, when you don't know exactly what to say, everyone repeated what she said, except in different words. I didn't raise my hand. I haven't talked in class for a while. It started after Gidi's *shivah*, when I came back to school and didn't understand what they were talking about in class because I'd missed so many lessons, so I decided I'd rather be quiet so nobody would notice that I didn't understand, and after that, I got so used to not talking that even if I wanted to say something – let's say at the trial they had in *Bible class* for King David, when they got to the part where he sends Uriah the Hittite to war – the words stuck in my throat and I had the feeling that if I opened my mouth, I'd stutter. Even though I'd never stuttered in my life.

When Alon said that the murder was terrible and horrifying, and Rinat said that the murder was horrifying and terrible, I thought to myself – when you don't talk, you have more time to think – that it was weird how my world had turned upside down in the last few days. Till the assassination, my world was made up of my house, where we weren't allowed to listen to music or laugh, and everybody else, who tried to be really nice to me but kept doing their own thing, kept being happy when Beitar won on Saturday, or complained about the prices at Doga. And now everything had turned upside down. Everybody on the street is worried, they walk slowly, talk quietly, and in my house everything is as usual, they don't turn on the TV, they don't care. Like Mum said to Nitza Hadass last night, everyone cries over their own dead.

Does anyone want to add anything? the teacher asked and looked around at the class. My elbow started to rise on its own, but I forced it back down on to my desk. Why bother. They won't understand anyway. And besides, I'll stutter. I'll be better off waiting for backgammon with Amir, he has patience with what I'm thinking, even if it's weird. And he always has something interesting to say. The day before yesterday, for instance, I told him that I think people who die aren't really dead, but they live somewhere up there in the sky and watch us down here. He said that the first time he was on a plane going to America and they flew above the clouds, he really did look for the souls of dead people up there, or for God. And he didn't find them. But maybe he didn't look hard enough.

*

A red Egged bus is racing through the streets with a dull roar. It doesn't pull into bus stops, its doesn't open its door. It's three a.m. The driver is Moshe Zakian. His passengers have long since gone home to bed. Moshe is the only one in the bus, clutching the wheel and staring straight ahead. No one is taking out money to pay his fare. No one is asking if the bus goes to here or to there.

He leaves the neighbourhood, turns right at the Mevasseret bridge and starts driving towards Tel Aviv. The road is empty, the air is sharp and darkness swallows up the trees flying past. After the descent to the Castel, he steps harder on the accelerator. A truck coming from the opposite direction has its full beams on. His face grim, Moshe turns his up his too: I'll show him. The miniature Beitar menorah hanging from the rearview mirror jumps around like a football fan after a win. He presses the radio search button. The Voice of Music. The Voice of Ramallah. There's nothing he wants to hear. He settles on Non-Stop Radio, Hebrew songs all night, including the greatest hits of this year. And still, the words Sima shot at him that night keep sounding in his brain. 'Forget it', 'Let it go', 'Over my dead body'. Over and over again. You'd think he'd suggested something terrible. All he did was say that they opened a nice kindergarten up the street. Half price, twice the hours, good food for the kids to eat. Two of his friends had already transferred their children, and they said the kindergarten was good. Menachem, in Tiberias, thought they should. It wouldn't hurt the boy to absorb some Judaism. The education he was getting now was a disgrace. Not to mention that the money they'd save would help them buy a bigger place. With a room for guests to stay. But Sima's as stubborn as a mule. What exactly had she said? 'For you, religion is a house, but it's a prison for me.' A difficult woman, as difficult as can be. Moshe fans the flames of his anger and slams his foot down. The red bus hurtles from Sha'ar Hagai and Latrun zooms past. OK, she doesn't want to go to the rally with him. And she wants Liron to stay in the kindergarten he's in. But is that a reason to talk about splitting up? We can talk. Compromise. Make up. What'll the children think when they see their father in the living room in his underwear? Lilach's a baby, but Liron's old enough to understand what they said. And why should it be him, Moshe, who has to leave their bed? He's the one with a bad back, and sleeping on the hard living-room sofa will make his bones crack.

Wait, his brow furrows in a frown. They say there's a camera here, after the turn. Maybe I should slow down.

From the airport control tower, a light flashes. Once. Twice. The miniature Beitar menorah is still. A passing plane illuminates a cloud in the sky. Suddenly tired, suddenly limp, he decides not to go into Tel Aviv after all, and he knows why. When he was a child, he wandered away from his parents on Frishman beach and waited hours at the lifeguards' station for them to come and get him. It's dark in the city now, and he could lose his way. Besides, he has to be back at the wheel at seven the next morning. He has to be alert and steady. And God knows how late it is already. He takes the Gannot exit and starts driving back. More and more of the songs on the radio are in Rabin's memory: Shlomo Artzi, Aviv Gefen, Yehuda Poliker singing sadly about taking back terrible things he said. Overcome with shame, Moshe remembers things he said during the fight, before he ran out. It was out of weakness that he'd said what he said. Sima knows how to twist words, she comes out on top in every little dispute. He understands perfectly, but when it comes to talking, well, it's not exactly his strong point. As he approaches Latrun, he starts missing her. He sees her in his mind: in the delivery room, her plump, contented face, holding Lilach in her arms and kissing her. She is home for him. And he can't breathe without her.

Eight years ago, he talked to her for the first time during break. On the way to the water fountain, he felt he was walking crookedly and thought he looked a mess. At Hanukkah, they started exchanging looks. At first, quick flashes, as if accidentally. Then she smiled. And he was hooked. He already knew every feature of her face. He already knew that her light-coloured jeans were a little too short and a beautiful part of her leg was exposed in the space between the edge of her trousers and the top of her socks. Based on her smile, he thought she might be interested, but how could he really tell? In any case, he felt that if he didn't ask her out by Passover, his life would be hell. As for her, she finished drinking, wiped the last drop of water from the corner of her mouth and leaned against the concrete wall behind the fountain, in the shade. He walked the last few steps that separated them and practised one more time the words he'd spent the night before planning to say. But when he was standing in front of her, a gust of wind carried the thick, intoxicating scent of her hair to his nostrils, and instead of 'I wanted to tell you that I think you're very pretty' or 'You look beautiful in this light', what came out of his mouth was, 'Do you want to go to the cinema tomorrow night?'

He drove across the Mevesseret bridge and turned right.

The red bus is racing through the streets with a dull roar. It doesn't pull into bus stops. It doesn't open its door. It's four-thirty in the morning. Soon, Moshe thinks, he'll get into bed. He'll hug Sima from behind, whisper sweet nothings in her ear, and she'll forget the terrible things he said. If she wakes up, maybe they'll go to look at the children together. There they'll stand, hand in hand, in the kids' room. He'll remind her of how they once stood together at the water fountain in the playground. He won't mention the kindergarten. He'll be on his guard. Where's the fire, tomorrow's another day. She'll admit she's wrong after she hears what he has to say.

*

When the programme on Rabin is over, the men kiss at the door and my father takes all the sections of *A-Nahar* that were lying around the living room and goes to read them in bed, leaving only me and my mother there watching an Egyptian movie, and I want to say to her, *Ya umi*, I saw the house. I saw it with my own eyes. But I know that whenever anyone mentions the subject, it makes her ill. Forty years have passed, but the hurt she feels in her heart is as wet as the ground after rain.

A few weeks after the Six Day War ended, people started visiting their old homes. Quietly, not making a big fuss about it, they'd pile the whole family into a pickup, sometimes ten people in one small truck, and go. Back then, they didn't have to pass five checkpoints every hundred metres like today.

Some people only found a pile of stones where their houses used to be. Some people, like the ones who lived in el-Castel, found their houses still there and in good condition, but Jews were living inside. They would stand and look at the houses from a distance, and if someone asked what they were looking for, they'd just turn around and leave.

The ones who came back from al-Kuds brought plums from the plum tree, the crooked one near the square, and figs from the *muzawi* tree, the one that had fruit as big as pears, and they told us that the Jews had built ugly buildings that didn't fit in with the mountain, and that they gave all the streets the names of wars, Independence Street, Victory Street, Six Day War Street, and they told us about Aziz, the only man who stayed in the village to wait for the soldiers, and after he was killed, he turned into a black demon that entered into the body of the Jews and made them crazy.

We were the only ones who didn't go back. My mother wouldn't let us. She said she didn't want to see. Didn't want to know. Didn't want to hear. With eyes glittering with anger, she would say, I will only go back to my home to live there. I won't be like those *fellahin* who stand around like beggars, waiting; maybe some Jew will invite them in to sit in the living room and drink coffee, in their own house. She'd say to my father, and you too, don't you dare take the children there, or else find yourself another wife.

Even now, sitting in front of the TV, my mother's eyes are glittering, but not with anger. In the Egyptian movie, Mahmoud Yassin comes home to his village after six years in Cairo and only the dog recognises him. *Yekhreb baitak*, she curses Mahmoud Yassin's father, who's looking at him through the window, how can you not know your own son?!

My mother, she has something to say to everyone, even to people in films. Usually, Arab women are silent, hiding behind their husbands, but with us, ever since they took away my father's land and he had to go out and work like a common labourer, he became weak, *ya'ani* depressed, and my mother talks for him.

I look at the dog that's licking Mahmoud Yassin's face, and remember my mother's story about Assuad the dog. It's a story she always tells when my aunts and uncles from Ramallah come for Ramadan or Id al-Fitr, and someone mentions the sweet *katayif* my grandmother used to make, and before long, they're talking about that house. Then she says: Do you remember Assuad, *al-kalb*, the dog? Everyone says, *taba'an*, of course, and they turn their chairs towards her to hear again about the night they ran away, about how Assuad, who was a big, black dog, refused to leave the house and how his howls filled up the whole wadi and even after they tied a strong iron chain around his neck he kept on pulling my father, who was holding him, back to the village and how he looked at the long line of people with the eyes of someone whose best friend had just tricked him, and how at one of their stops, when my father wasn't watching, he managed to break loose and ran to the village with the iron chain trailing after him and never came back. They never saw him again. 'Even a dog was more faithful to his home than we were. Even a dog!' My mother always ended the story with those words, and all my aunts and uncles lowered their heads in shame. Then they sang *mawal* to the village. My father usually started quietly and all of us gradually joined in:

Ya dirati ma lakh aleinu lom, lomackh ala menkhan. Do not be angry with us, our village, be angry at those who betrayed us.

I think he'll apologise to his son, my mother said and pointed to Mahmoud Yassin's father, who was sitting in the dark smoking a *nargileh. Mazbut, ya umi,* I say, even though I'm thinking about something else: should I tell her or not? Where is your dignity, she'll yell, how could you build houses for Jews in our village? Aren't you ashamed? Don't you know that the land is registered in your name? Don't you know that it's your land? That's what she'll say. So why should I tell her? Besides, how can I tell her if I'm still not sure? And how can I be sure if I still haven't gone into the house? We'll be finishing Madmoni's frame soon, and I still haven't been inside, God forgive me.

*

If you think I've forgiven you, you're making a big mistake, I told Moshe and turned my back on him. Two minutes before that, I had been crazy with worry about him. It's not like him to go out like that, in the middle of the night, when he has to drive in the morning. I looked at the alarm clock every five minutes, then every minute, then I got up and went to the kitchen and finished off a whole bag of cornflakes, even though I knew that Liron would be disappointed in the morning when he saw there were none left. I read two magazine articles about Sigal Shahmon, one in *For Women* and the other in *Modern Times* – she said she didn't want to have children yet, but family was the most important thing in life for her – and from so much Sigal Shahmon, I was ready to forgive Moshe just as long as he came home quickly and didn't fall asleep on the road, God forbid, and have an accident, like Turji, his friend from work who fell asleep on the road to Eilat and now he parks his car in the handicapped spaces.

But as soon as I heard the bus turn into the street and knew he was OK, I didn't feel like making up any more. I put the box of cornflakes back in the cabinet, jumped into bed, covered myself and pretended I was sleeping. I heard the bus door closing and the front door opening and Moshe humming an Ehud Banai song, 'Maybe after all this, we'll sail off to an island. The children will wander along the shore.' Why's he humming? I thought. What's he so happy about? And our whole fight came back into my mind, all the ugly things he said – not said, yelled – what's good for the whole neighbourhood is good for us too. If you don't have God, you don't have anything. He'd yelled all kinds of things like that in an extremely loud voice, like a person who's not sure he's right. Like my father yelled before he left.

By the time Moshe finished in the bathroom and came into the bedroom, I had forgotten that I'd softened up and just waited for him to say one wrong word or forget to turn off the light in the living room so I could stick him with some sharp words, but he didn't say anything, and he turned off the lights and got undressed quietly, without banging into the wardrobe, and got into bed carefully and lay down next to me without stealing the blanket. But still, I couldn't control myself and said what I said, turned my back to him and pressed my nose up against the frozen wall. When he tried to stroke my hair from behind, I said to him, Moshe, don't touch me, in a tone so full of disgust that I even scared myself a little.

*

When form time was over, I put everything into my bag and locked the buckle. Rinat reminded me that we still had a catch-up English lesson. I told her I know and I don't care. Lately, I bunk lessons a lot, but no one says anything to me because I lost my brother. The headmistress even

74

took me to the grove behind the field for a talk and leaned her elbow on a tree and got dirty from the sap. She told me about what a good student Gidi had been, as if I didn't know, and told me that her door was always open – which is not true, it's always closed – and that I shouldn't hesitate to come to her about anything, anything at all.

It was very cold outside, it was even drizzling a little, so I decided to run, but I stopped after a few metres because my bag bounced around while I was running and my pencil case dug into my back.

When I got home, I didn't feel like going inside. Mum was probably in bed, she rests every day and stares at the ceiling or at Gidi's picture. If I went in, she'd say hi, Yoti, there's food in the fridge, warm it up for yourself. And I'd sit alone and eat cutlets and mashed potatoes, and the potatoes'd be hard around the edges from being in the fridge for a hundred years. I can't go to see my friends from class either, they're still in the catch-up English lesson, and besides, lately, it's no fun with them. All the things they do, like sneaking looks under girls' dresses with a mirror or setting up a secret camp in the Mevasseret woods, don't interest me any more. I mean, I drag boards with them from Madmoni's construction site and exchange Beitar cards with them, but I have this bland taste in my mouth, like old pitta, and sometimes their talk makes me really pissed off like yesterday, when Dor said he hates his big brother because he always hogs the computer to play Doom and doesn't let him play, and I wanted to tell him, Dor, you jerk, say thank you that you even have a brother. But I didn't say anything.

I'd rather go straight to Amir's.

I knocked on his door. While I waited for him to open it, I pressed my ear against the far wall to hear if Moshe and Sima were still arguing. Last night, Mum and Dad went out to the garden and all the way up to the fence so they could hear the shouting better. Dad said: They've been living next to us for six years and I never heard them raise their voices even once. Mum said: It's a good thing that Gina can't hear very well, it would break her heart. I stood behind them and was glad. Since Gidi, I haven't heard them talk quietly to each other like that. I hoped that Moshe and Sima would keep fighting all night.

Noa opened the door. She's so tall, I barely come up to her bellybutton. Are you looking for Amir? Yes. He's not home. Is he at the university? No, he's at the club. What club? She gave me that look grown-ups give you before they decide whether what they have to say is for children's ears. He volunteers at a club, she said, but tell me, Yotam, maybe instead of standing outside and getting wet, you'd like to come in and wait for him here? She brought a dry towel and spread it out under me so I wouldn't get the sofa wet. What club does Amir volunteer in? The Incognito? I asked again. When I want an answer, I know how to be stubborn. She laughed, no, it's not a dance club, it's a club for sick people, I mean, sick people who are already starting to get better. I didn't understand. What does that mean? Sick with what? Noa offered me a glass of Coke. I didn't give up. Sick with the flu? With strep? No, she sighed. More ... more like sick in their minds. In their hearts. Crazy? Not exactly. Sort of. Half crazy and half normal. Half crazy, half normal? I remembered an episode of *Star Trek* when Captain Pickard comes back from the planet of the Medusas and starts acting weird on the ship. Instead of being serious, he laughs, instead of being decisive, he's confused, and the whole crew is scared, that's not the Captain they know, until Data the robot discovers that the Medusas on the planet secreted something that got absorbed through the Captain's skin without his noticing it, and that's what made him act like that.

I thought that Noa probably didn't watch *Star Trek*, so I didn't tell her about the Medusas. I didn't say anything and just kept on fiddling with the sofa cover. Tell me,

Yotam, would you like to help me with my homework? she asked me out of the blue. Why not, I said even though it annoyed me that she said homework, like she was a kid. She took me into the bedroom, to a glass table that was lit up by a lamp under it, like a moon. There were camera films on the table, arranged in rows. These are negatives, she said. And this table is called a light table. If you put the negatives on the light table, you can choose which picture on the film is the best and then scan it on the computer. Want to help me choose? OK, I said.

Every picture showed more or less the same thing: the display window of a shoe store. But there was a different high-heeled shoe in the middle of every picture. Sometimes, the price tag was in the middle and the shoes were around it. This is a project we have to do on the subject of religion and God, Noa said. I didn't understand what the connection was between God and shoes, but I picked out two pictures that looked nicer than the others and pointed at them. Why those? Noa asked. I don't know, I said, it's like the things are arranged better in those pictures. Composition, Noa said. What? Composition. That's what we call the relationship between the different elements of a picture. Truth is, you're right, Yotam. The composition of those two really is special.

We went on picking out pictures according to their composition, and meanwhile, Noa told me about other things that have to do with photography: the camera shutter, the light meter, the special light at the beginning and end of every day that's called 'magical light', and her photographing days when she just goes out into the street and waits for something special to happen in front of her eyes. Sometimes a whole day can go by without anything happening, and sometimes a fantastic picture falls into her lap right away. Like for instance yesterday, the minute she went out, Madmoni's workers were getting out of the pickup that brings them to work and one of them, who'd fallen asleep, stayed in the cab. He was wearing a woollen cap with a brightly coloured Indian design, the kind you see only on people who have come back from trips to South America, and then she had this feeling in her stomach that she has when she sees something she wants to photograph, and the only feeling that comes close to it is the way you feel when you see yellow peppers in the supermarket, so she asked the worker if she could take his picture, and he said yes. She loves those kind of mistakes in the world. Let's say, a plastic bag swimming in water like a jellyfish, or a stone sticking out of the wall of a house, like the one in Avram and Gina's house, or the empty lot between their apartment and ours, which in her eyes is one big mistake. I didn't understand why the lot was a mistake, but I felt funny about asking her, so instead I asked about the black container that was standing in the corner of the bedroom. That's the Jobo, Noa said. You put the film in the Jobo and it turns it into a negative. Without Jobo, you can't start the developing process. The third time she said the word Jobo, I had a laughing fit. That word, Jobo, made me laugh hysterically, and no matter how hard I bit my lips, I couldn't stop. Noa tried to control herself, but in the end, she caught it from me and started laughing and pushing her long hair from side to side with her hand so it wouldn't get into her open mouth. I suddenly noticed that she really was beautiful, like Amir told his friend on the phone. Especially when she laughed. After a few seconds, I started to hiccup the way I always do when I laugh for a long time without stopping, and that only made us laugh more. If Mum could see me laughing like that, she'd probably make an 'aren't-you-ashamed-of-yourself' face, like she's been doing since Gidi whenever I watch a comedy on TV, even if I turn the sound off. But Mum didn't see, so we kept on laughing until the laugh muscle in my stomach hurt and Noa's eyes glittered with tears. And then Amir came in. The minute we saw his face, we stopped. Even though he smiled at me and kissed Noa on the lips, you could still see right away that the half-and-half club had made him a bit crazy. How was it, Noa asked him, and he started zigzagging around the room, saying, it's not easy, it's not easy. I picked up a picture and looked at it so he'd think I wasn't listening. Nava says that it's because of the Rabin assassination, he said, and I watched him over the top of the picture, like a detective. The thing is, he went on, talking with his hands, that they don't care about Rabin himself. Some of them don't even know he was Prime Minister. But all those memorial ceremonies, and the sad songs and the special programmes on TV, it's like their emotional antennae are picking up the idea that something in the order of things has been disrupted, and that pulls the rug right out from under them. Do you see what I mean? he asked Noa. Without wanting to, at the worst possible moment, I hiccuped and she didn't have time to say yes, she understands, because Amir asked me in a worried voice if I felt OK. He's fine, Noa said and smiled at me as if we had a secret we couldn't tell Amir. Good, he said in a nervous tone that didn't sound like him. I'm going, I said. I felt like I was sitting in the stands at a Beitar game when too many fans had gatecrashed and you can't breathe. I felt like I was keeping them from doing something, although I wasn't sure what. Thanks for the explanations, I said to Noa. She smiled. I should thank you, she said. Because of you, I chose really beautiful pictures. Won't you at least have a drink of water? Amir asked. No, I answered, they're probably worrying about me at home.

*

At night, after I came back from the shelter, I had a dream. It must've been important because I remember a large part of it. Shmuel, a man of about sixty who has hair like straw and wears cracked glasses, was standing in the middle of our living room and explaining his theory, the same theory he had explained to me a few hours before, in reality, in the club's coffee corner (a peeling Formica table, two chairs, one with a broken back, lumpy sugar, Elite instant coffee, containers of UHT milk, spoons that had already seen a lot in life). The world, he explained excitedly, is divided into three colours: red, white and transparent. Red and white represent the two human extremes, and transparent represents the middle road, the divine compromise. In politics, for example, the far right is white, Rabin may he rest in peace, was red, and the true path, the transparent, runs between them. The same is true of love. Men are white. Women are red. That's why hearts break. Now – in the dream – Shmuel bent to whisper into my ear: Look at your apartment, my friend. Everything here is red, white and transparent. I looked around the apartment. The dream's director shifted the camera so I could see, with horror, that Shmuel was right. The chairs were red, the table white, and the wall that separated us from the Zakians was transparent. Through it, I could see that Sima and Moshe were in the middle of an argument, but I didn't hear what they were saying. There was a transparent plate on the table. On its right was a red knife, on its left a white fork. But why red, white and transparent? I asked. What's the logic behind it? Shmuel shrugged and nodded in the direction of the picture on the transparent wall, the picture that bothers Noa so much, of a man looking outside through a window. Its original colours, purple, black and orange, had changed to haphazard areas of red and white. I didn't like that kind of modern art, and suddenly, in my dream, I didn't understand why Shmuel was standing in the middle of my living room instead of being where he belonged, in the club. I turned to him to find out, but he'd disappeared. Or maybe he hadn't? Maybe he was just transparent? The thought passed through my mind as I dreamed, but I didn't have time to check it out because I suddenly heard pounding on the window. I went to see who it was, but I couldn't see because the window wasn't transparent. It was white and opaque. From the voices, I could tell that Noa, Itzhak Rabin and some child, maybe Yotam, had lost the key and wanted me to open the door for them. I went to the door and tried to open it. It didn't open. I pressed my shoulder against it, but it didn't open. I gave it a karate kick, but it didn't open. And that's where the part of the dream I remember ends.

*

When I woke up in the morning, his side was already empty but still warm, and the pillow had an indentation in the shape of his head. In films, in scenes like this, after a fight, the man always leaves the woman an emotional letter saying he's sorry, or he buys her a bouquet of flowers, and even though I know that Moshe isn't into writing letters or bringing flowers, I did expect something to be waiting for me on the kitchen table. That's how it is with films – they have an effect on you even if you know they're stupid. When there was nothing there but a half-empty cup of black coffee, I was disappointed. Lilach, who's usually calm and laughing in the morning, was whining and wouldn't stop. That little one is an antenna. She picks up everything. That's why we always try to argue in the bedroom, behind the closed door. I changed her nappy and cut up a banana for her, the way she likes it. Meanwhile, Liron came in and asked me to help him tie his shoelaces. I heated up some cocoa for him and added two squares of chocolate to it, to make up for eating all the cornflakes. I put cuts in his orange so he'd be able to peel it during the morning break, explained to him for the thousandth time how to loop one lace and put the loop of the other lace through it, and the whole time, I was looking for signs of yesterday's argument in him, but I didn't find any. As usual, he drank the cocoa too fast, and as usual, he burned his tongue a bit. As usual, he forgot to pull out the points of his collar, and as usual, he got cross when I reminded him. It wasn't until he got to the door and kissed me on the cheek, as usual, that he suddenly turned around and asked, I'm going to Hanni's kindergarten, right? Then I realised that not only had he heard us, but he had also understood, so I said, of course to Hanni's, and I gave his hair a quick pat to get him moving, and he looked up as if he wanted to tell me something, but then turned around and went out. I watched him till he went into the kindergarten at the end of the block and the minute he disappeared, I was sorry I'd let him go like that, without explaining to him. But what could I explain? I didn't even know how to explain to myself. All of a sudden, I wanted to talk to a friend about what happened. To ask her advice. But who? I put Lilach into her carriage, gently, so she wouldn't start crying again, and thought about all my friends. Galit always says yes, yes on the phone, and then you realise from a question she asks when we're about to hang up that she hasn't listened to a word. Calanit just had twins and you have to talk to her in short sentences because one of the twins always screams when you're in the middle of a sentence and you never get to the end of it. Just last week, Sigal transferred her son to the kindergarten Moshe's talking about, so she probably has a speech about it all prepared. For it, of course. People are always ready to boast about what they've done, otherwise why is that people always come back looking so satisfied from trips to other countries? Really, I'd like to meet one person who comes back and says it was awful. Then there's always my sister Mirit, but I know what she'll say about anything before she says it. A story like this, for instance, would get her all upset right away. Why did you fight? Why was he driving in the middle of the night? Why didn't you give in? Mirit was always for giving in. Her husband's been cheating on her for half a year with his secretary in the army, and she turns a blind eye. She says he'll get over it, as if it's the flu. If my mother was alive, she'd tell her a thing or two about the flu.

In my mind, I could hear Mirit say, but Mum was alone

in the end, have you forgotten that? My mother had a heart attack and it took three weeks for one of the neighbours to notice. The medics who came said that if they'd reached her in time, there might have been a chance. Do you get it? Mirit goes on in my mind, I know that Doron is cheating on me, but at least I have someone in the living room who asks if I'm OK when I cut myself with the salad knife in the kitchen.

A second before I answered Mirit in my head, the door-bell rang. Noa, the student. They were out of milk. Come in, please, I told her, don't be shy. She came in and before I could warn her, she banged her head on the new lamp-shade. What can I do, I said and straightened the swinging lampshade; we're all midgets in this house. Everybody's short in my family too, she said, rubbing the place where she got hit. So how did you turn out like that? I asked. I don't know. My grandmother's slightly taller, so maybe it's from her, she said. There's not much left, I apologised, waving the almost empty milk carton in the air. How about having your coffee here, I suggested, and without waiting for an answer, I filled up the kettle and took out a couple of cups. She talked to my back: She actually likes being tall. She was very introverted when she was a child, hardly ever spoke, and people noticed her just because she was taller than the others. Without her height, she would've been completely invisible. Well, I said, people probably notice you a lot now. With your legs, you could be a model without even trying. Don't be silly, she protested and patted her thighs, and I thought: I'd take those thighs any day. I poured the coffee and milk, moved the carriage closer to the table and sat down. And what were you like as a child? she asked, blowing on her coffee. Me, I laughed, just the opposite. I was always the smallest, the last one in line in gym class, and that's why I didn't have a choice, I had to learn how to talk, to make myself heard. I had an opinion on everything from the minute I was born. I made sure everyone knew who Sima was. Besides, that's how my mother brought me up – if you have something to say, say it. Don't be afraid of anyone. Later on, when I was older and I used to argue with her for hours to let me stay up and watch *Dallas*, she was a little sorry she'd taught me that, and she'd say, *raskh pehal hezar*, your head is as hard as a rock, but I really think she was proud of me. And I'm like that to this day, stubborn. Like yesterday, for instance . . . I started to say and stopped. What happened yesterday? Noa asked. I liked her tone. Interested, but not pushy. Wanting to know, but didn't have to know everything. So I started to tell her about the argument with Moshe, and before I knew it, I found myself talking about his family, how from the first minute, from the first family dinner, even before Moshe and I got married, they adopted me like a daughter. But on the other hand, they always gave me the feeling that I was a disappointing daughter, that I didn't know how to make Moshe *kubeh hemusteh* the way he liked it, that I had too many opinions, that I didn't know how to do up the house so it looked nice. If I offered them coffee when they came over, they'd get insulted and Moshe would explain to me quietly in the kitchen that I shouldn't offer coffee first because that means I'm being stingy with food. But if I didn't offer them coffee, they'd also be insulted. I've been with Moshe for eight years and sometimes I have the feeling that a whole life won't be enough for me to learn his family's rules. Yeah, Noa says and touches my elbow, I know exactly what you're talking about. I waited for her to tell me a little about Amir's family, but she didn't say any more, so I told her about my mother, what a special person she was, and how she raised us by herself after my father 'got religion' and took off, and how she used to wear the same dress all summer so she'd have enough money to buy us books and notebooks, and how she'd sit with me and Mirit a week before school started to cover them with coloured paper and put stickers on them. She had a special folding technique, I don't know how she did it, but the teachers would always say what beautiful covers I had, hold the books up and say, look at these, children you can all take a lesson from Sima.

I went on and on without a break, and Noa sat there quietly with attentive eyes, and Lilach was quiet too, probably from shock. She'd never heard her mother talk so much at once, and when I finished – I didn't really finish, it's more that I got tired – I saw that the coffee was cold and I got up, not only to make us black coffee, because there was no more milk, but also because all of a sudden, I don't know why, I was ashamed to look Noa in the eye.

*

Whenever Amir has to deal with a glitch, he develops a twitch. Strangers might make a mistake, but Noa sees clearly when his lower lip starts to shake. And Noa herself? With her, it's her face. Whenever it's time to hand in work at Bezalel again, all her features scrunch up into a single focal point of pain. With the landlord, on the other hand, it's his digestive tract. Loose bowels, to be exact. He was so stressed out during basic training that he had a constant case of the runs. And this last week too, the business with the kindergarten caused him so much aggravation that he felt the same heavy, burning sensation in his gut. And Sima, his wife? No sign at all. Not even when Liron drives her crazy, or Moshe drives her up the wall. Maybe because she won't settle an argument with a kiss and a hug, she won't sweep anything under the rug.

On the other side of the empty lot, every day Yotam's mother sweeps her falling hair into a dustpan. Right after Gidi's death was when it began. And her hair used to be so long and thick. Yotam's father liked to run his fingers through it when he lay beside her in bed. Or smooth it down gently, starting from her forehead. Now they're both so grim. He doesn't touch her, and she doesn't touch him. Only sometimes at night, unintentionally: his stomach

85

presses against her back, her head rests on his chest, limb brushes limb. And in the morning, they go their separate ways with nothing to share. She brushes her teeth. He gets dressed. She combs her thinning hair. He cuts himself shaving but doesn't swear. Sometimes, at work, his wheeze gets worse. He had asthma when he was a child, and it has come back now that he's mourning his son. The doctor told him to get an inhaler, so he went out and bought one. Every night he takes it out of his shirt pocket and puts it on the table next to his ring. But he doesn't talk about it, so she doesn't ask him a thing.

*

I knew it would happen. How long can you not do home-work and not participate in class and not bring an atlas to geography? I knew that someone would finally get fed up with it. And today, after I left citizenship class four times to go to the bathroom and met my form teacher in the hallway one of those times, it really did happen. She came into the lesson just before school finished and gave me a letter in a white envelope with the school logo on it addressed to Mr and Mrs Avneri – and even though I didn't open it, I knew very well what it said. Grades deteriorating, behaviour deteriorating, social involvement deteriorating, deteriorating, deteriorating. Funny word, deteriorating. You can hear what it means when you say it, like crunch or splash. I didn't give the letter to Mrs Avneri. Why bother? I knew what she'd tell me. I can actually hear her voice: you know how hard it is for us, Yoti, so why are you giving your father and me something else to worry about? Instead, I pushed the envelope under the monument I built for Gidi in the empty lot. For a minute, I had the feeling he was sitting on one of the branches of the big tree near Noa and Amir's house watching me, disappointed at the way I was acting, but I ignored it and kept adding stones on the sides so the letter wouldn't show, and I spread a few smaller stones and some earth in the spaces between the larger stones. My form teacher will probably call Mum, but I have another few days till then. I went into my room through the window, grabbed my draughtboard and ran across the lot to Noa and Amir's door. I hoped one of them would be there alone, it didn't matter which one.

Amir was really glad to see me, but his cheeks were all stubbly, like he was in mourning. It's great that you came, he said, and stroked my cheek, I'm just taking a break from studying.

Wanna play backwards draughts? I asked and tapped the board with my fist.

You know what, Yotam, he said as if he was making an announcement, no. I think you're ready for chess.

*

A few weeks after the assassination, there's an outbreak of 'N-Na-Nach-Nachman-From-Oman' stickers on the streets. Cars infect each other with the sticker, and then it moves to pieces of white cloth hanging on balconies. An authorised commentator explains on the radio: this is the formula for a prayer written by Rabbi Nachman from Breslau, which appeared in this riddle-like form at the beginning of the twentieth century and tends to reappear during times of public anxiety.

Driving to Tel Aviv, Amir whispers to himself a couple of alternatives:

S-Swe-Swee-Sweet-Sweetheart

Or

P-Po-Pot-Pota-Potat-Potato Chips

If he worked in an ad agency, he might have made a sticker out of it.

But he didn't. He didn't work at all. He took time off this term so he could devote himself to his studies. (Which means he has time to think. Maybe too much time.)

*

Maybe it wasn't such a good idea to stop working. These long days alone in the apartment. For the first few hours,

I can still study: summarise chapters, mark passages, choose the right word from the ones the electronic translator offers. But after a while – and every day, that 'while' gets shorter – I get restless and start wandering. Gorge myself on raisins. Peel oranges and eat the peel. Throw a tennis ball against the wall above the computer and hope it hits something on the rebound, breaks something, so there'll be some drama. Otherwise, without drama, the poisonous thoughts begin. I already know. They're just waiting for the opportunity, lurking, dying to fill the void, like the less secure participant on a date. They make me jealous of people who work, people whose days are full and who can happily repress, at least for a few hours, whatever is troubling them. Yes, what's wrong with repression? Entire psychological theories are based on the assumption that repression is bad for one's mental state and that people should be liberated from their repression mechanisms the way an occupied region is liberated from its occupiers. After half a term at home, I say: repression is wonderful. Denial is great. Long live sublimation! I say it and keep pacing, vulnerable, inside these four walls. The bile of my soul rises in my throat. The theories that Shmuel from the club told me about return to haunt me. His red-white-transparent world menaces and attracts. His cracked glasses wound me. I can't get the completely unimportant, completely irrelevant 'what's going to happen' thoughts out of my mind: What's going to happen when my savings are gone? What's going to happen with college? What's going to happen with the stain that's been growing on the ceiling since the water heater exploded? How can I be a psychologist if everything gets to me? I'm influenced by everything. I don't even have a laugh of my own. I keep taking over the laugh of whoever I happen to be close to. Once I used to laugh like my father, then like Modi, now like Noa. I'll probably end up laughing Shmuel's strangled, jerky laugh that collapses in on itself.

If it wasn't freezing outside, I'd go for a short walk around the neighbourhood, up to Doga's and back through the playground with the broken swing and past the stationery shop that's never open. The last time I did that, my cheeks hurt from the cold. If it snowed, at least there'd be something romantic about the whole business, but Maoz Ziyon is located right on the dividing line: cold enough to preserve people in stone jars for three months, but not cold enough for white flakes.

I remember my first snowfall in Jerusalem. I was the new kid in class again, and nobody bothered to tell me about the unwritten rule in that city: if it snows, no one – not pupils and not teachers – goes to school. The guard at the entrance smiled pityingly at me as I went inside. I didn't understand why. I walked down the empty hallways, expecting that someone would come running towards me with a basketball in his hand, or that a teacher would come walking down the hallway with her high heels clacking on the floor. It wasn't until I went into the classroom that I figured it out. The chairs were upturned on the desks. Yesterday's Bible homework assignment was written on the board: describe and explain the fall of King Saul. Outside the window, snowflakes continued to curl around in the air, like my father's signature. I took my chair off my desk and sat down. Every movement I made – moving my schoolbag, shifting my position in the chair, coughing – was tremendously loud in the empty classroom. I waited a few minutes; maybe one of those nerdy girls who sit in the front row would come. When that didn't happen, I got up, turned my chair over on the desk as noisily as I could, on purpose, and went home. On the way, I trampled on the lumps of snow that had piled up on the edges of the pavement, my eyes tearful from the wind.

Now, I also feel like turning my chair over on my desk and going. But where? I could always call someone. But who? At this hour, the world is playing musical chairs and

I'm the only one left standing. Noa's unreachable, running around between Bezalel and the café. David's up to his bald head with rehearsals for Licorice's first show at the Pargod. He usually calls me between one and two in the morning, whining about how much he misses Michal in a voice hoarse from singing. I calm him down, remind him of her bad qualities (she'd better not go back to him, or else I'm in deep shit) and send him back to the rehearsal. And crazy Modi is trekking around the world. Man, I could really do with a tennis game with him now. One or two sets. A backhand smash on the line. An easy, well-placed volley that he can't get to, and then we'd sit in the pub, sweating and thirsty, drinking and laughing, laughing and drinking. But he's so far away now, my best friend. His letters get more and more funnysophical, filled with an intoxicating sense of freedom, and cut off. Very cut off.

Which leaves me every day with the voices of Moshe and Sima arguing on the other side of the wall.

There's something embarrassing about this vocal voyeurism, so the minute they start, I cover the water-heater hole and turn on the radio. But still, probably on the sub-threshold level (we learned about that in Cognitive Psychology – your brain absorbs impressions without your being aware it), I realised that the argument was about their son. And it was serious. Even Noa, who's become friendly with Sima lately, mentioned a crisis. I hope our landlords don't suddenly separate on us. It happened to David once. The woman just threw him and his guitar out of the apartment with a week's notice. On the other hand – the thought flashes through my mind – I hope they do separate and we leave and finally there'll be a change. No! I get my balance back. Just so I don't have to move again. Now that I've finally got used to this apartment. To the neighbourhood. To Yotam. To his soft, hesitant knocking on the door.

On days like this, I find myself waiting impatiently for him.

When I see him, with the hems of his trousers folded up and his hair falling into his eyes, and the mischievousness that sometimes bursts out of the sweater of sadness he wears, something inside me smiles. Yesterday, for example, in the middle of an especially poisonous thought (Noa and I are frauds. We palm off on the world, and on each other, the pretence that we're so calm, so cool and self-contained. But inside, we're both in utter turmoil.) he appeared with his draughtboard. I was getting tired of draughts – we play it a lot in the club – so I offered to teach him chess. He agreed happily. It seems that Gidi had promised to teach him, but never got the chance. I stopped myself from asking about Gidi. He'll tell me when he wants to, not a nudge sooner. I took the board out of the cupboard and opened it on the table. The bishops shook themselves off, the knights stretched. I hadn't taken them out of the box in a long time. I took my old chess stopwatch out of a drawer and put it down next to the board, even though I didn't think we'd use it. What colour do you want to be, Yotam? White. Kids always choose white. But for some reason, from the first time I played with my father, I preferred black. OK. Now you arrange the pieces on the board. For every one I put down, you do the same. First the pawns, in the second row. They're the least important. Then the rook. The bishop. And the knight. Then the queen and the king. How can you tell the difference between the queen and the king? That's a good question.

*

Lately, when Noa comes home, Amir's happiness at her return is diluted with a kind of pre-insult. Before he has a specific reason, the insult is already lying in wait, ready to spring. He's waiting for the kiss that doesn't last long enough, for the careless way she drops her things. For anything that will give him an excuse to make a nasty crack. And Noa stands in front of him unprepared, taken aback. Her feet hurt her so much that she can't restrain herself, try and understand. So she answers him back. And for a few minutes they repel each other, like magnets pressed together on the wrong side. He goes to his study. She goes to the shower. He tries to read an article, but can't manage to understand. The soap keeps dropping out of her hand. And when she finally comes out wrapped in two towels, he gets down on one knee. I'm sorry, Noa baby, he says, I don't know what came over me. I wait for you all day, thinking of what I'll say, and then when you come, instead of being nice, I'm mean to you. She runs her fingers through his hair and says, I had a crazy day too. You know what, let's decide to be nice to each other from now on. And he thinks: how can anyone think that you just decide, and all the bad feelings are gone. But he swallows his irritation and tries to change the subject. You know, he says, following her to the bedroom, Sima and Moshe fight all the time. I try not to listen, but the walls are so thin. Yes, she says, it's that business with the kindergarten. I can't see him backing down and she certainly won't give in. I just hope they don't separate and force us to look for another apartment. It would be just too much, Amir says, after we opened a credit account at Doga. Right, Noa laughs and continues, after I learned how to navigate the tile path to the house. After drivers finally started giving me a ride to the big bridge. Wait a minute, Amir says, suddenly angry, since when do you hitch rides? Everyone does it here, Noa says, brushing his worry aside. It's not dangerous. You stand on the road and if they know you, they take you to the bridge. It's really very close. OK, Amir says in a gentle voice that smoothes away the wrinkle that has suddenly appeared during their conversation. *Yallah*, do we ever talk a lot. *X-Files* is starting, he says in excited anticipation.

They go into the living room. He sits down on the armchair. She sits down on him. So he moves a little to the side. The opening music sounds loudly in the air. The subtitle appears: 'The truth is out there.'

A rebellious thought passes suddenly through Noa's mind: I'm out all day trying to make a buck. If Sima and Moshe separate and we have to leave, I'll tell him goodbye and good luck. I'll find myself an apartment in a good part of town. With a girl for a room-mate. And none of these problems to weigh me down.

A rebellious thought passes suddenly through Amir's mind: It's pretty crowded, the two of us on this small armchair.

The camera zooms in on a clearing in the woods: a group of robed people are praying to the devil. Mulder isn't around, of course. Scully's hiding behind a bush. And the music gets louder. Louder. Louder. The violins screech. The drums boom. Amir wriggles around on the chair trying to find some room.

*

A fifteen-minute stop, Moshe announces on the loud-speaker. Someone yells from the back of the bus: how long? Moshe bends forward again: fifteen minutes, he repeats, and waits patiently for the last passenger to get off. He looks in the mirror, checking all the seats in the bus. The old people usually get off first, their steps small and slow. This time, it's a soldier who's been sleeping since he got on the bus an hour and a half ago. He's walking down the aisle, his rifle bouncing on his back and he grabs the barrel so it won't bang against the exit door when he gets off to buy a snack. But it does anyway. Moshe extricates himself from the narrow space between his seat and the coin dispenser, takes a last look to see that no one's left behind and gets off the bus to unwind. A nasty wind blows hard against his face. Masmiya junction looks as if there's been an earthquake there. The iron support of a bus stop shelter, without the shelter, is lying on the black asphalt, flyers for 'Dr Roach – Exterminators Inc.' are strewn everywhere. Even though there's no supermarket in the area, an over-turned supermarket trolley is lying half under a car. Just a

93

huge, slightly menacing petrol station and a snack bar. You can buy pitta filled with an omelette, hummus and hot sauce there. Moshe has never eaten a sandwich that could compare. He stops here just so he can have one. But today, his appetite is gone. Worry keeps rising in his gorge. The fight with Sima never seems to end, and when he came home yesterday, she turned her back on him again. What'll he do now? Without thinking, without deciding that this is what he'll do, he goes to the payphone nearby and calls his brother, the rabbi.

I hope I'm not disturbing you, Rabbi Zakian, he says, and his brother replies, laughing to reassure him: heaven forbid, you caught me between lessons and besides, dear brother, I always have time for you. For you, anything. Moshe begins to tell him, first in half-sentences, as if he were hesitating, and then it flows out of him like a spring. All the words that he didn't have the day before with Sima are miraculously there and he tells his brother everything. For me, God is home, he says, and for Sima, a prison. For me, God is peace, and for her, it's like having someone watch her every move. Menachem listens patiently for a long time, hmming every once in a while so Moshe will know he's still on the line. He lets his brother finish telling the whole story before he sighs and says: I am here for you. Then Moshe asks: but tell me what you think I should do. And Menachem replies: What I think is of no importance, and this is all I will say – the way will be illuminated for the righteous and joy will come to the upright. Moshe, not sure that he understands the meaning of the verse, persists and asks again: but what exactly should I do so things don't get worse? Before Menachem has time to answer, someone knocks on the phone booth glass. The soldier, his eyes still red, is trying to tell him something. He uncovers his watch, presses it against the glass and shows Moshe the time. Moshe looks and is horrified. The break ended long ago. Shivers of shame run down his spine.

He has to end the conversation right now. He thanks his brother, says goodbye and hurries after the soldier to the bus. The passengers are already waiting there, and one of them shouts at him: what a disgrace. How could you forget about us, the passengers on your bus? Someone else says: it's because Egged's a monopoly, so they do whatever they want. Mortified, Moshe makes his way through the crowd to the bus door. Nothing like this has ever happened to him before.

*

So, what do you think? I ask Noa a few mornings later, when she comes over for coffee again. Her eyes are wandering over the walls as if they are cameras and I feel bad that I didn't have time to tidy up before she came. The only pictures we have on the walls are paintings of vases we got as gifts from some distant uncle of Moshe's who thinks he's Van Gogh, and giant photos of Moshe's brothers and his parents at our wedding. So the place should at least be neat. *Nu*, I push her, I'm the one who talks the whole time. So what about you? What do you think? I lean on my elbows and wait for her verdict. She starts talking. Stops. Starts talking. Stops. What are you afraid of, I say and laugh at her. Tell me what you feel, from your guts, don't think too much. But who am I to express an opinion, I'm not . . . she protests. I roll my eyes up to the ceiling. Don't worry, I won't take it like the Torah from Mount Sinai. All I want is another opinion. OK, she says, giving in, and she takes a toothpick and holds it between her fingers like a cigarette. First of all – she starts taking puffs of the tooth-pick – I think you should go and see that kindergarten before you decide about it. By the way, I wouldn't mind going with you. We have a project to do on religion and God, and the truth is that we've already handed it in. I took pictures full of shoes in display windows to symbolise the western world's worship of brand names, but the lecturer said I was running away from an emotional confrontation with the subject. And second of all? I ask, urging her on, and I take a toothpick too. Second of all, I think that this whole thing is deeper than whether you choose this kindergarten or a different one. Which means . . . ? I'm still pulling her opinion out of her like you pull a tissue out of a box with an opening that's too small. It means, she says, chewing on the toothpick, based on how strongly you feel about it, that this is all about . . . About a principle and you have to see whether you're ready to give up on it. Whether you're really ready to give up on it. Because if you're not really ready and you give up on it anyway, it'll keep on eating you up inside. Ow! The toothpick stabbed her tongue.

Thanks, I say. Feel like something sweet? She stares at me, surprised by the quick change of subject. She doesn't know me yet. With me, there's no going on and on about nothing. Once I get it, I get it. We both put our smoked toothpicks in the ashtray and I get up to empty it and bring a few biscuits. How's things with you and Amir, I ask on the way, do you feel good in our apartment? Yes, she says, sure. You know, I tell her, that's the first place we lived in. Right after we got married. It's our first apartment together too, she says. There's something strange about the way she says that. Her tone gets lower towards the end of the sentence, like lips that open up to smile and then drop at the corners. No, more like a smile that disappears too fast. I go back to the table with a full plate. She eats a biscuit and it knocks her off her feet. How . . . what . . . what is this incredible thing, she asks and takes another one from the plate and brings it up to her nose. It's *baba*, I explain. Moshe's mother taught me how to make it. Dough with a thick layer of date spread and nuts and all kinds of spices. I just have to take some for Amir, he loves sweets, she says. But again, instead of saying it happily, she says it as if she should take him some biscuits but she doesn't really feel like it. She wets a finger and picks a few *baba* crumbs off the plate with it, puts the finger in her mouth and gives me a different kind of look, like she's sizing me up, the look of a personnel manager. I fill Lilach's bottle and wait. If she wants to, she'll tell me. She keeps on picking up crumbs and doesn't say anything. What's her problem, I ask myself, insulted, I'm not good enough for her? I didn't pass the test? So I don't have a degree, so what. You don't need a degree to understand people. And besides, why should I tell her about myself and about Moshe if she doesn't tell me anything? I shush myself and put the teat into Lilach's mouth. A minute ago you said she'd decide whether to tell you or not, so what's your problem? I scold myself. Calm down. Just don't blurt out some nasty remark, like you do sometimes when you feel insulted. Sharona hasn't talked to you for two years because you told her that her little boy was fat, after she had the nerve to say something about Liron's haircut. Better change the subject.

Do you remember that Arab who came to ask for water, I ask. Noa nods. So listen to this, I say. Day before yesterday, Gina, Moshe's mother, comes back from Doga with bags full of food, and that worker jumps out from behind her, asks her if she needs help and offers to carry her bags to the house. She says no, thank you. But he insists. Free delivery, lady, free delivery, he says. Then he grabs the handle of a bag and starts pulling it. But she doesn't let him. I don't need delivery. I don't need any help. So the two of them keep tugging at the bag till it tears, and everything in it – oranges, pears, onions, a box of eggs – falls out all over the pavement. The minute the Arab sees that, he gets scared, does an about-face and disappears, leaving Grandma Gina standing there in the middle of the street, in the middle of the day, with one shoe covered in egg yolk and oranges all around as if she was the tree and they all fell off her. Lucky I was home. I heard her screaming *hutmani! hutmani!* – which is oh my God in Kurdish. I went outside, helped her pick up everything – not that she said thank you – put it all away in the fridge and then I went right to Madmoni to complain. Naturally, he wasn't there. Or the workers either, because they have some kind of holiday and they knocked off early. His wife said they'd take care of it right away, but today I saw that worker get out of the pickup. How do you like that? He has a lot of nerve, don't you think? All the dust on the windows and the hammers banging in the morning isn't enough, now this?

*

The book of books in Noa and Amir's apartment: *One Hundred Years of Solitude*. Amir started reading it first, but Noa commandeered it. Ever since, they've been arguing, half jokingly, half seriously, about who has the right to read it. Unhand that book, Jose Arcadio Buendia, Noa says and throws a pillow at Amir. Sorry, Amir replies, but it's too late, Remedios Moscote, my dear. When he informs her one day on the phone from Tel Aviv that he might be late, she tells him to hurry up, but she's really thinking, this is great. Now she can dive into the pages of the book without worrying he's about to come back. It isn't nice to say, but lately, she has to admit that she has a much better time when he isn't here. She can sit quietly at her light table. She can spend hours choosing negatives. She can just rest and play around with ideas without worrying that he'll interrupt. And screw things up.

For Liron, the book of the year is *Atlantis, the Kingdom under the Sea*. Moshe suggests to him gently, over and over again, how about trying a different book today? But Liron's soul is bound to Atlantis, and he won't agree. His eyes gleaming with excitement, as if this were the first time, he listens to Moshe read to him once again about the lost kingdom. About dragons breathing fire so hot that even water can't put it out. About knights talking together at the bottom of the sea, with no bubbles coming through their lips. About whales that live in wrecked ships. And more. So much more. From her cot, Lilach the baby is also listening to the adventures of the deep. It's not clear whether she understands, but the story helps her fall asleep. And Sima, the mother, is enjoying a few rare moments of rest. She glances at Moshe and the children and, despite herself, a feeling of warmth surges through her breast. It's not easy to be angry at a father like him. On the other hand, she hardens her heart. Which kindergarten Liron goes to is a matter of principle because it will determine his future. She can't give in. She has to fight for the boy and she has to win.

Yotam's parents, for their part, aren't thinking about the future. For them, the future has no meaning. Every night, before she goes to bed, Yotam's mother prays that she'll wake up in the morning and discover she's been dreaming. So how can she think about the future. Or the present. Before Gidi died, they used to go out on Saturday trips with friends, the Lundys. Before Gidi died, she used to take Yotam's father ballroom dancing in the community centre on Sundays. Now his head is always down. He can barely drag himself around. He comes to life only when the newspapers call. Or that damned Forum for Peace and Security. And she can barely move from place to place. She can hardly get through the days. She'd been a bookworm once. The people at the bookshop used to put aside selected titles they thought she'd need. But now she finds she just can't read. She puts on her glasses, she tries, God knows. But thoughts slip away from her. Like shadows.

At the Madmonis', there isn't much reading going on either. Sometimes Nayim brings a Jewish newspaper with him. Saddiq already knows that he shouldn't read the front page. It give him bad dreams. Since Itzhak Rabin died, everything seems to be coming apart at the seams. (And fate laughs: the Jews always said they couldn't make peace with the Arab countries because too much depended on a single dictator who might suddenly be forced to flee.) So

Saddiq leaves the headlines and takes the sports pages. He checks the English football scores, to see how his team, Liverpool, did that day.

And he peers over the top of the newspaper at the house across the way.

*

I climbed up the ramp that Amin built so I could read the sports pages where no one would bother me. And then, all of a sudden, I saw the door. I couldn't see it before because we hadn't built that high yet, but now, standing at the height of the electric wires and looking down, it stood out between the branches and leaves of the tree. A heavy door, made of iron, with engravings on the sides. Just like I remembered it. When we lived there, the door was at the front, naturally. With the Jews who live across from Madmoni, it's the back door that leads nowhere. I slapped my forehead, why didn't I think of that? I remembered the house from a different direction, and whenever I looked at it these last few months it was from the wrong direction. That's why I couldn't decide. I was so excited that I finally understood, I almost fell off the ramp; it's a good thing I didn't, because we don't have insurance. I grabbed one of the iron bars, wiped my forehead with my shirt and looked at the house and the street. I tried to picture how the house looked when you saw it from the other side. And then, all of a sudden, while I was stretching myself to see better, I saw the old Jewish lady, the one who lives in the house, walking down the street carrying bags full of shopping. Without thinking too much, I jumped off the ramp, squeezed through the concrete pillars, crossed the street and ran up to her. I wanted to ask her to let me in, just for a minute, to see what was inside, to be sure, but my running scared her and she dropped all her bags on the pavement.

I was ashamed of myself, the way I scared a lady my mother's age, so I bent down and started picking up all her stuff to put it back in the bags – cottage cheese, oranges, onions – but she started yelling thief! thief! and she hit me on the head with a baguette. I put my hands on my head and she kept on hitting my fingers, the way Ali Ahvis, the arithmetic teacher, used to hit us with a ruler. Stop, madam, stop, I'm helping you, I'm giving you a free delivery, I said, trying to explain to her, but she kept on hitting me with a baguette in one hand and a carrot in the other, and meanwhile, people started looking out of windows all around us. So I left her – who needs trouble like that? – and ran back to Madmoni. Luckily, the pickup had just come to drive us home before the neighbours had a chance to come outside and kick up a fuss. I even saw the old lady's daughter – I think that's her daughter, the one with the tiger eyes – come running over to her, before the pickup turned the corner. *Ya* Saddiq, *inta majnoon*, are you crazy? Amin asked and twisted his finger in the air like a screw. You want to get us all in trouble? And Nayim said, *dahil allah*, God help us if Rami the contractor hears about this, we're finished. They were sitting across from me in the pickup and their eyes were red from the dust that gets into them every day. *Allah satr*, I reassured them. Nothing happened. All I did was help an old lady carry her bags. Is it my fault that she's crazy? And besides, Rami needs us. To finish the building. Who else can finish the building? Angels?

*

The paper boy isn't an angel or a cherub or a Beitar fan. He's an older man. A factory manager who was fired two months ago and would rather deliver papers than be unemployed. And, besides, the early mornings when he doesn't have to reveal his shame to the world are a time he enjoys. His wife is the only person to whom he told the truth. To his son he explained that the factory had a big order and he had to go in early because there was a lot of work to do. His voice shook when he lied, but the son – his mobile pressed to his ear – didn't even hear.

Four-thirty in the morning. The sun is still only a rumour in the sky. The father is chugging along the street on his scooter tossing newspapers at the houses as he passes by. On the corner of Victory and Convoy Streets, a speeding car comes hurtling towards him out of the blue. He veers away and avoids a collision at the last moment. That's the only thing he can do. But the street is slick and the scooter is old, and before he realises what's happening, he's sprawled face down on the ground, which is wet and cold. The car screeches to a halt. Three young men get out and walk tentatively towards him. He gets to his feet and waves his finger at them, ready to tell them it's all their fault. What do you think you're doing! In the middle of a residential street! You're lucky I don't call the police! But before he begins to speak, he sees through blurry eyes that one of the three is his oldest son. What are you doing here?, he shouts, why aren't you at home? The boy goes up to him, clasps his hands behind his back, and replies with some questions of his own. Are you OK? Are you hurt? Are you OK? I think so, the father says, feeling a bruised thigh, I just got knocked around a little. I'll be all right. But why are you riding around at this time of night? We were at a party, is the son's stammered reply, we just didn't notice the time. You just didn't notice . . . just didn't notice . . . The father repeats his son's words and one of the boys, probably the driver, lowers his eyes. But Dad, what are you doing here at four in the morning? the son asks, his voice full of surprise. And what are all those newspapers for? He picks a paper up off the street, looks at it and then gives his father a look he can't ignore. Now it's the father's turn to be silent, to become reacquainted with his shoes. He steals a glance at his son's friends in the hope they'll understand that the answer won't be given while they're there. And after a few moments of silence (four people standing in the middle of the street, awkwardness filling the air) the friends say a polite excuse-us, and disappear into the darkness in their car.

Crickets chirp. Dogs bark. A father and son stand facing each other in the dark. They don't know what to say to each other. The son is thinking: so this is why his father has been going to sleep so early and hardly speaks to his mother. This is why his eyes are so sad and you hardly ever hear him laugh. The father wonders whether it's time to stop hiding. Or maybe he should say he's doing a favour for a friend. But he decides to tell the truth in the end. The son doesn't say a word, and he can feel his lower lip quiver. When his father has finished, he looks at the newspapers scattered on the street and asks, do you still have a lot more to deliver? It looks like we really ruined your morning. Maybe I can help you out. The father presses the light switch on his watch, and is upset to see how late it is. He really doesn't need to get fired again. Getting fired from the factory caused him enough pain. When he hears what his son says, he hesitates: no, it's too late. Go home to bed. You know your mother will be sitting up waiting for you. Don't worry, the son insists, it'll go faster if we do it together. He bends down and gathers the newspapers, one by one. The father picks up the scooter and opens the box on the back for his son. The boy arranges the newspapers neatly inside. The father locks the box and thinks: maybe things aren't as bad as they seem. There they are – a team.

The dawn is hinting at its arrival as the first strips of light over the mountains begin to show. If there were roosters in the Castel, they'd be starting to crow. The son hugs his father from behind on the scooter, and the contact makes them both feel good. The wind blows through their hair and brings tears to their eyes. Sometimes they stop in front of a house and the father explains: we have to go around the garden and put it through the bars. Here, the lady of the house asked me to put the paper in a vase. Her neighbours steal it and sometimes she doesn't see one for days. There's a loose tile here. There's a dog over there, so steer clear.

Towards the end, they reach the apartment where Noa and Amir live.

For these people, the father explains, you have to throw the paper on the roof. Why? Look at all those rocks. The guy I replaced broke his leg here in the dark. That I can do without. Besides, at first I saw that the papers were accumulating up there, but not now. They figured it out.

The son pulls a newspaper off the decreasing pile, takes aim and sends it flying through space. But he throws it too hard, and it lands in the wrong place.

*

Thwack. Moshe Zakian is woken up by a blunt object hitting his forehead. He opens his eyes in surprise. He's not in his own bed. For a moment, it's not clear how he got into this situation. What am I doing here? he asks himself in frustration. Suddenly, he notices a newspaper on the floor. He feels his forehead where it was struck a moment before. From where he's lying, he can read the headlines, something about a security warning. Outside, it's almost light. It's cold, so he wraps the blanket around his body. Gradually, the morning clouds surrounding his thoughts disperse and Moshe Zakian is fully awake. What a shame. For a few days, his thoughts had given him a break. He'd fixed the dripping tap in the sink. Sima had baked a cake. He'd read bedtime stories to the children. She'd looked at him longingly from the living room. It had seemed that they were putting an end to their feud. But yesterday she went with Noa, the student, to the kindergarten on Elijah the Prophet Street and came back in a fighting mood. He sat in the living room, hugging a pillow, avoiding her eyes. He absorbed one volley. Then another. And he could feel his blood pressure rise. Finally, he answered her, still trying not to offend. But instead of focusing on the argument at hand, she'd attacked him for his pronunciation. The word's *dai-dactic*, not *dee-dactic*, she'd said with a sneer, and he tightened his grip on the empty glass of juice and snapped, why can't you stick to what we're talking about, why do you keep trying to insult me? But she wouldn't stop.

You don't understand, Moshe, that's exactly what it's about. If you want him to talk that way too, send him to that kindergarten and he'll turn out just like you.

If only – he thinks, counting the parts of himself that hurt – if only you'd stopped there, you'd be sleeping in a warm bed right now. If only he'd managed to get the conversation back on track in time, they could have reached an agreement somehow. But no. He insisted on charging through a bright red light with a bus full of rage. Like me? What do you mean, like me? It wouldn't be so bad if he talks like me when he gets to be my age.

*

Talk to me, I say to Noa, I want to hear. But she scoots to the edge of the bed and curls up into a ball. She folds her long legs under her, and her black hair hides her face and twists around her neck. The brightly coloured top she wore to Bezalel today suddenly seems out of place. Her thighs, so white and delicious, are showing from under her dress, but this isn't the time. She must have got a bad mark for something she handed in. I move closer and envelop her in a hug. More accurately, in the contours of a hug. She's trembling in my arms. Probably crying. Like in Bob Dylan's song, she acts just like a woman, but she breaks like a little girl. I hold her tight and whisper in her ear. Don't worry, what do they know. What kind of people decide to be lecturers in Bezalel? The ones who don't have enough talent. And then they take their frustration out on their students. She's trembling harder. I try from another angle. You know I believe in you, don't you? Don't you? She nods slightly, almost imperceptibly, but it gives me hope. I kiss the part of her cheek that's exposed. My lips linger on the salty skin. Noni, I really think your project was great. Your friends thought so too.

So one lecturer didn't like it, so what? In another five years, when he wants to see your exhibition in New York, tell him you're sorry, but there are no more invitations, OK?

A tiny smile appears on her salty face. Appears and disappears. I keep on weaving the fantasy. You'll walk around the hall that's filled with your photographs and you won't say a word, you'll just listen to the hum of admiration coming from all those New York phonies. And in the morning, we'll get up early and buy the *Times*, and there'll be a review of your exhibition with the headline; Biggest Israeli Surprise Since Entebbe Raid. Or something like that. And the text will make special mention of the brilliant project on religion and God, and of the artist's beautiful legs.

Smash.

One of those beautiful legs kicks me in the knee.

Sorry, not her legs, but her compositional skill.

And what if they clobber the New York exhibition too, she asks, and turns over on to her back. She's not curled up into a ball any more. She's not crying. She's looking at me with a half-bitter, half-grateful look in her eyes. We'll go back to the Hilton, I suggest, wrinkle their sheets a little. And you'll start working on your next exhibition. OK? OK, she says, mollified. Then she waits for a minute and asks me, looking completely serious: You'll love me even if I'm a total failure for ever, won't you?

*

After Amir drags Noa's pain out of her, some of it remains in him.

And accumulates in his heart.

That's how the law of the preservation of sadness operates, subtly.

*

It's true. I shouldn't have mentioned that Moshe never took all his exams. I know that's a sensitive point with him, and it isn't really fair to bring up something a man whispered to you once at night so you can win an argument. And anyway, there was only one test he didn't take, English, and he's planning to take it when Lilach gets a little older. Or when Liron starts school. I don't remember. But with all due respect, none of that justifies what he's doing. Not when there are two children in the house and one is pretending to be sleeping while he's actually listening to every word. Not after the woman you're planning to marry in a week took you to the Armon Hanatsiv promenade, sat you down on a bench and explained to you that she didn't want any of that stuff in her life. That she'd had enough when she was a child, before her father left. The looks the neighbours gave them from their windows, the questions the children asked at school, eating supper the next day, trying so hard to chat and to smile that the muscles around their mouths hurt.

After he smashed the glass with his foot, the house was quiet. The only sound in the background while we looked at each other was the students' happy music on the other side of the wall. I said to him: I want you to leave. Now. He didn't say anything. I think he was just as shaken as I was. I went to the door, opened it and said: Come on. Go. I don't want to see you. He closed it, leaned his back on it and tried to explain: I didn't mean it, I don't know what came over me. I'm sorry. Let's talk. I moved him away, opened the door again and pushed him out with both hands. He didn't resist, lifted his arms in the air, OK, OK. I slammed the door. I slid the bolt into place and stuck the key in the lock. I got a broom and a dustpan and swept up the pieces. The handle of the glass and another few large pieces were lying close to where he'd stepped on it, but the smaller splinters were scattered all over the living room: on the rug, behind the TV table, in the space under the sofa. While I was looking for them, I found Lilach's plastic hammer. I've been looking for that toy for weeks. I put the broom and dustpan away in the space between the refrigerator and the wall and went to see how the kids were. Lilach was sleeping like a baby. I put the plastic hammer on the night table, a surprise for her in the morning. Liron was completely covered up, except for an elbow that stuck out. When he was younger, I was afraid he'd suffocate like that, without air, and I used to pull the blanket off his head every single night, but I saw that he did it himself anyway, in his sleep, and there was nothing to worry about. I walked over to his bed. The blanket was rising and falling too quickly. He was breathing too lightly for someone who was asleep. Could he have heard everything? And if he did, did he understand? It's too bad we can't ask him what he wants. Give him the chance to decide. After all, at a certain age, even children whose parents are divorced can decide who they want to stay with, the mother or the father. But Liron is still young. And anyway, what made me think of parents who are divorced? I stroked his back through the blanket. That's our regular signal. If he's awake and wants to, he turns over, opens his big eyes and starts talking: about the kids in kindergarten who always fight over who gets the purple paint; about the new computer game Daniel has and he wants too; about what's hiding behind the stars in the sky. He didn't turn around. He was entitled not to. I let him be and went out of the bedroom.

Moshe knocked at the door.

What do you want?

I have nowhere to go.

Very tragic. Go to your parents. (Tragic was Noa's word. Was I actually starting to talk like Noa?)

They'll ask me questions. Do you want them to ask me questions?

I don't care.

OK, I get it. You've gone completely crazy. But I want you to know that it won't help you.

We'll see.

Then it was quiet outside. I couldn't see anything when I looked through the peephole. But I could feel that he was still close by.

Sima?

What?

It's freezing here. Could you please get me a blanket?

I'll think about it.

OK, just think fast.

I went to get him a duvet. I climbed the ladder to the top shelf of the cupboard and took down the thin mattress we use for guests. And while I was doing it. I was thinking, maybe I'm exaggerating. We've been together for eight years and he's never even once raised his voice to me. He was always calm and reasonable. Even now, it's not as if he threw the glass at me. God forbid. He just put it on the rug and stepped on it. It's a good thing his shoes have thick soles, or he would've cut the bottom of his foot. My sister Mirit's voice was talking inside my head: Sima, did you lose your mind? You're pushing things too close to the edge, men don't like women with opinions. In the end, he'll get sick of you and take himself a passenger, one of those women who sits behind the driver and laughs the whole way. A woman who won't give him any trouble. So what'll you do then, smartass? Where will you get the money to send Liron to private kindergarten? Give in, Sima, let him have his way. You saw what happened to Mum.

I don't want to give in, I answered Mirit, and remembered those colouring books in the kindergarten on Elijah the Prophet Street, page after page of pictures of boys with skullcaps and prayer books, as if they were the only children in the world. Moshe's being stubborn with me? So I'll be stubborn with him. If it means I have to be alone, well, there's nothing I can do about it. Besides, there are lots of men who'll want me. I see how they look at me. Even Amir, the student, looks at me. I'll go to work, what's the big deal? I'll manage, no one scares me. If my mother managed, so can I. Rabbi Menachem doesn't know who he's dealing with.

I opened the window and dropped the duvet and the mattress out. Then I went into the bedroom and got a blanket. The air blowing in from outside really was freezing. I'll open the door for him in a little while. Or in the morning, at the latest. Before the Arab workers get here. The worker who attacked Gina keeps wandering around outside our house and I don't want him to bump into Moshe by mistake.

*

Winter love in the Castel begins under the covers. First a little cuddling, a little snuggling till warmth begins to flow through the lovers. Then they peel off their clothes, piece by piece. Amir removes Noa's pyjamas, the ones with the sheep. Then he wraps his arms around her. She sucks on his neck and dives under the heavy cover (Amir's hug feels good, but it's still cold in the room and she still has goose pimples all over). They lick and kiss in the dark, airless space under the blanket. Warm tongues find their way into ears. Slowly, they take off all their clothes except for their socks. Now they can pull down the upper part of the blanket, very gingerly, of course. Amir tries it. Noa doesn't object. They blink in the light and take a deep breath. Their skin shines with sweet sweat. A sudden wind bangs against the windows and their desire grows. Their separateness comes undone, their souls intertwine, they blend into one. Later on, there might be pain, who knows. A fingernail might scratch. A hand might strike. Amir is into that. Noa isn't crazy about those games, but lately, her partner seems to get carried away. For now, she tries not to care, as long as he doesn't pull her hair. As long as he whispers loving words into her neck while he's doing it – my darling, my only one –

And as long as he doesn't steal the blanket away when they're done.

*

I didn't take a lot of pictures in the kindergarten. The teacher finally agreed after I pleaded and explained that I'm not from a newspaper, but I sensed that she didn't trust me, and I didn't want Sima to get thrown out because of me. But I did walk out of Shulamit's Kindergarten with a few pictures, not good enough for my teachers, but interesting enough to keep for myself in a separate bag between the pages of my album. One picture shows a kid, shot from the back. He's wearing a Chicago Bulls T-shirt with the number 23 – the number that Michael Jordan, 'God', wears. His black skullcap has slipped to the side of his head and he's reading from a big book that, from its size, could be either a prayer book or a children's book. There's a picture of a rabbi hanging on the wall above him. Not Ovadia. Not Kaduri. Someone else. The framed *rebbe* is looking at the camera; the child isn't. Then I took a series of pictures, not too many. Most of them are pretty ordinary, except for one that shows a boy whose curled sidelocks have fallen on to his cheeks and his little hand is resting on his heart as he stares longingly at a girl with a red hairband sitting next to him. But the most striking picture – which I added to my portfolio later – is of Dina, the teacher's assistant. I asked her if I could take it when we were about to leave. I used a wide-angle lens to include in the frame the cardboard sign listing the advantages of the kindergarten. The sign said: Open from seven to four. Three full meals. Certified teachers. Under the supervision of the Ministry of Labour and Welfare. Reasonable prices.

Dina herself looks like another advantage of the kindergarten.

Looking at her, with her denim dress, her white long-sleeved top and the green shirt over it, you can't help imagining how a pretty girl like her would look in a low-cut mini dress with her hair loose. I guess that she herself wasn't concerned about that, because in the picture she's completely relaxed. And beaming. Usually, when you look at a picture, you try to find the light source: the direction of the sunlight or the side the flash is on. In that picture, the light source is Dina herself. Her face is illuminated, her neck – the part that is exposed – is glowing, and her enormous green eyes (which are looking straight at the lens, just like I wanted) are gleaming. Dina was with us the entire time we were there, and I liked her from the first minute. The sound of her voice reminded me of my aunts on my father's side, the side I liked, and I thought: if I had a child, I'd want him to have a kindergarten teacher like her. She walked around the kindergarten with us slowly, as if we weren't disturbing her in the middle of the day, explained patiently how special the kindergarten was and answered Sima's questions sincerely, even the provocative ones: Do they have to wear skullcaps? We don't force anyone. The children themselves want to wear them. Could it happen that a boy comes home from kindergarten and tells his mother that she's not dressed properly? Yes, things like that have happened. But on the other hand, we make it very clear to the children how important it is to honour their father and mother. Go to the kindergarten in Mevasseret, see how disrespectful the children are to their parents when they come to pick them up. You won't see that here. And in Mevasseret, they'll always look down on your son because he's from the Castel. Here, everyone's equal.

Sima nodded slightly, and I thought she was agreeing. Even I was having second thoughts when I heard what Dina had to say and especially when she stopped next to a boy who'd fallen in the sandbox and stroked his head until he calmed down.

*

On the way home, we didn't speak. I let Sima absorb what she'd seen, kept my eyes on the uneven pavement and said to myself that I should fill all those holes with white sugar or salt and photograph them. I rolled around in my mouth the names of the streets we passed – Palmach Street, Convoy Street, Victory Lane – and thought that the War of Independence still hadn't ended here. I thought that the empty basketball courts, especially the ones that had torn nets, could be an interesting subject for a project on loneliness. I smiled at the group of toothless old men watching us from a bench and, in my imagination, posed them for a class picture, with a little girl as their teacher standing beside them. And I planned an answer in case Sima asked my opinion.

But when we went into the house, she didn't pour out her heart. All she did was ask me to keep an eye on Lilach for a minute, and went to have a shower. She stayed in the bathroom a long time – Lilach had already begun her pre-crying whining – and when she came out, she stood in front of the mirror in the living room combing her thin hair and said, I think best in the shower. Me too, I said. Every time I have to decide something important, I go into the shower. And she laughed. Ah, now I understand why we don't have any hot water, and before I could fake an apology, she asked, one sugar, right? I said, don't worry, I'll make it, take Lilach for a while, she's about to cry. Sima said, don't be silly, those sounds are a sign that she's happy. Can't you see that she's crazy about you? Don't exaggerate, I protested, even though the compliment made me happy, and Sima took Lilach out of her cot and held her to her beautiful breasts, which were surprisingly firm after two babies, and asked, so what do you think about in the shower, Noa? I laughed: what do you mean? And she said, I tell you everything about myself, and you don't tell me a thing. I'm starting to feel hurt. Don't, I said, it takes me time to open up to people. And suddenly, as I was turning to take the milk out of the fridge, I wanted her not to give up, to keep on asking me. To get me to open up. Lately, I haven't had any long talks with friends. After so many disappointments, Liat finally has someone serious, and although we met for coffee a year ago and she made fun of the women who ignore the rest of the world the minute they have a man, that's exactly what's happened with her. And Hila just came back from a trip to India, loaded with clothes in bright colours and black-and-white clichés – whatever happens is what's supposed to happen, all rivers flow to the Ganges, that kind of stuff. I love her dearly, but if she tells me to go with the flow one more time when I tell her about something I'm upset about, I'll just pull her short, annoying braids. No. I need someone who has no preconceived notions about me, someone who doesn't already think Amir is fantastic, someone who won't be worried about hurting my feelings, who'll say what she thinks.

I brought the coffee over to the table, and before I could sit down, Sima's question mark was already hanging in the air. So what happened with Amir? Nothing, I said, suddenly put off by the very directness I was hoping for from her. What makes you think something happened? I asked. She rocked Lilach and said, woman's intuition, and I didn't deny it, I didn't try to gloss over it, but I didn't really know what to tell her either, because it wasn't really clear to me what, if anything, was bothering me, or how to translate the abstract feelings into concrete examples. But I started to talk anyway. I told her that I was a bit worried about that club for former mental patients where Amir volunteered. And that I thought it was having too much of an effect on him. Every night he has horrible dreams about the people there, dreams I can't even listen to any more, but he keeps telling me every little detail anyway and he expects me to give him clever, carefully thought out interpretations. A few days ago, when I came home, I saw him through the window sitting in the living room talking to himself. I couldn't hear anything, I just saw his lips moving, and maybe he was only singing along with the radio, but on the other hand, maybe he wasn't. And then there's all that time he spends with Yotam, the neighbour's son, the one whose brother was killed. When I left the house, they were playing chess, and they probably still are. There's something nice about it, true, but the boy's in our house more than in his own, and sometimes, when I come home late, Amir acts weird, as if something is locked up inside him, and last Saturday we hardly touched each other, I mean, he came home from the club really down on Thursday and I was wiped out from Bezalel, and we didn't actually fight, but every conversation we started turned into an argument and I found myself supporting experiments on animals and objecting to treating depression with drugs, or the opposite, just for the sake of argument, and the whole time, I felt something humming and buzzing in the background, like in the morning when Madmoni's workers are drilling, do you know what I mean?

During that whole muddled speech, I was feeling that I couldn't tell her the real truth. That there was something else behind all of that, something inaccessible to me. Like when you try to remember a word in English and it's on the tip of your tongue but doesn't come out.

Sima tasted her coffee and said: I didn't know that he and Yotam were friends. It's very nice of Amir to spend time with that boy. And I thought, oh no, it's happening again, she's falling in love with him, captivated by his good deeds, like my friends, like my parents. Like everyone.

*

It took me three months just to learn the functions of the chesspieces. I remember my father showing me over and over again the peculiar way the knight moves, two forward, one to the side. The sound of disappointment in his voice: What? You still don't understand? Yotam, on the other hand, mastered the whole game in two weeks. He even caught on to castling very quickly. Maybe children today are used to that kind of thinking because they're always on the computer. Maybe I was especialy slow because my teacher was too set on making me a champion. I don't know. In any case, with Yotam, I very quickly moved from the status of omnipotent master to the status of an opponent who should be respected, but whose days of having the upper hand are clearly numbered.

There's only one thing I can't get him to understand no matter how hard I try: the idea that sometimes it's worth sacrificing a pawn in order to achieve a greater, more important goal like defending the king or taking a bishop. He refuses to accept that and puts up a fierce fight to save the life of every one of his pawns.

Last Saturday, a winter sun suddenly appeared over Maoz Ziyon and we carried the folding table with the chessboard on it out to the empty lot. Yotam wanted to go outside and I was glad of the chance to get out of the field of high tension that had been buzzing between me and Noa since Thursday. They'd shot her down at school again, and I'd just come back from the club all shaken up: Dan, a shy, quiet man who spends most of his time playing draughts wasn't there, and when I asked Nava why, she said he'd had a relapse and was back in the closed ward. When she said that in her cold, professional voice, I felt slightly dizzy and my knees shook. Dan was the sanest crazy person in the club. Conversations with him were a refreshing change from the strained talks with Shmuel, and I had the feeling that I was actually getting through to him and encouraging him. Obviously, I wasn't. Obviously I didn't understand anything. I went outside to inhale the fumes from the buses, and for the whole day, I couldn't get myself to stay in the club for more than a few minutes at a time. I felt as if the walls were closing in on me. As if the drawings were laughing at me. And the cigarette smoke was winding around me like a rope. During the training session we had after the members left, I tried to talk about Dan, but Nava kept on shifting the discussion to the relations between the trio of volunteers until I gave up and said to myself that I'd talk to Noa about it instead. She'd help me put the crosshairs of my internal camera on the right spot. But when I got home and stumbled into the living room and said that Nava is driving me crazy, all Noa could say was that my shirt stank of cigarettes, as if I didn't know, and that I should go and have a shower. I deliberately kept the shirt on and sat down on the sofa, and she said, OK, if you're not going to have a shower, I will. I had a killer of a day and I have to wash it off me.

Yeah, I could've followed her, put the toilet seat down, sat and asked her in a sensitive tone what happened, but I felt as if I'd given her an opening that she hadn't taken, so why should I take hers. I stayed sitting in the living room and looked at the blank TV screen, and a few minutes later, when she called my name, I pretended not to hear, but I was thinking what if something happened to her, what if she fell, but I still didn't answer her. I stared at the walls and didn't answer. I thought about how small the apartment was and didn't answer. I thought about Dan from the club and didn't answer. When she came out of the shower, dripping, she walked past me without saying a word.

*

Moshe is racing to Tiberias. It's the only thing he can do. There's rain on the window and it's hot inside – inside the car and inside Moshe too. How could his wife have left him outside all night after their fight. How could she have thrown the blanket at him. How, how, how. He coughs. Vapour rises. He tries to consider possibilities, but everything melts in the blaze of his wrath. He's not thinking about the kindergarten any more, he's not thinking about the boy. All he wants is to be right. The bus descends to the Dead Sea; on the left is the tempting new casino in Jericho. He vacillates. Maybe he'll stop there and play. Menachem's in the *yeshiva* now anyway. No, he rebukes himself, and turns to the Jordan Valley Road, this can't wait. I need help, without doubt. Menachem got him into this mess, so he'll have to get him out. He reaches Tiberias, earlier than expected. The city is sooty and neglected. Balconies are on the verge of collapse. But the large *yeshiva* building is freshly painted. Even though he has no skullcap, he goes inside. Young students walk past him, looking at him in surprise. He stops one and asks if he can tell him where to find Menachem Zakian. If you mean Rabbi Zakian, the student says in a tone filled with awe, of course I can. Yes, Rabbi Zakian, Moshe confirms, and the student directs him to the end of the corridor. That is the Rabbi's office, the last one. Moshe walks past the pictures of the *tsaddikim* quickly, to overcome his chagrin, hoping the door is open and his brother is in. But the door is closed and he has to tap hesitantly with his finger. There's no answer until he knocks again, and then he hears his brother's voice from inside: Come in! Come in!! He goes in, words of apology all ready. But when Menachem sees his face, he gets up and takes his hand. It's an honour, he says, and pulls his brother to his chest in a warm embrace. He explains to his students: this is my brother, Moshe, who has come all the way from Jerusalem, the holy city. To what do we owe this honour, my brother? Moshe blushes. How can he reveal his shame in front of all these students. He doesn't want their pity. No ... that is, if we can talk, he begins to apologise. Menachem smiles into his eyes. Please, my brother, sit with us. We'll be finished in a minute. In the meantime, you can listen to pearls of wisdom from these young scholars. Moshe obeys and sits down on a chair that's a bit small for him. The students go back to praying, looking at the Rabbi with reverence in their eyes. On the agenda: Genesis, chapter 44, verse 18. Joseph pretends not to know his brothers, who are standing before him in Pharaoh's palace, until he can no longer control the cries of longing rising in his throat. 'Then Joseph could not refrain himself before all them that stood by him; and he cried: Cause every man to go out from me. And there stood no man with him, while Joseph made himself known unto his brethren. And he wept aloud; and the Egyptians and the house of Pharaoh heard.' Menachem reminds his students not to forget that these are the same brothers who threw him into the pit. Just because they were jealous of him. They threw him into the pit and walked away. But Joseph does not hold a grudge against them, God forbid, he forgives them. And why does he forgive them? What gives him the strength to forgive? 'Now therefore be not grieved, nor angry with yourselves,' Joseph said to Reuven, 'that ye sold me hither; for God did send me before you to preserve life.' And what do we learn from this?

Moshe hears the words, but he's preoccupied with last night's fight and he doesn't really absorb what they're talking about. He waits impatiently for the lesson to be over and for the last student to go out. When they're alone in the room, he pulls a chair over to his brother's desk and looks at him, his eyes filled with gloom. His brother asks: is everything all right? No, Moshe replies, too tired to pretend. Now he tells Menachem the whole story from beginning to end. How Sima went to the kindergarten. And how she came back. What he said to her. What she said to him. How he put the glass under his foot and smashed it. When he comes to the part where Sima threw him out of the house, his voice cracks. It's so hard to tell his brother these facts. But still, he plunges ahead: the bitter cold, the newspaper landing on his head. When he's finished, he feels as if he's run a marathon. All his strength is gone. He looks up at his brother: If you don't help me, I can't go on. Please give me some advice, and if possible, don't quote some biblical verse that has more than one meaning, because the situation at home is getting worse. Menachem, who's been silent till now, forgives his brother for his remark about the verse. He simply strokes his beard and shakes his head to some hidden tune. So what do you think you should do, he asks, and the question hangs in the air of the room. Moshe replies: I don't know. Otherwise

I wouldn't have come here. Maybe I should take the boy to that kindergarten without asking her if I can? Maybe I should keep sleeping outside till she realises she's made a mistake? I even thought of leaving the house tomorrow morning without giving her any warning. Leave the house? Without any warning? Menachem says, raising his voice, and Moshe recoils in alarm. Then he repeats his threat, but less convinced this time. Yes, leave. You don't think it's a good idea, Rabbi? And Menachem stands up, walks around the desk and bends forward until his face is close to his brother's. Tell me, brother, without meaning any disrespect, did you hear what you said? Have you completely lost your head?

*

The first to greet me is Mordechai. He's waiting impatiently in front of the entrance to the shelter, holding a photo album. I already know that the album contains pictures from his glory days as a goalkeeper for Ramat Amidar's junior team. With the ball, without the ball, leaping across the goal, hugging the goalpost. And one picture of him with his father, after a game, their arms around each other's shoulders, looking alike the way only a father and son can. Mordechai doesn't remember that he's already shown me the album several times, and he doesn't remember my name either. He has some idea that I'm one of the student volunteers. But that's all. When I cross the street and approach him, he introduces himself, asks if I'm on my way to the club and then opens the album for me. I listen patiently to his explanations – here we were playing against Bnei Yehuda, here I caught a ball that would've been a goal for sure – and I know that when he gets to the picture of him with his father, he'll stop, look all around as if he's revealing a top-security secret and then he'll tell me about the night his father had a heart attack and he, Mordechai, the son who was always sick, suddenly had to do everything himself: call an ambulance, give his

120

father artificial respiration according to the instructions they gave him on the phone, go to the hospital, wait on the bench outside the emergency room. Maybe you can tell me the rest inside the club, I suggest, taking a quick look at my watch. Nava the co-ordinator doesn't like us to be late. Not that she's openly angry at them, that wouldn't be 'psychological' on her part. But she has her ways – a look here, a word there – to make you feel like a traitor. Mordechai refuses my invitation. He'd rather breathe a little more fresh air outside. He'll probably try his luck again on the next person to arrive.

I open the iron door and start walking downstairs.

My steps are heavy, hesitant. My shoulders are stooped. Over the years and all the times I moved, I've discovered that I have two noticeably different ways of walking: the tense, stiff way when I hold all the air in my chest – the way I walk when I'm in a new place; and the open, confident walk when I throw my legs forward nonchalantly – the way I walk after I learn the rules and see that things aren't as bad as I thought.

Inside, a strong odour assails me. Over the next few hours, my shirt will absorb it and then Noa will wrinkle her nose when I come into the house. It's hard to describe that smell: cigarettes, sweat, but something else too, something unique to that place. Maybe loneliness. Joe is the first one to come over to me, waving a draughtboard. Wanna play? Since Dan was hospitalised, Joe has been my partner. He mops the floor with me. If draughts were an Olympic sport, the man would have a medal. Our games don't usually last more than a few minutes, and between games, I try to get him to talk so I can understand what brought a man like him, who looks like an accountant, to a place like this. It was most likely a crisis with his ex-wife, but he doesn't volunteer any details. Hold on a second, I say to him, I just got here. Let me put my things away. He takes a step back. I take a quick look over his shoulder and see that Shmuel isn't there. I'm relieved and disappointed at the same time.

Nava and the other two students are standing in the other, smaller room. Right on time, Nava says. Somehow, coming from her, it sounds like an accusation. I walk past them and lean my bag and the big, card crossword puzzle against the wall. In our opening talk, Nava explained that each one of us had to organise an activity that involved something we're interested in. Chanit jumped in and said she wanted to give a cooking course. Ronen, who's also studying computer science, suggested something that had to do with science and I said I'm interested in lots of things, but none of them seem right for an activity here so I said I wanted to think about it. Nava raised a plucked eyebrow. Amir, she said, you should take into account that activities begin next week. No problem, I said, but it stressed me out a little. What'll happen if I don't get an idea? What am I, an idea man? It's a good thing I have Noa at home. She has that ability to come up with nice, simple ideas like the kind that make you say, 'How come nobody thought of that before?' A crossword puzzle, she said. And she was right. The crossword puzzle idea turned into a great success, and even Nava, who didn't show any particular enthusiasm at the beginning, was forced to admit that it was interesting to see how they co-operated with each other. Every week, I had to think up harder and harder clues to challenge the participants, whose number was increasing. Occasionally, they had surprising solutions that challenged me too. For example: Five letters, ending in *y*, what you feel when you do something wrong. Sorry? No. Worry. Or: Five letters, with an *e* in the middle, what you do when you're not awake. Sleep? Of course not. Dream.

Shmuel only came to the first meeting of the crossword puzzle group. I think it's childish, he explained. He was more interested in conversing (not in 'talking', but in 'conversing'. He, like me, prefers beautiful words.)

Is Shmuel coming today? I ask Nava, and she nods. Yes, he went to the shop to buy milk for coffee. It's his turn. Interesting, he asked about you too. What's so interesting about that, I think. What?! I hate that remote, insinuating tone of hers. But I don't say a word. She has to give us recommendations for a Master's programme at the end of the year.

I already know that Shmuel will be waiting patiently for me till the crossword puzzle group breaks up for the day. He'll sit in a corner, drink tea and he won't talk to any members of the group. Every once in a while, he'll smile, sometimes at a joke someone tells, sometimes at a silent, internal joke. Every once in a while, he'll clean his scratched glasses on the collar of his shirt. When we're finished, he won't come right over to me, but he'll give me time to roll up the card, to wash my face in the bathroom and have a short conversation with Chanit and Ronen. He's in no rush. He knows that in the end, I'll go over to him. He already understands how attracted I am to his complicated theories, to nice words. I've been musing over our last conversation: Amir, he'll tell me when I sit down next to him, thereby cleverly touching on another one of my sensitive points: my need for continuity, my sense that there's a point to all our conversations. Share your musings with me, I'll reply, and rest my chin in my hand as a sign that I'm listening.

Cutting a piece of Scotch tape with my teeth, I remember that last time he explained to me again why God is transparent. How the entire Bible split into two and God passes transparently through the middle, between the red and the white. Man is always drawn to the edges: taking a bite of the red apple from the tree of knowledge, or a white apple from the tree of life. And God does not permit it. When he saw that I wasn't attacking his theory – the way others who couldn't control themselves undoubtedly had – he went on to explain in a different, lower tone that God had been revealed to him three times, on three junctions of pain (his expression). He described how God had appeared to him in three different forms at each of these junctions – as a dog, a beggar, a picture of a girl in a museum – and despite myself, I heard in my mind the voices of my socialist-bourgeois parents scornfully dismissing anything related to God. Wait, I replied to that voice, for this man, God is a surfboard. For this man, on the verge of drowning in a sea of churning emotions, God or, in this particular case, the primary, healthy inner voice appears and rescues him. What's wrong with that? Why jeer at it?

I wonder what Shmuel's going to talk about today, I ask myself and move away a little to check that the card is hanging straight. Will my heart pound in inexplicable terror again while we're conversing?

The devotees of the crossword puzzle group – except for Dan, who probably won't be coming – slowly gather around me. They say hello, shake my hand. They all have very limp handshakes and are quick to pull away. As if they're afraid to infect or get infected with something. Malka with the messy hair has something to tell me, something important about her sister again. Her eyes are filled with longing, but I ask her to please wait until after we're finished. Everyone sits down in front of the *puzzle* on the kind of squeaky, too-small chairs that even schools aren't using any more. Amatzia, who keeps changing his mind, peeks into the room and asks if he can join the group. I invite him in, and he immediately sits on his heels and starts muttering to himself, no, no. He'll do that another few times during the next hours, and every time, I'll welcome him all over again, in the hope that this time he'll work up the courage.

I ask if anyone wants to read the clues today instead of me. As usual, no one volunteers.

I point to the puzzle and read: one across, eight letters, quiet endurance.

*

124

Patience, my brother, this is not the way to be, Menachem explains to his younger brother and sits down across from him, knee touching knee. Those who are far from the Torah must be brought closer, not by force, but by wile. Moshe protests. But when we ate at your house, you said that I have to insist on getting what I want because this concerns the future of the family. Yes, Menachem says, his self-confidence still entirely intact, but let me tell you a parable from life, nothing abstract. When you're swimming in the Kinneret and a wave comes towards you, you can smash it with your fist and fight against it, or you can give in, dive under it and then continue forward. What are you trying to say, asks Moshe, who didn't like swimming a lot and wasn't crazy about analogies either, abstract or not. What should I do, give in to Sima about the kindergarten? Just surrender? For now, Menachem suggests, let it go, put it aside. Let time take care of it. Bring home some books on Judaism, make sure you celebrate the holidays the way you should. You'll see, if you do all that, the rest will take care of itself. Sima is a believer, and it's only fear that's keeping her from coming closer to religion. Give in to her now, and with God's help, her heart will open in the end. Her heart will open in the end, Moshe repeats, shaking his head in disbelief. But Menachem puts his hand on his heart as if he's about to swear an oath. You know, my brother, until five years ago, there were only four hundred *yeshiva* students in Tiberias? And now, may God be blessed, there are three thousand five hundred students, three large *yeshivas*, four kindergartens. Five seats on the city council. And, as God is my witness, we did it all through peaceful means. Without coercion. So what am I saying? Sleep at our place tonight, until your anger cools off. I'll tell Bilha to make some *kubeh khamusta*. You'll take some for Sima too, if there's any left. And tomorrow morning you'll say the morning prayer with me. We'll pray for Father's health too. He'll be having the operation soon, and his health is more important than anything we've said here, that is certain. Then you'll shave carefully, drive home and give in. What are you worried about? A little patience, my brother, and you'll see that everything will work out.

*

You see, I say to Noa while I'm cutting a tomato – first slices, then along the length, then the width – I did a little thinking when Moshe was in Tiberias. And what did you decide? Noa asks, and on the other chopping board she cuts the yellow pepper she brought. I didn't exactly decide, I say and slide the diced tomato into the bowl. She puts the pieces of pepper in too. Her pieces aren't small enough for my taste, but I don't say anything. So what conclusion did you come to? she asks and picks up an onion. She'll be crying soon. I have this kind of exercise, I tell her, something that I always do when I can't make up my mind about something. I close my eyes and picture every little thing about the two possibilities I have to choose from. Let's say, in this case, I closed my eyes and pictured what my life would be like without Moshe. What it would be like to raise the kids without him. What it would be like to sleep without him. What it would be like to watch TV without putting my head on his shoulder when the programme is boring. And what did you feel? Noa asks in a voice choked with tears from the onion. Dizzy, I say. Dizzy. I felt like I was in an elevator going down the floors of a building and it keeps on going down past the parking floors, minus one, minus two, minus three, and it doesn't stop going down even when there are no more parking floors. What did you feel when you pictured the other possibility? she asks me. That's just it, I explain and add olive oil to the bowl, I didn't have to picture the other possibility any more. Are you saying that you gave in? That Liron is going to the kindergarten? Noa asks, and the disappointment in her voice is as bitter as lettuce. No, I explain and mix the salad. The tomatoes that are on the bottom rise to the top. The corn that was on the top falls down to the bottom. How can that be? Noa asks and spreads her arms in confusion. We sit down at the table. I put some salad on her plate, check to see that Lilach is still sleeping, and explain. Moshe comes home yesterday, and before I can say anything, he takes my hand and his face is as serious as that man's on the nine o'clock news. He sits me down here, at the table, and says, listen Sima, I thought about it, and I asked my brother Menachem's advice, and I don't think it's a good idea to move Liron to a new kindergarten in the middle of the year. Let's wait till next year and see how things develop, OK? O-ka-ay, I say as if I'm doing him a favour, but inside, I'm cracking up laughing. Do you get it? If he'd only let me talk first, I don't know what I would've said. Oh Sima, Sima, Noa says, soaking up the salad dressing with a piece of black bread. With you, nothing's sacred. Well I wouldn't say that, I tell her with a little smile and get up to slice more bread. I cut another three even slices and one crooked slice that starts off thick and ends up thick. When I come back, I find Noa with her eyes closed, her lashes trembling, and a smile of pleasure on her lips. Is the salad that good, I ask her, and she opens one eye into a slit and says don't disturb me, Sima, I'm in the middle. In the middle of what, I ask. Be quiet, she says, I'm picturing every little detail of my two choices.

*

No one mentioned my birthday. Not that I expected to be taken to Kenya on safari like Daniel from Mevasseret was, but I didn't think they'd ignore it either. They actually know the date very well, and just to be on the safe side, I mentioned three times the week before that my class was arranging a party for me and I put a note on the fridge with the date written in huge numbers so even Mum without her glasses couldn't miss it, but on that day, the guys from Gidi's platoon came over at lunchtime. They were on their first leave since the incident and had decided to come to our house straight from the base, so there wasn't time – they were sorry about that – to let us know in advance. Mum said, don't be silly, you don't have to let us know, and called Dad and said, Reuven, come home right away, Gidi's friends are here, and Dad, who Mum always says wouldn't leave work in the middle of the day even if World War III were starting, was home within fifteen minutes, even less, shaking the hands of all of Gidi's buddies and saying to Mum, why don't you offer them something to drink? She said, I did, but they didn't want anything, and Dad said, make the boys some lemonade; don't be shy, boys, make yourselves at home. He sat down on an armchair across from them and asked questions about the situation in Lebanon, about their commander, the redhead, how is he, and Mum came in with the lemonade and called me to come and see them, but I didn't want to. I knew exactly how the conversation would go, they'd say again how much Gidi loved the company, even though every Saturday night he used to close the door to his room and cry because he was so miserable about having to go back to the base. They'd say again that he wanted to sign up for the regular army although I'd heard him say to his friend, Sarit, that even if they gave him a million dollars, he wouldn't stay in the army one more day. And after they'd finish telling all those lies, which even my parents knew were lies, they'd give a blow-by-blow description of how he was killed in an ambush, which was something I didn't want to hear.

OK, I'm just coming, I told Mum. Then I climbed out my window and started walking over to Amir and Noa's place.

There was a strong wind, ice-lolly wrappers were blowing around in the air, and I almost fell twice. The Arab worker, the one all the mothers have been warning their kids about recently, was walking around in the empty lot. Up close, he looked old and not at all scary, but still, I didn't understand what he was doing there. Should I get the soldiers who were in our house? I hid behind Gidi's monument and watched him for a while, but he didn't do anything interesting, didn't bury a bomb, didn't take out a knife, all he did was look at Avram and Gina's house from a few different angles, then limp back to Madmoni's site. No reason to get the soldiers, I thought, just a weird old man. I came out of my hiding place and ran to Amir and Noa's apartment. Amir opened the door with a big smile: you beat me to it by a minute, he said. I was just on my way to your place to give you a present. A present? I said, surprised. How do you know it's my birthday? A little bird told me, he said. What bird? I asked. Just kidding, he said, laughing. Last week, you only mentioned three times that Wednesday was your birthday. No way I could've missed it.

He took a large gift-wrapped box off the top of the TV and gave it to me. You can probably guess what it is, he said. Inside the wrapping was a shiny new chessboard. I opened it, and inside the board were the pieces, bigger than any of the ones we'd played with till now, and more nicely sculpted. The knight really looked like a horse, the rook really looked like a fortress. And the king's crown was like the crown you see in educational TV programmes about Richard the Lionheart.

Next to the pieces was a small plastic bag. Open it, Amir said, handing it to me, it's for you too. Inside the bag was a Beitar Jerusalem scarf, not like the nylon one I had, but a thick, woollen scarf with the menorah logo of my favourite football team, Beitar Jerusalem, printed on both ends.

Thank you, I said. It sounded like too little to me, that 'thank you', but I didn't know what else to say.

T-h-a-n-k-y-o-u, Amir imitated me. Is that all? Do you know what it means for a Hapoel fan like me to buy a Beitar scarf? Do you know what they'd say in Bloomfield if they knew? Hey, gimme a hug.

After we broke in the new board with two straight games – I made Amir swear not to let me win just because it was my birthday, so I lost them both – Noa called and Amir said he had to meet her at the shops soon, in the supermarket, to buy flowers and candles for his friend David's show. I gave him a normal hug goodbye, quicker than the first one, and went home with my new board. When I came in, Gidi's friends were gone, and Dad was back at work. Mum was sitting in the living room looking at a new album I hadn't seen before. I thought about slipping away to my room without talking, but she looked up from the album and asked, where were you? She didn't say it as if she were planning to tell me off, but as if she'd been worried about me while I was gone. So I told her the truth, that I was at Amir's. That student? Yes. Do you go there a lot? Yes. It's a shame you didn't sit with us for a little while, Yoti, you would have heard a few stories about Gidi. Do you miss him sometimes? Yes. And that Amir, tell me, what do you do together? Play chess. Chess? Since when do you play chess? Since he taught me how. OK, it looks like I have to meet him, that friend of yours, let's go and see him. Now? Now. We can't, he's at the shops, buying things for his friend's show. How do you know? He told me. Come on, Yoti, let's go to his place together. But he went to the supermarket. Let's try, the worst that can happen is that he won't be there.

Mum put on her long black coat and we left. Walking down the stairs, it occurred to me that I never actually take this route to their place, along the street. I always take the shortcut through the lot, and now we went out to the pavement, turned left and walked on the road, close to each other, but not touching, and we went up the stairs that lead to the Zakian house – the strong wind almost blew me into my mother, but at the last minute I managed to stay on my feet – and as we climbed, I kept hoping that Amir had already left. Sure enough, when we got to the Zakian house, Moshe was standing outside with a cigarette in his hand and he said, welcome, and my mother pointed to the grey-tiled path and asked: is that the students' apartment? Moshe said yes, but he just left and she's not home, do you want to leave them a message? And Mum said no, we'll come back another time, and Moshe said, you can come inside and have something to drink at our place, and Mum said no, thank you, another time.

That expression, 'another time', is the one my mother's been using the most since Gidi. She says it to all her friends when they call to invite her over, and also every time I ask her to help me with my homework, and now, I thought, it looks like she's going to celebrate my birthday 'another time' too. We did an about-face, and as we were walking down the steps to the street, Mum stroked my head. At first, I was so surprised that I didn't know what was touching me and I almost hit her hand with my own, but when I understood, it felt good, and I walked more slowly to keep pace with her stroking, and she said, Yoti, tell that student to call in when he has a chance, OK? I said OK Mum, even though I knew I wouldn't tell him because I wanted to keep Amir all to myself.

*

When Noa and Amir come home from the supermarket, the house is full of cooking smells. So what do you think, Amir asks as he uncovers the hole in the wall, did Moshe and Sima decide to make up? Did you hear anything at all? Yes, I think so, Noa says, otherwise Sima wouldn't be making him chicken breasts on the grill. With mushroom sauce, Amir whispers, and tiny potatoes with dill. They stand there under the hole for a few minutes and try to see if they can tell – it's a kind of game they play – exactly what the Zakians are going to eat tonight from the smell.

Later, maybe because the game has made them hungry or maybe because the documentary on TV is about animal abuse, a kind of gloom seems to pervade the air of the living room. And they become immersed in their own worries. Noa is listing in her mind the names of the people who have already chosen a topic for their final project. And she's torturing herself again because she hasn't even picked a subject yet. Amir is thinking about the club and transparent Shmuel. And about the fact that tomorrow will be another grim day spent at home alone. They can't talk over the TV announcer's loud voice, and they don't touch each other, out of choice. The bowls of tasteless soup they made in such a rush are sitting on the table, untouched. The sofa is hard, the heater's dead and the water stain on the ceiling overhead is getting bigger. I might as well go to sleep, Noa thinks, but makes no move to go. Moods shift here like the weather in Modi's letters, Amir thinks, and buries his fist in a cushion. Let him go to bed first, Noa thinks, I want to have some time without him. Let her go to bed first, Amir thinks, immediately surprised by the venom in his thoughts. He gives Noa his hand and their fingers interlock. Then he rubs his foot against the bottom of her sock. She looks at him and asks: is everything OK? And he answers – a shadow passing across his heart – yes, why are you asking me? No reason, she says, sounding panicky. He asks: is everything OK? Then watches her lips as she replies with a line from Boaz Sharabi's song: Yes, no one dies of love any more. And he sings the next line, imitating Sharabi's guttural voice: But without love, what is life really for? She smiles a superficial smile, turns off the TV and says: What a terrible programme. And a few seconds later, she adds: a real downer. And he swallows a surprising I'm-out-of-here thought that rises up from somewhere deep. You're right, he says. Come on, let's go to sleep.

*

I don't want to wait for her on Zakian's steps. It's too cold. And besides, why does she always have to be late? And then she'll want to get changed and put on make-up, and I'll end up missing David's show. I'm going alone. If she doesn't come in the next five minutes – I'm going alone. She just has to have all those scenes, so there'll be a little tension, a little drama, otherwise she can't create, right? Look who's talking, Mister I'm-Out-of-Here. What was that supposed to be last night? You're sitting in the living room, all cosy and comfy, eating soup – what could be more wintry than that? – and you start with those prickly thoughts. What happened, things started feeling homey and you got scared? Addicted, that's what you are. Addicted to change. You pretend that all you want is four walls, a home, and then, the minute it happens, you start planning your getaway. Wait, hold on a second, maybe I'm putting the wrong spin on things. Maybe I really do need to get away for a couple of days, to breathe the air of solitude. But how? I sink without her, revert to being a spectator, a moaner, a masturbator, and when she comes home, my whole body reaches out for her and I want to devour her, to peel and eat her, then listen to her stories with all those little details only she sees. But that's not actually a contradiction, not at all, she can be fantastic and still suffocate you with that dissatisfaction of hers that bubbles over on to you too. Oh come on, what are you, a symbol of serenity? A logo for *shanti*? Get serious, don't put it all on her. But it's a fact that before we moved in together, it was different. Before you moved in together? It was a lie, a pretence sprinkled with enough bits of truth to make it work, and now – now you want to close the boot on her. Yes, don't deny it. When you came back from the supermarket and she bent over to take the bags out, that's exactly what you wanted to do, close the boot on her. That's right. Your hand itched on the red metal and you almost slammed it shut. OK, it's because you're in the house all day, you don't run, don't play sports, and your best friend hasn't had his bar mitzvah yet. You go on like that and you'll end up being accepted into the Helping Hand Club. So, it's time to get out of that loop before it winds itself around your neck. Get out of it, get out, get out. How did you fall into this anyway? When did it start? Noa's late. She's late. So what. Cool it.

All these shows start late anyway. I wonder what the songs will sound like. I know them from the guitar version. David used to play them during our long guard duty shifts in the army in a small sentry box with a broken window, and now we'll hear how they sound with a group. I wonder what kind of audience there'll be. Probably fans. It'll probably be fun. I love going to shows with Noa. Music really turns her on. She flows with it. And when she dances, she closes her eyes, not like those girls who dance as if they're paying taxes. If she's wearing a dress, then you can just stand there and look at how beautiful she is, how her legs show when her dress lets them, how the lights flicker on her shoulders.

On the last night of the trip where we met, we all went to the disco at Kibbutz Mitzpe Shalem. We'd spent every day of the trek in the desert circling each other, throwing out a sentence, a look, a word, lingering on sarcastic remarks. But when I saw her dance, tossing her hair from side to side, pulling an imaginary rope with her elbows and swaying her hips, I felt something in that spot in my body that tells me how I really feel, the small delta made by the two arteries in my neck where they meet my chest, and I started wanting her.

Well, what do you know, here's the van that brings her home. I recognise the squeal of its brakes. Eight thirty-two. Unbelievable. There's still a chance we might get there on time.

*

The first photograph of the show is of the poster. Red background. Black letters (a combination of colours that rockers starting out seem to like). Their funny name, Licorice, is in huge letters, and under it, the names of the group members. David's name is the same size as the others because 'Just because I write the songs and sing them doesn't mean I'm more important than the bass player.' That's what he told Amir when he showed us the sketch a week earlier, as excited as if the show was just about to go on in our living room. On the right of the poster, I managed (taking a professional risk, I went out into the street) to catch part of the door to the Pargod Club: a heavy wooden door with an arch on top and iron buttons on the side, the kind of door that, if you pass it during the day when it's closed, you might easily think is a monastery door. Below the Licorice poster is a poster for a different show – you can see the date and one word of the group's name, Shabess. I think the whole name is Shabess Dance, but I'm not sure. Behind, as background for the posters, is a greenish kiosk covered with notices. Behind that are a few Jerusalem stones that are part of a large wall, and behind the wall – this you can't see in the photo – is the beginning of the Nachlaot neighbourhood, or more accurately, the nice part of Nachlaot, the one with the narrow lanes.

It was in those narrow lanes that Amir and I almost had our first kiss. It was two weeks after we started going out. We'd just come out of the cinema – *Fearless* with Jeff Bridges, which I saw not too long ago on the movie channel and it turned out not to be such a bad film – and we talked and talked about almost every possible subject: about the importance or unimportance of archaeology – on the one hand, what's the point of digging up the past, but on the other, without the past, how can we understand the present; about Jerusalem as a place to live – on the one hand, it's so beautiful, but on the other, a little too intense; about my dream of becoming a photographer, and about his dream – which he still wasn't sure he could call a dream – of becoming a psychologist. We talked for hours, covering up the simple tension of when the kiss would come with long, complicated sentences. Every once in a while, we stopped next to an entrance with ornate ironwork, or a window through which the sound of a saxophone was coming, or an announcement about a special prayer meeting to be held in a square in front of a synagogue before the Sabbath. Finally, we sat down in a small park between buildings, on a bench that still smelt of fresh paint. The kiss was in the air, we even looked at each other's lips while we talked, but we kept drawing out the tension longer and longer. Later, at four in the morning, when we were lying in my bed exhausted and purring after three times, one of them with the addition of mocha-vanilla ice-cream, Amir said that he hadn't been sure I wanted him. That he was afraid I was interested in him only as a friend. I don't know. I think we both – after all, I was there too, and in the past, I'd bent first to kiss guys – waited with the first kiss because we knew that after it, there'd be no going back.

After I took pictures outside the club, we went inside with our heads bent so as not to bump into the low ceiling. I'd already been to the Pargod a few times (in my freshman year, I saw the Brera Tivit group three times, each show more thrilling than the others), but still, even this time, going into the club was a surprise: This is the whole deal? This is the Pargod? A small, cramped space with ten rows of plastic chairs, a narrow aisle, damp walls. If it had stalactites and stalagmites, it could officially be called a cave. While Amir was buying tickets from the club owner, I studied his face. For the first time in months, the light was back. Those visits to the Helping Hand Club, the pressure of his studies, and something else, something he doesn't talk about, had made him seem stooped. Three grey hairs had popped out in front, about five years too early. His twitch was twitching again. And the deep furrow on the right side of his face seemed to be getting deeper. But that night at the Pargod, everything was reversed. He smiled at everyone, hugged David's mother in excitement, danced lightly as we walked to our seats and kissed me on the neck once a minute. I don't believe it, he said and pointed at the lit stage where all the instruments were, I just don't believe it. He drummed on his knee and mine, as if they were bongo drums, to the rhythm of the pre-show music, and I found myself again, for the millionth time, amazed by his ability to be really happy, with his whole heart, for other people. Without a drop of jealousy. Without a smidgen of egoism. He was just happy for David. So happy that when Licorice came hesitantly on to the stage, he leaped out of his seat as if they were nothing less than U2 and he dragged the whole audience in that little cubbyhole along with him into a cheering session – including David's mother, who was trilling along with the cheering crowd – that went on for two straight minutes.

The show itself started with feedback – grating guitar squeals that startled the audience and caused a wave of embarrassed muttering. That's what happens when your soundman is a teenager. But it got better. Licorice got more confident with each song, David's voice opened up, the bass blossomed, the drummer came out of his hiding place behind the cymbals and reinforced David's voice with his own soft, almost feminine voice, the audience of fans applauded during the choruses and lit their Zippos during the ballads, and the bald critic from the local newspaper – everyone knew who he was, but they tried not to show it – nodded at least twice in satisfaction. Every once in a while, through the screen of distortion, you could make out a few lines of the songs, such as 'Love is a jittery DJ', or 'The dam on the I river has collapsed', making me think that they should consider handing out lyrics during the performance, not just with the CDs. I had my usual attack of jealousy of musicians because they can create together and help each other create individually, because they can signal each other with a look, with the strum of a guitar, that it's time to end the song, while photographers have to make all their decisions alone and make mistakes, mistakes all the time.

Towards the end of the show, I even managed to forget that I was at the performance of someone I know. I closed my eyes and just let the music fuse with my body and take me off on a trip. During one instrumental passage, I was on a yellow hill in the Negev leading a herd of red goats. In another, stormier passage, I found myself in the middle of a brightly coloured festival in a village from *One Hundred Years of Solitude*, and Modi appeared in front of me and handed me a purple cocktail.

After the last song – a weird reggae version of Benzine's 'Freedom is completely alone' – the audience naturally called for an encore. Licorice didn't bother with the usual ritual of walking off and then walking back on to the stage at the audience's insistence because they didn't exactly have anywhere to walk off to, so they stayed on the low stage. The guitarist exchanged his electric guitar for an acoustic one. David took the microphone in his hand and spoke. His voice was hoarse from so much singing. His forehead glistened with sweat from the heat of the spotlights. I remember almost every word. 'I want to thank everyone who came tonight. I won't say you were a wonderful audience, because that's bullshit. You were a loving audience. I only hope we have audiences like you at all our perform-ances. (Wild applause.) I want to give special thanks to three people without whom I wouldn't be here today. Yoni, Matan and Amir (here, Amir squeezed my thigh). Without their love and affection, I wouldn't have survived the last few weeks and I wouldn't be standing here now. I dedicate this next song, "Spread your Grace", to them. I think that this is a time when a little grace wouldn't hurt any of us.'

In the second photo of the show, David and Amir are hugging. After 'Spread' – I'd heard its hymn-like chorus many times in our living room, so I could join in – the lights were turned on and the audience went up to congratulate the members of the group. There was a short line, like the kind you have at weddings after the ceremony, and I waited with my flash for the minute that Amir came up to David, moving around constantly to find a place where no one could come between me and them. The picture itself shows David's face over Amir's shoulder. His eyes are closed, his eyebrows a little wild. His lips are stretched almost into a smile. Amir is slightly bent, his shirt pulled up, exposing a little bit of his back. His right hand is reaching out, pulling David to him for a manly hug. In the background, some guy is making a speech to a woman – the fabric of her trousers is the kind older women wear, so she must have been David's mother – and his mane of hair spills out of the frame. The kid who did the sound is behind them, bending to pick up a cable. And all the other details are swallowed up in darkness. In the black hole. Not the photograph of the century in terms of light, but I still like it because of David's half-smile and because if you bring it close to your face, you can actually smell that smell, the one that exists only at shows like that: a combination of cigarettes, sweat and excitement. On the way home, we tried to guess which of Licorice's songs would be a hit on the radio. Amir remembered other details from the performance and recreated them with shining eyes. Did you notice how their bottles of water stayed full? They didn't drink a drop. Did you see the drummer, the power he had? David says that in real life, he's a pussycat. And the critic, did you see him? He went up to David after the show and said thank you. Thank you is good, right?

Of course thank you is good.

Amir took the turns going out of Jerusalem so fast that I was afraid his enthusiasm would propel us straight into the Mevasseret wadi, but I didn't say anything. I enjoyed seeing him that way so much – excited, elated, alive – that I didn't want to spoil it.

Back then I still thought I had control over what gets spoiled and what doesn't.

*

You know, *ya ibni*, there's something else I didn't tell you, Mother says and closes her eyes. The rusty old key to that house is sitting between us on the small stool with the gold edging. She took it off her neck for the first time in forty-

139

eight years – she never even took it off in the shower – but I still don't take it. I've already told her about the house, and she didn't yell. I've already described to her what it looks like from every angle, and she didn't gesture with her hand for me to leave. Just the opposite. She added more signs for me to look for – there are two fig trees in front, a pomegranate tree at the back – so I'd be sure that was the place. But to reach out and take the key – I didn't have the courage.

I was too ashamed to tell you this story, she goes on. But you, *ya ibni*, will be an old man yourself soon, and who knows how much time I have left to live. You have many years left, I want to say, but she silences me with a look. On the day the Jews came, she begins – but not in her story-telling voice, her large voice that makes you bend over and listen, but a quiet voice that I don't know – on the day they came to drive us away, we didn't take many things from the house. There was no time. The soldiers were already standing on the hills, and the stories about Dir Yassin were spreading through the village. You've heard about Dir Yassin, haven't you? Everyone said that now, Dir Yassin would be here, in el-Castel, and fear entered out hearts. We were not thinking clearly, do you understand? We took a little rice, a little olive oil, a few pots, put it all on the donkey and started walking. I didn't remember until a few hours later that I'd left something at home. The most important thing. I wanted to go back. I had to go back. But the soldiers fired over our heads and yelled *yallah*, go to Abdallah, the King of Jordan, and your father said, *ma'alish*, we'll be back in the village in another two weeks anyway. That's why it's remained there, since then, in the walls of the house.

What is it, *ya umi*? What are you talking about? I ask, and she puts her hand on mine and says, I can't tell you that. You'll see for yourself. Her hand shakes. I cover it with my other hand, and she covers that hand with hers.

And we sit like that, with a tower of four hands, one on top of the other, for a few minutes without talking.

The muezzin starts calling, and his words come through the window with the wind. Children are yelling in the yard below. My father is coughing in the bedroom.

Finally, she takes her hand away, picks up the rusty key and hands it to me. Here, *ya ibni*, go to that house you are talking about and open the door. Maybe it's from Allah that they took you to work in our village. I'm a stubborn old woman, but go there if you want to so much, and Allah will watch over you. Go, go and say hello to the spirit of Aziz. People say he's still wandering around there, making the Jews crazy. Go and bring back black figs from the fig tree, go and pour lime on the ground near the mosque so the ants won't get inside. And then, when you go to the house, go inside, don't be ashamed, it's your house, don't apologise. If the Jews say anything, show them this. She goes to the cabinet, takes out the *sura*, the sack, and pulls a document out of it. I know that document: the last time I saw it was thirty years ago, when my wife's family wanted to know what land the groom's family owned. That's how it was then. People believed that we'd all go home very soon and get our land back.

The certificate from the land registry office, Mother says and hands it to me. Her hands shake and the paper dances. People die, trees die, but the land stays for ever, she says. *Mazbut*, that's true, I reply and use my sleeve to wipe off the dust that has collected on the paper. You guard this very very carefully, OK? She waves a threatening finger at me. I will, I promise, and put my hand over my shirt pocket.

Now listen well, she says, and lowers her voice as if she's about to tell me a secret. I bend down to her. Above the door, under the ceiling, there's one loose brick. Look for it and you'll find it. I trust you, that's your job, isn't it? When you find it, take it out carefully. If that's the right house, you'll find a bag behind it with a lot of rolled-up newspaper inside. Wrapped in the newspaper is something that belongs to me. To my mother. *Ya* Saddiq, if you can, bring it here. And Allah will be with you.

Chorus

When I was ten
And Beitar was taking it on the chin
I'd promise God to obey His commandments
If only He'd make them win.
I'd keep the Sabbath
Wear a *yarmulke* on my head
And say the blessing over bread.

And now I call to him come back,
Come back to me
Spread your grace over me.

When I was fifteen
And my father was sick in bed
I'd beg for him to get well
And swear to do what the rabbi said.
I'd put on my prayer shawl,
Pray every day
And join a *yeshiva* not tomorrow, but today.

And now I call to him come back,
Come back to me
Spread your grace over me.

The dam has collapsed over the river I

Rivers of longing are drowning me alive
I'm about ready to say
I'm done for, no more
Spread, oh spread your grace over me.

I've broken my promises, the whole long list
And maybe You don't even exist
But come back, come back to me
Spread your grace over me.

Music and lyrics: David Batsri
From the Licorice album, *Love As I Explained it to My Wife*
Produced independently, 1996

3

All of a sudden I heard a boom, says an eyewitness in a cardigan who was breathing heavily. All of a sudden I heard a boom, says a salesman from the shoe shop, an involuntary smile twitching on his cheek. A boom? What boom? An explosion doesn't go boom, just like a dog doesn't go woof-woof. At the café they say Noa never got there, and the shift manager tries to allay my blatant fear. The police blocked off the street, so even if she wants to, there's no way she can get through. Among the casualties are women and children, the announcer says, his face all puffed up. And the thought flashes through my mind, what about Noa? Is she considered a woman? The ticker moves across the bottom of the screen. City centre telephone lines crash from overload. But more than an hour's gone by. She's had enough time to get out of there and call. The telephone shrieks. Is it her? No, her mother. More uptight than I am. Yes, I heard. No, she hasn't called me. No, she doesn't take the number eighteen bus. She takes the one-five-four. She's probably stuck there and can't call because the lines are down. At Bezalel? There's no one there to talk to. The office is only open on odd-numbered days, and only for an hour or so. Yes, it's outrageous, I know. No, Tel Aviv's no better. You're right, Yehudith, those should be our biggest problems. Right, the first one to get the all-clear signal will let the other one know, OK? OK. I put down the receiver and start pacing, unable to turn off the TV and unable to watch it because I'm afraid there'll suddenly be a close-up of a stretcher with Noa on it. The man in the picture on the living room wall is still staring at nothing at all. Maybe he's waiting for a phone call too. Noa's right. That picture is a depressing sight. If she gets out of this OK, I'm taking it down. Why did I say 'if'? I look in the fridge for something to eat. The sticker 'Create or Stagnate' screams at me from the corkboard. I find two rubbery dried apricots. I sink my teeth into one of them, toss the other into the air. And catch it. Sima's Lilach is sobbing, screaming. Her crying splits walls. In my little workroom, the book *Psychopathology* is open at the chapter on post-traumatic stress disorder. I browse through it till I get to the chapter on behavioural therapy for worry. I don't read, just put it down belly up, open at the right chapter. The phone screams. Now it has to be Noa, and I am going to give her a piece of my mind. Why didn't she call sooner? It's Hila. Noa was supposed to have called her in the morning from the café to set up a day for Reiki, but no sign of her yet. And the café isn't far from Jaffa Street, you know. Yes, Hila, I know. Are you watching TV? Yes. The mayor's giving a speech into a sea cucumber. 'The horrendous sights . . .' 'On a day like this . . .' 'We did everything we could . . .' People are crowded around him like fans around a football player. It's terrible, Amir, Hila whispers into my ear, just terrible. How much hate does a person have to have to do such a thing? It spreads so much bad karma in the world. Didn't they ever hear of non-violent protests? If they would just march, lock arms and march, no one could stop them. I don't know, Hila, I don't know if things like that work in the Middle East, I say, and hear myself sounding as hollow as a political analyst on TV. She'll be OK, won't she? Hila begs. Let me know if you hear anything from her, Amir. Promise? Yes, I promise. Bye, Hila. Bye. The Minister of Something-or-Other Affairs promises, on live TV, to bring the full weight of justice to bear on the terrorists and those who send them. The fans are pushing. The camera is shaking. The broadcast switches back to the studio. They rehash everything we already know. What if she doesn't call? Scenarios start to sprout in my mind and I can't trim them down. Noa with an amputated leg, Noa with crutches, Noa in a hospital bed with me beside her reading her the end of *A Hundred Years of Solitude*, trying to absorb the fact that I have a handicapped girlfriend. And another one: Noa's dead, someone informs me, a police officer. He calls and offers me his condolences. (Is that how it works? They offer their condolences even before you know you need them?) Then he asks me to come to the hospital. My trip to Shaare Tzedek Hospital – no, to Hadassah Hospital in Ein Kerem – is ceremonious. Cars make way for me as if they know. Her family is already waiting at Hadassah Ein Kerem – it's not clear how they got here before me. A quick hug with her father. A three-way hug with her mother and sister. They're all weepy and I can't shed a tear. Why not? And why does that whole scenario infuse me with a kind of sweetness, why does it excite me? A knocking at the door saves me from the answer. Three quick, demanding knocks. I open it. Sima apologises for bothering me. I just wanted to ask if Noa's all right, she says, brushing her hair from side to side with one hand. In the other, she's rocking Lilach. Why are you standing outside? Come in, I extend an arm and she comes in. Dressed nicely, sharply creased black trousers, a pink shirt with buttons down the front, one of them open right over her cleavage. Is that what she wears at home? I take a quick look at the living room through her eyes. The two pillows on the sofa. No underpants on the floor. It's a good thing I managed to tidy up a little in the morning. Did you hear anything from her? she asks, putting Lilach down on the rug. The fear starts creeping again. No, I haven't heard anything. Tell me, that café of hers, isn't it near . . . ? Yes. And . . . ? She never got there, I checked. *Allah yestur*, God help us, Sima says and puts her hand on her breast, her fingers slipping under her shirt through the open button. Meanwhile, Lilach discovers my tennis ball. She feels it with her fingers and tries to eat the yellow fuzz. Sima bends down (plain white bra) and takes it out of her hand. It doesn't taste good, she tells her gently, it doesn't taste good. She hands me the spit-soaked ball and says, with the same gentleness, don't worry, it'll be OK, it's not her bus. Sit down, why are you standing, I say to her and ask myself till what age will my heart respond so quickly to maternal gentleness? I wonder if even when I'm eighty, I'll want to rest my head between the breasts of every woman who talks to me that way. Have you called the emergency numbers yet? Sima asks and points to the screen. I look for a pen that works and manage to copy down only one number before the broadcast switches to 'our correspondent, Gil Littman' with the first pictures from Shaare Tzedek Hospital. Gil Littman taught us field studies at school, and all the girls in the class used to put on lipstick before his lesson. Now he's talking to the hospital's Deputy Director, with drips and white gurneys racing past in the background. They'll probably postpone Avram's operation again, Sima mumbles to herself. Who'll have time for his kidneys now? You never know, I try to reassure her, staring at the screen and thinking: just don't let any black hair pop up now. No black hair. I start imagining again: I'm at Noa's bed stroking her hair, kissing the veins on the back of her hand, and she doesn't wake up. Doesn't wake up.

Thirty-four injured, Sima says, repeating the number the

Deputy Director has just said as if it were a mantra for self-relaxation. Thirty-four.

As I dial the first number on the page, I recall those stories from Memorial Day programmes about mothers who feel in their bodies, even before the army officers knock on their doors, that their son has been killed. Did Yotam's mother feel it too?

I check to see what I'm feeling inside my body, and find turmoil.

*

On days when there's a suicide bombing, Jews don't answer you. Even if you ask, 'How much does this juice cost?' they don't answer. And if they do, you can tell from their voice how scared they are. On days when there's a suicide bombing, wherever you go, the radio is screaming words like 'savages' or 'murderers'. And you want to scream back at the radio. On days when there's a suicide bombing, I feel shame in my heart, and pride too, and I don't understand how I can feel both those things at the same time. On days when there's a suicide bombing, I calculate how to save more money than Nehila and I are already saving. Maybe we should rent out a room in the house. Maybe we should sell some of her gold jewellery. Maybe our oldest boy should leave school and start working. On days when there's a suicide bombing, even I am afraid of buses. Every time our van is behind a bus, I think there's going to be an explosion and I picture the back of the bus flying through the window and the glass slicing into our throat. On days when there's a suicide bombing, I say to myself: calm down, Saddiq. There's already been one bombing. It's not logical for there to be two on the same day. On days when there's a suicide bombing, I think about my cousin Munir, who went to study medicine in Italy and met an Italian girl from a rich family and married her. He sends us pictures of his big house that has a beautiful garden and a pool, and he's standing there with a completely shaven face, and even though it's only a picture, you can smell his expensive cologne. On days when there's a suicide bombing, I think about my mother and what she always calls Munir: a traitor. She says: a person should die in the place where he was born. On days when there's a suicide bombing, I want to go back to bed and get under the winter blanket and be a child again, not a father who has to go to work, put food on the table and think every day about what tomorrow will bring. On days when there's a suicide bombing, I love my wife again. Even though she's fat from all the babies she's had, even though she has wrinkles around her eyes. On days when there's a suicide bombing, I stroke her hair before we fall asleep and kiss her forehead. On days when there's a bombing, I want to smoke, even though I gave up, and drink a bottle of whiskey, even though it's not allowed. On days when there's a suicide bombing, I don't listen to music, but I eat a lot. I eat everything my wife puts on my plate and go to the pots to see if there's anything left. On days when there's a suicide bombing, I remember the chief prison guard, Eli Barzilai, and hope that asshole was on the bus that exploded. But I also remember one girl soldier who heard me crying in my cell and gave me a Marlboro Light from her pack, and I hope she decided to take her car today.

*

At first, I ran around taking pictures of everything like a madwoman. Small groups of people, large groups, bloodstains on glass. The area looked like the palm of someone who squashed a mosquito that had food in its mouth. I finished three rolls of film one after the other without stopping, without thinking. Without even feeling. It's a good thing Schwartz Photos was open and he still had Fuji 200. Schwartz's son gave me a you-must-be-crazy-to-be-taking-pictures-today look, but I didn't care. The main thing was to get back to the scene and start looking for mistakes. I saw a sign on a shoe shop right above the skeleton of the bus that said EXPLOSIVE SALE. I noticed other photographers, like me, who were looking for the right angle, hiding behind their cameras. I tried to document the first signs of life going back to its regular routine. The first violinist to take his violin out of its case and play a heart-rending melody to the cold stones, and to me. The first falafel stand to reopen. The first man to buy and eat half an order, tahini dripping down his chin. The first European traveller to stop and look at the frame of the bus for a few minutes and then continue walking down the pedestrian area. And I wasn't the least bit scared. Not that I'm brave or anything. Just the opposite. Every little noise in the house at night scares me. Once I even convinced Amir that there was a burglar in the living room, and he went to see, armed with a tennis racket, and found that it was a small plastic bag making all the noise. But during all the time I spent on Jaffa Street, I wasn't worried for even a minute. I was completely engrossed in my work. It wasn't until the end of the day, on the bus going home, that I suddenly got scared.

And that was when I took the best picture, the one I'm looking at now.

At that hour, the number one-five-four bus is usually full, and I have to stand for half the trip, holding on to a post or the back of a seat and regretting that I'm not wearing more comfortable shoes. But when I got on this time, most of the seats were empty. The few passengers looked suspiciously at me and tried to figure out how dangerous I was and what was in that bulging bag I was carrying (a camera, folks, calm down). I sat down in the seat behind the driver, the one reserved for old or handicapped people, and hoped that more people would get on at the next stop. No one did. The driver, wearing a blue sweater over a white button-down shirt, passed the empty bus stop without pulling in to it. I remembered

A.B. Yehoshua's story, 'Galia's Stop'. The hero is on a bus, going to see his childhood sweetheart, and at some point the ride becomes a total hallucination, and it turns out that the bus is moving through the streets without a driver.

Suddenly, I had an idea. I went to a seat at the back of the bus, attached my flash, switched to Fuji 800 film and started snapping. I explained to the astonished passengers that it was for a project I was doing at photography college and I promised not to photograph their faces. They were too exhausted to argue with me. Two or three raised an eyebrow, but the rest just ignored me and sank back into their coats.

The pictures turned out to be grainy. Slightly blurry. From the people sitting and standing, you might guess they're on a bus, but it's only a guess. The backs of two necks fill the centre of the frame, one thick like a man's, the other thin and wrinkled, like an old woman's. The windows reflect each other, and my image with my camera in front of my face is caught in one of them. The driver isn't in this shot. The angle I took it from makes it seem as if the bus is moving along without a driver. The 'Break in Case of Emergency' hammer is in the upper corner of the frame. An ad for the Kupat Holim Sick Fund is on the left. And the blurriness anaesthetises everything. It's hard to explain. When I developed the picture, I felt that I'd succeeded in doing what's so hard to do when you deal only with the external, only with what you can see: catching the inner sense. A week later, I named the picture 'After a Terrorist Attack' and hung it proudly on the wall of our classroom.

My fellow students actually complimented me on it before the lesson, but the lecturer stared at it for a while, sniffed twice and said: aesthetic, very aesthetic, in a tone that was leading up to a 'but', so I beat him to it and said, but what? He didn't smile. He just said, I'm asking myself, Noa, where are you in all this? And I, a perfect idiot, pointed to my reflection in one of the bus windows, and he, his bottom lip drooping in disappointment, said, yes, very nice, but that's not what I meant. What's missing here is the emotion, Noa, what do you feel about all this?

*

After a suicide bombing, they usually put up a roadblock and don't let us go out to work. And there are no surprises today either. I wipe the steam off the window and look out. Najib and Amin are trying to convince the soldier to let us pass. They show him all the permits, all the papers, but he keeps moving his head from right to left and smiling an evil smile. I told them it was a waste of time, but they're stubborn. What can you do, the *shabab*, the boys want to make all their mistakes on their own. Now the soldier is fed up and he points his rifle at Amin and yells something at him. I can't hear what it is, because the window's closed. Najib and Amin fold their papers and put them in their pockets, turn around and jump into the car. Cold air rushes inside when they open the door, and I hug myself to stop shivering. They curse the Jews, the *rayis* and the rain. Because of the rain, the car keeps sinking deeper into the mud. I get out to help them push. The rain trickles in between my shirt and my neck, and a drop rolls down my back to my ass. *Yallah*, I say, trying to get Amin and Najib, who are getting tired, to push harder. They push a little more and the car starts to move. Good for you, *ya* Saddiq, they tell me when we're back in the car, you have the strength of a young man. *Shukran*, I thank them, but their compliment doesn't make me happy. Not even a little. On an ordinary day, it would, but not today. Today, the land registration certificate and the large key are in my bag. Today, I'm supposed to go into the house I was born in and take something that belongs to my mother. Today was supposed to be an important day. A special day.

And in the end – a roadblock.

And that word, roadblock, *machsom*. A Jewish word that the Arabs use all the time. As if we didn't have a word for it in our own language. The same thing's true of the words for fruit-picking and cream and the word for rolls, which I can see now on the right, written on the sign over a store: *Manayish* Rolls and Arabic *Kubez*. At least we use our own word for traffic light, *ramzon*, even though we only have one *ramzon* in the city, the one we're stopped at now.

Shwaya, shwaya, take it easy, I tell myself when the light turns green and the driver tries to go around a puddle in the middle of the intersection. Be as patient as a *sabra*, *ya* Saddiq. You waited fifty years. You can wait another week.

*

The morning after the terrorist attack, the teacher came into the classroom, bit her lip and said, children, Daniel won't be in class today because his brother was hurt in the bombing yesterday and he's with him in the hospital. I am asking and sincerely hoping that all his friends will help him in the days to come and save him a copy of all the handouts I give you. Wait a minute, I thought, and took a good look at everyone's face, was it like this when she told them about Gidi? Did Dor keep digging around in his ear? Did Maya keep on drawing those blue butterflies in her notebook? Did the teacher not say anything for a couple of seconds, and then ask, in her normal voice, for everyone to take out their bibles? Yes, I answered myself, and instead of feeling hurt, I actually felt good. As if a fat man who'd been sitting on my chest suddenly got up. Which made me think that if Daniel's brother dies from his wounds, maybe Daniel will be the class's new bereaved brother and everyone'll feel sorry for him and whisper about him and watch him all the time to see how he acts, and they'll finally leave me alone. Then I was ashamed for thinking that, it's not nice to want someone else's brother to die, but I knew that after school I'd go to Amir's place and tell him exactly what I'd thought because that's what's so great about being with

Amir, that you can tell him things like that and he doesn't get all upset like my mother, who says her eyes are swollen from an infection, but it's because she cries all the time, or like my father, who sleeps on the sofa sometimes, not in their bed, or like when they hardly talk to each other.

The teacher asked us to open to the First Kings, Chapter 21, about Naboth's vineyards, that we'd started studying last week. 'And Ahab spake unto Naboth, saying: "Give me thy vineyard,"' she started reading, and I asked Dor to put the book in the middle of the desk because I forgot to bring mine. '"Give me thy vineyard, that I may have it for a garden of herbs, because it is near unto my house; and I will give thee for it a better vineyard than it; or, if it seem good to thee, I will give thee the worth of it in money." And Naboth said to Ahab: "The Lord forbid it me, that I should give the inheritance of my fathers unto thee."' After those two verses, she stopped, closed her book and asked: who can explain why Naboth refuses to give his land to the king?

All of a sudden, without my thinking too much about it, my hand moved away from the desk and my finger was waving in the air. At first, the teacher didn't notice. She was so used to my not participating that her eyes skipped over me. But no one else wanted to answer, and when she looked around at the whole class again, she saw me. Yotam?! she asked, looking like she was sure I was raising my hand just to scratch my forehead. Yes, I said, and started talking. Without seeing them, I could feel everyone turning to look at me. I said that Naboth can't take the King's offer because he was born and raised on that land, and giving up his home would be like wiping out everything his father and mother did, and then he would be violating the commandment to honour his father and mother, which is one of the Ten Commandments, like we learned, even though his parents might be dead already. I said all that without stuttering even once, and the words didn't get stuck in my throat like I thought they would, and none of the letters got switched around. Very good, the teacher said when I was finished, you've raised an interesting and definitely original point. Maya, did you want to add something?

I didn't listen to the rest. I was so tired from talking that I couldn't concentrate. I wanted the lesson to end so I could go to Amir's apartment. I knew he'd be really happy that I spoke in class. The last time I was at his place, after I beat him twice in a row in chess – once was the fool's mate, he hasn't been focused at all lately – I told him that I didn't talk in the lesson because I was afraid I'd stutter, and he said he'd been like that too: every time he moved to a new city, a new school, he wouldn't say word at first, he'd just watch how the other kids acted, like a spy hiding behind a newspaper. So when did you get over it? I asked and tried to imagine him as a kid my age. It went away by itself, he said and started setting up the white pieces for another game. Don't worry, one day you'll have something really important to say, and then you'll talk. Meanwhile, you're learning how to listen, which is just as important.

*

Listen, Amir,

How can I explain this to you. It's like you're driving in a car, and all of a sudden there's a bump and the car leaves the road and floats in the air for a minute, and your stomach sinks and electricity flashes through your temples. Or like when you dive right in and kiss a girl for the first time, and you don't know whether she even wants to. Or like . . . OK, enough comparisons, bro.

Yesterday

I

Bungee

Jumped!

Hold on. I know you're not crazy about stuff like that. But listen for a second. Listen and then you can put me down. Yesterday, we came to a small town called Palacio, near the border with Peru. The minute we got off the bus, they shoved flyers at us with a blurry picture of the bridge you jump off. All those big operators had the same flyer with the same terrible picture. It's incredible how they don't have the slightest bit of business initiative here. Please, I said, and pushed them out of my face, talk to me the day after tomorrow. But the New Zealanders who got off the bus with me went wild about it. Where is it? How much does it cost? When does the shuttle leave? Seems they've been bungee jumping from the day they were born (did you know that bungee jumping was invented in New Zealand in the 1940s?), and they get their thrills collecting certificates saying they bungeed at bungee-jumping sites all over the world. Sick, yeah? I thought so too. But the next day, I went with them anyway because there was nothing else to do here and also because of Jenny, a very dark-skinned girl from New Zealand who I liked from the minute she got on the bus with a backpack that was twice her size.

I sat down at a table at a small kiosk by the foot of the bridge. It looked out on to the bridge you jump from and also the river where the boat waits after you jump (you can ask the operators to plan the length of the rope so that your head lands in the water or not). I watched the New Zealanders climb on to the bridge, one by one, tie the ropes and rings around themselves, stand right on the edge of the ramp, bend forward a little, and then (with the help of a little push from the operators), jump. The first to jump, a huge guy named Rod, let out a bloodcurdling shriek that echoed and re-echoed through the mountains. I stood up like the fans in Bloomfield who stand up when they think there's going to be a goal. I was sure he'd crashed on the rocks and that the parts of his body were like islands in the stream. But no. His bald head dipped slightly in the water and he bounced back a few times like a human yo-yo till he got steady just slightly above the river, and the boat picked him up and brought him to shore. That stomach-flipping shriek of his convinced me that my decision not to jump had been right. But the ones who jumped after him were a lot calmer. Some of them blew kisses into the air before they jumped, like movie stars. Some stuck their hands out in front of them like they were diving into a pool, but my Jenny was the absolute best. She stood like a stork, one leg raised behind her, and spread her wings before she jumped.

After she jumped, my lower back started to itch. If that tiny little thing can do it, maybe I could get over my fear?

Wait a minute. Do you even know that I have a thing about heights? I don't think so. Big surprise, right? There are things you still don't know about me, even after seven years of friendship. It's not exactly a fear of heights, more like the desire to jump. Every time I'm standing in a high place (like on the balcony of your old apartment in Ramat Gan) I get this strong desire to jump. Not to float. Not to fly. To jump and crash. I remember the first time it happened. It was in Italy. My mother and I went up the Tower of Pisa, and on the seventh floor (the Tower is built like a wedding cake, every floor is a layer that you can walk on), I suddenly had the urge. There was no railing. Or barricade. I could've taken three steps forward and found myself in the air. I was so scared I might do it that I flattened myself against the wall and pressed my hands against the concrete. I remember the cold feel of the stone. My mother was pestering me to get going: there are two more floors, she said. I told her I couldn't move. What do you mean, you can't move? she asked and came over to me. I can't, I repeated. I knew for sure that if I moved, I'd jump. There was a small commotion. Tourists pointed at us. A Japanese guy took pictures. Finally, they had to bring two security people to peel me off the wall and drag me downstairs.

From that day on, everyone in my family knew that I had a fear of heights, and I went along with the diagnosis, even though I knew I had no fear, just the strong desire to jump.

Weird, huh? Just doesn't make sense, does it? After all, I love life and never, not even during the worst parts of basic training, not even after Adi and I split up, did I ever have thoughts like that.

I'll be damned if I understand it. Psychology probably has a name for it, right?

So why am I telling you all this? One: because it's night here and Jenny has a boyfriend in Auckland so she'll do a little kissing, but she won't come to my room, and my room's small, no windows, and someone's snoring on the other side of the thin wall and I'm in a confessional mood.

And two: so you'll appreciate what I did after Jenny jumped.

I got up, paid the kiosk owner for the three Fantas I drank and started walking towards the bridge. The New Zealanders, who'd all finished jumping and were drinking beer at the table next to mine, cheered me. Go, Modi, go! Rod yelled in a thick, hoarse voice that didn't have the slightest resemblance to the shriek that came out of him when he jumped.

As soon as I got to the jumping-off spot, I started to change my mind. The operators were three young guys, and when I got there, they were just starting to chew coke leaves. The ropes lying around looked old, with split ends. The iron rings were in an advanced state of rust and the whole bridge looked too narrow to hold the apparatus they'd put on it. OK, Modi, I thought, bungee jumping is cool, but why here, of all places? There's not a single bus on this whole continent that leaves on time. The men are almost always drunk. And a week ago, the train you were on stopped for two hours and the driver poured cold water on the tracks to cool them off (what the hell's the point of cooling off train tracks?).

I took a quick look at the river. It was a lot further down

than I'd thought and the rocks were too close. One little swerve, and I get banged up. The New Zealanders waved at me from the kiosk. Jenny was with them already, her hair still wet from her quick dip in the river. That's it. Too late to change my mind.

I let the young guys tie me and hook me up and put cuffs around my legs. I put on the ridiculous protective vest they gave me and I told the one who asked that I didn't want my head to touch the water. I hate it when my head gets cold.

We moved forward, me and the guy who was helping me, step by step until we got to the edge of the ramp. He grabbed me hard by the arm and asked if everything's all right, if I feel OK. I looked down. First at my knees. Then at my shoes. One shoelace was loose, so I tightened it. And then, very gradually, I moved my eyes downward a bit more. The whole flowing river was spread out in front of me. The boat that was supposed to pick me up was waiting. Near a rock. And then – it came over me again. That same desire to jump that I'd had on the Tower of Pisa. That same craving to take one more step. But this time I could do it!! The guy with me asked me in English: Are you OK? I nodded. He said to me: you can jump now. And then I fell.

It's hard to describe what happened then. I closed my eyes, so I can't tell you what the river looked like. I can only say that after about ten metres I felt help-me shivers or orgasmic shivers settle on a spot on my lower back and spread from there like two arrowheads through my body. Then, before I had a chance to scream, the cable pulled me up. There was another second or two of hovering, and then, the landing. And the jerking around. And the nausea. And there's the boat, ready to pick me up. They offer me some papaya juice, but I don't take it. Then they bring me back to the kiosk. Jenny kisses me on the cheek. I collapse on a black plastic chair and put my feet up on another chair. I drink water from someone else's glass. And look at the next guy standing on the edge of the ramp waiting to jump off. It doesn't faze me in the least. Just the opposite. That nice 'after' feeling flows through my body, from head to toe, and suddenly I have the feeling – and it's an even more wonderful feeling than what I felt when I actually jumped – that no tall building in the world, no balcony without a railing, will ever scare me again, because I've already been there, I've satisfied the urge – and come back (although I still have to check out this dramatic announcement in reality).

It's weird, but I hadn't really absorbed that it happened until now, when I'm writing, as if someone has to say or write it in Hebrew for it to be true, and if it's in English – which is the language I've been speaking here for the last week – it can only be a scene from a film.

It isn't only Hebrew that I miss, bro. It's you too.

Maybe you can still find a break in your timetable and come here between classes?

Even with all the munchies and the bungees, the nights on a trek can be pretty long. And the days too. In one really infinitely long trip, I've been alone so much that I've starting talking to myself out loud.

By the way, I've noticed an interesting anthropological phenomenon. Hostels have three kinds of room: with a double bed (for lovers), with twin beds (for friends) and one bed (for singles). In the first two kinds of room, the walls are bare, there's nothing on them except nail holes. But in the rooms that have one bed, the walls are full of graffiti – curses and declarations of love and confessions and quotes from songs by Pink Floyd, Kurt Cobain and even Aviv Geffen.

Bro, what you wrote about the assassination was very moving. The truth is that the rumour got here before your letter did. New *muchilleros* brought newspapers from 5 November in their backpacks. But I couldn't connect to what people were feeling until I read your letter about the graffiti they wrote all over the square where he was killed. But still, I'm sure I can't even begin to understand what you're all feeling. When the most important decision you have to make is whether to order scrambled or fried eggs for breakfast, and the worst war you find yourself in is with the hostel owners about how much to pay for a night, everything looks far away and blurry. Like when you watch the world news round-up and see something horrible that's happening in Somalia and then forget it two minutes later.

But maybe it's good to forget sometimes, right?

Which reminds me – be careful with those nutcases of yours. I don't know, something about the way you write about them has me a little worried. Especially that Shmuel. Sounds just like a cuckoo's nest. I'm not saying you have to leave, just tie a cable to your back so you can pull yourself up if you fall into the abyss. I don't want to remind you what happened the last time you weren't careful, and this time, bro, it'll be a little harder to get there from South America to shove the barrel aside.

By the way, have you told Noa about that yet? You have to fill me in so I won't blurt out something by mistake in front of her when I get back (if I get back).

And now that we're talking about her, how is she, really?

I was surprised when you wrote that she's a lot more difficult than you thought and that you're not sure she'll ever be happy. Well he-ll-o, Amir! You're just finding that out? Of course she's difficult. Like all your other girlfriends were. That's how you like them, right? I mean, if she was cuddly and easy, you'd be bored, right? Admit it.

I see you nodding slowly and smiling a little smile to yourself, and swearing at me for being right, and then going to the bathroom, stroking Noa's hair on the way, and sitting down on the toilet, reading this letter from the beginning and thinking: what happened to Modi? What's with this letter? It's not like him to make speeches. The truth is that you're right. I just read it over from the beginning and noticed that it's a little different. It must be this window-less room. And Jenny's boyfriend from Auckland. And the rain that's been coming down for two days.

But it's not so bad – that's what's so great about travel-ling –

I'll be in another place very soon.

Yours,

Modi

*

Modi bungee jumped.

Wow.

From some bridge in Ecuador. He's ecstatic. I got a five-page letter from him about it.

Lunatic.

Look who's talking. You wander around Jerusalem looking for terrorist attacks. Don't you get scared some-times?

Truthfully, no. When I have a camera in my hand, I work. All I think about is light and composition and stuff like that.

And it doesn't drive you crazy, all that glass and blood and tears?

Are you any better? With all your loonies?

I didn't say I was better.

You didn't say it, but you thought it.

No I didn't.

OK, you didn't. Tell me, why are you so aggressive?

I'm aggressive?

Yes. Why are you against me?

I'm not against you, I'm worried about you.

No you're not, you're worried about yourself.

That's not true, I'm worried about you. Promise me you'll call next time.

I'll call.

Do you swear by Diane Arbus?

I swear by Diane Arbus. Why are you making such a big deal about it?

Because I think you're putting yourself in danger on purpose, that you're looking for it, that you like flirting with death.

It's not fair, what you're doing now.

Why not?

Because I told you already, I was a different person at sixteen, and there's no way it'll happen again.

Okay.

Besides, I asked you not to mention it.

OK, I'm sorry. (How is it that this ends up with me apologising? Unbelievable.)

(What does he want from me? He should give me some space.)

(Why is she quiet now?)

(He'd like me to sit home all day, like him.)

(Why do I always have to be the one to apologise? Let her do it for once.)

(Why is it his business what I do? He should leave me alone.)

(She should be the first one to say something.)

(He should be the first one to say something.)

What are you thinking about?

Nothing, this conversation is making me tired.

(Terrific, now she's turning her back and here we go, another night without sex. We haven't had sex for two weeks. We haven't had sex for two weeks. We haven't had sex for two weeks.)

(We haven't laughed for two weeks. All that death around us has crept inside us.)

(That's why I walk around starving, even a strip of Sima's white bra turns me on.)

*

Those doctors. They act like they're God, dressed in white, looking through you like you're a window, but when something goes wrong, all of a sudden they're the smallest, the most pathetic, the most sorry-but-things-like-this-happen. Damn them. They let Avram wait three months for the operation, even though he hasn't been able to sleep for a year and a half because of the pain. They promised it'd be a simple operation, no complications. One of the most common operations in the hospital, Dr Zehavi told Gina, you have nothing to worry about. He'll be home in three days, a new person.

The minute I saw the doctor walking toward us after the operation, I knew something had happened. It was as if the whole man had turned into a back. No face. No stomach. Just a back. All four of us went over to him together, but for some reason, he decided to talk to me. Maybe because he saw that I wasn't part of the family, and he had less to be afraid of with me. It's going to be more complicated than we thought, he said and sank further into his back. Avram's blood pressure dropped during the operation, probably because of the anaesthetic, which means that the amount of oxygen to his brain decreased dramatically for at least five minutes. And it seems that he's allergic to one of the anaesthetics, which adds a toxic effect, that is to say . . .

But the stones, what about the stones? Gina burst out, demanding that he look at her.

We removed his gall bladder, but we'll have to wait and see how his brain function is affected by what happened.

What brain? What does the brain have to do with it? Gina asked, waving her finger in the air, it's a stomach operation, isn't it, doctor? That's what you told me. You said it's a simple operation, that's what you said!!

Mama, calm down, don't yell, Menachem said and put his hand on her arm. It's a good thing he came, I thought. He's the only one in that family who can handle her.

Can we go in to see him, doctor? Moshe asked and pointed to the locked door.

No, it's too soon, the doctor said. Actually, he's still being operated on. I suggest that you go home to rest and come back early tomorrow morning.

And I suggest, doctor, that you don't make any suggestions, I was surprised to hear Menachem say, so angry that his beard was shaking. The doctor swallowed the insult. I could see it pass through his Adam's apple to the indentation between the arteries in his neck and settle in his chest. No problem, he said and put on his gloves, you can stay and I promise to keep you informed of developments.

He went back to the operating room with the same stooped walk, and Gina collapsed on to a bench. I sat down right next to her. That woman had been mean to me so many times, had put me down for the way I cook, had contradicted me in front of Liron, kept talking to Moshe about single women even after we got married, but even so, I couldn't help feeling sorry for her now. Avram was everything to her. She married him when she was fifteen and he was thirty, and she's looked up to him ever since, even though he's short. She doesn't know how to write a cheque without him. Doesn't know how to change a light bulb. Now she swore at the doctor in Kurdish, out loud, so the whole department could hear. And she also grumbled a few words to Moshe. Sometimes, it's probably easier to get angry than to be worried, I thought. And put a hand on her shoulder.

*

Sima asked Noa to watch Lilach for just a few hours at their house. And now Lilach's fingers are drumming on Noa's face. She holds her close and inhales her smell. Drowns in the green of her eyes, and feels a shiver of pain deep inside. But only a shiver for the time being, and she can push it aside. There's still a fire burning inside her that water can't put out. She still wants to know what it's all about. To shout. To run through the streets. Far. Very far. It's too soon for her to keep her passions inside.

Not to mention Amir, who doesn't even know what his passions are. And now he's afraid that psychology isn't one of them. And lately, the air between them has been leaden. He's as quiet as a school during the summer vacation. And she comes home late on purpose, to avoid confrontation.

Noa puts Lilach back into her cot and slowly lulls her to sleep. Despite everything, she's glad Sima asked her to babysit. It's nice to know that she's good at it. That there's at least one little creature in the world who doesn't think she's hard to be with.

Suddenly, there's a knock at the door.

She walks across the room to the door and looks through the peephole. The Arab worker is standing there. Breathing hard, as if he's been running. Lilach starts to cry, startled by the unexpected visit. Noa picks her up and asks: who is it? It's Madmoni's worker, Saddiq replies, without adding another word. What could he add, his name? What could that possibly mean to her? She goes back to the peephole. And looks through it again. Madmoni's worker is standing in the same place. He has gentle eyes. And grey stubble on his face. And he's wearing a funny, long belt that reaches the floor. But still, because of Lilach and the number eighteen bus, she doesn't open the door.

*

A day later, the Zachians occupied the Surgery Department at Hadassah Hospital. The eight brothers plus all their wives plus the older grandchildren – they all came and took over the waiting area. The men prayed with Menachem, the women made a circle around Gina and whispered stories to her about this one's cousin and that one's nephew, who went through exactly the same thing and ended up fine. The children ran around in the hallway and kept asking for coins to put in the snack machine.

We were all waiting for our turn to go in and see Avram. The first ones to go in were Gina, Menachem and Shuli, Oved's wife, who was once a nurse in Poriya Hospital and so everyone thought she was a big expert. They stayed in the room for maybe an hour, and when they came out, Gina was leaning on Menachem and Shuli looked at us and twirled her finger next to her temple. Without saying a word, they split into two delegations. Menachem, with Gina on his arm, went to update the men. Shuli signalled the women to gather round her and she spoke in a low, self-important voice: *Papuka* Avram. He's *majnun* now. They poured all kinds of stuff into his brain, and now he's talking crazy. We went in to see him. He didn't say hello. Didn't recognise us, not even Gina. He kept asking if we knew where his son, Nissan, was. You know who Nissan is? All the women nodded obediently, but Shuli told them anyway. He was their first child, even before Menachem, and he died of some sickness on the way to Israel. Now, all of a sudden, he can't stop talking about him. He has a demon inside, *papuka*. The whole time: where's Nissan? where's Nissan? who took Nissan? Shuli described Avram's pale face, his dreamy look, the deep wrinkles in his face, which she thinks are even deeper now. Meanwhile, I went to look for Moshe. I saw him standing on the edge of the group of men and I watched his reactions. I know him by heart: the way his eyes close, really fast, when something hurts him. The way he beats his fist on his thigh twice when he's cross. The way he scratches his ear when he doesn't know what to do. I also knew that at some point, when Menachem finished giving his speech, his eyes would look for me.

On the way home, he held the wheel tightly with both hands. People always drive carefully when they're coming home from a hospital, and besides, the road from Ein Kerem to the Castel is narrow and covered with all that slippery sand that spills out of the trucks leaving the quarry, and it was a dark night (the Mevasseret council has enough money to light every little street and alley, but not enough to light the main road to the Castel? Who are they kidding?). He started to relax a bit when we got closer to our neighbourhood, and he took one hand off the wheel, put it on my knee and said, thank you. For what? I asked, and he kept on stroking my knee and said, for everything you've done these last couple of days. I didn't do anything special, I said, and he turned into our street and said, yes you did, don't argue, do you always have to argue? He smiled, and so did I, because I really am like that, and after we parked behind the bus, Moshe switched off the headlights, switched on the small light inside the car and turned his whole body around to me. He asked if he could put his head on my lap for just a minute and I said, yes, even though I was thinking it wasn't nice to keep Noa waiting, it had already been three hours, and he bent down slowly to the right until his neck touched my thigh, and I stroked his hair without saying anything, because I felt that he wanted to talk, and after a minute he said, I don't understand how it happened. The man goes in for an operation and comes out sick. I know, I said. And Moshe went on: besides, why's he talking about Nissan all of sudden? I haven't heard that name for twenty years. Did he love him very much? I asked. I don't know, Moshe said, he never talked about him, only once, when my mother saw some boy on television and said he looks just like Nissan, and he said to her, what are you talking about, Nissan was a lot better looking. And that was it? He never mentioned him again? I drew a question mark on Moshe's forehead. He said no and went on: my mother says there's demon inside Papa. That's why he's talking about Nissan now. A demon? I kept myself from laughing. I think it's stupid too, Moshe said, but she wants to call an exorcist, some old man who used to do that in Kurdistan. An exorcist?! I said, shocked. You know my mother, Moshe said, just try talking sense to her. Yes, I agreed, and smoothed down Moshe's right eyebrow. I could have made fun of her, but I didn't want to spoil the mood, so I just said: let her call him. The worst that can happen is that it won't help and it won't hurt. Moshe said: you're right, it won't help and it won't hurt. We sat in the car like that for a few minutes, not helping and not moving.

Once, we used to do that a lot. Sometimes he'd fall on me and sometimes I'd fall on him. But for the last few weeks, with this whole business about the kindergarten, we'd pulled away from each other into ourselves. Now, in the car, I could feel again how much he's mine and how much I'm his, and I let that feeling spread through my body like hot chocolate. Let's go, he said and opened his eyes, Noa's waiting, and I was glad he was the one to say it, not me. All of a sudden, I was ashamed of the dream I had about Amir the day before yesterday – his hand slipping under a dress that wasn't one of mine, stroking the inside of my thigh. Who needs Amir when I have such a teddy bear, I said to myself, and helped Moshe get up. We got out of the car, closed the doors quietly and walked together to the house, close together, not the way we've been for the last few weeks with him half a metre in front of me. While I was looking for the key, he leaned on the door and looked at me gently, as if he couldn't care less if he had to wait like that the whole day, his whole life, but when my fingers got to the bottom of my bag, Noa opened the door and said, I'm glad you're back, I was beginning to think something had happened. Before I could ask, she answered, the kids are fine, Lilach's been sleeping for a couple of hours and Liron's in the shower. I'm going to dry him off, I said, but Noa grabbed my hand: wait, you didn't tell me, how's Avram? Not good, I said, and Moshe added, not good at all, and he started to tell her the bad news. Meanwhile, I went to check on the little prince, and when I came back Noa said, I just told Moshe that I have an uncle, my grandfather's brother, in fact, who had the same thing and a month later the effects of the anaesthesia wore off and he was fine. Yes, we're all praying for that to happen, Moshe said and started to peel off his coat. Here, I said and took a fifty-shekel note out of my wallet and handed it to Noa. Are you crazy?! she said, pushing my hand away, don't be silly. I insist, I said. What's the matter? she said; if anything, I have to pay you for letting me be with that sweet little girl. Anyway, if you really want to pay me back, bring us some of your cooking. The smells that come in through the hole for the water heater make our mouths water. It's a deal, I said, laughing. Then Noa grabbed her head. How could I forget?! she said.

What?! Moshe and I asked at the same time.

That Arab, Noa said. Madmoni's worker. The one who tore Gina's bags. He knocked on the door and wanted to know where the old man and woman who live upstairs were, why they're not at home. I asked him what he wanted with them. He said he needed something from the house.

That's it, Moshe said, I'm going over to talk to Madmoni right now. What does he mean, he needs something from the house? It's his house all of a sudden?

Really, he looks pretty pathetic, Noa said, trying to calm him down. He's an old man.

Pathetic my foot, Moshe said and put his coat on again. I don't want him here hanging around the children.

*

Amir already knows how it'll end. One day, when he takes his eyes off the road to fiddle with the radio, he'll swerve right into an oncoming truck. And smash. That'll be it. Over in a flash. The radio will stop on the classical music station and the sounds of a requiem will fill the air. An ambulance siren will blare. Traffic will pile up in the opposite lane because of drivers slowing down to stare.

He's already been saved from similar scenarios at the last minute. He's managed to pull the wheel to the right or the left. And prevent disaster. But he knows it doesn't matter. He can follow all the safety rules and drive slowly all the way: in the end, it'll happen anyway. He can see the head-line in his imagination: 'Died Trying to Change the Radio Station', or 'Musical Death' (if the editor doesn't have enough space). Yes, it's no use fighting it. It's a lost cause. Even if they send him to Gaza on reserve duty, even if he gets a disease that has no cure. It'll end because of music. That's certain.

(And, he thinks, there'll be a circular justice to it, because music is what saved his life twice in the past. Well, saved his life is a slight exaggeration, but whenever his spirits had sunk as low as they could go, in basic training, for example, he grabbed on to a song that was being played on the radio at the time, or a tape that Modi had edited for his twentieth birthday, and let the sounds flow through him, to start the countdown from the begin-ning again, to remind him that he didn't have to be so sad, that not everything in his life was bad, not every-thing was black.)

As for Noa, she'd already visited the cold side. And come back.

When she was sixteen, she'd had enough and taken almost a whole bottle of Advil. And thought: a few minutes of nausea, and I won't have to suffer any more. I'll just lie down and die. And thought: Mum won't cry. Not even when she finds me dead in my bed. And her conscience? Half a pang at best. And her dad? I wonder how many days it'll take before he's out the door. Two? Three? No more than four. And the people at her school. For two years, they've been acting as if she isn't even there. They think she's weird. She dances like a boy, philosophises about everything. And the whole world – evil at its core. Hopeless. Corrupt. Why live in such a world any more? A world without love.

In the end, her stomach was pumped. The doctor agreed not to put 'suicide attempt' on her file so the army would take her (funny, he thought he was doing her a favour). Her parents sent her and themselves to the most expensive psychologist they could find. And agreed that it would be best not to let the story get around. People wouldn't understand, and they might put a label on her. They'd have to waste energy on an explanation instead of dealing with the real situation.

Even six months later, no one could define the real issues. They formulated a few rules. Made promises. Her mother surprised her by wetting a few tissues. Then they bought the psychologist a plant, a farewell gift, and spoke about the subject as infrequently as they could. Her parents went back to their comfortable routine. Suddenly, without a word of complaint, they had enough money to buy her materials and she started to paint. She splattered the canvas with all the colours bubbling inside her.

For hours, she'd sit in front of her easel, dipping her brush, drawing a line, losing her sense of time. There was always another painting to finish. Another painting to start. Another reason to leave the Advil bottle in the bathroom and focus on her art. Meanwhile, the boys in her class started showing an interest. Her beauty, which was beginning to show, saved her from loneliness. Her eyes looked straight ahead into other eyes. Her dresses got shorter and shorter, showing her thighs. In no time at all, she didn't have to hide behind trees at breaktime. In no time at all, the boys were showing off for her every day. Pimply-faced teenagers hanging on every word she had to say.

Of course, she didn't tell anyone what she'd done. She preferred to pretend the Advil night had never happened.

If she could keep up the pretence that life was great, maybe she'd really start feeling that way before it was too late.

(It wasn't until years later, when she and Amir were lying on top of the blanket in a rented bungalow, that she suddenly had a feeling that made her happy and frightened at the same time. She had to be totally open with him, he had to know. So she said: there's something else I haven't told you. And he said: so you're really a man who had a sex change operation that really worked? She laughed and said, don't be an idiot. Not that kind of something. She moved closer to him so she could whisper the rest. And spoke the words. Straight into his chest.

*

Rami the contractor said that if I show my face around there one more time, I can forget about all the money coming to me, even though he likes me and even though I'm his best worker. I don't know what your story is, he said, but it has to stop, *tifham*? Rami likes to mix Arabic words into his speech, *ya'ani*, to show that he's an ordinary guy. And no one corrects him, even though he makes a lot of mistakes every time he opens his mouth. OK, I told him. You have nothing to worry about, Rami. You won't hear any more complaints. Anyway, I said to myself, the old man's in the hospital and the old lady's with him, and I don't want to sneak into the house like a thief. I want to walk in and say: hello, the land you're living on is mine. Your cooking, your fighting, your lovemaking – you do it all on my land, *fahmin*?

Ever since my mother said that the house I saw was ours, everything that used to be has come back to me. Not *shwaya shwaya*, not slowly, but all at once, as if a wall fell down in my mind and let everything in. All of a sudden, I remember the house where our neighbour, Salman el-Sa'adi, lived. His door was always half open,

174

at night too, and he kept chickens in his yard. On very windy days, chicken feathers would fly over to our place and a brown feather would come in through the window and drift slowly on to the floor. I also remember his son, Wasim, who was the first friend I ever had. We used to climb trees and chase each other and have fist-fights, and after every fight my mother would lock me in the house, *ya'ani* to punish me, but only for a day, and then we'd go back to running around together and playing marbles and looking for ants' nests so we could block them up with stones and see what the ants would do.

I also remember the day everyone ran away. I'd forgotten that day for almost fifty years. Maybe it was too painful to remember. How Mama put all our belongings into two big sacks – clothes and small pots, and some rice and olive oil – and sent me to Salman el-Sa'adi to ask if they had something that we could carry water in and I ran through the field and tripped on a stone and my knee bled, but I still kept running. Everyone around me was running, loading things on donkeys, swearing at each other, pointing to the hills. That's where *el-yehud*, the Jew, would come from, they said. From there. I looked at the hills but didn't see anything but the sun setting, and I kept on running till I got to their house, and Wasim's mother gave me a big leather pouch covered in fox hair and said, give this to your mother, may Allah protect her, and on the way back – my knee was still bleeding – Kamel, who drew the water for the village, grabbed my hand, stuck his fingernails into my flesh and yelled at me, *lawen*, where to, where are you running to? Anyone who leaves his land has no life, no life. *Halas, ya* Kamel, leave the boy alone, someone who was tying a mattress on a donkey yelled at him, and Kamel swore and let me go. I ran all the way home, sure that my mother would be happy that I'd brought her a container for water, and she'd be proud that I kept running even though I was bleeding, but when I came in, she didn't look at me. She was busy with Marwan, my brother, who was crying, why aren't you taking my football? It's all right, she told him, we'll come back in two weeks and your ball will be waiting for you here. No it won't, *inti cazab*, you're lying! he said and kept on crying. Then my father went over and slapped him hard and said *uskut*, shut up, *ya walad*, you baby. That was when I started to understand that something serious was going on, that this wasn't a game. My father never hit us. He was a quiet, shy man, and if he slapped Marwan, then something important was happening. Keep an eye on your little brother, my mother said, and pointed to Marwan, whose cheek was still burning from the slap, and go and pick some figs we can eat on the way. I took Marwan by the hand and we got a small bag. I climbed on to a branch and handed him a fig, then another fig, and he ate one and put one into the bag, ate one and put one into the bag, and we didn't go home until the whole bag was full.

I'm looking at the fig tree now, from the ramp. They completely knocked down Salman el-Sa'adi's house and built a big villa where it used to be, three storeys. Only stones are left from the mosque, at the bottom of the wadi. They built a synagogue where the village square used to be. But the tree is still there, in the same place.

When we went into the house with the figs, our fingers sticky sweet, we found my mother and father and Nabil sitting on a crate, trying to lock it but they couldn't, so we sat on it too to help, then we walked through the house to check that we hadn't left anything important, and then we closed the door and loaded the sacks and crates on to two donkeys and started to walk in the procession with everyone else. First, we walked very quickly, then slowly. I remember – *yallah*, it's amazing how fifty years suddenly shrink in my memory, as if someone put them between two rollers and pressed – I remember that I asked Mama: where's Wasim? Because I didn't see him there. And she said, Wasim's father has a brother in Gaza, and they're going to stay with him. It'll be better for them there, but don't worry, *ya ibni*, we'll all come back to the village in two weeks and you and Wasim will be able to fight again.

Fifty years passed and I still haven't seen him. To tell the truth, I've never had a friend like Wasim since then. That's the way things go. The friendships you have when you're a child, they're the strongest. In prison, when I was there, I asked the Gazans if they knew Wasim, but no one did. No one had ever heard of him. I wonder what he looks like now. Whether he got married. How many children he has. What kind of job he has. Maybe he went to Egypt. Or Qatar.

And I wonder what Mama left in the house when we ran away. What didn't she put into the two big sacks we loaded on to the donkeys? What is it that's so important to her that she wants me to bring it back to her?

Halas, as soon as the old man and woman come back to the house, I'll go in and find out. I don't care what they say. And I don't care what Rami says. Let him fire me if he wants. Let him kill me if he wants.

*

When Sima thinks about 'the end', she thinks about her mother, even though she doesn't believe in such things, it's nonsense and she knows that very well. She likes to imagine how it would be to meet her in heaven (that *tzaddikah* would never be sent to hell). How she'd kiss her on both cheeks (if her mother only kisses one, she knows she's about to get told off. How she'd disappear into her arms, like a gift into its wrapping. How she'd rest on her large breasts for a moment and listen to her heart beating. Then she'd tell her about all the things she hadn't lived to see. How much her grandson loves to climb trees. How her granddaughter is already crawling around on her hands and knees. And how her daughter Sima listens to songs in French and is never scared. Later, when darkness falls on the trees in the park, she'll tell her secrets she's never shared. Like she used to when she was little and they sat in the kitchen. Oh, if only she were sitting in the kitchen with her now with the clock ticking quietly on the shelf, she'd tell her things she never even tells herself. For instance, that sometimes she's sick and tired of Lilach's crying. That sometimes she asks, why did I need another child, why was I in such a hurry to have more? And if her mother wasn't shocked by that confession, she'd tell her about the students who were living in the apartment next door. About Amir who, she was embarrassed to admit, she was slightly attracted to. When she'd stood next to him a few days ago, his elbow had touched hers. Unintentionally, that's true. And she felt a kind of flash in her chest she hadn't felt in a long time. Naturally, she didn't do anything. Didn't make a peep. His girlfriend is lovely and she babysits for Lilach. Almost every week. And that day, there'd been a terrorist attack. But still, Mum, a flash in my chest. What do you think of that?

Moshe almost killed his buddy in basic training. During an exercise with the whole platoon. The buddy was supposed to jump, but he did it a second too soon. Moshe was shooting at a cardboard figure and didn't see that someone had walked into his line of fire. Stop! Stop! someone yelled. He froze on the spot. Put the safety catch back on. The commander came running over like a madman. He slapped Moshe's helmet: what did you do, you idiot?! Then he leaped right into the ditch where Moshe's buddy was lying in a pool of blood. The wind whistled. Dust clouds whirled. All the soldiers stopped breathing, couldn't believe what they were seeing. Moshe closed his eyes and for a long, long, long minute, he was sure he'd killed a human being.

It turned out that the bullet had scratched his buddy's ear and he needed a stitch or two. The next day he was back in the field, as good as new. They kept Moshe in detention for twenty-eight days. Inspections all day long, inspections of every kind. When he got out, he wiped the entire event from his mind. When his friends in the neighbourhood asked why he'd been confined to the base, he told them that the military police had caught him without a beret. That was the only thing he could think of saying. And he never talked about it again.

Not until this week, when he took his hallucinating father home from the hospital in the afternoon. He suddenly remembered it, the exercise with his platoon. He bit his lip. Why was he remembering it now, of all times? And he had that same strange feeling he'd had when his commander jumped into the ditch to see if the soldier was dead: as if an ice cube were climbing slowly up his back to his head.

*

Come over, Sima called me through the water heater hole, you have to see this.

Gina brought an exorcist to get the demon out of Avram. What?!! I said, shocked.

Yes, it's really amazing, Sima said. It might be good for that project of yours? On God and all that.

I wanted to tell her that the project had been scrapped a long time ago, but I grabbed a camera and ran out instead.

In the end, of course, they didn't let me take pictures. The exorcist, *Hacham* Yehieh ben Amar, Yehieh ben Amar the Wise, said that demons don't like cameras and asked me politely but firmly to put the camera back in its case. I also remembered that the witches in Bolivia wouldn't let anyone photograph them either, so I didn't argue (one of those witches sold a yellowish love potion in a small bottle to a friend I was travelling with. We laughed about it for hours, trying to decide whether to put it in the tea or just pour it down the sink, and the next day, she met the love of her life).

Gina, tie Avram's hands together, *Hacham* Yehieh ordered, and Gina did what he said. Now his feet, he said. Gina raised an eyebrow. Sorry, *Hacham* Yehieh apologised, it's so that if the demon wakes up, he won't kick us, God forbid.

Sima and I stood on the side smirking at each other. *Hacham* Yehieh saw us smiling and gave us a strange look that seemed to rebuke us but also hinted that we were accomplices. He looked pretty weird, that *Hacham*. I would've expected a certified exorcist to have a tangled beard and wear a long white robe, but Yehieh had on stonewashed jeans and a rainy-grey sweater, and he fussed around Avram with quick steps that made him look almost like he was dancing.

Avram was passive, completely out of it. Somehow, his eyes followed what was going on in the room, but without offering an opinion.

Now, *Hacham* Yehieh said and sat down at a safe distance from Avram, now bring . . . but before he could finish the request, a tub full of water was put in front of him and Gina handed him a towel. She knows the drill, I thought.

Hacham Yehieh put his hands into the tub and asked Gina to cover it with a towel. Sima jumped up and did it for her. She tucked the edges of the towel carefully under the tub and shot a look at Gina to check that she was doing it right.

Hacham Yehieh closed his eyes and started mumbling in a language I didn't understand. I think he's calling the demons now, Sima whispered in my ear. Even though I'd been warned not to, the temptation to pull my camera out of its case was enormous: a ray of sunlight had just come through the window, with dust motes drifting through it, and there was *Hacham* Yehieh, with his intense piety and

Gina, with her wrinkles, and in the background the colourful cloth hanging in their living room, and a picture of Avram looking twenty or thirty years younger, wearing an old-fashioned white undershirt and holding one of the boys, maybe Moshe, in the air.

No, I told myself, and kept my hand close to my body. Gina would get angry. And Sima would never forgive me.

For a few minutes, nothing happened. *Hacham* Yehieh mumbled. The towel moved a little. Outside, two dogs barked a conversation. And then, all of a sudden, Avram started to tremble. At first, it was a slight trembling in his bound hands, then it got stronger and moved to his arms, his shoulders, and finally his whole body was shaking violently. Gina let out a terrified scream. It really was very scary. No external force was shaking him. He himself was looking at his arms in total shock.

Now *Hacham* Yehieh went from mumbling to shouting. I didn't know what he was saying, but some of it sounded like pleading and some of it like threats. His hands were moving under the towel as if they were battling something. His face contorted in real or fake suffering, and shrill, chirping sounds came from the area of the tub, although we couldn't tell who was making them. Calm down, Noa, I told myself. Those can't be the voices of demons. There is no such thing as the voices of demons. *Hacham* Yehieh must be a ventriloquist and those voices are coming from his stomach. It's coming from his stomach, I gestured to Sima, but she was totally mesmerised by what was going on under the towel and didn't notice me. Small bumps began appearing on the surface of the towel, like the kind you see on boiling hot pizza, hills rose and fell, rose and fell, as if someone or something was trying to get out and couldn't. OK, I thought, trying to calm myself down, maybe it's his fingers, maybe he's pushing his knuckles against the towel to create that effect. But no, there are too many bubbles.

It can't be that he's raising his fingers in six different places, unless . . . unless what?

Very slowly, the hills flattened out and Avram's shaking subsided. And *Hacham* Yehieh stopped suffering and spraying water all over the place.

Amir won't believe me when I tell him about this, I thought. He's at home all week, and the day they have their own episode of *X-Files* here, he goes to Tel Aviv.

Hacham Yehieh opened his eyes and motioned with his head for Sima to untie Avram's hands and feet and take the towel off the tub.

I almost fell off my chair: the water was full of blood.

He wounded me, that *momzer*, *Hacham* Yehieh grumbled and asked Gina to bring him a bandage. Sima was so shocked that she cried out when she saw the deep cut that split one of his fingers. OK, that doesn't mean a thing, I thought sceptically, he could have cut his finger himself. All you need is a paper-cutter up your sleeve.

Gina wound the bandage around his finger, shooting worried looks at her husband, who'd gone back to staring at the world with vacant eyes.

He'll be fine, *Hacham* Yehieh said. You have nothing to worry about, Gina. There was an old demon inside him, a stubborn old demon who's been wandering around here for almost fifty years. The demon cut me, but I drove him away, and now he knows not to start up with Yehieh. I'll write something for you to put in an amulet he can wear on a chain around his neck so the demon doesn't come back.

Gina nodded admiringly. I started to nod too, automatically, but caught myself in the middle and stopped.

Won't you be fine now? *Hacham* Yehieh asked Avram, to prove what he'd said. Avram nodded obediently. Now do you remember what happened to Nissan? *Hacham* Yehieh asked him, and we all tensed up. Avram didn't say anything. The sunbeam, which had been getting shorter the last few minutes, made its final retreat from the room.

182

I suddenly remembered that there'd been a time when all the kids in my Girl Guide troop used to talk about seances. None of them ever took part in one, but everyone knew someone who'd been to a seance and seen the glass move across the letters.

Nissan's dead, Avram said, interrupting my nostalgia. Nissan's dead, he repeated and gave *Hacham* Yehieh a puzzled look. What made you mention him now?

*

There's a demon wandering around Maoz Ziyon. From nightfall till dawn. And he's black, not white, like you picture a demon. And he's all alone.

For the first few years he tried to be likeable, initiate a dialogue, squeeze through open doors. But everyone –men and women, old folks and children – screamed when they saw him and drew back. When he tried to compliment one woman on the aroma of her cooking, she promptly had a heart attack. They saved her in the end, but he decided: he wouldn't try to be anyone's friend any more. And that meant giving up the pleasure he held most dear: listening to the residents whispering to each other, the demon was there, the demon was here.

Sometimes, sitting on the park bench, the old people still talk about it: how a ghost used to wander around the Castel at night. And they start arguing, each one trying to convince the other that he's right (while the demon listens with pleasure from a safe distance, behind a tree): I saw him myself, my eyes can still see. He's something the women and children made up, so how could that be true? He's a refugee from World War II. What are you talking about, he first showed up here in the fifties. What fifties? Your memory's out of control. *My* memory's out of control? *Your* memory's like a fisherman's net with an enormous hole. A fisherman's net with an enormous hole? Nothing you say is true. You were born crazy, Simon, and you'll be crazy when they bury you.

When the conversation collapses on its own (the old people are tired and the sun is glowing gold high in the sky), the demon withdraws. He disguises himself as a shadow and slips through the alleyways until he reaches the palace he calls home: the cage of used cartons behind Doga and Sons.

Only once or twice a year, when a gap opens in someone's soul, does he take advantage of the opportunity and slip into it. Such a perfect place to hide. So warm and pleasant inside. He can play all sorts of pranks, make them all look like fools. Scramble memories. Break rules. And hope that stupid *Hacham* Yehieh is called upon. So he can trick him: retreat and come back again later on.

*

And while I'm trying to stop the Arab, to push him out, and Gina goes to the kitchen and comes back with a frying pan to hit him on the head with, and we're both yelling terrorist! terrorist! so the whole neighbourhood can hear – Avram, who's been snoring on the sofa all morning, stands up suddenly, looks at him, barks *uskuto!* at both of us and walks over to him. He touches his shoulders, his hands, then his face, moves his finger over his cheeks, his nose, his forehead. The Arab is so stunned, he doesn't move. Just stands there with his certificate and his rusty key. Not breathing. Then Avram gives him two light slaps, the affectionate kind, and moves a little bit away from him, the way you move away to look at a painting, and then he moves back, looks at him with dreamy eyes and says, Nissan, *ya ibni*, my son, welcome, and hugs him tight. Over Avram's shoulder, the Arab gives us a what's-with-him look, and Avram squeezes him tighter and keeps on saying, *ya ibni, ya ibni* Nissan, and the worker, who's starting to feel uncomfortable, hugs him back with one hand, and with the other, points at Avram and says, my name is Saddiq, not Nissan. I never heard of this Nissan, and what's wrong with this old man? Gina recovers first, curses Yehieh under her breath and explains to the Arab: Nissan was our first child who died when he was two, the day we moved into this house, and Avram, he's my husband, he has a demon inside him this week, he thinks Nissan's alive and that we all know where Nissan is but we hide it from him on purpose, but Nissan's dead. Avram, Gina says, putting her hand on his shoulder and trying to pull him gently out of the embrace, Avram, Nissan's dead, *kapparokh*. Don't you remember what you said to Yehieh? I didn't say anything to Yehieh! Why are you lying?! Avram yells and pushes her hand away, Nissan's here! This is Nissan! He moves away a little and points at the worker. Come in, *ibni*, he invites him with a sweeping gesture of his hand, sit down, we'll get you something to eat, something to drink, we'll make a place for you to sleep.

Avram, listen to me for a second, I say, trying a more direct approach, he's not Nissan, he works for Madmoni, you know Madmoni, your neighbour, the one who's adding on to his house now? This is his worker, and his name's not Nissan, it's Saddiq. Who's she? Avram points at me with a surprised look, then asks Nissan-Saddiq, who's this woman who talks so much? Do you know her, *ya ibni*? Did you ever see her before? The worker looks at me, embarrassed. Avram, that's Sima, Moshe's wife, Gina says trying to remind him, and she points at our wedding picture hanging on the wall. Avram stares at the picture. Little Moshiko? He has a wife already? How could that be? You know about this, Nissan? Avram asks the worker.

Halas, I tell them. With all due respect, like they say, enough is enough. I'm calling the police now. Let them come and take you out of here, Mr Saddiq. How can they take me out of here when it's my house? Saddiq asks quietly and waves his certificate in the air again. I ignore him and go to the phone. Avram rushes over – just a few minutes ago he was lying on the sofa and couldn't move a finger – and steps between me and the phone. You're not calling anyone, he yells, no one is going to take my Nissan away from me, do you understand? No one! If you call now, I'll grab a knife from the kitchen and cut you and myself, do you understand? I stand still and look at Gina. She signals me with her eyes to let it go. OK, I say to Avram, OK, you don't need a knife, no one's going to take Nissan away from you. Avram doesn't calm down. He stands between me and the phone for a while to show that he doesn't trust strangers. I don't move. Gina doesn't do anything either. Slowly, his eyes stop darting back and forth and he goes back to fussing around the worker. You want something to drink? Maybe black coffee? How many sugars do you take in your coffee? And Saddiq answers: no sugar, I like my coffee bitter. Avram gives him a big ear-to-ear grin and says, just like your father. The worker nods and says *Aiwah*, and starts walking around the house. He knows that we can't do anything to him now, so he allows himself to touch the stones, to go in and out of the rooms, to open and close the windows. He touches the wall that separates the bedroom from the living room and says to Gina, this wall didn't used to be here, right? Gina says yes, we built it twenty years ago, and he nods without enthusiasm and says, I knew it. Look, I'm starting to remember, there, where the television is, that's where my mother's cooking stove was, that's where she cooked so the smoke would go out. Where you cook is no good, madam, the smoke stays inside. Gina doesn't answer him, no one answer him, we all look at him, hypnotised, starting to understand that maybe he isn't lying, maybe he really did live in this house once. He goes into the bedroom and the three of us follow him. He points: look, this is where my mattress was, and that's where my big brother's mattress was, and my little brother's next to it. We slept very close to each other because it was cold at night, not like now with the heating you have. We only had a little coal heater, and sometimes the coal would get used up and we had to rub each other's back and hands to get warm. My mother would go to the neighbours to get more blankets, but the door to the house wasn't where it is now. It was on the other side, behind your sofa. It's still there, an iron door, you know that, don't you? Of course we do, Avram answered quickly in a voice full of pride, you remember everything, *ya ibni*, you remember, and you, Avram said, turning to me, you lunatic, aren't you ashamed to say that to Nissan? Look at how well he knows the house! Only a child knows his house like that, isn't that true, *ibni*? Yes, *abui*, the worker answers him, playing the game and calling him father, knowing that as long as he's Avram's son, no one can touch him. He takes a few sips of the black coffee Gina gives him with hands that shake from old age and says, thank you very much, really, thank you, and then he puts his bag down on the floor and pulls out a toolbox. He takes a hammer and a chisel out of it and explains to us while he works. Fifty years go, my mother left something in there, above the picture where you put that *hamsa*, so if you don't mind, I'm going to take it out now.

Before we can answer him, Avram says, of course, *ya ibni* Nissan, what's mine is yours, take what you need, do you want me to bring you a ladder? Gina and I look at each other. The chisel is about to gouge the wall, but we're both afraid to open our mouths because if we do, Avram will cut himself, and meanwhile, he goes to get Saddiq a ladder and comes back and they both open it in front of the wall and start taking down the *hamsa*, and Gina comes closer to me and whispers, Sima, *ileh amokh*, don't you have to get back so the babysitter can go? I jump at the chance while the two men are busy and won't notice, and I tiptoe to the door, put my hand on the knob and press it quietly to open it, then I close it behind me without shutting it all the way, and run down the steps to our house without looking back. I go inside panting and say to Noa: call the police.

*

I touch the stones, stroke them like you stroke a woman you love, but I don't feel anything in my heart. I tell the Jews, there was a wall here, this is where my mother used to cook, that's where the mattresses were and the heater next to them. I just say it, without feeling, like I'm telling Rami the contractor about how we're doing on the frame. How long I've waited for this day, this moment, how much I've dreamed about touching these walls, walking on this floor, and now I don't feel a thing. Here's the old door. Here's the window I used to look out of to see Wasim waiting for me, whistling. Everything's here, even the old fig tree. But the smell, the house is full of their smell. The smell of that old man who thinks he's my father, and of that woman with the wrinkles around her eyes. Their smell is in the walls and the floor and the sofa and the door and in the air and everywhere, even in the coffee. So why did I come here? My mother was right not to let us go to the old house when everyone else went, in '67. What for? It's better to dream. To sing songs. It's better not to smell this smell. Not to see that they've taken down the pink curtains my mother made and put up new blue curtains, that they've built a new wall in the middle of my parents' bedroom, that all our things have disappeared, the small rug from Damascus, the lamp from Hebron, the one I almost broke once, everything's gone. The crazy old man says that only his son who grew up in this house could know everything so well. Right? he asks me, right, my Nissan? Of course it is, I tell him and ask him to bring me a ladder. *Aiwah*. Of course, he says. At least I can do this. At least I can bring my mother what she asked for. This, I won't give up. It's a matter of honour. I don't care what that young one with the tiger eyes says. I don't care if she goes to call the police now. They're like putty in my hands, all of them. I'm Nissan, the crazy man's son. And no one can touch me. I'll set up the ladder in front of the old door, the door that doesn't lead anywhere now, take the *hamsa* off the wall, take the chisel out of my toolbox and start banging.

*

In the end, the policemen came, three of them, and their chief, who was even shorter than me, almost a midget, asked immediately: where's the intruder, miss? I pointed upstairs and said, you hear that banging? That's him, there, taking apart the whole house. Armed? the midget asked. No, he doesn't have a weapon, I said, and I don't think he wants to hurt anyone, even though he has a chisel in his hand. O-o-kay, he said, and turned to the others, who drew their guns: no shooting without a direct order from me. Is that clear? Shooting?!! I said, scared, what do you mean, shooting? You don't have to shoot anyone, officer, they are three old people in the house. With all due respect, miss, let me decide whether they're dangerous or not, the midget said and signalled his men to follow him. I asked Noa to stay a tiny bit longer with Lilach and went out straight after them.

A bus that had pulled into the stop across the street let passengers off, and they all came over to see why a police car was parked here. That's the way it is around here, everyone has to know everything. It's OK, I gestured to them, everything's fine. The policemen started going up the stairs and I grabbed the midget by his sleeve just before he got to the door and said that maybe I should go in first, so they won't get scared. Absolutely not, he said and smashed the door hard with his shoulder, like you see in those TV series, but the door was slightly open – that's how I left it when I sneaked out – so he kept right on going all the way into the living room. The other two policemen tried not to laugh and went in after him, and I locked the door. Thank God, Gina said and blew a kiss to the ceiling, thank God you came. Thank God for what? What are you talking about? Who asked them to come? Avram said, letting go of the ladder and walking over to the midget. Ah . . . the midget stammered and pointed to me, this lady here called us, she said an Arab broke into your house. Broke in? Who broke in? Avram said and grabbed him by his shirt. *Ya ahabel*, you idiot, this is my son, Nissan. I invited him in, and I'm overjoyed that he's here. And who's this? the midget asked, pointing at me. Avram looked at me and a spark of recognition flashed in his eyes. No one, he said, some crazy woman. She talks a lot but doesn't understand much. She's my daughter-in-law, Gina interrupted him (and I thought: the Messiah must have come, Gina's saying something on my behalf?), and this is Avram, my husband. He's a little . . . he had an operation, you know, and since then, he has a demon inside him, he thinks this Arab in Nissan, our son. He's not your son? the midget asked, rubbing a button on his shirt. Of course not, Gina said. Nissan died when he was two, when we first came to Israel and moved into this house. And you claim that he *is* Nissan? the midget asked Avram, who was nodding impatiently as if even asking the question was an insult. O-o-kay, the midget said, walking over to the ladder and looking up at the Arab, who was standing on the highest rung. So all I can do is ask you, sir, who are you? I'm Saddiq, the Arab answered without stopping his work even for a second. And what are you doing here, if I may ask? This is my house, Saddiq said, and picked up the key that was hanging around his neck. Your house . . . interesting . . . the midget said, smiling crookedly. So if it is, maybe you could explain what all these people are doing here? They're my guests, Saddiq answered as he pulled out the first brick and pointed to us: he's my guest. She's my guest. And that woman's also my guest. They've been guests in my house for fifty years now. O-o-kay, the midget said and stuck his finger in his belt, I'm beginning to understand. And you have some papers that prove this claim of yours? Yes sir, Saddiq said and pulled the certificate out of his pocket, bent down and handed it to him.

This is the land registry certificate from the Turks, he explained to the midget, it says here that this house belongs to the A'adana family, which is my family, and also all the land around it, half a *dunam*. The midget studied the certificate for a few seconds and then, as if he'd suddenly lost his patience, threw it on the floor and started waving his hands in the air: I don't give a shit about the Turks! If you don't have an official document from the Israeli government, then as far as I'm concerned, you're trespassing! And you – he pointed at us – have to decide if you want to file a complaint against him. If you do, I handcuff him right now. If not, don't waste our time. The Israeli Police has enough work without you wasting our time.

If that's the case, I said, then I want to file a complaint. That man has been wandering around outside our house and bothering people for five months already, and now he has the nerve to . . .

No one is going to file a complaint against Nissan!!! We heard a voice shouting from the kitchen, and Avram came out with a bread knife in his right hand. I warned you, miss!!! he barked at me with murder in his eyes, I warned you not to do it!!! The two patrolmen jumped between me and Avram. I was so scared that I took a step back. Gina tried to calm him down, she put a hand on his shoulder. He pushed it away, put the knife on his Adam's apple and said in the voice of a guy selling ice lollies on the beach, I'm cutting! I'm cutting!

In the name of Allah, say something to him, Gina begged Saddiq, you're the only one he'll listen to.

Saddiq hesitated for a minute, shot a quick look at the policemen and got off the ladder. *Ya abba*, he said and walked over to Avram, put the knife down. We don't settle things with knives in our family. That's not what you taught us. Avram looked at him, stunned, and then broke like a vase. He fell on to Saddiq's shoulder with a heartbreaking scream: did you see? Did you see how he called me father?

I told you he's my Nissan. And you didn't believe it, you didn't believe me! Saddiq hugged him back with one hand, and with the other he gently took the knife from him and handed it to the midget. But the gesture scared the midget, who jumped back, whipped out his gun, fired a shot at the ceiling and then aimed at Saddiq.

That was the first time I'd ever heard a shot. I didn't know how much it hurt your ears.

Why are you shooting? Saddiq yelled in panic and threw the knife on the floor, I wanted to give it to you, sir, just give it to you!

Plaster fell from the ceiling into the midget's eyes. These contact lenses, he hissed to himself, why the hell did I buy them? and tried to take out a stubborn speck that had lodged under his lashes. One of the patrolmen went over to him, and while the midget pulled his lower lid down, he blew gently into his eye. They seem so good at it that they must have done it before. Thank you very much, Zabiti, the midget said, blinking. Sir, Zabiti said in an intimate tone that suited the moment they had just had together, I think, sir, that you're making too much of a big deal out of what happened here, sir. Oh really, the midget said nastily, and what exactly do *you* suggest? We all tensed up waiting to hear what Zabiti, who had a tiny little scar on his forehead, would say. I think, sir, that we just have to arrest this Arab and figure out what to pin on him later. Why take risks, sir?

The midget nodded and Saddiq grabbed the ladder. Yes, the midget chuckled to himself and pulled the handcuffs off his belt, if the worst comes to the worst, we can charge him with interfering with an officer in the performance of his duty. Sure. Didn't he interfere with us taking our lunch break? Wait a minute, Avram shouted and stood in front of the ladder. What do you think you're doing? No one is taking my Nissan. That's enough, sir, the midget said and signalled for his assistants to get into the act, that's enough.

Zabiti and his buddy walked up to Avram and each took one of his arms and dragged him to the side. Zabiti's scar was blazing in the middle of his forehead as if it had suddenly come to life. Don't hurt him, Gina cried, he's an old man. If anything happens to him, I threatened, we'll file a complaint against you, do you hear me? Avram kicked the air for a minute, then gave up and stopped moving, but he kept on yelling: Help! Help! They're taking my Nissan! The midget ignored him and went over to Saddiq. Saddiq, an older man with soft eyes, made no sign that he was going to fight, and the midget was about to handcuff him when all of a sudden, the television crew came in.

In seconds they'd all burst into the room like locusts: a cameraman, a lighting man, a reporter wearing a tie and a man who was holding a big furry microphone. I couldn't work out where they'd come from, but then I remembered: the community station has this hotline. If you give them a story that gets on the air, they give you a fifty-shekel coupon for the shopping centre. Someone must have heard the shot and called them.

Ladies and gentlemen, the tie started talking to the camera, and all the people in the room shut up, out of respect for the occasion. Ladies and gentlemen, drama at high noon. Our neighbourhood, which went through a difficult time a few months ago when it lost one of its sons in Lebanon, is back in the headlines tonight with gunfire in a private home, apparently related to terrorist activity. All the details are not yet known, but we are trying to find out now: what happened? Why were shots fired? Is this incident related to the recent suicide bombings? This is Sharon Dadon, *Mevasseret On the Air*. We'll be right back with the latest updates.

The cameraman turned the camera on the midget. The tie told the microphone man to start recording right away, what was he waiting for. The microphone man looked down and pressed whatever button he pressed. The tie looked into the camera and said: we're here with the highest-ranking police officer in the field. What details can you add, sir?

The midget cleared his throat twice and smoothed down a couple of rebellious eyebrow hairs: Unfortunately . . . he said with his chest puffed out self-importantly, but then he stopped talking and rubbed his chin. Avram was standing very close to Gina, as if the demon inside him was also afraid of the cameras. Saddiq kept on banging the wall with his chisel, trying to attract attention to himself.

I ran my fingers through my hair and thought about how when Moshe comes home at night, I'll tell him about all of this and he won't believe me. Not a single word.

Meanwhile, the midget tried to get started again: Unfortunately, he said, for obvious reasons, I am prevented from saying any more about this incident. All I can say is that the police will do everything it can to wrap up this case quickly while looking out for the interests of the public.

But even so, sir, the reporter persisted, perhaps you could shed a little light on what happened here during the last hour. Is there any truth to the rumour that shots were fired? Was anyone injured?

No comment, the midget answered authoritatively, and in order to stress that he meant it, he closed his eyes and repeated: no comment.

I can tell you what happened here, sir, Saddiq said suddenly from the top of the ladder.

The cameraman moved quickly towards him, bumped into the sofa and swore in English. The lighting man, the man with the microphone and the reporter followed him and stood around the ladder. Then perhaps you'll tell us, the reporter said, how everything started?

Everything started an hour ago, Saddiq said. No, actually everything started fifty years ago, when the Jews came in and threw my family out of this house. On the night they drove us out, my mother left something here. And today I came here, to my house, to get what belongs to me.

I un-der-stand, the tie said in the tone of someone who didn't understand a thing. So how did things deteriorate into shooting?

The shooting's because of him, Saddiq said, pointing his chisel at the midget.

Because of me?! He threatened me with a knife, the midget said, breaking the official silence he'd imposed on himself just half a minute ago. That man broke into a private home, harassed the tenants and threatened to kill me with a knife.

Liar! He didn't threaten to kill you, Avram broke away from Gina's embrace and all the media's attention switched right over to him. That man on the ladder is my son, Nissan. He came home to see me, his father. And all these people want to take him away from me. So I came out with the bread knife and told them that if Nissan goes, I cut.

And that's when the shot was fired? the tie asked, and you could hear a little bit of disappointment creeping into his voice.

No, what are you talking about? Avram explained slowly, as if he was speaking to a child. Nissan here took the knife out of my hand and gave it to the policeman, and then the policeman shot at him for no reason.

The tie turned to the camera and motioned for the lighting man to turn the lights on his face. He squinted and said: It's still too early to say, but from the testimonies we've heard in the field, it is possible that we're talking about a police foul-up. And if so, it won't be the first foul-up the Israeli Police has made recently, and perhaps, perhaps we're talking here about a syndrome, a syndrome that some higher-ups are calling 'the shoot first, think later syndrome', while others are calling it . . .

What syndrome? What syndrome?!! the midget interrupted and tried to squeeze between the reporter and the camera.

Hey! the cameraman yelled.

Please, the tie said to the midget, you're interfering with the media trying to do its job.

And maybe you're interfering with me trying to do my job? the midget said, not moving from where he was. The two of them stood facing each other, like in a western. You could have cut the tension between them with a knife. A bread knife. But before either one could draw, some neighbours from our street burst into Avram and Gina's living room. Somebody must have seen the television crew coming in and called everybody. Dalia's Nissim was there. And Razi, who used to deliver for the supermarket. And Avi from Avi's Flowers. And some other old people who always sit on the bench near the park and hassle the girls walking by. They stood in the middle of the living room, took a quick look at Saddiq, another one at the cameraman, and started yelling: Death to the Arabs! Death to the Arabs!

The lighting man turned on the spotlights. The cameraman rushed around trying to arrange the setting. The policemen started pushing the demonstrators out. By force. Watch the lamp! Gina yelled, watch the lamp, but everyone knew that Razi the delivery man was not the calm type. Once, he cracked an egg on the head of a woman who wanted to give him a tip, and now he gave Zabiti a little whack right on his scar, and Zabiti pulled out his club and a commotion started. Gina and I ran into the kitchen, behind the counter, and watched what was going on from there. I had a weird feeling – as if I was watching a film, the kind they show on the movie channel at two in the morning – as if none of it was really happening. Avi Flowers jiggled Saddiq's ladder to shake him off it, but Avram went over and slapped him. Razi the delivery man and Zabiti had grabbed each other's collars and were shouting at each other, don't touch me! don't touch me! The tie reported to the camera on the violent demonstration. The horny old men from the park bench started chanting: Po-lice State! Po-lice State! And everyone else joined in. The midget chased after Dalia's Nissim, trying to get handcuffs on him. Gina said, call the police! Call the police! I told her that the police were already here and dragged her a littler further into the kitchen, just in case. The big picture fell off the living room wall and the glass frame shattered into a million pieces. Avi Flowers stepped on one of them and started screaming, I'm hurt! I'm hurt! And his blood dripped on to the carpet. That's the end of our carpet, Gina said and called to Avram to let go of the ladder and come into the kitchen. A big black dog ran into the living room and started barking at the cameraman, of all people, and the tie raised his voice so he could be heard over the general uproar: the Israeli Police have once again demonstrated how powerless they are when dealing with situations of this kind. We are seeing once again how lack of judgement creates new problems instead of solving existing ones. Once again . . .

Halas with that 'once again', Zabiti said and snatched the camera with one hand (the other was still holding Razi's collar). The tie suddenly looked helpless without the camera. The cameraman mumbled in English: this is un-fucking-believable, un-fucking-believable, and then went up to Zabiti and yelled at him in English: are you out of your mind, man?! Do you know who I am?

Chief, Zabiti suddenly called in a scared voice, there's this guy here talking English. The midget, who was busy chasing the black dog, dropped everything and went over to Zabiti, his face pale. You know what the orders are about foreign media, chief, Zabiti said. Sure I do, the midget said, but are you sure he was speaking English? Zabiti nodded. Ask him where he's from, the midget said, ask him who he works for. Vere are you, pliz, Zabiti asked in English. First give me back my fucking camera, then we'll talk, the cameraman answered. O-o-kay, the midget said, climbed on to the coffee table, stood on tiptoe and announced: attention, ladies and gentlemen, until further notice this area is declared a crime scene and is off limits to the media. That's denying us freedom of speech, the tie protested. Shut up, Zabiti told him, grabbed him by his tie and pulled him toward the door.

The rest of the people followed them out. The horny old men got tired. Dalia's Nissim must have had to go back to Dalia. Avi Flowers was a little dizzy from the slap Avram gave him and he wasn't sure now who was against who. And, besides, now that the television was gone, nobody was having fun any more. They left, one after the other, mumbled I'm sorry in Gina's direction, wished Avram good health and kissed the *mezuzah*. Even the dog went out with its tail between its legs. Only the cameraman kept on demanding his camera back. But the midget refused to give it to him and told him, in Hebrew, that the Police Department's office of confiscated property was open on Mondays, Thursdays and Fridays, between nine and one, and on Tuesdays till two. Fuck you, the cameraman said and left too, without kissing the *mezuzah*.

Zabiti, the midget, and the third policeman who hadn't said a word, leaned on the wall and licked their wounds. The midget talked to someone on his walkie-talkie and his tone got more apologetic by the minute.

Avram and Gina's house looked like those houses you see on TV after a tornado has passed through them, or maybe a hurricane, I don't remember what they call those storms. The carpets looked like rags. The table looked like a chair. The chairs looked like beetles lying on their back. And with all the plaster sprinkled on the sofa from the shot, it looked like a doughnut covered with powdered sugar.

I wanted to get out of there and get back to Lilach, but I knew that if I left now, Gina would never forgive me for not staying to help. So I took the broom out of the cupboard and started sweeping. Saddiq, who'd kept trying to make himself small during the whole commotion and let the Jews fight each other, went back to working with his chisel. I watched him working quietly, and all of a sudden I could see what he must have been like as a child. That happens to me with people sometimes. It happened to me with Moshe when we first met. It happened to me with Amir only a week ago (what a handsome little boy he was!), and now it was happening to me with that Arab. I could see him running around this house with laughing eyes, bringing his mother water from the well and fighting, not seriously, with his brothers. I was ashamed about pushing him and shouting like I did when he asked to come in. After all, what did he really want? To walk around the house he was born in and take something that belonged to him? When I went to Ashkelon a year ago and asked the family that bought our house if I could take a look around, they treated me very well and even invited me to stay the night. On the other hand, I thought, how could I have known? Today, any Arab could be a terrorist. After another few bangs, he dug out the second brick and exposed something behind it. *Allah yasidni*, God help me, he mumbled to himself and shoved his hand into the wall to take out what he'd found.

I stopped sweeping. Gina stopped crying that her house was ruined. Avram stopped asking Saddiq if he wanted more coffee.

Even the midget asked his chief on the walkie-talkie to call him back in a minute.

*

The minute the television people left, I knew I didn't have a chance, that without the camera I was finished. It didn't matter whether they called me Nissan or Saddiq, a dog's tail can never be straight, and a policeman won't fight an Arab without putting handcuffs on him.

But I still kept on working. I banged with the chisel till there was a crack between the bricks, and then I pulled out the loose brick the way you pull out a slice of cake. There was an empty space behind it, as quiet and cold as a grave. I stuck my hand inside and at first I didn't feel anything, but when I stepped on to the next rung of the ladder and pushed my hand in deeper, I touched something. A bag. I pulled it out, and everyone in the house stopped talking. The policemen. The old man who thought he was my father. The young woman with the tiger eyes. They all wanted to see what was in the bag.

Inside the crumbling bag was another bag. The second bag was made of stronger cloth, the kind they make cement bags out of. The opening was held together with a thick rope tied in a complicated knot. I opened it, twist after twist. I used my teeth too.

The chief stopped talking with his generals and came over to the ladder too to see what was in the bag.

My mother hadn't told me what she'd left there, but I could already see it in my head. What do people usually hide inside walls? Either weapons or money.

I pulled a gold chain out of the bag. A thin, delicate chain exactly the right size for a small woman's neck. Even though almost fifty years had gone by, it still glittered in the light. *Allah carim*, dear God, I thought with fear in my heart, this is Grandma Shadia's chain. All the old people in the family, my mother's brothers and sisters, always used to talk about this chain. It had been handed down from mother to oldest daughter, from mother to oldest daughter for maybe a hundred, two hundred years, from the time the family was living in Lebanon. And no one knew where it had disappeared to during the war. Except for my mother, who knew and kept quiet about it. The chain slithered through my fingers like a snake. Why didn't you tell anyone, *ya umi*? Maybe you were ashamed of leaving it behind like that. Of forgetting the thing that was most important to the family and running away. And now what? Maybe you don't care any more. Most of the old people are dead already, and the ones still alive, their memories disappear like salt in water.

I'm asking you to hand over that chain, the short policeman said, coming closer to me and putting a foot on the first rung of the ladder.

I looked at the old man, at my saviour. I waited for him to wave the bread knife around again, to yell and save me. But suddenly his eyes were empty, and he looked at me as if I was air. Then his expression changed again, as if I was another one of those people he didn't know, and all he said was, I'm cold. Then again, I'm cold. His wife said, come Avram, you've had a long day, maybe you should rest, and then she took him by the hand like he was a little boy and pulled him along to their bedroom.

I demand that you hand that chain over to me or I'll be forced to arrest you, the short policeman said and took his handcuffs off his belt again.

I looked at the young woman with the tiger eyes. She looked back at me. I felt as if she wanted to say something on my behalf. I even thought I saw her lips move. But she didn't say anything, and in the end, she even stopped looking at me and fixed her eyes on the hole in the ceiling made by the bullet.

This chain is mine, I said and put it into my pocket, it belongs to my family.

The other two policemen also moved closer to the ladder. That chain is stolen property, the short policeman said, and you'll give it to me now. Later on, if you win the trial, you can go to the confiscated property department. It's open on Sundays, Mondays and Thursdays from nine to one and on Tuesdays till two, he said and smiled like an asshole.

Suddenly, my mouth was full of the words I hadn't been able to say when the television crew was there, all the sentences that had been stuck in my throat like cement. That's a sad joke, I said in a strong voice, like Gamal Abd al-Nasser in his good days. What's happening here is a sad joke, but one day it'll end, one day the strong will be weak and the weak will be strong, and then none of you will laugh any more, believe me, none of you will laugh.

Maybe some day that'll happen, the short policeman said and grabbed my arm hard, but meanwhile, mister, you're under arrest.

They put the handcuffs on me, dragged me out of the house and slapped me when I tried to resist. They pulled the chain out of my pocket and threw me into the police car. They blindfolded me with a handkerchief and slapped me again, harder, for the fun of it, and cursed me in Arabic the whole time – the Jews always curse in Arabic – and took me to the Russian Compound, to an investigator who wanted to know what organisation I belonged to, Fatah or Hamas, or maybe to the Popular Front, and I told him I'm just one man, alone, no organisation. He slapped me – the third slap – and kept at it. Isn't it too bad for your family? he said, your children? Give me the name of your chief now and I'll make sure you won't get more than a year inside, and I said, what chief? What do you want? I didn't do anything. What are you charging me with? And he said, oh man, we've got ourselves a smart-arse here, and without warning, like a football player kicking from where he's standing, he gave me the fourth slap and yelled, who do you think you are? You have two choices, either you co-operate willingly or you co-operate unwillingly, which will it be? And I said, I didn't do anything, no one sent me, I don't know what you want from me. He got up and paced around the room to make me nervous. Then he went out and said to the guards waiting outside, take him to a cell, and the guards came in and blindfolded me again and dragged me through hallways that smelt of detergent. They took off the blindfold and gave me a fifth slap, you stinking Arab, and threw me into a small cell with Arabic writing on the walls and the smell of piss. But I didn't care, because my heart was filled with happiness that I'd been in my house, that I'd gone back to my home and did what my mother asked. I'd gone into all the rooms and found the chain and made a big stink and they filmed it and it would probably be on television, on the evening news. For the first time, they'd see an Arab talking on television about his home, and the whole world would listen. The whole village would be proud of me.

There was a small TV set outside the cell, for the guards. I couldn't see the screen because the guards had turned it towards them, but I could hear. From the kind of talking I heard, I guessed the news would be on very soon. First there was a quiz with organ music and loud applause after every sentence. Then they talked about food, and a woman talked about a British film they made in a large castle not far from London. Then there was the sports announcer, and I put a hand behind my ear so I could hear how many goals Liverpool had scored against Everton. Then, half an hour before the time I guessed the eight o'clock news would go on, there was trumpet music all of a sudden, and the guard called his friend, hey, there's a newsflash. Looks to me like something happened.

There was hope in my heart: maybe the newsflash was about me? Maybe they'd tell about the policeman who shot at an Arab inside a house?

It turned out to be a suicide bombing. In Jerusalem. Lots of injured people. The number of dead unknown. The second bombing in the capital coming hard on the heels of a previous attack, the broadcaster said, and then the rest of the news started. I kept on listening. I hoped that maybe between reports from one hospital and another, they'd stick in a little item about what happened in el-Castel today, but they didn't say anything about it. *Abadan*. A lost cause. I was done for. I felt like someone who tried to jump on a donkey and fell off the other side. What did I make that whole scene for? What good did it do? I couldn't even bring my mother the chain. And what would Nehila do now? Where would she get money to buy food? There was nothing left in the house that she could sell. And little Imad would be starting school next year. We needed money for his books, for clothes. And who'd bring the money if not his father?

One of the guards who was watching television came over to my cell, looked at me with red eyes and spat in my face. You son-of-a-bitch, you're all sons-of-bitches. Force is the only thing you understand, only force.

I went to the back of the cell and sat down on a stained mattress.

He kept spitting at me and called his friend to join him: come on, man, a little target practice.

I covered my face with my hands. I felt as if someone was sticking a needle into my vein and injecting me with hatred.

They kept on spitting, collected all the saliva they had in their mouths and throats and hurled it at me. It was a 'bulls'-eye' when they got my face, a 'hit' when they got my body. I knew that game from my days in prison.

*

A storm is raging around us: Ovadia goes over to Ronen to ask him something about black holes, then changes his mind. Then goes over to him again. And changes his mind again. Joe and Zachi are having a loud, aggressive argument about whether you can move backwards to capture a piece in draughts. Nava tries to calm them down before one of them grabs someone else by the throat. Gideon the speechmaker is making a speech to the entire room. He's holding a tattered book he took from the club's small library and reading, putting the stress in the wrong places, something by A.D. Gordon. Some of the people in the room cheer him on. Some order him to shut up. Shmuel and I try to ignore all of it. We're engrossed in conversation, our heads bent, our voices lowered. A thin, invisible bubble surrounds us, separating us from the commotion in the room. But what hurts *you*, Shmuel? I ask him, and he suddenly stops talking. He's just finished giving me another lecture on his theory of colours, and out of an uncontrollable urge – how many times can you listen to the theory that the world is divided into red, white and transparent – that direct question suddenly comes out of my mouth. He takes off his cracked glasses and wipes them with his shirt. Without them, he looks younger and more lost. He puts his glasses back on, stares straight ahead and says nothing. His knee is jerking nervously, and he says nothing. It's possible that he didn't hear. And it's possible that it's too soon. That not enough trust has been created between us for him to share with me what's really bothering him. But how can trust be created when every week I have to remind him all over again what my name is? Besides, maybe his theories were not meant to hide anything deeper, maybe the theories are the thing itself. And why is he the one I've latched on to? Of all the suffering people here, why him?

Look, my friend, he says, trying to please me, as if he senses that I'm about to give up on him, you asked me a tough question. And it's not that I don't know the answer. I know it very well. So what's the problem, Shmuel? I ask, and immediately regret the question because there he is, taking off his glasses again and turning his face away from me, wrapping himself in that silence of his. Don't push him, idiot, don't push. The problem is, he says to me – thank God, I haven't lost him yet – that what I'm about to say will make you doubt me. You'll say to yourself that Shmuel is crazy, disturbed. And what do you think I say to myself now, with all your weird theories? the cynic inside me replies, while I myself am silent. If he wants to, he'll talk. The pain, he finally says after another silence and a twitch that closes his right eye, the pain isn't actually my pain, but all the pain that exists in the world. Oh no, I wince, he's going to come out with a new theory. Should

I interrupt him now? I don't mean the 'world' in cosmic terms, he reassures me, but more the people who fill the world with their pain. You see, in every person's chest there is a sun of pain and sorrow, and that sun radiates fiery rays. If you're well protected, those rays don't penetrate you. But if you're not protected, the pain of the people close to you enters you and burns you from inside. And you just don't have any sunblock to slather on your skin? I ask, and realise right away that my tone is wrong, that my attempt at humour is inappropriate here. I don't have that layer of skin, he corrects me without any anger. There's no protective skin between me and the misery in the world. To tell you the truth, he says, bringing his mouth to my ear as if whispering a secret, I did have skin like that. But a few years ago, it melted away and left me exposed to all the rays that strangers radiate at me. Wow, I say and put my hand on my chest to stop the pounding of my heart, what you're telling me, it doesn't sound easy. No it isn't, Shmuel nods, scratching his head fiercely, hurting himself. From the other side of the room, Nava signals to me with her hand on her watch that the time is almost up, we have to start arranging the chairs. Why the pressure? Doesn't she see that I'm in the middle of a conversation? Tell me, I say, ignoring her and turning to Shmuel, can you give me an example? An example of what? he asks, watching Nava fearfully as she hurries the other members to leave. An example of a person, I say, talking faster, a person you find it hard to be near because you feel that his pain is too strong, that it's blazing too hot for you.

You, he says, and smiles a nasty little smile. Since when has Shmuel been nasty?

Me?! I say, my voice choked. I was sure he'd mention someone in his family or that girl who shattered his heart when he was seventeen. But me? Yes, he says, and his smile spreads to the sides like hands. When you came here, your sun was sending out pleasant, caressing rays. But lately, my friend, I sometimes have to stop talking in the middle of a conversation with you just to relieve the pain you make me feel. O-ka-a-y, I say, stretching out the 'kay'. I don't have anything else better or cleverer to say. Shmuel is quiet and I think: am I hurting him even now, this minute? He sees Nava approaching and stands up, frightened. I squeeze his hand – again that limp handshake of his – and he moves away, leaving me and Nava with a weak wave of his hand and his usual parting words: see you next week, God willing.

After he disappears up the steps, I go over to the coffee corner and try to stabilise myself: calm down, Amir, he's crazy, he's talking bullshit. Your question must have been too nosy and he decided to hurt you deliberately. I say all that to myself, but deep inside me, I suspect he's right, and that shakes up all my inner organs. One of my kidneys crashes into my spleen, my liver into my pancreas, my pancreas into my appendix. I feel it happening inside my body even though I don't know exactly what the appendix is, but during our training session, when Nava asks if everything's all right because I look a little pale, I say yes, everything's all right because I don't trust her enough, I don't feel that I can share anything intimate with her without being afraid that she'll apply one of her theories to it. But still, she probes: I saw you and Shmuel having a long conversation, she says. Yes, so what? I attack and she retreats, gives up and goes on to Ronen. Suddenly I'm sorry she doesn't insist, because how can you keep something like that to yourself? You have to talk to someone about it. But Ronen is chattering excitedly about his science class, and the conversation moves away from me, further and further away, until it ends with Nava looking sharply at her watch, and a minute later we're all climbing the urine-saturated stairs. She locks the heavy door and we each go our own way, Ronen to his motorcycle, Chanit to the bus and

Nava to the large, mysterious van that's always waiting for her outside.

The Fiat's right headlight has popped out again, and I push it back into place. I toss the rolled-up crossword puzzle into the back seat, sit down behind the wheel, try in vain to get my heart beating normally again, and start the long drive back to Mevasseret.

*

It's outrageous, Dad said. And Mum said, yes, that an Arab should walk around the neighbourhood for months like that without anyone stopping him? And Dad said, a fiasco, a plain fiasco. I was eating an omelette and thinking that this was the first time they'd agreed on something since Gidi. Dad thinks that it's time to take apart the museum in the living room and move it to Gidi's room, and Mum says over her dead body. Mum wants them to keep meeting with that woman from the Ministry of Defence, and Dad doesn't. But they don't talk about all that. They have this way of arguing without words. Mum takes out Gidi's yearbook to look through it and Dad gets up and leaves the room. Dad makes appointments with the Parents' Forum for Security and Mum makes noise banging pots in the kitchen on purpose to show him what she thinks about it.

But they agreed about the Arab and I was so glad that they finally saw eye to eye on something that I didn't want to spoil it, so I didn't tell them that the Arab was just an old man with a limp, and that's why no one suspected him. All I did was take a slice of bread and put a piece of my omelette on it along with a slice of tomato and two olives and hoped they'd keep on being nice to each other and maybe after breakfast they'd even sit close to each other in front of the TV like they used to, but then Dad said, it just goes to show that we have to chase those terrorists down everywhere. Here, in the territories and in Lebanon. Mum sighed and said, but so many children die doing it. Dad declared as if he was giving a speech in front of his

Forum, that's how it is, that's the sacrifice we have to make for security. Mum said, I don't believe you really think that. It's only talk, right? Dad said, what do you mean? Mum looked at him and decided to hold back and not tell him what she meant. But Dad started to cough, a little cough at first, and then with his whole throat, and Mum asked, should I get you the inhaler? Dad got up, his face red, and said, I don't need any favours from you, don't bring me anything. And Mum started to go to their room anyway to get the inhaler, but Dad grabbed her hand and said, I told you not to go, didn't I? They looked at each other as if they'd act differently if I wasn't there, and the truth is, I really didn't want to be there any more. I didn't want to hear him tell her to say again that it was his fault and that's that. I didn't want to hear her answer as usual, what are you talking about, that's not what I think. I got up from the table and Mum asked, where are you going? You haven't finished eating. The truth was that I wasn't planning to go anywhere, just up to my room, but the minute she said the word 'going', it made me feel like going, so I put on my coat and she said, you're running away to those students again? I said, yes, so what? Dad tried to say something, but instead of words, coughing came out, and Mum said, really Reuven, go and get your inhaler, and he ran to their room, coughing without a stop, leaving the two of us alone. Mum stood in front of me and didn't say anything for a minute, trying to decide whether to let me go or not. Then she took the Beitar scarf off the hook and gave it to me, saying, wear this at least, so you don't catch cold. I put it around my neck and held it by the ends, and she asked with an angry expression on her face: tell me, have you told that student that I want to talk to him?

*

The traffic's moving, but I'm all jammed up, even when I pass the airport (the thought flies through me, I could fly to Modi now). I drive past Ben Shemen. Past Latrun. On the radio, a woman broadcaster with a feathery voice asks the listeners, tell us what's happening on the roads, and I think that if I had a mobile I'd call and report on the internal jam that I've had for a month already, without any visible accident, but I don't have one. There's no money for airtime when you live on air, and anyway, I'd already reached Shaar Hagai, with the hills close to the road on both sides, which feels different every time. Sometimes it's like a woman's vagina taking you in warmly, and sometimes, like today, it's grey and threatening and suffocating and you feel as if snipers from the Jordanian Legion from the War of Independence are standing on the hills. In another second, they'll shoot out your tyres and you'll end up like one of those rusted tanks on the side of the road. You wonder, where's the Burma Road, where's the Burma Road, but here's the turn to Shoresh, and I'm still driving, still alive. The radio isn't picking up anything now except for the stations devoted to the newly religious. A woman is home, as we say, her honour is in the home, the announcer whispers into the microphone, with God's help, he hopes . . . but I turn off the radio before he can say what he needs God's help for. I start up the hill to the Castel, and the Fiat sputters a little but keeps climbing. With God's help, Noa will be home and I'll be able to tell her about Shmuel. Yes, she'll know how to put the crosshairs on the target. She'll take me in her arms, soft and perfumed, I think and turn on to the bridge, ignoring Doga, glide down Anonymous Hero Street and park the car behind Moshe's bus. From the end of the paved path, I see that there's a light on in our house, which means nothing because Noa always forgets to turn off the lights when she goes out. Lately, when I walk up the path, I imagine going into the house and catching her cheating on me. I don't have an exact picture of the man. I can only see his back, and her face, peering over his shoulder, is contorted with passion, then surprise when she sees me.

And the weird thing is that the whole scenario doesn't make me angry. Just the opposite. It gives me a feeling of intense pleasure, especially when I imagine myself waiting contemptuously until the guy gets dressed and goes. Then I put all my CDs into a bag and take down the picture of the sad man and leave the apartment without looking back. This time too, the closer I get to the door, the springier my steps get. Excited, I decide not to peek through the window and burst right inside. Noa isn't in the living room, but I feel her presence in the air. And I think someone else is here too. Amir?! she calls from the shower in a voice that's too innocent, and I start walking to the bathroom. Maybe they're already having their 'after' shower. The curtains hide their bodies and I suddenly remember that scene from *Psycho*, but I don't have a knife. Hi, she says, pulling the curtain open. There's no one with her. She's alone. Alone. My fantasy shatters into a thousand pieces that fly into the air in slow motion. I lower the toilet lid and sit down. You won't believe what happened, she beats me to it. Almost every one of her stories starts with 'You won't believe what happened', and then it turns out to be about a cup of coffee that spilled on her in the cafeteria or a report on Hila who, for the fifth time this week, has found the love of her life. But this time she tells a story that really sounds unbelievable. Some Arab, she says, one of Madmoni's workers, went into Avram and Gina's house and claimed that the house belonged to his family in '48, and that his mother left something of hers in one of the walls. Gina wanted to throw him out, but Avram jumped up and said that the worker was Nissan, their little boy who died when he was two, and that no one was to touch him.

What?

I swear. Avram's been loopy ever since his operation. Did I tell you about the exorcist Gina brought? It turned out that he didn't help a lot.

Wait. Where are you in this whole story?

I was babysitting for Lilach. And at some point, Sima came downstairs and called the police because the Arab started taking bricks out of their wall.

And the police came? I ask, licking a drop of water that had splashed onto my lip.

Only the police? The whole world was there. I mean, at first the police came and went upstairs with Sima, and then, a few minutes later, there was a gunshot.

A gunshot?!

Don't get upset. No one was hurt. It was just a stray bullet one of the policemen shot.

But right after the shot, the whole neighbourhood showed up. You wouldn't believe it. A demonstration, yelling. Then even a TV crew came in.

TV crew? How did they know to come?

I don't know. But they came pretty quickly. Maybe they'll show it on the news today.

Wait a minute. Did you photograph anything?

Are you joking? I wish. I was stuck downstairs with Lilach. She cried the whole time and I had to calm her down. Except for pulling out a breast and letting her nurse, I did everything. But don't worry, I have an idea for a project.

She turned off the water and asked me to hand her a towel.

What idea? I ask and move aside so she has somewhere to stand.

To get in touch with Arabs who were driven away from the Castel in '48, she says. And ask to photograph them, their whole families, against the background of the house they used to live in. The house that has a Hebrew street sign next to it. And a sign over the door in Hebrew. And a laundry line that has army uniforms hanging on it. They'll stand the way families stand in classic family portraits, and maybe I'll even ask them to smile, to make the point even sharper. What do you think?

A gorgeous body, I say. She's standing in front of me, naked and smooth.

About the idea, she says and flicks me gently with her wet hair.

A great idea, I say truthfully, and add: but I'm not sure about the smile. That could look cynical.

You're right, she says, walking past me on the way to the bedroom. I'll just photograph them both smiling and not smiling. Then we'll see what works better.

Just a minute, I say, wanting to clarify something that bothers me, you didn't tell me how the business with Madmoni's worker turned out.

A disaster, she yells, and her voice is swallowed up momentarily in the sweatshirt that she must have been pulling over her head. They confiscated the chain he found in the wall and arrested him too. Not that he's dangerous or anything. You should've seen him, an old man who just wanted to visit his house. Even Sima felt sorry for him in the end.

While Noa's getting dressed, I think about that worker and remember that when my family moved to Jerusalem, we had to move again three months later to a different apartment on the same street. I don't know why. Something about the lease, if I understood correctly the English my parents spoke in cases like that. Anyway, we piled up boxes again and wrapped glasses in newspaper and waited for the Chen Brothers, the movers, who were actually father and son, not brothers.

A few weeks after we settled into the new apartment, I was coming home from school deep in thought, and instead of going to the new place, I walked unconsciously to the old apartment. The buildings looked pretty much alike, and I went into the hallway without suspecting anything. I slowly climbed the stairs to the second floor. Maybe I was even humming a Tislam song to myself on the way up. When I reached the door that used to be ours, I opened it and breezed inside. The new tenants hadn't changed the interior of the house, and an old brown sofa that we'd left behind was still in the centre of the living room. I was immersed in thought, and the scene I was seeing was probably familiar enough not to make me suspicious, so I threw my schoolbag down at the door, like I always did, said hi to my mother and collapsed on to the sofa. All of a sudden, a woman I didn't know ran out of the kitchen wearing an apron over her clothes and looked at me, shocked. Excuse me, she said, who are you?

Who are you? I retaliated.

What do you mean? I live here! she said, putting her hands on her hips.

I looked around at one piece of furniture after another, one picture after another, and comprehension started to sink in. And with it, the burning sensation of shame rose in my throat. Wait a minute, she said with a new spark in her eyes, I know you. You're the son of Danny and Zehava, the couple who lived here before us, right? Yes, I admitted and stood up. So what happened, the woman said amiably, did you miss your old house? No, of course not, it's just, ah . . . I'm sorry, I stammered and ran out of there as fast as I could.

What are you thinking about? Noa asked, coming into the living room and interrupting my escape.

About your idea, I say, thinking that I still haven't talked to her about what happened in the club today.

Let's turn on the TV, she says, maybe they'll show what happened at Avram and Gina's.

OK. I obey, and look for the remote under the cushions, thinking to myself that I have to talk to her about what happened with Shmuel I have to talk to her about what happened I have to talk.

By the way, she says before I can say anything, Yotam was here and said that his mother wants to meet you.

Fine, I say, turning on the TV. A small map with street

names appears in a corner of the screen. Suddenly I heard a boom, an eyewitness wearing a cardigan says, breathing heavily. Suddenly I heard a boom, says a salesman from a shoe shop, an involuntary smile twitching his cheek. A boom? What boom, I think, why a boom now?

Chorus

Dying to live one
'Cause of Liat
Two
The view
Three
To be free.
Four
I want more
I want more.

Don't wanna die
in a terrorist attack
No way.
Not today.
I like my life.
I wanna stay.

Dying to live five
Wanna survive
Six
All those chicks
Seven
My idea of heaven
Eight nine,
I like it here just fine.

Don't wanna die
in a terrorist attack
No way.
Not today.
I like my life.
I wanna stay.

To fall asleep on the beach
one more time
would be sublime.
Eat ribs that are prime
And make love till the end.

Till the end.
Don't wanna die
in a terrorist attack
No way.
Not today.
I like my life.
I wanna stay.

Music and lyrics: David Batsri
From the Licorice album, *Love As I Explained it to My Wife*
Produced independently, 1996

4

_____

In the end, she came to call on me. She knocked on the door in the morning, when Yotam was at school, and said in a low voice: Yotam's mother. I opened the door. I'd seen her before, hanging washing up, getting out of the car, getting into it. But now, for the first time, all of her was standing in front of me. Grey hair. Dark lakes under her eyes. Shoulders stooped. A woman who had once been attractive. You could tell from her features. Would you like to come over for a cup of coffee? she asked, and I said, yes, sure. She didn't say anything about why she wanted me to come to her house for coffee. There was no need. I'll just change my clothes, I apologised, and she wrung her hands and said, I'll wait for you outside. I changed from tracksuit bottoms into jeans, and from a stained sweatshirt into a clean one, thinking: it was clear this would happen, what did you expect? It's a wonder it didn't happen sooner. I saved the work I was doing on the computer and went out. It was very cold. The wind blew into my sleeves, giving me chills up and down my back. Yotam's mother gestured for me to walk behind her and she took the long way, not the shortcut through the lot. Of course, I thought, hugging myself, she won't start jumping over stones now. When we reached their door, she stopped, turned to me and said: you've never actually been here before, have you?

Only once, I thought, during the *shivah*, by mistake, but I said: no.

Then we went inside and my blood curdled.

Dozens of memorial candles flickered in the living room. Not a single lamp was lit. A picture of a soldier wearing a beret hung on the wall opposite the door. The picture was the size of the posters they put up at bus stops. There were another three pictures of Gidi: one on the TV of him saluting someone; the second one on the cabinet, next to the bowl of artificial flowers, showing him carrying Yotam on his shoulders, and in the third, he looked younger. From the *yarmulke* he wore and the way his hair was parted on the side, it was probably his bar mitzvah.

How many sugars do you take? Yotam's mother asked from the kitchen. Two, I answered, and continued walking around with my hands behind my back, as if I were at an exhibition.

*

No one answered, but I remembered that Amir once told me that the key was under the flowerpot on the right and that if I feel like it, I can stay there even when they're not home. It was weird going in like that, without Amir giving me a hug or Noa giving me a kiss, but I said to myself that this was better than seeing my mother now and telling her that I got kicked out of lessons again. It'd be better to tell her that at supper, when Dad's there too. Maybe it'll make them talk to each other. I closed the door behind me and started walking around the apartment looking for interesting things to do. I found an old tennis ball. I threw it against the wall a few times and caught it, but then it accidentally hit that picture of the sad man and I stopped. I went into the kitchen to look for something good to eat, but the only thing in the fridge was a jar of mayonnaise, and there's nothing you can do with mayonnaise by itself. I looked at the noticeboard across from the fridge, trying to find something interesting, secret. But the only things there were electric and water bills, a picture that Noa must have taken of a place with a lot of clouds, a sticker that said 'Create or Stagnate', a few drawing pins without papers, and a drawing of a couple sleeping in bed – he's trying to pull the blanket to his side and she's nailing it to the bed so he can't – and under the drawing was a small piece of paper and someone, maybe Amir, had written on it, 'My love is sometimes a hot baguette and sometimes a broken baguette', and next to that was another piece of paper that said, in different handwriting, 'My love is chocolate I'm allowed to eat, and sometimes chocolate I'm not allowed to eat.' In other words, nothing interesting. I went back to the living room, sat down on the sofa and turned on the TV. That's when I noticed the letter on the table.

The first words of the letter were, 'Amir my love'.

This is wrong! I told myself, but my eyes darted back to read it. I turned my head in the other direction on purpose, but my eyes darted back to peek.

Amir my love,
Lately, our words get tangled up.
Why can't it all be simple?
I love. You love. It should stop, shouldn't it?
Have a wonderful, simple morning.
Kisses and hugs,
Your Noa

*

I have *mamoulim* if you want, she said and put the little plate of filled biscuits down next to the coffee. Thank you, I said, and remembered that I hadn't eaten anything all morning. She sat down on the chair next to me and looked me over silently. Her eyes moved over my body, slipped away to the ceiling, the walls, then came back to study my face. I wanted to break the ice, to compliment her on how nice the house looked, the way people do in situations like this, but it seemed strange to compliment her on the armchairs or the curtains when the whole house looked like a memorial site. It's warm here, I finally said, and that was a lie too. Somehow, despite the candles and the humming heaters, the air I inhaled between sips was dark and chilly.

Yotam spends a lot of time at your house, doesn't he? she said, ignoring my dubious compliment and getting straight to the point. Yes, I admitted. How is he? she asked, making me swallow the apology that was on the tip of my tongue. I took one of the biscuits, and while I was taking little bites, I thought about how to answer her. He's a great kid, I finally said. Sensitive, sweet, smart. I taught him to play chess two months ago, and now he's beating me.

Yes, she said, an almost unnoticeable bit of maternal pride in her voice. But what I'm asking is, what's happening to him? What is he feeling? He doesn't talk to me at all, you know?

I took another biscuit and crumbled it with my fingers. He doesn't talk to me about Gidi either, I admitted. It probably hurts too much. Or he still hasn't taken it in. He's only a boy and . . .

So you don't talk about him? she said, interrupting me. Her chin dropped in disbelief.

No, I confirmed. And a second later, I added: not yet.

She stroked an embroidered cushion that was lying next to her and looked at one of the pictures of Gidi, the one on the TV. They were very close, she said, Yotam and Gidi. They were nine years apart, but very close. Gidi was like a father to him, she whispered, and a shadow crossed her eyes, as if she were remembering a bad dream. Yotam's father spends a lot of hours at work every day, you know? So Gidi actually raised him.

I nodded, but only once. Two or more nods is Nava.

She picked up the cushion and held it against her stomach. The whole week, Yotam would ask me if Gidi was coming home for the weekend, and if I said yes, he'd go outside on Friday morning and sit on the steps to watch the bus stop for hours, waiting for him to finally get here. Every time a bus came down the street, he'd call out to me: Mummy, the bus is coming! And he'd stand on tiptoe so he could see. In summer and in winter. He'd sit and wait.

Like I used to wait for Noa, I thought.

Once, Yotam's mother went on, there was a hailstorm and I made him come into the house so he wouldn't catch cold, God forbid. So he pretended to do what I asked and then went out the window and sat in the bus stop shelter without my knowing it.

That's just like him.

You should have seen them. She released the cushion slightly and looked encouraged by my smile: Yotam would jump on him and hang from his shoulder, like a handbag. And Gidi would peel him off gently and stroke his head and let him drag one handle of his duffle bag – he never let him touch his gun, never! – and that's how they walked to the house, a big boy and a little boy, and when I hugged Gidi at the door, Yotam would wrap his little arms around us and hug us hugging each other.

She put a hand on her waist, as if she were trying to feel that touch again. I held my cup with both hands and tried to inhale the last vestiges of heat from it.

More coffee? she asked. No, thanks, I said. Biscuits? she asked, pointing to the plate, which had only a few crumbs left on it. No thanks, they were delicious, I said, and she rubbed her hands together in embarrassment, as if she'd hoped I'd give her an errand to do so she could take a minute's rest from herself. Or from the conversation. Or maybe she wanted to postpone the minute she'd have to ask me something she wanted to know, but was afraid to ask.

You're a psychologist, aren't you? she finally said, looking straight at me.

No, I said. I mean, yes. I'm studying psychology, but I'm only working for my B.Sc., so you can't say I'm a psychologist. I mean, I'm not. Her eyes moved away from me again and started wandering around the walls. Her face, which had brightened a little when she talked about Gidi, fell again, and her cheeks dropped over her mouth.

Probably the fact that I wasn't a psychologist really disappointed her.

Two voices argued inside me. One wanted to satisfy her, to pretend I was an expert, to console her, and the other called out for me to be careful.

They sent us a social worker from the Ministry of Defence, she said and turned her face to me again as if she'd decided to ignore the new information I'd given her. Maybe you know her, Ricky Be'eri? No? Never mind. She sat with us a few times. Here, in the living room. She said it was important for us to talk about things and not keep them inside. But Reuven didn't want to keep having the meetings. He told her that after every time we sit with her, he feels a lot worse, so what's it good for? He said it just like that, right to her face. No shame. And she said to him: maybe you're afraid that if you look into your heart, you'll find things you don't like. And I thought that was true, what she said, and I even nodded my head so she'd see that I wanted her to continue. But it just made Reuven mad. He said to her, who are you to tell me what I have in my heart? Then he got up angrily and started pacing around the room. Did you ever have a child die? Do you even know what it's like? You think you can come here with your nice clothes and the car your father bought you and tell us what to do? Listen carefully, Miss Social Worker – he could never remember her name – I'm asking you nicely, don't come here any more, we don't need your help.

What did she say?

She wrote her phone number on a piece of paper and gave it to me, not to Reuven, and said that we could set up a different arrangement for our talks. And that was it. She left.

Did you call her?

I wanted to. Here, look, I still have her number.

So why didn't you?

I didn't have the strength. I started dialling the number so many times, but I got tired in the middle. As if in my heart I didn't believe any more that anything good could come out of trying. And that's how I am all the time, I have no patience with anything, I can't read a book, can't watch a film to the end. I can't believe how Reuven goes to work every morning, and two nights a week he runs to those meetings of the Parents' Forum for Security. How can he? I can hardly do the laundry. Only Gidi's clothes. I washed them three times, like an idiot, and folded them and put them in his wardrobe, as if he only went to sleep and he'll get up in another minute and put them on.

Yotam's shirts really do smell mouldy, I said to myself, and then was immediately ashamed of the thought.

But why am I telling you all this? Yotam's mother said with real amazement in her voice, as if another woman had been talking the last few minutes, not her. You poor man, what did you do to deserve this?

It's all right, I said, then kept quiet. I didn't know what else to say.

You probably have to get back to your studies, right? she said, getting up and taking the cups and the plate. Psychology is hard, isn't it? Pretty hard, I admitted, still looking for something clever and sensitive to say. Go back and study, she said, so you can finish college and help people.

Finish? I thought, I still have at least seven years to go. I waited for her to come back from the kitchen. The window was slightly open, and the draught coming through it made the candle flames dance. Some of them went out. Some kept twisting until they straightened out and went back to doing their job. I shifted my position on the sofa. I bit a nail, even though I don't bite my nails. Gidi watched me from four different angles. I looked down.

She came back from the kitchen holding a piece of paper in one hand and a fridge magnet in the other. Look, she said, I got this from school yesterday. I looked. Written at the top of the page was, *Re: Complaints About Your Son's Behaviour.* Then came the details of a few instances when Yotam ignored teachers' requests or talked back or missed lessons without permission, but the zinger came at the end: *We are all aware of the tragedy that struck your family a few months ago, and we are doing everything we can to take these special circumstances into consideration, but we cannot accept this kind of behaviour on a long-term basis since it has an adverse effect on other pupils.*

If they're being so considerate, they should leave him alone, I said, handing back the letter. I think so too, but this is the second letter already, she said and put the paper on the table between us. The magnet she kept, switching it from one hand to the other.

Can you talk to him? she asked suddenly, looking straight at me.

Me?

You're the only one he seems to listen to.

He doesn't want *me* to talk to him, I thought. He wants *you* to talk to him. To give him attention.

OK, I said, and her body, which had been waiting tensely for my answer, suddenly relaxed. OK, I'll try.

*

Noa and Amir's word of the month: scene. Noa had a bad scene during her shift on Sunday. Amir had a strange scene in the club on Monday. And there's also a good scene. And a dangerous scene. And a wild scene. Sometimes they run through a series of scenes (though lately, this hasn't been part of their regular routine). Then one day, Noa announces that the word 'scene' was annoying and she'd never use it again. Right after that, she blurted out, what a weird scene! when she saw someone from her school on TV in a commercial for an exercise machine. And a few days later, she whispers to Hila on the phone: lately, Amir and I have been having a bad scene. And Hila says: amazing! Lately, a lot of couples I know have been going through the same thing. I wonder how it'll end? And Noa thinks: why does she always think that everything has to be part of a mysterious, general trend? While Amir, in bed, is filled with suspicion and doubt: why is she whispering? What's she hiding? What's this all about? Noa listens patiently to Hila, who needs to explain. Then she gets quietly under the covers again. She turns her back. Can't fall asleep. And Amir is busy thinking and doesn't know what to say: if all these are scenes, when do they turn into a play?

Rami the contractor's word of the month is *heideh*. Which means 'let's go' in Romanian. And he also knows how to say 'money' in Romanian (*badeh*). And tomorrow (*mineh*). That's how it is – new workers, new words. But you can't say he's a happy man. He waited three weeks for his Arabs. But the border closure was as tight as the day it began. Employers who smuggled their workers out had to pay fines, so what could he do? Romanian workers were better than none. Without them, work on Madmoni's house would never be done. And sometimes, when he sees a crooked iron rod, he says out loud, *ya* Saddiq, why did you Arabs have to make this mess and then disappear? Where are you now that I need you here?

In prison. Learning Hebrew with Mustafa A'alem. Mustafa is an old man, but he recognises Saddiq right away. He remembers all his outstanding students as if he'd seen them just yesterday. Saddiq A'adana, you still have a lot to learn, he tells him when he's in the tent that serves as their cell. We still haven't done any grammar. And you don't know how to spell. I know, that's why I came back, Saddiq says and kisses Mustafa on the cheek. After they smile at each other, Saddiq bends his head, humble and meek. That's how it is. Mustafa A'alem is a famous hero of the Intifada and the young prisoners treat him with great respect. They wait months for the chance to become his students, hoping to be the ones he'll select. You're not a boy any more, are you? Mustafa A'alem says. Come to me tomorrow at three. We'll see what we can do. Then Saddiq remembers to call out Mustafa's famous slogan: Know your enemy! *Ta'aref el ado!* When he's said those words, he can turn around and go.

And the next day (after being humiliated and harassed) they're already sitting together over their books as if no time at all had passed. Mustafa takes out a package of newspapers that was smuggled into the prison especially for him. And he takes out two pens. Then he dictates to Saddiq a list of new words in Hebrew that are easy to understand. And Saddiq writes the Hebrew letters with an unsure hand. When they're finished, Mustafa goes over the words, one by one. Proof. Pardon. Solution. Retribution. Power. Payment. Compensation. Expectation. Longing, *gagua*, in Hebrew. It's such a beautiful word, Saddiq says, like a baby crying for its mother. But Mustafa scolds: What's beautiful about it? Saddiq tries to explain (he'd hardly slept all night or the night before) and says: because longing is, like you said, when you want to be in another place. When you've fallen from grace. When you've lost something that nothing else can replace.

Yotam's father longs for his son Gidi. Every time his name is mentioned, his face turns blue and his wife thinks he's going to choke. She brings him a glass of water and holds it to his lips while he drinks. But he's afraid he knows what she really thinks. He believes that deep in her heart, she thinks he's the guilty one, because he had the strongest influence on their son. He pushed Gidi to go into a combat unit, always talking about this battle and that war when the family went out together for a drive. Maybe if he hadn't encouraged him to be a fighter on the front line, he'd still be alive.

*

I was in the late stages of pregnancy. My stomach was swollen and crisscrossed with stitches that looked like varicose veins. It turns out that Noa and I had agreed that because she couldn't, I'd do it for her and be – what can I call it – a kind of surrogate father. But suddenly I found myself in Haifa, and my mother, who's in charge of anxiety in our family, felt my stomach and said: Amir, you won't make it. Right then, the space of the dream was filled with the sentence 'you won't make it' in various fonts, with the white sheep that came off Noa's pyjamas squeezed together between the letters, and the warning siren that later turned out to be coming from the alarm clock. When I woke up, I didn't say anything to Noa. Her interpretations of dreams are usually accurate. This time, I was afraid they'd be too accurate.

*

Even now, when I look at that picture, I'm sure it could've turned into a wonderful final project. It's true that, in the end, I didn't find any Arabs and had to photograph a Romanian worker standing in front of a house, but what could I do? Madmoni's Arabs stopped coming because of the border closure, and the other Arabs at the university who I asked to pose mumbled that they were busy. So I found a Romanian with dark skin and gave him a framed black-and-white photo of an Arab house. I posed him in front of a real Arab house in Talbieh. And I asked him to hold the picture against his chest and smile. And I asked him to cry. And I asked him to be angry. I opened the shutter. And I closed it. I knew that it didn't come out exactly like I wanted it to, but I thought it would be enough to get the idea across.

The lecturer, on the other hand, thought it was sloppy and launched into a speech about the fact that anyone who does sloppy work is abusing his art and that we're not great enough to ignore small details. If he'd said that in our third year, I wouldn't have kept quiet, I would've told him that great teachers recognise the heart of the work and don't get bogged down in petty details. But with all the put-downs I'd been getting the last few months that had made me feel as small as a slip of paper, I let him go on. And when he had finished trampling on everything I'd done, Yaniv, who came on to me in our first year, raised his hand and said that even if we ignore the execution, the basic idea is still problematic because art doesn't operate in a vacuum, and doing a project like that at a time when buses are exploding is a bit cynical, especially if the Romanian, excuse me, the Arab, in the photographs is smiling.

I expected there to be uproar in class, that at least one person would defend me and say that the Romanian's smile wasn't cynical but sad, and that there was no better time than now to deal with the subject. But everyone just nodded and the lecturer started to move on to someone else's work, panoramic shots of Austrian forests, and he complimented Tamar Frish on the composition, on the courage it took to photograph in that light, on the meticulous attention to aesthetics that runs through all her work, and I wanted to yell, who cares about Austrian forests? But I knew that anything I said would sound bitter, so I took my bag, got up and walked out of the room and wandered towards the cafeteria because I suddenly felt as if hot chocolate could solve all my problems. But there was some very irritating music playing in the cafeteria, and two drag queens came up to me and shoved invitations to a Purim party into my hand. The year before, I won second place after I'd dressed up as Miss Obsession. I worked on the costume for weeks. I went to second-hand clothes shops, I cut and dyed and sewed, but now those invitations with their screaming colours just annoyed me. I threw them in the rubbish bin and gave up on the hot chocolate because someone I knew was standing in the queue and I was in no mood to hear her ask me how my final project was going. I pushed open the doors, where a poster about the party was hanging, and walked into the driving wind outside – that's what Amir calls strong winds. I wanted that wind to pick me up and carry me away, up over the Augusta Victoria Hospital, over the walls of the Old City and the Golden Dome and put me down gently on a large bed in an expensive hotel, let's say the King David. I waited a few seconds, maybe it would happen, and when it didn't, I zipped my coat up to my neck and trudged towards the station where the number twenty-four bus stops, thinking about what I used to say to people whose work was put down in the first year – remember, there are the pictures hanging on the wall, and there's you and your talent, none of which gets wiped away when someone criticises you, even if the criticism is terrible – and I tried to say all that to myself at the bus stop, but it didn't work. The only thing I could think about was that it was the middle of February already and we had to hand in our final projects in June. If they hadn't approved any of my ideas by now, they wouldn't approve anything and I wouldn't finish the year, I would never graduate and I'd be a waitress till I was fifty, like those pathetic waitresses in American films with that hard look in their eyes, like those people on the bus who don't smile. No one in Jerusalem smiles. I sat down and they all looked at my bag, afraid I'm going to blow up on them. They're right, I am about to explode, but not on them, I muttered to myself, wiping the steam off the window and thinking: if I lived in Rehavia, I'd be home in fifteen minutes. Why did we go to live in the Castel? What would've happened if we'd waited till I graduated, when I could move to Tel Aviv? Why the big hurry to cram ourselves into a small space? And why haven't we been happy lately? Everything between us is so cramped and crushed and cranky. He has bad dreams and doesn't tell me what they are. He just says, I had a bad dream last night, and doesn't describe it. He's so down when he comes back from the club that he can't even tell me why. On the other hand, last night he woke me up and suddenly told me a horrible story about something that happened to him in basic training. He had to stay on the base for the third Saturday in a row. He was so depressed that he couldn't grab on to anything, any song that would help, and he found himself aiming his rifle at his leg so he could fire, be injured, be discharged. It was only thanks to Modi, who ran over at the last minute and shoved the barrel aside, that the bullet hit the wall and not him. Amazing. Amazing how together he looked on that hike when we first met, and actually, until we moved in together, I kept thinking he was a rock. Even now, if he's in the mood, he can hug me until I stop shaking inside, but it's been a long time since he was in the mood. It's been a long time since I felt his tennis player's muscles pressed against my body. And in the shower yesterday, I suddenly felt a twinge of desire, a longing for a simple, single-layered man. Like Liat's Zachi. Someone whose pain won't seep into me. Someone I wouldn't have to be so cautious with. Who'd give me ground so I could take off. Because that's what I want, to create art. And since we've been in this apartment, I can't. Maybe because it's impossible to create when you live with someone. I read an interview with an American writer who said he can't work when there's someone else in the house; that the very presence of his wife, whom he loves, bothers him. So every year he goes to a cabin in the woods for three months, leaves everything and holes up alone. Maybe I need to leave everything too. And maybe not. Maybe I just don't have it, and it's convenient for me to blame it on Amir. After all, without him, I wouldn't have the strength to go on. He's the only one who still believes in me, who really understands me. With Assi and Nadav, my two ex-boyfriends, I always felt that I had to translate everything I wanted to say into a different, more masculine Hebrew. With Amir, we can run hand in hand through the forest of nuances and he makes me laugh when I'm bitter and sings me love songs that he puts my name in, like 'Without love, where would you be,

Noa'. And we have private words that only we understand, like 'worvous', which is a combination of worried and nervous, or 'you're limirossing', which means 'there's a limit, and you're crossing it'. And when I left him a love note on the table a week ago, he called the café and asked for me, then disguised his voice and said that he hadn't been able to sleep at night since he saw me on the street, and when could we meet, and I played the game and said, tonight, and he asked where? I said, in bed, and when I got home, he was waiting for me outside on the Zakians' steps the way he used to. Oof, I thought and got off the bus, let him be waiting on the steps for me now. Let him open his arms for me. Let him comfort me. Let him whisper things in my ear the way he knows how. I closed my eyes and imagined his smell, the taste of his smell. I imagined how he'd hold me and I'd bury my nose in the hollow between his shoulder and his neck, and sniff.

But no one was waiting on the steps, and when I opened the door and he came over to hug me, the only smell coming from him, from his shirt, was the smell of the club: cigarettes, sweat, loneliness, and a new element I didn't know what to call. I didn't say anything about the smell because I remembered how he responded the last time I did that. I gave him a quick, cursory hug, and he said, what's this, a brief military hug, and I said, that's all there is. Then I was sorry for the tone, for the content and the timing, and reached out to stroke his cheek in compensation, but it was too late.

*

I didn't shave. I always shave before I go to the club, even if there's no more shaving cream, but this time it completely slipped my mind. I realised it on the Mevasseret bridge, but I thought that if I went back I'd be late. So I kept driving, running my fingers over the stubble, and then I started having other thoughts. No one at the club said anything about the stubble. Nava gave me a very significant look, as usual. Shmuel greeted me enthusiastically, as if a week ago he hadn't accused me of causing him pain, and the devotees of the crossword puzzle group asked me impatiently when we could start.

We started quickly. That conversation with Shmuel still stung me, and hanging the crossword on the wall and escaping to the definitions was just what I needed.

Two down, five letters. The capital of Ecuador.

Quito. That's right, Gideon.

One across, four letters. The symbol of peace.

Dove. Right.

Five across, four letters. The opposite of despair.

Hope. Very good, Malka. What did you say, Gideon? Love? But love is with a 'v', and our third letter is 'p'.

Gideon got up. What difference does it make, he suddenly yelled, what difference does it make if it's a 'v' or a 'p'? Just write what I tell you. The group waited tensely for what I would say. If I'd been feeling myself, it would have ended there. I would have given in and fixed it later. But I was having one of those days when the ground was splitting open under me. So I insisted.

I won't write love here, I told Gideon, because it's wrong and it'll mess up the rest of the puzzle.

He got up, walked around me contemptuously and tore the card off the wall. Who are you to tell us what's right and what's wrong? He threw the puzzle on to the floor. Look at what you look like! Not shaved, a stain on your shirt. You look like a crazy man, so where do you get off pretending to be normal, huh?

I rubbed my stubble in embarrassment and looked at the members of the group, hoping they'd come to my rescue. But they thought the whole scene was entertaining. They grinned admiringly at Gideon and he, encouraged by their support, stamped on the puzzle, covering the card with the imprint of his soles and screamed: we don't want your puzzles! We don't want you. Get out of here!

I looked at the door – maybe Shmuel would hear the screaming and come to defend me. Maybe he'd stand at my side with his cracked glasses. But Nava came in instead.

Is everything all right? she asked, looking from me to Gideon to the crushed puzzle on the floor.

Nothing's all right, Gideon answered her. The quality of the students gets lower every year, and this year it's the lowest. You brought us a crazy student. Look at him, look at the way he looks. Not shaved. He should be a member of this club, not an instructor.

Murmurs of agreement came from the group. Traitors, I thought. I'd sat with every one of them for hours. I'd listened to Malka's hatred of her sister, to Amatzia the vacillator's sexual fantasies, to Joe's paranoia about the General Security Service. And the minute I need them, they turn their backs on me.

These students invest a great deal of time in you, I heard Nava say to Gideon in an authoritative voice, and what you are doing now is completely unfair. Gideon shrank into himself, rebuked. I suggest that we disperse the demonstration, Nava said, looking at me. I don't see much point in continuing with the group at the moment. I gave a slight, confirming nod. The members of the group filed out of the room. On the way out, each one of them gave me a look, as if they still expected the *coup de grâce* I was supposed to give to Gideon, but it stuck in my throat.

Amatzia the vacillator was the last one out, and a second later he came back in, pointed to the floor and said: but what about the puzzle? Who'll solve it? An unsolved crossword puzzle is not good! Then he turned on his heel and went out.

Nava gave a quick look to make sure he wasn't coming back this time, and said, I can see that you just went through an unpleasant experience. Yes, I admitted. Her eyes were soft and understanding, and for the first time since I started volunteering at the club, I felt that I could share something important with her. That I wanted to. I think they're especially sensitive now because of the tension all around us, in the country, she said, and her look went back to being professional and cold. And also, maybe you're having a problem with limits. But I suggest we talk about it during our training session, OK?

OK. No problem. Of course. I understand.

The window of opportunity closed. I was left alone in the room. I picked up the crossword and tried to fold it, but all I did was tear it some more. There was nothing I could do. I had to throw it away and make a new one for next week. Not that anyone would come to do a puzzle next week. All of them know now that the student from the crossword puzzle group is crazy. *He should be a member of this club, not an instructor.* Gideon's words pounded at my temples. Maybe he's right. What actually is the difference between me and them? Everything they feel, I feel, only at a slightly lower volume. I'm like Dan, shifting back and forth between elation and depression. I'm like Amatzia the vacillator, who's always thinking one thing and its opposite at the same time. And I'm like Shmuel, feeling Noa's sun, on her bad days at Bezalel, radiating beams that pierce my skin and burn me on the inside. Like them, I've been displaced, a man without roots, pretending to be confident but swept away with every wind. A thin line separates me from them, and I've crossed that one too. In basic training. If Modi hadn't been there to save me, I would've ended up on the army shrink's sofa, and who knows, I might've wound up here, a member of the Helping Hand Club.

I took the drawing pins off the board, and for a minute, I wanted to press them between my hands till they bled, but I put them and the Scotch tape into my bag and thought: what the hell am I going to do for the two hours until the training session? How do I go out of this room now and look those people in the eye? Shmuel will probably want to talk, and he won't remember my name again.

He'll comb his hair from side to side again and complain about how full of pain I am and how bad that makes him feel. No. I won't be able to take it standing up. Or sitting down. It's too much for me. Much too much. I have to get out of here. Fast. Wait a second, the voice of reason flickered. If you go now without waiting for the training session, you can forget about a recommendation from Nava at the end of the year. How can she recommend someone who can't cope? Fuck coping, a different voice answered. There's no chance she'll recommend me anyway, in light of the darkness between us. And besides, who wants to be a psychologist? My image wants it, all the girls I've known who always told me I should be a psychologist want it. But do *I* really want it? The only thing I want to do, that I have to do, is leave. Now.

I took my bag, left the room, ignored Nava's raised eyebrow and Shmuel the Cracked, who was coming over to me. I didn't answer Ronen and Chanit, who'd stopped their flirting for a minute and called out to me. I signalled a quick no with my hand to Joe, who was on his way over to me with a draught board. I went up the steps and made way for Gideon, who was just coming back from the bathroom and ignored me as if the fight we'd had was all in my head. And maybe it was? Maybe I hallucinated the whole thing? I thought, and felt a slight dizziness that threatened to toss me down the steps, but I kept climbing, stopped to breathe, leaned on the right-hand wall, leaned on the left-hand wall, until I was out in the open air, in the deserted park, and started running down the street, running, running, not knowing where.

*

And these are troubled times. In Lebanon, cannon blasts resound. At Ben Gurion airport, there are no tourists to be found. Agricultural projects have been halted and cucumbers tremble in the cold. Abu Dhabi has broken off diplomatic relations (please Abu Dhabi, take us back into the fold). Jerusalem is celebrating its three thousandth anniversary, but no one comes to the celebration. The suits, who can't agree on a date for the elections, can barely hide their frustration. A Jordanian couple who named their son Rabin flee to Israel to escape their countrymen's ire. An unemployed man attacks a social worker with an axe. Children dream about terrorist attacks. And on the bridge to Mevasseret, a white cloud of thought appears, large and clear: for a minute, only a minute, it seemed that things could have been different here.

*

I held the letter that came for Amir and Noa, but I didn't want to throw it to them through the hole. I wanted to listen.

And we have to throw out that picture, Noa said. I could finally hear her clearly.

What's your problem with that picture? Amir asked her. His voice was strange. Different from the voice I know. Shakier.

It drags us both down, Noa said. It's like the nymph of grief enticing us to drown.

Come on, Noa, a man is sitting on a bed and looking out the window. Where do you see drowning here? Amir said, and his voice moved away a little. I pictured them standing in front of the picture with their hands on their hips.

Look at his shoulders, Noa said. Look at how they're drooping. And the hands are so heavy. He isn't even looking at us. He's looking out. That's why you hold on to this picture, because he always wants to be outside, like you.

He doesn't want to be outside, Noa, he misses something.

Do you miss something too?

Always.

What do you miss now?

You.

I miss you too, Amir.

But I'm here.

No, I miss the way you were before we moved to this apartment.

How was I?

I don't know, Noa said. Rounder. I imagined that there was a big, warm circle in your body.

Sorry to disappoint you, but I also have corners. When people tell me I'm crazy, I can't help it, but I just can't round off the corners of that.

*

I covered the hole and leaned against the wall. What happened to the way they were yelling before? How can they suddenly be talking to each other so nicely, suddenly so understanding. I never had a conversation like that with Moshe. He misses her, she misses him. So what's their problem? And who said he's crazy? And why were they smashing glass half an hour ago?

I uncovered the hole again. I know it's not nice, but I couldn't control myself.

*

And what about you? Why don't you dance any more? Amir asked.

But I do.

When?

When you're not home.

Why? Do I bother you?

No, I just have more room when you're not here.

But you have an aerodynamic build.

God, Amir, it's not physical. It's more of a feeling.

So maybe I'll leave, and you'll have lots or room. Endless room.

Do you see how you always want to take off?

OK.

That last 'OK' of Amir's was a killer, and I was waiting for the action to start again, for them to yell and break glasses and plates. The question even crossed my mind what would happen if Noa leaves and Amir stays in the apartment alone, and his landlady goes to comfort him, and that made me angry at myself. Enough, Sima, what's wrong with you, and I covered the hole in the wall once and for all and went to the kitchen to load the dishwasher and wash the sink, but I had one ear cocked to hear what was happening on the other side of the wall. They talked for another few minutes, first him, then her, then him. Then it was quiet, as if they'd left the house. But the door didn't open and I didn't hear footsteps on the tiles. And then, a few minutes later, I heard those sounds that Noa makes, the ones that give me a twinge down below, and I started to picture them lying in bed together, his long white body on hers, hiding it. Or maybe she's lying on top of him, leaning on his strong shoulders, kissing his completely hairless chest, the kind of smooth chest I love. And maybe he's lying on her back – who knows what those two could be doing – maybe he's lying on her back, holding on to her hips, those narrow hips of hers, and . . .

Lilach started crying like she always does when she hears those noises of Noa's. I went and picked her up. Her body was hot, but mine was hotter.

*

As if this were the last time. Holding on with our fingernails, with our feet, clinging to anything we can to keep from slipping. I press her tightly to me, the way people hug each other at the airport before one of them goes up the escalator, and she coils around me, gets entangled with me, turns me on my back, on her back, and then, using my little finger as a brush, I slowly paint a line from her cheek to her collarbone, the way she likes me to, circles, circles, a kiss, circles, circles, sucking. She draws me inside. First my tongue is swallowed up, then my cheeks, my mouth and now my whole head is inside her, my thoughts are inside her, my memories are inside her. I pull myself out by the skin of my teeth and bite my shoulder, then hers, and she says aiee. Then she says, look into my eyes, and she pulls my head up so I'm facing her and I look into her eyes and feel like a cheat, even though I've never cheated on her. I dive into her neck to hide and she trembles slightly, chilled, but she insists, look into my eyes, Amir. I rise along the serpentine path from her neck to her cheeks until our faces are level again, my nose facing hers, and she smiles. I love your eyes when you're horny, they shoot yellow sparks as if smoke is about to come out of them. I blink in embarrassment like a model and say, thanks. Now that she's said that, I feel like my eyes really are burning, that the sheet, the blanket, the wardrobe are about to catch fire and the flames will spread to the living room and burn the picture of the sad man, who'll try to escape through the window but won't make it. The flames will pass through the hole for the water heater switch to Sima and Moshe, to the empty lot, to Yotam. Come, Noa says, saving me from the fire, come to me. I hesitate for a minute just to make her crazy, draw circles around her bellybutton with my tongue, licking it as if it were an ice-cream cone, kiss the inside of her thighs once, twice and then, when I can't go on any more and she pulls my Samson-like hair, come up here, come on, I toss aside a corner of the blanket – and come.

When it all collapses, she gets up quickly and heads for the bathroom. Where are you running off to? I ask her. She apologises, so there won't be an infection, you know. And I think, it's not because of any infection, it's because we can't stay together in the same air for more than a few minutes, and I say to her, watch out for the pieces of glass. She remembers and says, oh yes, I still can't believe you did that. I chuckle and say, don't forget that I'm half Greek. And half frightened, she says, I still don't believe it. At least put on your slippers, I insist and throw her one of hers and one of mine. She puts them both on and walks out. I stay in bed and cover myself with the blanket. All the images of our fight pass through my mind, and I don't know whether to be happy that I finally fell apart or to be scared that I fell apart into such small pieces. Somehow, as the minutes pass and Noa doesn't come back, the emotional scale shifts more towards being scared and I think, maybe she and I really do need to take a break. This apartment closes in on us, squeezes each one of us into our own dark corner. What was that supposed to be, that blind rage that is so not part of my image? A sensitive psychologist is supposed to contain everything. A sensitive psychologist doesn't use words to hurt, doesn't expose his nasty side like that, and he never ever breaks plates. Fuck, maybe I really do need some distance so I can calm down. Terrific, Amir! I rebuke myself. You haven't run away in a while. You haven't moved in a while. The women are different, but the story is the same. You're just addicted to it. Addicted to muscles tensing up so you can take off. To the magic you use on new people who don't know you. But no, I won't let you push away the only woman who ever really got close to you. The only woman you let touch that black lump of yours, even stroke it.

Make room, Noa says, back from the shower and already wearing her sheep pyjamas. I squeeze up against the wall and lift the blanket a little so she can get in. Her face is very serious, her forehead wrinkled in a frown. I can feel her thoughts scratching at the edge of my consciousness, almost forming words, but I won't ask her what she's thinking about so she won't ask me.

Will you pick up the pieces of glass and put them in the bin later? she asks, and I nod. We have to buy new plates, she says, we won't have any to eat on. Yes, I say, and the bad buzzing that stopped when we had sex, the old buzzing that always stops when we have sex, is standing between us again. She turns her back to me and I think, what if this time I really do have to get up and go and all this talk about addiction is just a smokescreen, the fog of war, psychological warfare that I use against myself so I won't see the bitter truth that it's been awful between us lately, and if you think about it, we were never really good together, except for the first sweet-as-honey weeks, and maybe even the first month in this apartment. And there were a few days after Hanukkah. Fuck, the swing keeps swinging and I can't think anything without the opposite popping right up in my mind. The line is blurred between right and wrong, between one person and another, between us and the whole mess around us, the explosions, the retaliations. They sold us a bill of goods about thick, clear, solid lines. It's a lie. Everything's blurred. Look, even the line between sanity and insanity. One minute I'm healthy and authoritative, and the next minute I'm not shaved and they pull me over to their side, the sick side, like in a kids' game when they draw a chalk line, take your hand and try to pull you over it. But there isn't even a line here; at the most a small asterisk. A small asterisk separates me from the other me, a small asterisk that fades so easily and bam, like in basic training, before I can breathe or defend myself, my chest collapses back towards my ears, my back itches with anxiety, my throat fills up with glass, and a scream gathers in my temples, crazy, crazy, crazy.

Meanwhile, Noa is already breathing deeply, asleep. And the buzzing stops. The buzzing between us always stops when she falls asleep and I feel suddenly quiet too. A stream begins to flow inside me, like in the Ehud Banai song, and now I can bend towards her and whisper words of love in her ear. I tell her that our souls are intertwined and there is no other woman like her and I desire her always, always and without shame. And it's all true. She smiles in her sleep and I kiss her cheek, her earlobe, and raise myself up and over her carefully, so I won't step on her. I put on slippers, one of mine, which fits, and one of hers, which is too tight. I pull the broom out from behind the refrigerator and start sweeping up the pieces of broken plates I threw on the floor when our fight was at its most furious and I yelled, I don't want to hear about your final project now! I don't! It's amazing how far the pieces flew. There are some near the door and some behind the TV and under the sofa. And there's one piece near Modi's letter, which I see now for the first time. That's weird. When did Sima toss it in? Did she wait until we were finished? Did she hear it all? Who cares. Let her hear. Let her think I'm crazy. That's what they think at the Helping Hand. So who cares. The main thing is that I have a letter from Modi. I can put the broom aside for a minute. Sit down in the armchair alone. And read.

*

Amigo,

I have to tell you something. The best thing would be if you were here and I could actually tell you this, but letters are all we have for the time being and I have to share. So here goes. Keep quiet and read.

Her name's Nina, and she's Czech. She's gorgeous, something like Olga, that Russian girl who was a year behind us in high school, but much classier. We met at the agency that arranges one or two-day treks to the nearby volcano, Pacaya. We were both waiting in the queue for the agent to finish with a large group of Germans. There were aerial photos of the volcano hanging on the wall behind her, but no matter how hard I tried to look at them, I couldn't. My eyes were drawn to her over and over again, devouring another detail each time. The snub nose. The Greta Garbo eyebrows. The section of statuesque white neck (sorry for the poetic language, but after examining it up close, I can tell you that her neck really is a masterpiece). And the weird thing was that she had her eye on me too. To this day, I don't understand what she saw in me, but it looks like there's a type of girl whose taste runs to overgrown Israeli guys

243

with messy hair. Anyway, she looked at me and I looked at her, and the longer we had to wait, the longer and more openly we looked at each other. Then, when I'm in the middle of trying to figure out how to translate all the opening lines I know into English, the door to the agency suddenly opens and a skinny guy in ripped jeans walks in, sits down next to my future wife and starts talking to her in some strange language. I don't believe it, I muttered to myself, I have such shitty luck. When I finally find a girl who does it for me, she's with someone? I got up and started pacing around the room, nervous out of my mind. Back and forth, back and forth.

Excuse me, are you also interested in the trip to Pacaya? her asshole, Jew-hating boyfriend asked me in English.

Yes, I said curtly.

When?

Tomorrow. You too?

We started talking. *Muchillero* small talk in English. Turns out they're Czech. Turns out they've been travelling for two months already. They did Ecuador and Peru, and now they'd cut over to Guatemala, like me. True, not many Czechs travel. The Czechs don't have money. Their economy's down the toilet. But ever since they were kids, he and his sister had this crazy thing about Indians, and they worked their asses off for five years so they could travel. His sister?!! Now that I looked at them, there really was a resemblance. Something about the nose. Then I worked up the courage and asked her, how are you enjoying the trip? She doesn't know English, her brother apologised for her, just Czech and Russian. He'll translate my question for her. She gave a long answer and looked into my eyes during her whole speech.

Before he could translate, the agent called us to the counter. The three of us signed up for the next day's group and set a time to meet later for dinner at the only restaurant in town.

When I got to the restaurant, shaved and wearing the only unstained shirt I had, she was sitting alone at a table. In English, I asked her where her brother was, and she spread her hands to the sides as if to say, 'I have no idea what you just said, but it sounded interesting.' I pointed to the empty chair next to her and made half a circle with my hand to mean 'Where?' Aah . . . She looked relieved. She rested her cheek in her palm. He was probably sleeping.

On the one hand, I was glad. No one would keep us from creating a romantic atmosphere. On the other hand, how can there be a romantic atmosphere if we can't talk? The waitress came over. Nina ordered the huge salad that was pictured on the menu and I ordered *churrasco*, which is a cheap, local combo of meat, rice, beans, bananas and avocado.

When the waitress left, we stared at the tablecloth and laughed in embarrassment. Turns out that we both thought the situation was funny (and on top of all of Nina's great qualities, she also has dimples). After we calmed down, she caught my eye and then, for a long while, she just didn't let me avoid her look. She hypnotised me into that blue-grey lake until I forgot we were sitting in a restaurant and there were dozens of people around us, and for a minute I thought we were the only two people in the world, and also (you'll probably think I'm crazy) that I was swimming. I had a real physical sensation of swimming and almost started making paddling movements in the middle of the restaurant. When I felt like I was starting to drown, I shifted my eyes.

Before I could feel embarrassed, she pulled her Walkman out of her bag, put the earphones gently over my ears – lightly grazing my cheeks – and pressed the play button. Classical music filled my head, actually something light, with sprightly flutes and triangles and an over-active trombone. Dvorak, she said, pointing to the

Walkman. Dvorak, I said, nodding slightly, as if I'd known Dvorak since I was a kid. I had the feeling she'd given me that Dvorak to hear not only because it was pretty, but also to let me know – without words – what she was feeling. So I leaned down and pulled out my Discman with a flourish. I looked through my CDs for one that would suit the occasion, and finally picked Machina's *'Children's Story'*: 'The prince is in love with a golden-haired princess'. I'd never have the balls to play a song like that for an Israeli girl on a first date, but with a Czech girl, in a different country, what could happen? She listened, and the second time the chorus rang out, she hummed along with it in gibberish.

Meanwhile, the waitress came over with our food. And you know, bro, how I eat ('Like a disturbed child with no co-ordination.' That's how Noa described it, right?) To cut a long story short, I pulled out my best manners. I didn't stick my elbows into the sauce. I cut the meat slowly with my knife like a boy in a British boarding-school. But I must have got a little carried away, because after we'd been eating quietly for a few minutes, she burst into semi-asthmatic laughter and imitated me eating, so serious and focused on my mission. Then I imitated her, the way she took a little taste of each kind of vegetable but didn't actually eat anything. And that's how we started a lively dialogue with our hands, our thumbs, our eyes, our eyebrows, our necks and our intuition. What can I tell you, Marcel Marceau is Louis de Funès compared to what went on there. The funniest thing was that at some point, during one of the breaks, I looked around and saw that we were the most talkative couple in the restaurant. The other four couples – two locals and two tourists – sat across from each other without talking and looked up at the ceiling or stared at the menu, bored.

Later, we walked to my room. On the way, we ate burnt corn on sticks, even though *The Lonely Planet* doesn't recommend it. While we waited for them to heat the corn, she rubbed her hands together, so I gave her my coat to wear (chivalry, an international language). In return, she gave me a wet kiss on the cheek and wound her hand around my waist after we finished eating and started walking again.

About what actually happened in my room, I have only one thing to say: I'm speechless.

We've been together since then, six nights already. And I'm not bored even for a minute. What would Yossi Chersonski say (if Nina and I were a performance and he was reviewing us)? 'Original? Yes. Suitable for everyone? Questionable.' I have no idea how long it can last, this 'no words necessary' thing (remember how they used to write that under drawings in the newspaper?). All I know is that two of my biggest screw-ups in love, including Adi, were because of words spoken at the wrong time, and that this quiet lets me listen to Nina more than I've ever listened to any other woman I've been with. I listen to her nostrils (when they get a little wider, it means she wants me), her dimples (there are sad dimples and happy dimples, and I've learned to tell the difference). I listen to her walk, to her sudden stops. And I always listen to her inner music.

What is inner music?

Aha!

Funny you should ask, because I've just developed an interesting theory (when you don't talk all day, you have a lot of time to develop theories).

This is how it goes: everyone has his own basic internal music that's always playing inside his body, with the volume turned down, and that music is what determines the pace at which he thinks, loves, writes and gets enthusiastic (I just added the enthusiastic thing because of my inner music). If you stop reading and close your eyes for a minute, you can hear your own inner music (or the upstairs neighbour yelling at her kids). Anyway, that inner music affects the kind of external music we like. Usually, people look for external music that goes well with their inner music. For example, someone who's full of wild music will buy CDs that fit that wildness, that give it the appropriate background, that balance it without being too different from it. Someone whose inner music is full of hidden tension will seek external music that'll dissolve the tension. The same thing is true of people. If you think people choose their mates because of the way they look or how much money they have or how clever they are, you're wrong big time. A first date is actually a concert. People eat, drink, recite their CVs to each other, but the whole time, they're really only listening to the inner music of the person sitting across from them. They see whether they can play their music together, hit the right chords, and only then do their hearts decide. Later too, couples don't stay together because they have interesting conversations or because she's different enough from his mother or he's similar enough to her father, but because their inner music fits together over time, and if it doesn't, if it's too similar or too different or too noisy, the courts won't help. And relationship counselling won't help. At some point, it'll be grating, either to him or to her.

Or not. All theories flounder when it comes to love. Like, you write to me that instead of bringing you closer, the apartment in the Castel only pushes you and Noa farther apart. Does that make sense? OK, she's blocked on her final project and you're upset about the club, but you still go to sleep together and eat spaghetti with student-style sauce and scream 'Nirvana Unplugged' together (I got it here from some American, truly a fantastic CD). Don't you?

I hope it works out for you. Don't throw it all away and stop playing music together. After all, like you wrote, Noa gets into your soul the way no other girl ever did before. And she's wild about you. I saw the way she looks at you when you talk. And I saw the way you look at her when she dances. Ah! That's the problem with these letters. The crazy delay. I'm writing these things about Noa, and who knows what might have happened by the time you get it. And with me too. I'm writing to you about Nina, and by the time you get this letter, she might be back in the Czech Republic.

Meanwhile, thank God, she's sleeping in my bed. The blanket's trapped between her legs and she's hugging the pillow. Her inner music – slightly indistinct, slightly drifting – keeps playing even in her dreams (what is she dreaming about?).

I'm sitting on the table and carving on it so that later I'll have proof this week really happened. (I hear you saying, so you actually do need words. There's something to that.) Through the window, I can hear an occasional rumble from the direction of the volcano. The last time it erupted was two years ago. The city was covered in ash and people breathed through surgical masks. Ever since, there's a disaster-on-the-way feeling in the streets, and every time the volcano gives a little cough, people stop and cross themselves (they believe that the volcano is a god, the god of fire, and that the Christian cross works with him too. It's amazing how everything's all mixed together here.).

Anyway, tomorrow morning we're leaving for Lake Atitlan, so I hope the volcano won't erupt tonight, our last night here.

I hope I didn't dump too much stuff on you (I just had to speak Hebrew with someone).

(And I'm sorry about all the parentheses in this letter. I just reread it and got scared.)

Love,
Modi

P.S. (I remembered something important.) What's happening with Hapoel? The last time you filled me in, we were in fifth place. How far down have we gone since then?

*

I have an exam, Amir said. But you promised, I reminded him in my most poor-me voice. Besides, this is the last time Hapoel is playing at Teddy this year! No it isn't, he said, trying to argue with me, there's still the state cup games. You're wrong, I insisted, even if both teams get to the semi-finals, the game'll be in Ramat Gan, not Jerusalem. You know what, he said, you're right, but I still didn't think he was convinced, so I thought the word 'yes' really hard like I used to do when I wanted Gidi to take me to a game. I'd repeat the word 'yes' in my mind four straight times. And Amir really did smile and say OK, but on one condition, and I thought he was going to say that I had to behave better in school because it was hard enough for my mother and father as it was. But instead, all he said was, I want you to swear that you won't tell anyone in the stands that I'm a Hapoel fan, or else I'm a goner. I laughed, put my hand on my shirt pocket and said OK, I swear. On Saturday, wearing my black trousers and yellow shirt and the scarf he bought me, I knocked on the door and Noa opened it and said, we've been waiting for you, and asked me to come in. Today's the big day, isn't it, she said. Amir suddenly popped out from behind her and said, yes, today's the big day for Shalom Tikvah, three-nil for Hapoel thirty minutes into the game. You wish, I said, three-nil for Beitar, three goals for Ohana. Noa said, you're both losers, and Amir started jumping and singing, 'He's a loser, he's a loser, he's a loser'. I sang along with him, waving my scarf around my head like a cowboy, and Noa said, I have to get this on film. I thought that was a cool idea, and I started posing for the camera, holding my scarf stretched out between my hands like on TV, but Amir suddenly stopped jumping and said in a not very nice tone, you don't have to photograph everything, you can just remember. Noa got insulted and

250

said, OK, I won't bother you, and went into the kitchen. All of a sudden, I remembered the note she wrote to him about how, lately, their words get tangled up, and I wanted to make peace between them. Right then and there, I wanted to make them link their fingers and make up, but I thought that if I couldn't do it with my parents, why should I be able to do it with them. So I decided to forget the idea and said to Amir, are we going? Come on, he said, and opened the door. He didn't say goodbye to Noa, so I said it for him, bye, and Noa yelled from the kitchen, have a good time! Then he said thanks, but a weak, fake kind of thanks, and hurried me out the door, saying so what are you waiting for? I was already thinking, is this how he's going to act all day? What a downer. But the minute we got into the car, he went right back to being nice. He turned on the radio and said, I'm really in the mood for football now. You scored on this one, Yotam, it's a great idea. You know the last time I went to a game? Five years ago, the derby between Hapoel and Maccabee. We lost four-nil. And I said, Beitar won in the last game I saw. They beat Maccabee Haifa two-nil. And Gidi was still alive then, I thought, I still had a brother then. As if he was reading my mind, Amir asked, who'd you go with, Gidi? I said yes and remembered how Gidi would always ignore me on the way to the game because he didn't want his friends to think he was a nerd. But the minute we walked into the stadium, he'd forget that and say, listen up, Yoti, from now on, you don't leave my side, and he'd give me his hand and make a path for me through the crowd and make sure I had a place to sit and no one pushed me. Once, when some tough guy stepped on me by accident, he grabbed him by the collar and said, hey moron, watch where you're going. The tough guy poked him and they started shoving each other. Everyone in the stands stood up to see. But right then, Harazi scored a goal for Beitar and everyone was so happy that they jumped up and hugged each other, even Gidi and the tough guy, and Gidi said to him, the main thing is that we win the championship. And the tough guy said, and the state cup too.

*

He's remembering Gidi now. I know what colour his eyes are when that happens. I don't know whether to comfort him, to coax out the memory or change the subject. So I keep quiet. At times like this, I think that our relationship is a little risky. After all, I'll leave the Castel in the end. And then what? Isn't it enough that Gidi disappeared on him, do I have to disappear on him too? Enough, I flog myself and cross another traffic light, you can't let fear of separation determine everything.

Park here, on the pavement, Yotam suggests.

Isn't it a little too far? I wonder.

Everything closer is taken, he says with the confidence of someone who's been here a lot.

Once, I remember, I took a girl to the beach at night and at a certain point she stopped and kissed me and pulled me under some thatched shelter. Something about her movements, something' about how confidently she spread the blanket under us told me that she was recreating what had happened before, right there, with someone else.

This way is shorter, Yotam says, pulling me along a side path, and I obey. We are carried along towards the stadium on a huge wave of fans. We're surrounded by big flags around us, hats and scarves. All of them yellow and black. But still, I start to feel the thrill of the excitement I used to feel when I was surrounded by Hapoel red flags, hats and scarves.

Wanna buy sunflower seeds? I suggest. But he feels more like an ice lolly. A yellow one, right? What else. I buy him a lemon ice lolly and a raspberry one for myself so I can have at least one red thing after I left all the others at home.

Someone practises playing his *zambura*, and the crowd

shoving its way to the ticket booth answers with a weak 'olé'. We already have tickets. I bought them on Thursday so we wouldn't have to queue and get pushed and shoved. But there's a huge crowd trying to push through the gate too, so I put Yotam in front of me and wrap my arms around him to protect him. How thin he is, I think. How fragile and full of bones. We move ahead slowly. Brakes. A step. Brakes. The policemen are stressed out after all the recent terrorist attacks and spend hours checking everyone who goes in. *Yallah, odrob*, come on, move it, the game's starting soon, complains a father whose son is perched on his shoulders. What do you want from them, they're only doing their job, a pair of identical twins standing behind him have a go at him. I wonder what Yotam and I look like to them, the thought flashes through my mind. Father and son? Brothers?

The guy taking tickets takes my two and tears them. The way they tear football tickets reminds me of the way a son whose father has died tears his shirt to symbolise a heart broken in anguish, and I shove the tickets right down into my pocket.

We go inside.

The fans' songs resound strongly now, shaking the concrete walls and the heart. Confetti rain is falling on us from nowhere, washing away all thoughts. There's no club. No Noa. No itch. Football is such pure fun.

Yotam breaks free of my grasp and runs up the steps. I skip after him and roar silently: Go reds go! Go reds go!

*

That's the really cool thing – when you go up the steps and all of a sudden you see the whole field and the fans sitting in the stands on the other side and the players warming up. Like in Eilat, when you go into the water with your snorkel and – boom! you see all the fish and coral all at once.

There are no Hapoel fans here at all, Amir said, standing

next to me. I put a finger on my lips to remind him he's at Teddy. Right, he said, slapping himself on the forehead. Then he whispered in my ear, you have to teach me a few of your songs fast so they don't figure out what I am. There's the song, 'O-hana', I started to explain to him, and while I was talking, he led us to two empty seats in the middle of the stands. A tall guy was sitting in front of us and Amir asked him to change seats with his friend because 'the kid', which was me, couldn't see. Moshe Sinai walked past under the VIP stand on his way to the Hapoel bench and all the fans got up and sang rude songs at him. Amir smiled at me, but I could see that he was a little pissed off about it. Then the fans unfurled a huge flag from the bottom of the stands to the top, each one grabbing the edge and passing it to the person behind him. It was dark under the flag, and hot and smelly. Amir bent over and whispered in my ear, I don't believe that I'm under a Beitar flag. Next time, we go to Bloomfield. Fine, I said, happy that there was a 'next time' in our plans.

Then the game started and everyone yelled at everyone else: sit down! sit down! But no one wanted to be the sucker who'd sit down first, so they all stayed standing. During the first half, there were mainly fouls. The referee kept whistling and taking out yellow cards. No one kicked in the direction of the goals except for one corner that Pishont kicked which almost hit the net by mistake. The fans, who had sung a lot of songs before the game, gradually got quiet, sat down and started cracking sunflower seeds. They didn't get up again until half-time, when Moshe Sinai walked past under the stands on his way to the locker room and they threw plastic bottles at him and swore at him. There'll be goals in the second half, Amir promised. Ours, I said, and remembered a Yehuda Barkan candid camera programme I had seen that week.

I didn't tell Amir about it so he wouldn't get scared. On the programme, they put a Maccabee Haifa fan into the

Beitar stands wearing a yellow shirt over a green Maccabee Haifa shirt. After a few minutes, he took off the yellow shirt and started cheering for Maccabee Haifa in the middle of the Beitar stands, wearing green. Wow, did he get smacked around. They took him to the hospital and he had to have about ten stitches.

Just don't let Hapoel score, I prayed silently. I wouldn't want Amir to have to get stitches.

But as soon as the second half started, that's exactly what happened.

Shmulik Levy lost a ball on the side closest to us and Alon Ofir ran down the line almost to the corner and then kicked. Kornfein ran out to stop the ball, but Nissim Avitan jumped higher than him and butted the ball into the net.

Suddenly, the whole stadium was quiet. Complete silence. Like right after Adina, our form teacher, shouts that if we don't quiet down, she'll give us a test.

I looked at Amir. I hoped he wouldn't say anything. I prayed he wouldn't do anything. But he did. He opened his mouth and yelled.

*

Why?! Why?! Why?!

That's what I yelled. I was bursting with happiness about Hapoel's fantastic goal and I couldn't keep it inside, so instead of yelling 'Yes!' I found myself yelling 'Why?! Why?! Why?!' Three earsplitting shouts that thundered through the stunned stands. Yotam looked at me worriedly. A few heads turned towards me in puzzlement. How, I kept yelling, how did you let them score a goal like that?! Because we have lousy defence, someone sitting two rows below us answered. Because the coach is shit, someone sitting above us said. A bunch of fans got up and started singing to the coach: resign, resign, resign. The Beitar players looked embarrassed. The Hapoel players went right into a bunker defence. A little one-nil. That's all we need. That's our speciality. For years. Towards the end of the game, Beitar did have a few chances.

Abucsis kicked two balls that whistled over the goal, and Yotam grabbed his head in frustration. I patted him on the shoulder with a winner's generosity. Wait, he said, it's not over yet. But a second after he said that, the referee whistled the end of the game and the Hapoel players hugged Moshe Sinai and ran quickly to the locker rooms so the flying plastic bottles wouldn't land on their heads. Fans hung on the fences and swore at them, and when they'd all left the field and there was no one left to insult, the stadium started to empty out. Yotam and I waited in our seats till the last fan had gone. We sat there staring at the sunflower seed shells, the ice lolly wrappers and the special editions of the fans' newspaper published in honour of the game that were now being trampled on by the crowd.

We didn't talk on the way to the car. As a Hapoel fan, I know how you feel after a loss: you have no strength for anything, especially not a conversation with a fan of the winning team. But when we started driving, I said to Yotam, don't worry, it's not over yet. There are still seven more rounds to go. He said, yes, but we're really awful. And I agreed, yes, you really are pretty bad. Then he imitated me, why?! Why?! why?! Why are they so awful?! We both laughed hysterically while we drove. My nose started running and my eyes were so full of tears that I could hardly see the road. And every time I thought I was calming down, he started again: Why?! Why?! Why?! And I started bellowing all over again. God, that was funny, I said when we stopped at a light. Yes, he said, I can't wait to tell . . . and he stopped.

Gidi? I asked, and all the laughter drained out of me like water in a bath after you pull out the plug.

Yes, he said. I tell him things sometimes. I go to the empty lot and talk to him, but it's OK, you don't have to tell me he's dead and doesn't hear me. I know.

Do you miss him? I asked, realising that this was the first direct question I'd asked him about his brother.

Sometimes, he answered, pressing a finger against the window as if he wanted to leave a print on the glass.

I almost asked, when do you miss him especially? but I wasn't sure it was a good idea to draw him into that kind of conversation, as if he were a repressed adult who needed help opening up. If he wanted to talk, he would.

He kept his finger pressed against the glass, and we drove the rest of the way home like that, in silence. I parked the car, then turned and looked at him. He looked exhausted. His hair was all messed up, the front of his yellow t-shirt was stained, probably from the ice lolly, and instead of opening the door, he sank deeper and deeper into the seat.

Everything OK? I asked.

He nodded. Too slowly.

Is it because we talked about Gidi?

No.

Because Beitar lost?

No.

So what happened?!

He played with the seatbelt, tightening it and loosening it. Tightening and loosening. I took mine off and reached for the door – not so I could get out, just to open the window and let a little air in – but then he said, literally shooting out the words: I don't feel like going home.

He looked apprehensively at my hand to make sure I wasn't running away. I put my hand back on the wheel and asked: why?

He didn't say anything. A few months ago, when Noa and I were still having idle conversations, she told me that when people hesitate about what to say, if you look carefully you can see the words rising and falling in their throats. Sometimes a word can get to the tip of their tongue, and then at the last minute, it slides all the way back. I looked at Yotam's throat and thought: when I was his age, I didn't want to go home either, but if someone had asked me why, I wouldn't have known what to say.

It hasn't been very happy in your house for the last year, I said, and a picture rose in my mind: dozens of lighted memorial candles in the living room.

Yotam nodded, or just moved his head slightly.

And your parents aren't the way they used to be, I went on. Before Gidi was killed, I mean.

Now it was a nod. No doubt about it.

And they don't have time for you, I said. They barely notice what's happening with you. You could disappear for half a day and they wouldn't even care.

Yes, he said, and like a relay race runner who'd just been handed the baton by his team-mate, he took off on his own run:

My mother doesn't do anything all day, she just sits and looks at his pictures, and if you walk past her in the living room, she asks you to come and look with her, but how many times can you look at the same album, you get sick of it in the end. And my father stays at work till late, on purpose, and when he comes home, he doesn't whistle like he used to, he just closes the door behind him, quietly, like he's ashamed to come in. Then he eats a bit, usually alone, and watches the news on channel two and on channel one, and gives his opinion out loud, even though no one's listening. Then he turns off the TV and goes straight to bed. He hardly says a word to me and he doesn't come to sit on my bed. Once, he used to come and talk to me every night before I went to sleep, ask me how things were in school. And Mum too. She used to come in and cover me even if I was covered already, and now neither one of them comes. They don't care about me.

I'm sure they care about you, I said, hearing how hollow and formal I sounded. I *know* they care about you, I said, trying again. I was at your house last week while you were at school and your mother told me that she's very worried about your behaviour at school.

Yotam looked up in amazement. That's what she told you? And before I could confirm it, the spark in his eyes died and he continued, I bet she's worried. That's the only thing they care about. My behaviour at school. All week I'm invisible, like that Dannydin in the book Gidi used to read to me, and the minute I bring a note home from school, they put on this good-parent act, look up from the albums, call me over and talk to me in a serious tone.

A bus thundered over to the stop across from where we were parked. It emitted a single passenger, like the whale spitting out Jonah. I waited until the passenger disappeared into the darkness and thought about how to put into words the thought that had been nagging at me since my conversation with his mother.

I chose to be direct and said: so that's why you're acting up in school, Yotam? So your mother and father will pay attention to you?

No, don't be silly, he said with a smile that was too cynical for a child, I do it so they'll pay attention to each other.

*

Moments when Noa is glad to be Noaandamir:

When he thinks she's asleep and can't hear, and he whispers words of love in her ear. She fakes deep breaths of sleep and in the morning says she slept like a log all night. And when he takes Yotam to a football match, or patiently explains which chess move would be right. Then she has a thought that makes her glad: he'll make such a good father. And after another bad conversation with her mother on the phone, he looks at her in a way that makes her feel she's not alone. She's also happy when they play the new Nirvana disc, *Unplugged*, at full volume. She feels so good, so free, when they scream together with Kurt, 'Come as you are, as a friend, as I want you to be.' And when guys flirt with her at the café, she can tell them she has a boyfriend and it's not a lie. And when he surprises her and comes to pick her up from college the day after a big fight, all the girls are so jealous they could cry.

*

Moments when Noa is sick of being Noaandamir:

After her shift, when a guy holding a bouquet of flowers is waiting for her in the street. And unlike the other men who always come on to her, he has a smile that's very sweet. After five minutes of conversation, she knows that with this guy, unlike Amir, what you see is what you get. With him, it would be light and airy, simple and healthy, no sweat. In short, she didn't have to be herself, he was no threat. So when can I see you? he asks, and she replies, trying to end the conversation: maybe in my next reincarnation. I think you're very pretty, he says with a smile. Thank you, she says, blushing. He puts his hands together in a plea, and for a minute she's almost tempted to say yes. But something shaky yet strong still clings to Amir. Even though they're not having a very good year. Something inside her is curious about how this love will end. Without the interference of another boyfriend. Sorry, she says, I can't. I'm involved with someone. And even though he smells so sweet, she walks away, leaving him standing there on the street.

Later, she walks into the house and Amir is reading and taking notes. She hovers around him for a while, thinking: should I tell him or not? She decides not to, what for? It'll just make things even more tense than before. But as she turns to go to the shower, he looks up and asks: hey lover, did something happen at the café? And she thinks: it's amazing how well he knows me. Then she says, no, everything's OK. He looks at her for another minute and says, with some surprise in his voice: if you're hungry, there are some stuffed peppers you can heat. Sima had lots left over from Shabbat, and brought some over for us to eat.

*

No thank-yous, please. Come in! I tell Noa. But she hands me the Tupperware box and says, no, I have work to do. She turns around to go, and then, as if two different women were arguing inside her the whole time, she suddenly says, you know what? Why not?

I close the door behind her and lead her to the living room. So, how were my stuffed peppers? She puts her hand on her chest and says, oh, they were fantastic. I can still taste them. Thanks, I say with a smile, picking up Lilach and putting her on my lap. I don't know why, but I suddenly wanted to feel her close to me. I'll give you the recipe if you want, I tell Noa, and she gives a little laugh, thanks, but I have no time to cook. Lately, my life is ... I run around all day. I hardly have time to breathe.

You're right, we really haven't seen each other in a while, we haven't talked, I say. Lilach wriggles out of my arms and reaches a hand out to Noa. Noa gives her a finger and Lilach closes her little fist around it.

I missed you, I say, and Noa laughs in embarrassment then leans over and gives Lilach a kiss on the cheek. I missed our conversations, I say and sound to myself like a pest.

Me too, Noa says, and even though she's looking into my eyes, I don't believe her. I think that for her other people are the sauce, not the main dish.

So tell me, were all of Moshe's brothers here for Shabbat? she asks.

How do you know? I ask, a little surprised. Does she listen to us through the hole?

What do you mean how? she says with a laugh. From all those peppers!

Yes, I say and let out a breath, there were almost twenty people here for dinner. They all came to celebrate Grandpa Avram's recovery.

So that's it, he's completely recovered? No more demons?

Mafish, Finished. The doctors say that his brain

managed to get over what happened to it and that he's functioning perfectly normally now. But don't forget, they're the ones who promised that his operation wasn't dangerous.

That's doctors for you. Actually, they're always guessing. Sometimes they get it right and sometimes they don't.

Yeah, I know.

That brother of Moshe's, Noa says, softening her voice a little, was he here on Shabbat, the one called ... Menachem?

Very nice of her to remember the name, I think, and say: yes, of course he was.

How is it between you two now? she asks. You can hear in her voice that she's trying to sound more interested than she really is. But it's nice of her to even try.

I think he's afraid, I say, after all that happened with the kindergarten, because you wouldn't believe how careful he is with me.

So you won, Noa says.

Only for the time being, I say. After Passover, kindergarten registration starts for next year and I bet you a million pounds that it starts all over again. That Menachem is a stubborn mule. And Moshe keeps going to rallies and coming home with his eyes all lit up and saying Sima, come with me just once. Sima, would it hurt to try? No, it looks as if this is just something I'll have to live with. Like in Ashkelon, when we lived near the central bus station. At first, the noise of the buses drives you crazy. Then you don't hear it any more. Menachem and Moshe will keep trying to make Liron grow sidelocks and I'll keep trying to protect him. And her too, I say, pointing to Lilach. Tell me, sweetie, do you want to wear long denim skirts when you grow up?

Lilach, who already knows how to recognise the sound of a question, actually nodded her head as if to say yes.

What do you mean, yes? I pretend to scold her and say

to Noa, that's just the way I am. I can be the nicest person in the world, but when it comes to my children, I'm a tiger.

I can understand that, Noa said, nodding.

She can't, I think. Not really. There's a thick wall, a concrete wall between people who have children and people who don't. What about you and Amir? I ask, and the minute I say his name, I remember that I dreamed about him again yesterday. I went over to get their monthly rent and she wasn't there. He said they didn't have any money and asked if he could pay me in a different way. I pretended not to understand and asked, what way? He bent over and gave me a kiss, a gentle kiss on the lips, and I said, that could be a problem, and all of a sudden I didn't have any clothes on. But before we could touch, I heard Lilach crying and I couldn't work out where the crying was coming from because I didn't see her. I looked for her in the dream and when I couldn't find her, I got scared and woke up. Then I realised she really was crying because her dummy had fallen out.

What about me and Amir, Noa repeats my question without a question mark and then is quiet.

Yes, I push her and remember the big fight I heard through the wall.

She wants to say something, but she's hesitating. You can tell from the way she's staring at her shoes and the way her knee starts jigging up and down. Tell me, Sima, she finally says, does it sometimes happen, I mean, did it ever happen, I mean do you sometimes think about other men, I mean, other than Moshe?

My heart drops into my trousers and slides down into my socks like a coin. How does she know? I didn't tell anyone about my dream, not even Mirit, so how did she find out? Do they teach her at Bezalel to photograph people's thoughts? That's scary. I knew there was something strange about that girl. I told Moshe right from the start. *Allah yistur*. God help me. How do I answer her?

Why do you ask? I look her right in the eye. Like they say, the best defence is a good offence.

No, because . . . she mumbles, embarrassed, accusing, and I'm almost tempted to confess, to get down on my knees and say I'm sorry, I didn't mean it, I don't know what came over me. I have hormonal problems, maybe that had something to do with it. Or maybe it's because it's spring, with all the allergies, but I promise you, Noa, you have nothing to worry about . . .

But then she starts to talk. No, listen, it's just that in the café some guy came on to me, and I usually brush them off. I tell them I have a boyfriend and go on about my business, I mean, yeah, it's nice, but nothing more, and yesterday, I don't know, he asked if we could go out, and my heart whispered, yes. A second before my mind kicked in, my heart whispered yes, do you understand? Of course, in the end, I said no, but I haven't been able to get it out of my mind.

What does he look like? I ask her. I'm so busy breathing in relief that I don't have time to think of a less idiotic question.

That's not the point, Noa says and looks at me, disappointed with me for not understanding.

So what *is* the point, I ask, trying to correct the impression I made.

It's not that specific guy. I'll forget him in a minute. It's just that I don't think something like that should happen when everything's good between you and your boyfriend.

Why not? I protest, and want to go on: take me, for instance . . .

I think that if you're looking outside – Noa makes a fist, puts it in her mouth and bites it – it's a sign that something's missing at home.

264

But something's always missing. No man has it all, I hear myself saying. And I'm almost convinced.

True, Noa says, taking her fist out of her mouth. But that's not the thing.

Lilach, who fell asleep in my arms, wakes up suddenly and starts looking for my breasts. She still does that sometimes, and I have to move her mouth away gently to remind her that she's been drinking from a bottle for a while now.

Look, I say to Noa and don't know how to continue. I feel like giving her some really first-class advice, something that'll make her come to me for help every day, but the only thing that comes out of my mouth is: maybe you need to get out together more, you know, to add a little variety to your life. You're at home all the time, aren't you? Travel a bit. Go on holiday. Go away for a few days. I say all that and think: now she's probably saying to herself, advice like this I can get from women's magazines.

But she actually smiles. You're right, she says, we really have got bogged down. And we used to go out a lot before we moved here. But there's something about these walls that closes in on us, that pushes us so close to each other that we can't see. Maybe that's really a good idea, to go away for a while.

Yes, what's the big deal, I say confidently, like someone whose advice has been accepted, and think: if only I took a quarter of the advice I give to other people. Why a quarter, an eighth.

I forget how good it is to talk to you, Noa says, playing with the fuzz on Lilach's head.

It really is great to talk to me, I say, and we both laugh. I look at the sparkle in her eyes, at the small wrinkles dancing on her cheeks, and I'm jealous: he probably fell in love with her because of the beautiful way she laughs.

*

All those particles of emotion in the air, the fragments of

265

hurt feelings, the small, invisible insinuations, all the hidden balls we've passed to each other with the speed of light, I have the ball, Amir has the ball, the ball is rolling down the street, all the kindled memories, recent ones from yesterday, distant ones, my mother, the words that have been spoken, the words that will be spoken, the words that will probably never be spoken, the throat choking off the words, the little lamp that lights up in your chest and illuminates you from inside, the touching, your body's memory of it, the inexplicable longing, great expectations, the slight but stubborn desperation, the law of connected vessels, the law of scorched hearts, music, his inner music, quiet, solid and tense, my inner music, slightly more dramatic, the duet, the delicate ballet of compromise, someone always has to give up something, the small flash of disappointment, the lack of clarity, the knowledge that it was never really clear, that it will never be clear, the stone rolling down your back, the little stab deep in your stomach, the shared wound constantly bleeding inside, the transparent ties that bind, invisible, like in the circus, the ties you can trip on and fall, fear of falling, hope of falling, knowledge of falling.

You can't see any of those things in the picture of that trip to the hidden spring.

In the picture, we're hugging. Amir's hand is peeking from behind my shoulder, my hand is peeking from behind his waist. In the background is the red Fiat Uno with its tired right eye. Behind it are green bushes sprouting from the hill, and behind them, the sky and a cloud shaped like a hippopotamus. Amir is smiling a slightly tired smile, or maybe it's only now that I think it's tired. As usual, I don't photograph well. Or maybe I'm just not pretty. Our bodies are very close. Relaxed. And there's no sign of what would happen a week later. Maybe the heads. Yes, the heads. I didn't notice it until now. Instead of tilting our heads towards each other, we're tilting them away.

*

It can't go on like this, Mum said. I knew I wasn't supposed to hear this conversation. It was really late already, maybe one in the morning, and I just happened to get out of bed to go and pee, and I was about to go back to my room when I heard her talking. Even though I was half asleep, I heard the words and stopped, thinking they were talking about me because I'd brought a note from my form teacher that day – an invitation to an urgent meeting to discuss my marks this term – and I was sure they were talking about what punishment they should give me after all the ones they'd already given me hadn't helped.

I tiptoed quietly to where I could stand closest to the living room without their seeing me. I pressed my back against the wall, breathed through my mouth and listened.

So what do you suggest that we do? Dad asked.

There's that social worker . . .

I don't want to see her face.

If she's the problem, we can ask them to send someone else.

What for? So you two can sit here again and blame me?

That's not what happened.

That's exactly what happened.

All she said was, 'Maybe you both feel guilty.'

She was looking at me when she said it.

You're imagining that.

Don't tell me I'm imagining.

Dad got up – I heard his armchair move – and started walking around the living room. His steps came closer to me and my heart pounded like a drum, but then the steps moved away. Then came closer again. Then moved away again. I wanted to run away and I wanted to stay. To hear and not to hear. Like when you order too many scoops of ice-cream and you don't have any more room in your stomach, but you still keep licking.

It can't go on like this, Mum said.

You said that already, Dad said.

It's having a bad effect on the boy. The neighbour, that student, thinks so too.

What? What do you mean?

He was very polite, that student. He didn't exactly say what he thinks about it, but I think he thinks that maybe Yotam is causing problems to bring us closer.

That's ridiculous. What does he know.

He's studying psychology.

What kind of man studies psychology? That's no profession for men.

Why? There happen to be a lot of men psychologists. It's very common these days.

Anyway, who is he to tell me things about my own son.

He spends more time with him than you do.

Well, what do you know, you're right. I apologise. I apologise that I have to work. I apologise that someone has to pay the mortgage on this house. The bank doesn't care that I lost a son, right? Isn't that right?

With the last 'right', my father started coughing. One big cough at first, and then a few small coughs, one after the other. I went back to my room before she asked him whether she should get his inhaler, before he said he didn't need any favours, before she went to get it anyway and he grabbed it and said, I told you not to.

*

It can't go on like this. There's the smell of breaking up in the air of the apartment, like the smell of potatoes cooking. Noa puts on her tracksuit after she showers. I stay late in the library just so she'll be asleep when I get home. Instead of lying in the fork position (she climbs on top of me, puts her head on my chest and slides one leg between mine forming a kind of four-pronged fork), we sleep like inverted parentheses. Our conversation is limited to the bare essentials. She doesn't tell me any of those little stories from work. I report to her, without comment, that I've taken a break from the club. She says, leave me the keys. Buy low-fat cottage cheese. I remind her to turn on the water heater. And we both avoid saying things in the future tense.

How is it that in films there are always crises. And dramas. And everything is concentrated into one weekend on a country estate in southern England where the conflicts are sharpened, then resolved, and finally there's a moral. But with us, here in the Castel, you can't put your finger on the minute things started to go wrong because there was no minute like that. Just the slow leaking of tensions from the outside world to us, then from each of us to the other. Just a buzzing that got stronger until now we have to cover our ears with our hands and there's nothing left to hug with.

Still, when we went looking for the hidden spring this week and walked down the path that was supposed to lead us to it and I took her hand, just like I did on that trip to the Judean desert, and we both smiled because we both remembered that first touch, I felt for a few seconds that we could change everything, that under all that buzzing there was something still beating in both of us and all we had to do was sweep a little of the sand off ourselves, the way sand is brushed off a beautiful, forgotten mosaic, and we'd go right back to talking in bed as if we were dancing, and dancing in the living room as if we were talking. But after an hour of searching, we didn't find the spring and I didn't understand how that could be. After all, we'd turned right a little before Hadassah Hospital, just like David told me, and then we drove down a dirt road and took a left at the fork, then parked a hundred metres after it on a small patch of grass. We walked down a path that began across from the grass to the place where the spring was supposed to be.

But there was nothing there. Just dead weeds.

It's all right, Noa said. It doesn't matter. But I insisted on finding that fucking spring as if everything depended on it, and I knew I was acting like an idiot but couldn't stop. So I dragged us back to the car and raced back to the fork in the dirt road, and Noa said, you're ruining the car. I ignored her and kept driving fast. I turned right instead of left and cursed David, that musical scatterbrain, for not knowing how to give directions. But the right turn didn't lead us anywhere interesting either, just to a rubbish tip full of bottles, and Noa said, let's go back to where we were, at least it was pretty there. I said OK in a bitter tone, as if we wouldn't find the spring because she was so impatient, and drove back to the patch of grass. Noa said, let's spread the sheet here and have a picnic, and I said, OK, if that's what you want. She asked me if I'd rather go back and I didn't answer. We spread the sheet and put stones on it to hold it down. We ate our sandwiches and drank mineral water, then lay down on the sheet to look at the clouds and argued about whether one of them looked like a hippopotamus or a vampire. Then Noa drank from the bottle, pulled my shirt up, filled my bellybutton with cold water and said, you see, here's the hidden spring. I laughed, because I'd really been so stressed before, since when did I care about things like that, but before the pleasure of that thought could spread through my body, Noa said, let's take our picture, and I thought, that restlessness of hers is seeping into me. I didn't have the strength to argue, so I agreed, and she got up and started fiddling with her camera. A few seconds later she said, get up, I can't get the mountains in the frame if you're sitting down. I pointed to my bellybutton and said, what about the spring? But she came over, pulled me up and said, hug me, it's going to shoot the picture. And before I could cover my face with a mask of happiness, we heard the click.

On the way back, she said, it was great to get out of

the house, wasn't it? I said, yes, even though I didn't think great was the right word. Then she said, we have to do this more often. Go out for a drive, I mean. I tightened my grip on the wheel and said, so where do we feel like going on our next outing? There's a dam under Beit Zayit, she said, and we could walk around the lake that's formed there. Lake? Near Jerusalem?! I said doubtfully. A lakelet, she corrected herself. But the truth is, I haven't seen it myself, she went on. I heard about it. Ah-hah, I said, and felt the two of us giving a silent sigh of relief, because if we don't really know whether there's a lake there, then we don't really have to go. OK, we'll see, Noa said and turned on the radio. Yes, we'll see, I agreed, thinking: it can't go on like this it can't go on like this it can't. That smell of cooking potatoes was waiting for us at home, and Noa said, can you smell it too? I said yes, and she said, it must be Sima and her cooking. It doesn't make sense that she'd be cooking the same thing all week, I said, and Noa said, you're right, so what's that smell. I wanted to ask her, don't you know? That's the smell of breaking up. I wanted to tell her that I'd already smelt that smell at least once in my life, if not three times, and it had a thick texture, just like now. But instead of talking, I went to have a shower and under the drizzle I remembered how once, in the Sinai desert, I hooked up with a group of enthusiastic architects for one day, and one of them, who was wearing white flared trousers that had the logo of a local newspaper printed on them, explained to me that you can know a lot about a person from the thing that's most important to him when he builds a house. What, for instance? I asked, throwing the backgammon dice on the board. You tell me, she said and took a puff of her cigarette. What's the first thing you see when you picture your dream house? A balcony, I said, straight from the gut. A big, wide balcony facing the view. Very good, she said and scooped up the dice.

271

What's so good? I persisted, what does it say about me? She exhaled smoke so she could answer, but then one of the architects came over and asked her if she wanted to go snorkelling with him before it got completely dark, and she said, yeah, cool, the water's full of red-sea fish now. She handed me the dice, one after the other, and said, actually, you know the answer yourself, don't you?

Yes, I do. That's why I don't leave now. I've headed for the balcony enough times. I've convinced myself enough times that there was no point in getting attached because, in the end, you break up. When I was twelve and we were supposed to fly to Detroit for a sabbatical year, I pressed up against a column in the queue at the airport and said I wouldn't get on the plane. But in the end, my father seduced me into going by buying me a pair of Adidas trainers. I don't want to leave again. If she wants, let her leave. I'm staying. To the bitter end. The furthest I'm willing to go is to the shower. To the shower over and over again. It's been a week since we went to the spring, and I don't think I've come out of the shower the whole time. There are lines carved on my fingers. I'm cold. And I'm still under the shower.

She's knocking on the door.

Once, she used to come in without knocking.

I'm going to Hila's, she said.

Bye.

I have a treatment.

Enjoy.

Will you be here when I get back? she asks. And for a minute, I'm not sure whether she means in general or specifically.

No, I finally answer. I'm going to David's. He was all excited when he called yesterday. He said I have to hear their new song and read the lyrics to me on the phone. 'It's time you landed, Superman, it's time . . . to tell your mother . . .' Something like that.

Sounds nice.

I'll ask him to put it on a CD.

You don't have to.

It's not a problem.

Then OK. I have to get going.

Regards to Hila . . . Shanti . . . What's she calling herself these days?

*

I felt as if three hands were moving over my body. Not one. Not two. Hila suddenly had three hands: one was holding the back of my neck, the second was rubbing my forehead and the third was burning in the centre of my stomach, warming my bellybutton and finally making me relax a little. Until that minute, I'd been worried: what did she mean by a combination of massage and Reiki? I'd never heard of anything like that, and what was that phoney opening conversation all about – knees to knees, how am I, how do I feel. Bad, thank you. At Bezalel, they've already told me that if I don't hand in my proposal for the project by the end of the month, I've lost the year. My boyfriend is falling apart. He goes from breaking dishes to being weirdly quiet and I've already told you that he's plotting to leave the apartment. My legs are ruined from waitressing so much. The major pain is in my ankles, but it radiates up to my knees, and I have a splitting headache every other day and enough, Hila, you're probably sorry you asked. Actually I'm not, Hila said in a soft voice, not hers, and went on: and what do you expect from this treatment? The truth? I said without looking her in the eye, I don't expect anything. You know I'm not a big believer in these things. I only came because we set dates and cancelled so many times before. OK, Noa, she said, elegantly sidestepping my ingratitude, think of this as a gift. If you could ask me for anything, what would you want the most? The thing I'd want the most, I heard myself saying suddenly, is to hear that inner

273

voice of mine again that tells me what's right and what's wrong, what's real and what's fake, what's important and what isn't. There's so much noise that I can't hear that voice any more, do you understand? Yes, perfectly, Hila said in a way that made me feel she really did understand, and she added: I don't know whether one treatment can give you that voice back, but at least we'll try to get some quiet flowing through you, OK?

OK, I agreed, though I was still a little suspicious because how exactly can you make quiet flow? Hila gestured for me to get on a massage table and asked me to lie on my stomach. I asked her if I could close my eyes and she said, it's recommended. I wanted to ask her why it was recommended, but I didn't, I just closed my eyes. She clicked something that sounded like the button of a tape recorder and harmless, circular music filled the room. She came over to me and stood at the edge of the table. I heard her breathing next to me, and when I opened half an eye to peek, I saw that she was rubbing her hands together. Like a fly, I thought, and closed my eyes again so as not to embarrass her. Then she started to touch me, gently, a touch here, a touch there. At first, it made me shrink back because suddenly it felt weird that Hila, who has known me from the time I was born and never touched me, except for those little kisses on the cheek when we meet up and slightly longer hugs when we see each other after long trips, it suddenly felt weird that her hands were moving along my almost naked body, touching places I only let Amir touch, and I thought that maybe I should have gone to someone I don't know. I thought, what if all this touching gets me excited. Now, for instance, she's touching my neck and my neck is very sensitive, yes, right there. And what if all of a sudden I feel a pulse between my legs. It could be awkward, very awkward, and confusing, as if I really needed more confusion in my life now. But no, her touches were fluttery, not demanding, not 'those kind' of touches, and after all, this was Hila and I could loosen my bum a little, let my tensed buttocks relax, first the right one, then the left. I gradually let go. Loosened up. I took longer, deeper breaths, like Hila asked me to, and I let my eyelids drop. When I started to feel that there were three hands, not two, I said to myself, or more accurately, mumbled to myself, OK, now we really are in the twilight zone and anything goes, and I let myself go completely. I surrendered to the heat flowing from her fingers into my body, flowing from my knees to my elbows, from my thumbs to the top of my head. I almost stopped thinking; I mean, I didn't have any more coherent thoughts, just vague, general sensations like, for example, that Hila really loves me, that I could tell from every touch how much feeling she had for me. Now turn over, she said. Slowly, from your left shoulder. I rolled over heavily, limb after limb, till I was on my back. Again, I felt slightly exposed, but Hila put her three hands on my forehead, just rested them there and waited for me to start breathing slowly again. Then she moved to my collarbone, which Amir likes so much, and moved along the length of it, deeply under it, removing poisons I didn't know were there, made them flow out of me through her fingers, then removed them again and made them flow out again. Then she disappeared for a minute, leaving my body alone to enjoy the purification, and came back a second before I could feel abandoned, straight to my lower stomach. She kneaded it lightly, very lightly, and from there, she climbed to that spot between my stomach and my chest where you still can't feel any bones yet, but you can feel muscles. She pressed it long and hard, and suddenly I was flooded with a wave of clarity as if Hila had pressed a switch that had turned on a light in my chest. I said, that's good, there, press it again. She did, and I was flooded with whiteness again, and something started to itch inside me, something wanted to burst out of me through that exact spot. Hila kept on pressing there and kneading around that spot, pressing and kneading until she'd removed the thing that had wanted to come out so much, the thing that had waited so long – huge waves of wild laughter that shook my whole body and brought tears to my eyes. I was astonished. It was supposed to be weeping. All the early signs indicated weeping. But I kept on laughing and laughing and laughing, the way I hadn't laughed in months, the way I hadn't laughed since I moved in with Amir.

Then I was silent. Small ripples of laughter still shook my body, but Hila calmed them without touching, without speaking. She just put her hands on my chest and it stopped. I was breathing long, peaceful breaths again and she could continue in the direction of my feet. Weird. Every spot she pressed had a sister spot somewhere else on my body. She pressed my heel, and I felt it in the back of my neck. She pressed under my big toe and I felt it in my knee. Even spots in my hand responded. She finished pressing and pulled each one of my toes gently, as if she wanted to dislocate them, but not really. After she'd pulled the little toe on my left foot, she completely stopped touching me and I felt her suddenly far away, suddenly separate from me.

Two thousand years later, a hand touched my arm and her voice, right up against my ear, said, we're done, Noa, you can keep lying here if you want. Steps moved away towards the bathroom and I pulled the thin sheet over me. I felt it fluttering on me with every breath, and I remembered how, when I was little, I could lie that way for hours on summer evenings, raise the sheet in the air and feel it land on me, very slowly, caressing first my chest, then my legs, then my stomach. Then I'd raise it again. And again feel it land and land on me.

Drink a little. Hila was standing next to me with some

water. I took the transparent plastic cup from her, and it was only after I'd taken the first sip that I realised how thirsty I was. She went to get me another cupful, which I also drank quickly. Your treatment really makes a person thirsty, I said, smiling at her. And she said, yes. I sat up and she supported my back and said, easy does it. Your body is very vulnerable now. You shouldn't make any sudden movements. Thanks, I said. You're welcome, she said. I meant thank you for everything, I said, touching her elbow. She gave me a big smile, as if the whole time she'd thought I wasn't enjoying it, and now she was relieved. It was fantastic, I said. And she said, too bad there's no mirror here. You should see your face now. What about it? I asked, and when I touched my cheek, I could feel how soft and smooth it was. It looks beautiful, Hila said. And laughed. So take my picture, I said, a plan suddenly taking shape in my mind. No, I don't know how to take pictures, Hila said, suddenly talking in her old voice. There's nothing to know, I urged her. Just click the button.

I'm looking at that picture now. The first thing that jumps out at me, of course, are the flaws. The little spot on my left cheek. The small mark on the bottom of my right cheek. The black rings under my eyes. That's how it is with close-ups. They show everything. Still, maybe it's the forehead that tells the story. Yes. There's something more serene about the forehead. More open. And the eyebrows, as opposed to almost all the other pictures I have of me, aren't contracted. There isn't even one wrinkle in the space between them or above them, in the centre of the forehead. As if Hila and her hands had pulled tight the sheet of my forehead and smoothed out the wrinkles.

After Hila took the picture, she looked at her watch and said, sorry dear, I have someone coming in five minutes. Oh, I said, of course, and I quickly put on all the clothes I'd left on the chair earlier. Shirt, jumper, coat. There were a lot of things I wanted to apologise for. Neglecting our friendship, ridiculing what she did, not taking this appointment seriously and cancelling it three times at the last minute. But I could tell from her eyes that she was in a hurry, so I just said thank you again and hugged her tightly, more tightly than I usually hugged her. Then I backed away slightly, still holding her around the waist, and said, right into her almond eyes, I'm so glad I have you. That you didn't give up on me. And she laughed, completely relaxed in my arms. Give up on you? Never.

Without really wanting to, I let go of her waist, one hand after the other, and walked towards the door. She said, don't forget your hat, and handed me my woollen hat. I took it and blew her a kiss. Before I left, I gave a long bye – I don't think I've ever drawn out that short word so much – and went out into the street.

Oddly enough, it wasn't cold. A light wind tickled the trees of Rehavia, a pleasant sun cast its twilight rays and I suddenly started to skip instead of walk. Two ultra-orthodox men gave me a frightened look of disapproval, but that only made me want to keep skipping. So I skipped down Metudella Street and turned on to Ben-Serok Street. I skipped all the way down the odd-numbered side of Hatibonim Street, shedding my worries as I went. So there have been fewer customers in the café lately, so what. You'd think I was Rothschild before. So I won't hand in a final project this year, what'll happen? Will the world come to an end? No. I'll hand it in next year. I skipped a bit more and remembered Forrest Gump, who starts running one day without knowing where. At first, he runs alone, and then all kinds of admirers start running with him until gradually there is a whole cult of people running behind him through the streets of America. We'll start a movement like that here, but of skippers, I thought, skipping toward

Aza Street, and we'll tie it in with some kind of important cause. Let's say, 'Skipping for Peace'. Yes, 'Skipping for Peace' is good. Jews and Arabs skipping together along the green line, demanding that their leaders skip the unnecessary killing and go straight to peace.

When I saw the bus stop in the distance, I started walking normally. I'd got a bit cold, maybe because the sun had disappeared and maybe because, after all, this was Jerusalem. And it always gets cold here in the end.

I sat down on the bench. An old woman with a colourful little girl's hairband holding her grey hair was sitting on my left. On my right was a man who looked like a watchmaker. But I wasn't really focused on them. I was looking inward. My thoughts were relaxed and clear, like they are after a good after-lunch nap. As if, along with the wrinkles on my forehead, Hila had removed the wrinkles in my soul and now I could see clearly the things I'd been hiding from myself for the last few months.

By the time the bus came, I'd outlined out for myself what I wanted to do.

During the ride on the bus, I added the small details – when, how, for how long.

And when I reached the apartment, I took down my travelling bag and started packing.

*

A bus winds its way down Sha'ar HaGai.
On the sides of the road, spring dances.
Rusted tanks on purple expanses.
The dead on the living.
Election signs
scream candidates' names on high.
A bus
is
winding
its
way

down
Sha'ar
HaGai.
That's Noa inside
unravelling the knot,
Thinking, it's worth a shot.

Chorus

You can make a mistake, man
Leave something undone
Not finish something you've begun
Do only what you can
You can cry, man
Be full of regret
Make promises to yourself
And then forget

It's time to land
Superman
Time to tell your mama
That you're not the next Messiah.

You can make a mistake, man
Make a wrong move
There's nothing to prove
You can get close, man
Go all the way
without being afraid
Of being betrayed

There's a woman out there
Somewhere
Just waiting for you to appear.

She'll open her arms,
She'll open her heart
And you'll go to her without fear.

It's time to land
Superman
Time to tell your mama
That you're not the next Messiah.

Music and lyrics: David Batsri
From the Licorice album, *Love As I Explained it to My Wife*
Produced independently, 1996

5

Where's Noa? Yotam sailed through the rooms as if Noa were a tennis ball you'll find in the end if you look hard enough.

I already told you, she went to Tel Aviv.

But I thought she was only going for a short time.

She went for a long time.

How long?

I don't know, Yotam. Why are you being such a pest?

Because it was nicer when she was here. And anyway, I saw something on the way home from school today and thought that maybe she'd want to take a picture of it.

What did you see?

Two Ethiopians from the new immigrant centre painted their faces white and were standing at the entrance to the shopping centre.

With signs, like at a demonstration?

Without signs.

That really is the kind of thing Noa looks for.

So you'll tell her? Maybe they'll be standing there tomorrow.

I promised him I'd tell her. What could I say? That Noa and I weren't talking? That I had no idea where she was?

So why'd she go? Yotam kept interrogating me.

Because sometimes people need to go away, I said, in the hope that would satisfy him.

Yes, but why? Yotam persisted. That boy is growing up right in front of my eyes, I thought. And sometimes it's a pain.

Look, I said, trying to explain, it's like when you sit down to do your homework – I know you haven't done that in a while, but try to remember – first you're concentrating and all the answers flow right out of your head into the notebook. But after a while, you get tired and bored, and you start making spelling mistakes, and all of a sudden you see that you've skipped a whole question. So then you know that you have to take a break for a few minutes, to get recharged.

So Noa was bored with you?

Not exactly.

So I don't get it.

Maybe that wasn't such a good example, Yotam. Never mind. *Star Trek* is starting in another two minutes. Do you want to watch it or do you want to keep on asking me annoying questions?

Yotam took the remote control and turned on the TV. I leaned back in relief. It's hard to explain to someone else something you don't fully understand yourself. Good, for at least the next hour, till the programme's over, he won't bother me any more. I've had enough questions thrown at me over the last few days. Everyone who's heard that Noa left has been asking questions and I don't have the patience for even one more.

Tell me, Yotam said when the theme song started, how come we never watched this together till now? Before I could answer, he answered himself: I know! Because every Thursday you go to that club for half-crazy people. What happened? Don't you go there any more?

No.

Why?

*

Less than fifty kilometres, and I feel like I've travelled to another country. Even the light here is completely different.

284

In Jerusalem, the light is glaring and white, and it makes your eyes burn. Here the light is muddy, always mixed with something else. From Aunt Ruthie's apartment – she's my grandmother's sister – you can't see the sea. Or the tree-tops. Just other people's lives showing through their windows, so close to me that I can almost touch them. 'Tel Aviv – Take a Peep.' That's how they should advertise this city in the world and give every tourist who comes here a pair of small binoculars as a gift. From the bedroom window, for example, you can see what's cooking in the kitchen of the couple in the next-door building. At two in the morning, he sneaks into the kitchen and takes some hummus and pitta out of the freezer. Then she gets up and goes into the kitchen in her pyjamas, her hair a mess, and puts it all back before he has a chance to binge. She washes dishes in the evening. Standing behind her, he puts his hands under her shirt and holds her breasts. She shakes him off. Or gets into it, depending on her mood. Once, at lunchtime, I saw her in the same kitchen with a different man who was too old for her. He dipped his finger in some ice-cream and held it out to her, and she licked it. It was repulsive, but I couldn't stop staring at them. And I look at the balcony that you can see from the study. There are three old brown armchairs on it. One of them is torn. In Jerusalem, no one dares expose their ears to the cold yet, but here, the evenings are pleasant and the three guys who live in that apartment sometimes go out there to smoke. The sweetish smell reaches all the way over to me. They puff away and laugh with dry throats, but there's some-thing sad about them. As if they'd dreamed their whole life of the day they could sit like that, on a balcony in Tel Aviv, and smoke together, and they said to themselves, we'll be happy then, but now they're slowly finding out that they're not. Definitely not. Hi, you, one of them called out to me last night, what's with that camera?! Click away, we're living it up here, his friend said, getting up and leaning on the railing. A tanned chest gleamed in the moonlight. I stayed hidden behind the camera. Now the other two joined him and leaned forward towards me. Muscles, earrings, beards, muscles, earrings, a buckle. Hi, photographer, the buckle said, you're invited to join us. His tone was actually friendly. And also his choice of words: 'you're invited' instead of '*ya'allah* come on over'. I shook my head. A slow, hesitant movement. Third floor on the right, he yelled. On the left, you idiot, the one without a shirt corrected him. On the left! he yelled again, as if he wanted to be the one to give me the information. This isn't what you came here for, Noa, I reminded myself and waved goodbye to them like a movie star leaving her fans, and disappeared into the protected space of the apartment.

Since I arrived here, I hardly go out. Just to the shop in the morning to buy a roll and chocolate milk, and in the evening, to the avenue to stroll with the dog owners (and I always have strange thoughts while I'm walking down the avenue: today, for instance, I thought that sometimes our past keeps us on a leash and sometimes it sets us free).

I spend most of the day in the refuge of the apartment (what a nice word refuge is, Amir would say now). Aunt Ruthie hadn't been in any condition to take anything with her to the hospital. Everything stayed here. Her library is still overflowing with its unique blend of books: slim volumes of poetry, small comic books and paperback romance novels. On the cabinet in the study there's still a picture of her father when he was young. He was so handsome, she always used to say, touching the plastic frame with the tip of her finger. I always agreed with her, even when I'd grown up and knew she was exaggerating. Her paintings hung on the walls of the bedroom, the living room and the workroom, and there was a slip of paper next to each one with the name of the painting on it, just like in a gallery. Here's 'Self-Portrait', a painting of a woman who doesn't resemble Aunt Ruthie in the slightest. Once, I thought it was strange to paint someone else and call it 'Self-Portrait'. Hanging on the right is 'Family Tree', whose branches scream to the heavens like the arms of someone being taken out to be executed in the Holocaust. On the opposite wall is my portrait, and next to it a sign that says 'Girl'. I remember how she sat me down on a chair and told me not to move, and when I started to get bored and complained that my bottom hurt, she said, just a little bit more, Noa'le, and promised that 'after we finish, we'll go to Dizengoff and buy you a double chocolate ice-cream.'

From the first time my parents dumped me at her place, a line stretched directly between us that skipped over two stopping points: my grandmother and my mother. We used to play girls' games together and buy clothes on Dizengoff and come home and paste collages all night – cutting from magazines and pieces of clothes. All my parents' strict rules – you have to go to sleep at ten, you can't watch *Dallas*, you can't listen to music with the volume turned up – all those rules were cancelled for a day or two, on the condition, of course, that I didn't tell (she was scared to death of my mother).

She was the only one, except for my father, my mother and Yoav, who knew about the stomach pumping – I told her, even though my parents wanted to hide it from her too – and she was the one who sent me to paint. I started that way too, she said, and the shadow that passed across her eyes made it clear what she meant when she said 'that way'.

We continued meeting at her place for coffee and chocolate-filled biscuits until I went into the army. Then, I only left the base every two weeks, and spent the little time I had sleeping, eating, going dancing, sleeping, eating, going dancing. Call Aunt Ruthie, my mother would say. She has no children, you know. And she always asks about you. OK, I'd say, I'll call right now. And I really meant to, but something always came up, a guy, a party, and I never got around to it. Aunt Ruthie swallowed her pride and kept sending parcels of chocolate and biscuits and poems by Dalia Rabikovitch to me at the base. I'd promise myself I'd write to her, or at least call her to say thank you, but I didn't do that either, and right after I was discharged, I went off on my big trip. I promised to stop off and see her on my way to the travel shop, but I didn't. When I came back home, I had to find an apartment in Jerusalem quickly because I was starting Bezalel right away. I know those were all excuses. The truth is that I just forgot her. I pushed her to the edges of my feelings and made do with the vague knowledge that she'd be there for me if I needed help. Until one evening, two years ago, when my mother called and said that she didn't know whether I still cared, but Aunt Ruthie was in the hospital, unconscious, after she fell in the middle of the street and hit her head. I went straight to Tel Aviv. I dropped everything and went, but it was too late to talk to her, too late to tell her anything or say I was sorry. All I could do was sit next to her and hold her hand.

We don't know what to do with her apartment, my mother said a week ago when we'd reached the twilight of one of our conversations.

Why? I asked, drawn back to the phone after my thoughts had wandered to another place. We would have rented it out, my mother said, but we're not sure she won't suddenly wake up. The doctors say that the chances are very slim, but it's happened before. So where will she go back to? On the other hand, every day that passes, she's losing rent money. And we need every shekel now, for the hospital.

So what will you do? I asked.

I don't know, my mother said with a sigh. Maybe we'll wait another few months.

I think you should, I encouraged her. And pictured Aunt Ruthie's apartment standing empty and the woman in the self-portrait looking at the girl, who's me, and asking, so, how long will we be here alone?

After the session with Hila, when everything opened up, the idea flashed through my mind: that's where I'll run away to. I called my mother right away and asked. She started stammering, look, I don't know, and I cut in and said I think it would've made Aunt Ruthie very happy, and she said, but what'll happen if she wakes up? If she wakes up, I said, I'll be out of there in half an hour. Besides, she's been asleep for a year and a half already, so why should she wake up now, of all times? Come on, Mum, it's only for two weeks. But Amir's such a nice boy, she said, and that pissed me off, so I said, that's not the point, Mum. Either you want to help me or you don't. I don't understand, she said. Why don't you come here? Stop it, Mum, I said. Why do you always have to be so difficult?

I told Amir that I was going to Tel Aviv for three weeks, and he asked, where will you stay? At a neutral location, I said. But he kept on, and asked, don't you want to at least leave me a phone number? I told him the truth: there's no line. He gave me a crooked smile and asked, so we're having a 'trial separation'? No, I explained, we're taking a break, and you need one too, don't you? He sat down on the sofa under the picture of the sad man and said, yes, the truth is that I do. And suddenly, even though I was the one who wanted to get away from him, that hurt. He needs a break too? And what if he doesn't wait three weeks for me? All those psychology girls are just waiting for him to be available. And they're pretty. And smart. I almost put my rucksack down on the floor, but then he started to talk. I thought we should get some air too, he said, but you know, with me, all this separation business is complicated. I never know whether leaving is just a habit with me, he said, or whether I really need to go. So you're telling me to go? I asked, a lump already forming in my throat. No, he said, pointing to my packed bag, you're the one who's going. What difference does it make, really, I said, suddenly sick of all the tension. What difference does it make, I said again, putting the bag on my back and turning to go. So we'll see each other in three weeks? he asked, and his voice broke a little. Probably, I said, enjoying planting this final doubt in him, and left.

I've been here ever since. In moments of weakness, I take out my picture albums and look at them. I look at the picture of him and David at the Licorice concert. At the picture of us on that first trip to the Judean desert, staring at everyone else with the exact same expression on our faces. At the picture of him hanging the sign on our door in the Castel, which suddenly looked fake, too formal. At the picture of that day at Sataf. We argued a little afterwards and I thought then that it was a terrible fight.

Every time I see his laughing eyes, that ridiculous crest of hair, the invisible line that goes from his shoulders to his arms and his waist, every time I see those things, I want to run to the nearest payphone and hear his voice, tell him I want to change my mind and ask if I can come.

But then I remind myself of how much poison there'd been between us these last few months, and I remind myself of the night he broke the plates, and I remind myself that from the minute I moved in with him, I haven't been able to create anything, so I hide the album far, far back behind the encyclopaedias.

*

Bro,

I hope you're reading this letter alone, with nobody around. I hope you're reading it in the dark, with just a small lamp on so only you can see the words, because I'm about to tell you the biggest secret in the world, a secret that millions of travellers have sworn never to reveal, even if there's a gun pointed at their groin, a secret more jealously guarded than the Coca-Cola formula, a secret that could have stayed hidden for a lot more years if I, the

Vanunu of travellers, hadn't decided it was time to take off the mask, tear open the cover, crack the safe and tell you, only you, the shameful truth that everyone tries so hard to hide: that when you come back to Israel and develop the pictures and sit down to show your poor friends the albums, everything suddenly becomes 'fantastic', 'great', then 'fantastic' again, and it's hard to pick only one of the countries to recommend because each has its own special beauty, and it's hard to say which one has the nicest people, because they were all so nice (excuse me: fantastic), and even that time in the market when they stole your travel belt with your passport and all your money in it was actually an experience, and even when the train was derailed in the middle of a trip, that was an experience too, and really, from the distance of a week or two, everything melts into one big lump, like rice cooked with too much water, and you can't separate the grains any more. But the naked truth is that there are also scary moments on these trips, and shitty moments and lonely moments. And the worst thing is the goodbyes. No one talks about that, but a long trip is just a collection of goodbyes. From the minute you get on the first plane, you start meeting people and you get connected to them fast and deep, because it's a trip. You talk to them about your family and your ex-girlfriend even though you met them half an hour ago, and there's a kind of magic in the air. But the minute the plane lands, you split. They planned to meet their friends at one hostel and you're supposed to meet some girl at another, so in the meantime you exchange your home addresses and phone numbers and promise to meet up with them during the trip. Then poof, you never see them again, and the truth is that at first it doesn't bother you. Just the opposite. You find the girl you arranged to meet at the hostel and she introduces you to the people she's been travelling with for two days. Naturally, they're her best friends. And you like them too. They'll be going back home in a week, but that doesn't bother you. You get the scene, you're into it, you know that after they leave, someone else will come. And sure enough, a minute after you help them load their bags into the taxi that's taking them to the airport, you meet a guy from Argentina in the lobby of the hostel. After a five-minute conversation, it turns out that he's your spiritual twin. He also started studying economics, he also gave up after the first year at Buenos Aires university, his girlfriend also dumped him a month before the trip, and he's also sure that *Zorba the Greek* is the best book he ever read. You travel together for two weeks or so, and it also turns out that you have the same taste in girls, the same uncontrollable lust for pork chops, and the same preference for hostels located far from the centre of the city. But a second before you start hearing the music from *The Double Life of Veronique* in the background, he tells you that he wants to go straight to Colombia, and Colombia is definitely not your scene now. So what's the big deal. He'll do Colombia later or you'll do it now. After all, it isn't every day that you meet your spiritual twin. But no dice. That's how it is on trips. The goodbyes come fast and easy, and when you pack your bag at four in the morning so you can catch the bus that'll take you to the border with Peru, he doesn't even get up to say goodbye. He just opens one eye and reminds you to leave the key to the room on the table, and you say, no problem. A shadow falls for a minute, but really only for a minute, because on the bus you meet two Peruvian *chiquitas* who tell you about the fiesta in their village, which doesn't appear in any tour guide but is a must, and in a last ditch effort to persuade you to come, they offer to put you up at their house. You ask if that won't make their father mad, and they laugh and say no, don't be silly. Our family loves guests. By the end of the trip, you've almost forgotten that Argentinian guy and get swept up by the giggling of Isabella and Felicia. When the fiesta – as colourful and wild as they promised – is over, you travel around with them for a while and sleep with both of them so as not to insult either one, and in the morning, even though the sex was nice (details in another letter), you're already feeling that itch at the base of your spine to go, to move on, to devour another place, another woman, and so it goes for three or four months. You feel like you're floating from one person to another, one city to another, and the goodbyes don't leave a scratch on you, they're not even recorded in the minutes. But you're wrong, you're wrong big time. And when do you find that out? When you've said goodbye to a girl who's been with you enough time, a girl you've really let into your heart. Suddenly all the goodbyes you've laundered come back to collect sadness-added-tax and you sit in the room you shared with her, which is yours alone now, and look out the window at the church and the square in front of it that's full of poor kids selling broken lighters, and suddenly you're tired, tired of everything.

If you still don't get it, Nina left yesterday. Her money ran out. I poured everything out of my wallet on to our bed, made two piles of all the dollars and travellers' cheques and said: *tuyo* (yours, in Spanish. We'd started stammering in that language, which we both hardly knew, but at least we *both* hardly knew it). No, she said and put it all back into one pile. Why not? I yelled in Hebrew, and she just shrugged her shoulders and kept on saying no, no, no possible. I got down on my knees. I put my palms together and begged. I pretended to be insulted. Crazy. Nothing helped. That stupid Czech pride of hers wouldn't let her take money from me. For them, she told me with her hands, a girl who takes money from a man is a whore. What whore, who's a whore, I said, getting upset and pounding on my chest. Don't you see that I totally love you? And if I understood the Czech she spoke, she said, I love you too, and gave me a long hug. She hugged me and stroked me the whole night, even in her sleep. But in the morning, when

I asked her if she'd changed her mind, that 'no possible' was even firmer than before, as if in the meanwhile she'd danced a tango with the possibility and rejected it once and for all.

So last night, I walked her to the bus stop. What else could I do? Aside from us, there were mainly peasants and chickens waiting for the bus. They travel to the big city at night, spread their mats on the ground and sleep in the main square to grab a space for market day. There was an unbearable smell of chickens in the air and grey feathers were scattered on the filthy ground. I crowed a little for Nina in a final effort to get her to change her mind, but she didn't even laugh. At eleven on the dot – all the buses on this trip were always very late, and hers had to come on time? – she climbed up to the roof to check that they were tying her backpack down tightly, then came down to me for a last hug. She handed me the Dvorak disc, the one she played for me on our first date, and said, *tuyo*. I refused to take it. Are you joking? I know how much you love it, I said, but she kept her lips clenched till I gave in. I didn't have anything to give her, except for a long letter in Hebrew – I hoped she'd find someone in the Jewish quarter of Prague who could translate it for her – and a kiss.

At eleven-fifteen, she wasn't waving to me from the window any more. I trudged back to the hostel. I was wiped out, as if I'd just finished the Eilat triathlon, and when I got back to the room, I fell on the bed and stared at the broken ceiling fan and had depressing thoughts, such as: love is like a cinema. The lobby is fancy, decorated with select posters from the film. But you leave the place through a twisting, urine-soaked corridor with dented walls and there's always some idiot usher who opens the door a few minutes before the end and you always try to ignore the invading light.

Enough of these thoughts, I told myself off before I fell asleep. The day after tomorrow's a new day.

But I didn't have strength for anything today either. There's a hot-water waterfall an hour-and-a-half walk from the village. I didn't go. Your letter is probably waiting for me at the embassy, an hour away by bus. I didn't go. And now I don't know what's happening with you and Noa. And I have no idea whether you made those crazies normal or they made you crazy. Even though I'm really curious about it. Really. But try to understand, bro. I could barely drag myself out to eat lunch. And even then, I didn't touch the meat and I only ate the guacamole. Would you believe that I ignored a steak that was sitting on my plate? Even worse. A French babe who was sitting at the table next to the wall kept showing me her dimples through the whole meal and I didn't go over to her. I didn't even smile back at her. I got up and started back to the hostel. All the people in the street looked like hostile, dangerous liars, so I walked faster and when I got to the room I lay down on the bed, even though I'd only got out of it an hour before, and suddenly started thinking about my family. It's been months since I invested even a minute in missing them, and all of a sudden I pictured all of them sitting down to eat supper without me, and I wanted to be there. To eat aubergine salad and potato salad with mayonnaise. To have those stupid fights with my mother. To laugh at my father's unfunny jokes. To take the dishes off the table after the meal and load the dishwasher.

And later, at night, I heard some music coming from the party in the bar downstairs. It was a song we used to like to dance to, 'Come on Eileen' by Dexy's Midnight Runners. My knee started bouncing to the rhythm, but that was all. I didn't feel like going down to dance. Why meet other people? So I could say goodbye to them two days later?

How does that Caveret song go: 'It might be over'? It might be. Or I might get up tomorrow morning and the sun will rise in my chest again.

Whatever happens, I'll fill you in so you know when to book a court for us. I can't wait to beat the pants off you.
Modi.

*

When I woke up on Saturday, I saw from the rectangles of light on the wall of my room that the sun was out. The sun! I opened the blinds and all the broken glass in the empty lot sparkled at me. The wind coming into the room was cold but nice. 'Great weather for football,' like they say on that radio programme, *Soccer and Songs*. And for taking a drive. Before Gidi died, we used to take a lot of car trips, mostly with the Lundys, to the Carmel, the Galilee, to all kinds of creeks whose names I don't remember. We get up early. Dad sits in the living room with the map on his lap and plans our route, Mum makes sandwiches in the kitchen and I fill empty Coke bottles with water and then help her wrap the sandwiches in foil. And always, a few minutes before we have to leave, the Lundys call to say they'll be a bit late and Dad sighs and says, as if we didn't know. And Mum says, I don't understand. Why can't we just plan to leave a little later? But when we meet them at the Sha'ar HaGai petrol station, no one mentions that they were late. They all hug and kiss each other. My father and Ami, who was under his command in the army, and my mother and Nitza. Then Dad switches to Nitza and Mum to Ami. Only Shira Lundy and I stand far away from each other. For the first few seconds, we don't have the courage to talk. She plays with her curls and I look at my shoes and neither one of us is brave enough to say hello. Then my mother says – she always says the exact same thing – Yotam, you know Shira, don't you? And Nitza laughs and says, Nechama, why are you embarrassing the children? Then my father says, let's go girls, we have no time for this. We have a long drive ahead of us today. We all get into our cars, fill the tanks and start driving. Every few minutes, Dad asks, do you see them? Do you see them? And Mum says, yes, they're right behind us, and goes back to humming along with the song that's on the radio. Sometimes Dad hums with her and they sing together, he with a deep voice that tries to sound like the singer and she with a mother's voice. He puts his hand on her thigh and strokes it and in the back seat, I try to find the best position for my legs and look out the window at the signs on the road that are full of the names of places I've never been to, like Elyakhin and Eliashiv, which always come one right after the other. Or Caesaria and Binyamina, which Dad always says are worth stopping at when we have a chance. But that chance never comes, and when the scenery changes and hills start popping up, Mum asks me what kind of sandwich I want, and I say, what kind do you have? She looks at me and says, cheese, pastrami with hummus and pastrami without hummus. I pick one and peel away the foil, thinking that soon we'll get to the place where we start walking, and then I'll see Shira Lundy again. That gives me a kind of scary but nice feeling in my stomach that makes me lose my appetite a little. But I eat anyway, so Mum won't say that she doesn't understand why she bothers to make sandwiches if I'm not going to eat.

The sun outside my room was so dazzling that I thought I might be able to convince my mother and father to go out for a drive, even though we're supposed to be sad. Maybe they saw the sun too and remembered the Lundys. But when I saw what my mother was doing in the living room, I lost my confidence. She was sitting under the big picture of Gidi, next to Gidi's memorial candle, browsing through Gidi's yearbook. There was a box of tissues next to her with one tissue sticking up out of it. But I took a deep breath and asked her if she felt like going out for a drive because it was so nice outside, and without looking up from the yearbook, she said, I don't know, ask your father. So I went and asked my father, who was lying in their bed reading the weekend papers and smoking a cigarette. He mumbled, I don't know, ask your mother. I coughed loudly to remind him that I hate it when he smokes and said, I already asked her. He looked up from the paper and said, Yotam, in case you haven't noticed, we're not really in the mood for trips and I don't think I have to explain why. I wanted to tell him that he really didn't have to explain, that they weren't the only ones who missed Gidi, I missed him too. But I didn't know how to say it, the words didn't come together into a sentence in my mouth, so I didn't say anything. He put the cigarette out in the ashtray on the nightstand and didn't say anything either. Then he went back to the paper. I coughed harder so he'd look up, but it didn't help, so I left without saying anything. I pulled a shirt out of the huge mountain of dirty laundry – Mum never has the strength to do laundry – and went out. Mum yelled after me, Yotam, where are you going? But I didn't answer. If she wants to know, let her get up from the sofa. I put a few more stones on Gidi's monument – I keep adding stones, but for some reason, it stays the same height – and talked to him. I told him that I miss him terribly and that I'm sorry that on the last Saturday he was home before it happened, I interrupted his phone conversation with a girl from his base, and I hope he forgives me, and if he does, if he forgives me, would he please tell Mum and Dad, give them a sign from heaven that he doesn't care if we go out on car trips, that he goes on trips up there and there's no reason we have to stay at home all the time. I felt a bit weird talking to stones, like one of those half-crazies in Amir's club, but when I finished, I waited for an answer anyway, for a stone that would fall and give me a sign that Gidi heard. No stone fell. So I left and went to knock at Amir's door. But no one answered there either, even though I thought I heard noises inside. I could've taken the key out from under the plant, opened the door and checked. But I didn't want to. I wanted to go out walking, that's what I wanted. And no one wanted to come with me. OK, I'll go alone, I said to myself. I walked down the tile path, crossed the street, and went past Madmoni's house, which was starting to look like a real house, except without doors. I went down on the path to the wadi. Bushes with thorns scratched me, but I didn't care. I was thirsty, but ignored it. I kept going down, down, down. I kicked small stones and sang to myself, I'm hiking, I'm hiking, I don't need anyone, I'm hiking. I passed the big tree, the one I once built a wooden house in. And I passed the rock that Gidi once told me was the border and that we couldn't walk past it. I kept walking and walking till I couldn't see the houses of the neighbourhood any more, and after a while, the path ended too. There was a big bush and no path behind it, as if it had got tired, and that confused me a bit, because till then, I had at least known where I was going and all of a sudden I was standing there, in the middle of the wadi, and I had no idea what to do. When that happens on a trip with the family, my father takes a map out of his pocket, looks at it for a while and then decides, 'to the right' or 'from here, we follow the red markings', but I didn't have a map, and even if I had, I wouldn't know how to read it because whenever Dad used to say, come here Yotam, look at the map with me so you can learn how to navigate, I'd lean over the map, put a serious expression on my face and think about other things.

And then I saw a small house.

At first, I thought I was seeing things because it was very hot and Mum once told me that if you don't drink enough water when you're out walking, you start seeing things. I took a few steps toward the house and after a few metres it really did disappear. I didn't see it at all. But I kept walking and there it was again. Then a whole bunch of trees hid it. But when I walked further down, I saw its walls made of dirty old stones, and its small, low door, and that gave me the courage to keep walking through the bushes and the rocks until I reached it.

Only when I was standing very close did I see that not only did the house not have a door, but it didn't have a roof either. Probably no one's lived here for years, I thought. And went inside.

*

Saddiq goes out to pee. Raises the side of the tent, bends over and squints so he can see. It's very cold now. The wind starts to howl. Walking over to a bush, he stumbles on a rock and his face sets in a scowl. Laughter comes from the guard tower. A huge projector lights hill after hill. If he runs, he thinks as he opens his fly, if he runs now and climbs the fence, the guards will shoot him. He'll fall. And it'll all be over, once and for all. No more humiliation. No more desperation. No more of that longing that fills his throat with a burning sensation. His whole body begins to shake. He remembers when he and his brother used to go out to pee in the winter, so cold that their bodies would ache. He zips up and once again, his eyes move to the fence. Maybe I'll climb it tomorrow, he says to himself. No. Doing it now doesn't make any sense. Maybe in another two weeks, or three, when Mustafa A'alem finishes teaching me. Then I'll take off and be free.

He walks back into the tent, lies down on his bed. His back hurts. The hunger in his heart makes him want to scream. But still, he sinks deeply into a dream.

Sometimes, when he wakes up in the morning, he reaches for his wife, thinking for one sweet, wonderful moment that he's back in his old life.

*

Is Yotam here?

His mother was standing at the door with a 'please-say-yes' expression on her face.

No. He's not at home?

He wanted us to go on a family outing today and . . . we couldn't. I was sure he came here.

No, I said, and was filled with shame. I knew that it was him knocking on the door and I didn't open it.

Where else could he be? Yotam's mother asked, looking at me with forlorn eyes.

Let's think, I said in an authoritative voice, and kept on kicking myself for not having opened the door. Maybe he went to a friend's house?

He hasn't been playing with other boys since . . . since it happened. I tried the houses of two kids who used to be his friends, but he wasn't there.

If it was a weekday, I thought out loud, I'd try the arcade at the shopping centre. But it's five o'clock now. The shops don't open till seven on Saturdays.

That's right, she said, and suddenly collapsed. Her knees buckled and she lost her balance. At the last minute, she grabbed my arm so she wouldn't fall.

Come inside, drink some water. It's very hot outside. I supported her until we got to the sofa in the living room. She sat down in silence and I went to the kitchen and came back with a glass of cold water and a napkin.

I don't know what I'm going to do, she said, wiping her face with the napkin. Enough, it's enough. It's too much. Reuven says he's not worried, Yotam went out for a few hours to make us angry because we didn't want to take him for a drive. But how can we? Our feet are so heavy, and all the places we could go to – the Galilee, the Golan – we went to with Gidi, so how can we?

Yes, I said, nodding, and remembered: just yesterday I didn't buy anything at Angel's because it was strange that Noa wasn't with me. And then I thought: how can you compare?

She looked at her watch and said, I feel like something bad could happen to him. When Gidi went to Lebanon that last time, I also felt in my body that it was dangerous. I told him that when we were standing at the door on Sunday morning, but he laughed at me. He said, Mum, you thought the training course was dangerous too, and when we went down to the territories, you thought it was dangerous. So it must be that your worrying keeps me safe.

I could actually imagine it – the woman sitting next to me and the boy in the huge picture hanging in her living room facing each other for a second before what they couldn't know would be their last hug. She's wringing her hands, he's shifting the straps of his backpack to get the blood circulating in his arms again.

I won't survive it, she said, getting up from the sofa abruptly, as if the very fact of sitting seemed irresponsible to her. I won't survive another one.

OK, I said, getting up too. Let's get a few neighbours and start looking for him.

*

Inside, there were two rusty cans, a pile of coals and a smell, like someone had done a poo. And there was a mattress that looked new and a long shirt that only had one sleeve. It's really kind of nice here, I thought. There's no fridge or TV, but there aren't any gigantic pictures of someone who's dead or memorial candles with a smell that makes you feel sick and parents who don't talk to each other. And not having a roof isn't so bad either. Winter's over already and it won't rain any more. So who needs a roof? Just the opposite. A house without a roof is cool, like the car David's brother has with the convertible top, the one we once rode in to a class party. You can sleep on the mattress at night and see all the stars, the Big Dipper and the Little Dipper, and the Milky Way that has no milk. Yes, I said out loud so it would be harder to change my mind later, I'll stay here until night-time. And if it's nice, maybe I'll stay here for ever. No one cares anyway. They even forgot my birthday. I could disappear for a year now and they wouldn't notice. Just the opposite. They'd be glad. That way they wouldn't have to talk about my problems at school and they could keep on being angry with each other. They probably think I'm at Amir's place. But he doesn't care about me any more either. He doesn't care about anything since Noa left. And he won't even tell me why she left. Every time I ask him, he makes up some stupid reason, like I'm a little kid who'll believe anything he says, like we're not friends. I'm sure he was home today when I knocked on the door. I'm positive. He was probably reading one of those fat books of his and couldn't be bothered to get up. Noa probably won't come back and he'll move out of the apartment soon and I won't have anyone to play chess with.

That's it. I decided. I'm going to live here. I lay down on the mattress and looked at the sky, waiting for the stars to come out.

*

I never saw anything like it in my life. Half an hour after the minute I knocked on Sima and Moshe's door, the whole neighbourhood was outside. Children on skateboards, old men on their way back from the synagogue, Beitar fans on their way to a game – they all streamed to Yotam's house. His father was standing on the steps leading the operation. Contrary to what his wife claimed, he didn't look calm at all. Maybe he'd just been trying to calm her before, and maybe the presence of all those people had roused him. I don't know. In any case, he was awake and alert, and he divided the people up into search parties. He sent Sima and me to search the area leading out of the neighbourhood, where the shops that sell building materials are. Where's Moshe? I asked her. He stayed with Lilach and Liron, she said and started walking. Isn't it amazing, I said, trying to keep up with her fast pace, how everyone came to help? Yes, she said. You probably don't know that the people here are divided up into a few clans, depending on what part of Kurdistan their family came from. There are Dahuks, Amadis and Zakus, and each one thinks they're better than the others. They're at each other's throats all year long, but when something like this happens, they put all that aside and come to help.

Dahuks? Amadis? What is she talking about? I've been here six months, I thought, and I still don't understand anything.

We were getting closer to the outskirts of town. From a distance, we could see the search party that had been sent to Doga's to check out the cage of boxes.

But the thing is, Sima said, following them with her eyes, that even when the pressure's at its worst, they never forget who's one of them and who isn't. I've been living here for six years, and they still consider me an outsider. Without even thinking about it, they sent me out to look with the only person here who's more of an outsider than I am. You.

I'm sorry . . . I started to say.

You have nothing to be sorry about, Sima interrupted. And besides, I kind of like being with you.

She touched my arm lightly when she said that, and immediately moved away, as if she'd scared herself.

You know, I said quickly, before she could break away completely, Yotam knocked on my door.

When, today?! she said, and stopped in front of Shlomo & Sons, Building Materials, and turned to me.

I could have lied. I'd left myself an escape hatch by not saying when. But I wanted to confess and expose my back to the lashes of the whip. Her whip.

Yes, I said. Around three. After he left his house and before he disappeared. I didn't open the door to him. I always do, no matter when he knocks. But this time, I don't know. I pulled the blanket over myself in bed and didn't move until I heard him walking away. You're the first person I'm telling this to. I'm so ashamed of myself. If I'd opened the door, he wouldn't have run away. I would've played a little chess with him, calmed him down . . . We talk, you know. I love that kid, I really love him. I should have opened the door.

What's done is done, Sima said, and her voice had no anger in it. Let's start looking. I don't think he's here, but look over there, behind the parking lot.

*

Yotam's mother circles the shops on the ground floor. She's already done it twice with her friends, but feels the need to do it once more. Her eyes dart all over the place, searching for her son, and in her heart, she's making deals with God. If you give him back in one piece, I promise to be a better person in every way. To light candles on Friday night. To recite psalms every day. OK, answers the God in her heart, I'll consider it. But a minute before their imaginary handshake, she gets angry and cancels the deal. Consider it?! she yells, out loud now – the hell with you. You already took my older son, now you're considering taking the younger one too!!

Enough, Nechama, her friends say, people are staring. They put their arms around her protectively. Let them stare, she says, I'm past caring. None of them knows how I feel. You're right, her friends say, but we should go, they say, trying one more appeal. Maybe Yotam's back already? Maybe he just went for a walk and lost his way? But we should go back anyway, because it's late. OK, she says, her strength suddenly drained, whatever you say. Let's go back, she says sadly. If they've found him already, then he needs me. Very badly.

Reuven, Yotam's father, is holding a large torch. The sun has set and it's a very dark night. Following him single file in the wadi are four other men. They have torches too, and they're hurrying along, yelling Yotam! Yotam! again and again. And Reuven thinks: I haven't wanted anything for six months. Not to eat. Not to drink. Not to dream. Not to think. Not to buy. Not to sell. The business is going to hell. Nehama asks, but he doesn't tell. Sometimes he gets up in the morning and doesn't know whether he's alive or dead. As if his head has been split open like a peach. As if his blood has been sucked out by a leech. But no more. Now he wants to find Yotam. That's all he's living for. He walks faster and says to himself over and over again: find him, find him, find him. Reuven, one of the men rouses him, the path ends here. Come on, he says in a voice loud and clear. We'll go this way. He walks around a big bush and climbs a slippery rock, the men right behind. He has no idea where he's going, no idea what he'll find. But he knows he can't give up, so he lets his instincts lead. He tramples through every thorny bush and over every weed. Now and then, he stumbles and grabs one of the men so as not to fall. Then suddenly he sees something and gives a loud call. Tell me, he says, pointing into the darkness, do you see an Arab house or am I just imagining it? There really is something there, they say in amazement and slow down a bit. It's strange, they say. There used to be an Arab village here, but not any more. Let's go, he says, running as fast as he can towards the door.

*

Hey, someone called. Amir and I walked out of the scrap yard to see who it was.

Are you looking for Reuven and Nehama's kid? a teenager with bleached hair standing across the street with his friend shouted at us.

Yes, Amir said, but a year went by until the bleached hair answered us. They found him, he finally yelled.

Where? What? Is he OK? Amir asked, running towards him.

Yes, he just got lost, the bleached hair said as if he couldn't care less, and his friend, the silent one, lit a cigarette. They found him in some old shack in the wadi.

But how . . . I mean, did anything happen to him? Amir asked.

Nothing.

Thank God. Thank God.

Yes, the bleached hair said, and from his tone, he sounded

more disappointed than anything else. Well then, we're gone, he said. If you see anyone else on the way, tell them too, OK?

OK.

After bleached hair and his friend had gone, Amir wiped the sweat off his forehead and said: wow, at times like this, even if I don't believe in God, I thank him.

Yes, I said, and looked at him. He'd been quiet the whole time we were looking for Yotam. He'd kept his eyes down, his shoulders were stooped and his bottom lip gave this weird twitch every once in a while. But now everything had calmed down. And he looked tall and handsome again.

I don't know what I would've done if . . . he said, and kicked a stone.

Once, I heard myself say, when Liron was little, I took him to the shops with me and when I went into the toilet I left his carriage outside and, like an idiot, I asked some security guard to keep an eye on it. When I came out, they were both gone. I thought I'd die. It turned out that the guard had gone to the loo as well and took the carriage inside with him. I almost killed him. The whole shopping centre came to watch me give him a piece of my mind.

I can picture it, Amir said and smiled for the first time in a long while.

We started walking back home. Amir hummed some melody I didn't know, probably one of those songs he listens to at full volume on the other side of the wall, and I wondered whether it would be OK if I asked him about Noa now. On the one hand, I thought, a stone had just been lifted from his heart so do I want to drop a rock on it? On the other hand, I thought, I hate not knowing things.

I was thinking so much that I bumped into him while we were walking. An electrical current ran through my elbow. Sorry, I said, and he laughed and said, it's OK.

So how are you getting along now? I found the courage to ask. And I was sure that he'd ask me, what do you mean?

Because all the men I know act like morons when you ask them about feelings. But Amir looked down at his shoes walking along the pavement and said: the truth is that it's not easy. All of a sudden, there's this emptiness, you know.

Yes, I said, thinking: why 'yes'? You married your first boyfriend and you've never been apart from him except for when he's in the reserves, so how do you know it's 'yes'?

And the hardest thing, he went on, is that I don't know what's going on. If I were sure that we're splitting up, I'd start hating her and focus on all the things that are wrong with her. But this way, it's one of those annoying neither-here-nor-there situations.

Wait a minute, I said, I don't understand. What exactly did you two decide?

I was sure she told you, he said, so surprised that he stopped walking.

No, I admitted. And the bitterness of knowing that she left without saying a word to me filled my throat again.

Amir was quiet, taking in the new information. Two dogs were rubbing against each other on the pavement in front of us, sniffing each other's bottoms.

She went to Tel Aviv, he finally said. For three weeks. And then we have to decide what we'll do.

Do you talk?

No, he said, and started walking again. I have no idea where she is, he said. She didn't give me the phone number.

Maybe it's better that way, I said, thinking: why are you giving him this bullshit? How could this be better?

Maybe, Amir said, and I saw his bottom lip give a slight twitch again.

We turned into HaGibor HaAlmoni Street, and I thought, we'll be at Yotam's house soon. There'll be so many people there that I won't be able to ask him anything, and who knows when we'll have the chance to talk again.

What do your parents and hers say about it? I asked.

Our parents?! Amir said, looking at me in amazement,

our parents don't . . . My parents have been in the States for a year now. And Noa's parents – well, she doesn't really let them get involved in things like this.

Right, I thought, I never really did hear her talk about her family.

I know it sounds funny, Amir said, but neither one of us feels connected to our family. Maybe that's what made us bond so tightly.

But there's something I don't understand, I said and stopped walking in the hope that he'd stop too.

What? he asked and stopped.

When you came here, you were like two lovebirds. So what . . . what happened? I hope you don't mind my asking?

Amir looked at me with the same expression Noa always had when she started talking about him. The truth is, Sima, that I don't know.

Strange, I thought. Usually, couples with problems know right away what the reason is. Mirit blamed it on her husband's cheating. My cousin Ossi always said, even before her divorce, that she and her husband were both very stubborn. But with these two, Amir and Noa, you ask for a reason and their eyes start flitting around all over the place. What is it with you two?

I don't know, Amir said again, as if answering the question I'd just asked in my mind, maybe . . . maybe we're too perfect for each other.

I wanted to ask him, what do you mean, too perfect for each other? But he started walking again and looked away from me, as if he was tired of talking, and a minute later, we could already see the people crowded around Yotam's house. This wasn't the right time for more questions.

They asked for you not to come in, said an aunt I remembered from Gidi's *shivah*. The doctor said that Yotam has to rest for a day or two without being disturbed.

Will he be all right? Amir asked, taking the words out of my mouth.

Yes, his aunt said. He was very lucky. That house where they found him was part of an Arab village that used to be here. They say that Arabs from the area still roam around there with their goats. I don't want to think about what would have happened if they'd found him there now, what with all the terrorist attacks.

He really was lucky, I said. And his aunt said, God must have been watching over him. He's just a little dehydrated. And the doctor said that he doesn't even need a drip. He just has to keep drinking and rest.

That's good, Amir and I said at exactly the same time, and then he said, so just send him hugs and kisses.

From who? the aunt asked.

From the neighbours, I said.

We said goodbye and started home. I walked slowly because I wanted to have a few more minutes with Amir. He didn't walk fast either, and I hoped it was for the same reason. When we got to our door, I stopped and said, all's well that ends well, and he smiled: yes, you can say that again. And I thought to myself that he has a really beautiful smile and that Noa is really a fool to let him go. If I had a man like him, who knows how to talk openly like that and who has broad shoulders like his, I'd keep him close to me and I'd never leave him the way she did.

OK, see you, he said, looking straight into my eyes.

I felt like telling him that he didn't have to wait for Yotam to go missing again for us to see each other. I felt like telling him that I'm alone in the house in the morning. And so is he. But right then I heard the voices of Lilach and Liron through the window, so I just took a deep breath to keep myself from speaking those thoughts and said: if you need something, don't be shy. Knock on my door, OK?

*

Yotam's father is sitting in his car, crying bitter tears. Crying as he hasn't cried in many, many years. If his employees could see him now, all they'd be able to say is wow. Their big boss is crying like a little child. He hasn't cried since Gidi was killed. All he did was cough. But yesterday, when they found Yotam, he was flooded by tears he couldn't choke off. Earlier, at work, he'd had a lump in his throat that wouldn't go away. Don't be such a baby, he kept telling himself all day. Be strong, he told himself again and again; without you, the business doesn't have a chance. But the lump kept growing and growing, and by lunchtime he was feeling unwell. He couldn't eat, and his partner said: go home Reuven, you look like hell. But he yelled at him, I'm not leaving till I've finished my work. He forced himself to keep at it till exhaustion was all he felt, hoping that hard work would make the lump in his throat melt. But it only got bigger and bigger. Late at night, on his way home, he felt he couldn't take it any more. So he stopped the car on the side of the road, turned off the lights and leaned against the door. He hid his face with his hands and began to shake. And cry as if his heart would break. He cried about so many things. About the morning he took Gidi to the bus station and they hugged goodbye with so much love. About the night he touched Nechama and she recoiled as if he were an enemy she wanted no part of. And about yesterday, when he found Yotam in that Arab shack. Lying there as if he were dead, on his back.

He wept and wailed for what seemed like a year, until a police car pulled up and someone yelled into a megaphone: Get going. You can't park here. OK, he signalled to the policeman and turned on his lights. He let a few cars drive by, then merged into traffic, trying not to cry.

But all the way to the Castel, the tears kept flowing. He cried so hard that he could barely see where he was going. And he thought: Nechama was right the other day when she said that things can't go on this way. I can't drive on these roads any more. Every traffic light brings up memories. And I can't stay at home, there's so much tension in the air. No, we have to take Yotam and run away. But where can we run to, where?

Right before the Mevasseret bridge, an idea popped into his head, but he said no, it'll never work. What's wrong with you Reuven, are you nuts? But the idea was persistent, it wouldn't retreat. It stayed in his mind when he drove up to the house, when he parked on his street. It was still there when he took a handkerchief out of the glove compartment to wipe his face before he went into the house. (He's a man, after all. The whole world doesn't have to see him bawl.)

He climbed the stairs considering whether to tell Nehama about the new idea he had.

And before he put his key in the lock, he decided not to tell her yet. It might make her upset.

*

It's as if I cried a lot, and now I feel relieved.

I flow with the streets leading to Frishman beach and think: it's so great that I don't have to be careful. That I don't have to feel Amir's pain enter me through a hidden tunnel that connects us. That I don't have to keep his hurt feelings deep inside my stomach. It's incredible how much room it leaves in my body. But on the other hand, at night, it's exactly that empty space that gets hungry and shouts: Amir! Amir! I try to fill it with peanuts or ice-cream, but it doesn't help. I walk around Aunt Ruthie's apartment terrified that Amir will give up on me and go to some other girl. I can see them together, hugging and touching each other, as if I'm standing at the window of the apartment in the Castel and taking pictures. She's a little shorter than I am. Her tits are nicer. And if I'm not mistaken, she's not as sad as I am.

Enough, I say, trying to push that scene out of my mind, you have to focus on the project, Noa. Go out. Look for interesting places in Tel Aviv. There must be some. All you have to do is raise your head.

*

I hear Sima washing dishes. Frying something. Talking loudly to Lilach. I hear her walking around the house in high heels (she has nice ankles. I noticed when we were looking for Yotam together). I hear her go out. Come back. Open the cover of the water heater switch, turn it on. Take a shower. I picture her body naked, very different from Noa's body. When Noa showers, the water flows from her hair down to her feet without interruption. When Sima showers, or so I picture it, the water pools in the indentations of her body. In the space between her large breasts. In her deep belly button, which she loves to expose. In the hills of her buttocks. I hear her step out of the shower and can actually see, through the wall, how she brushes her long hair, untangling the knots until it's smooth. I hear her talking, I can't tell to whom. I don't understand a word, but I like the tone. Full of energy, opinionated, always ready to burst into laughter. I think to myself: she's home alone too. Just like me.

A few days ago, I put on a 'Natasha' CD, and suddenly I thought I heard her singing along with it, 'One touch, then another, sadness, all so familiar.' I turned down the volume, and her singing stopped all at once. I pulled open the cover of the water heater switch and called: Sima! She came over to the hole in the wall and said: did you call me? Yes, I said. I just wanted to tell you to keep singing, I mean, you sing very well. She laughed and said: I didn't know you could hear me. Then she added: I love the music you put on today. Not like the noisy music you usually listen to. Nirvana, you mean? I asked. I don't know, she said, shifting uncomfortably on the other side of the wall. OK, I said, I'll try to edit my musical selections to suit the taste of the audience. You don't have to, she said, coming a little closer. I could hear her breathing. The scent of perfume wafted in through the hole, along with the aroma of frying cutlets. I wonder what's wafting through the hole from me to her, I thought, and said, well, I'm going back to my books. And immediately I regretted my words. OK, she said, I'm going back to my cutlets. Have a nice day. I put the cover over the hole and went back to the living room, intending to open my books again, when I heard the cover open again and her voice call me: Amir?

*

I asked him if he wanted me to bring over a few cutlets when they were ready, and thought, it's a good thing he's on the other side of the wall and can't see how I'm blushing now. Sure, he said, that would be great. And then I was sorry: what did I need this for? They're our tenants and it's not good to mix feelings with money. And anyway, he's Noa's boyfriend and Noa is my friend. But then again, she did pick up and leave without even saying goodbye. After all those talks we had, she couldn't come and tell me what was happening? Did she think it was beneath her?

An hour later, I put on my nicest trousers, the ones that give me a waist, put on a little make-up and walked up the path holding Lilach in one hand and a plastic box full of cutlets in the other, saying to myself: I'll just give him the box and leave without going inside and without talking. I have loads of things to do at home. The mountain of laundry is higher than Mount Meron. Besides, if Amir was ugly, that would be another story, but when he gets a haircut he looks like that tall American actor, I can't remember his name, the one whose films Mirit and I always went to see in Ashkelon, and when he talks to people on the phone he has all the patience in the world, and he speaks in a deep voice that passes through the walls and makes me feel good all over. When we signed the lease with them, I said to myself, he's a good-looking guy. Wild hair, light eyes, muscles in his shoulders. The way I like. And after we went looking for Yotam together, I liked him even more.

He opened the door and said, come in. And I forgot all

the promises I'd made to myself and walked inside, flustered by the smell of his aftershave. (What? Did he put it on for me?)

Thank you, he said, taking the box from me.

I put Lilach on the floor and she started crawling. I looked at the walls of the apartment. Here's that picture of the sad man I heard them arguing about. It really is a gloomy picture. And Noa must have taken those photos. Where's that from? India? Thailand? She really is talented. But why aren't there any pictures of them together? When Moshe and I lived here, there were three pictures of us in the living room, two from the wedding and one from our honeymoon in Antalia, and they don't even have one.

Amir came back from the kitchen, got down on all fours and started crawling in front of Lilach. She was so surprised that she stopped for a minute, then started crawling again, more slowly this time, until she reached him and touched his face with her fingers. He closed his eyes and let her investigate, put a finger in his ear, his nose, his mouth. Hit him lightly on the cheek.

Hey, I told her. Don't do that.

It's all right, Amir said, stroking the fuzz on her head.

I felt silly, standing when everybody was crawling, so I sat down on the rug too. I planned to sit far away from him, but the minute I crossed my legs, Lilach started crawling towards me with Amir right behind her.

She came to me, touched my knees, and he did the same. At first, I thought he was planning to climb on me too, and I got scared. I imagined what it would be like under his body, to grab his shoulders, to tussle with him a bit. To surrender.

He stopped a minute before his head touched my thigh, and sat up. I rubbed my thigh as if he had really touched it, and he said: does she always have this much energy?

Only in the morning, I said. Then I added: and also when Moshe comes home from work.

He leaned on his arms as if Moshe's name had pushed

him back. Lilach's fingers played with my nipples, and I could see how uncomfortable he felt about watching, but still couldn't pull his eyes away.

So, I said, moving her hand away, how's your studying going?

It's not, he said, sighing and picking up a fat book. You see this? I have to know all of it for tomorrow's exam.

Why don't you study with other people?

They're all in Tel Aviv, and I'm here, in the Castel. It's too far for them to come over and study with me.

Yes, it really is far.

You see? he said, smiling, and Noa claimed that the Castel was half-way between Tel Aviv and Jerusalem.

Well, there really is no such thing as the exact middle, I said, suddenly defending her. Like my mother used to say: you can't cut a watermelon into two completely equal parts.

Isn't that funny, he said and laughed, my mother says the same thing, but about grapefruit.

Lilach laughed too, and gave two short shrieks of happiness. He reached out to stroke her cheek, and on the way, brushed the exposed part of my arm. By mistake. It had to be by mistake.

I have an idea, I said. Pick a subject and teach me.

He gave me a funny look.

It's really a good idea, I said. You'll remember it better, I added, unfolding my leg. I was careful not to move it too close to him. But not too far away, either.

You know what? You have a deal, he said and started thumbing through the book. His shoulders contracted, and he rubbed his chin with his free hand. Most of all, I love looking at men when they're concentrating on something.

OK, he mumbled a minute later. What would you like to hear about? Franz Anton Mesmer, who treated people with huge magnets at the beginning of the eighteenth century? Or Joseph Breuer, who used hypnosis to treat people at the end of the nineteenth century?

What do you say, Lilach, I asked, consulting my little girl: magnets or hypnotism?

*

Sima's foot landed right next to me and kept me from concentrating. I wanted to bend over and put cuffs around her ankle. I could actually imagine the touch of her skin, but instead of doing that, I started talking to save myself. I tried to remember without looking at the book. I tried to explain it to her as if it were a story, not a collection of facts I had to memorise for a multiple choice test.

That Mesmer, I started, finished studying medicine at the age of thirty-two. He did his doctorate on 'The Effect of the Planets on the Human Body'.

Like the horoscope, Sima said.

More or less.

What sign are you?

Scorpio. What does that have to do with anything?

Just tell me what sign Noa is.

Also Scorpio.

A Scorpio with a Scorpio, uh-oh!

Lilach, tell your mother not to interrupt. Quiet in the classroom, please, I'm continuing. After Mesmer completed his doctorate, he began to enquire into the possible effects of magnets on the body and claimed he'd discovered something he called 'animal magnetism'.

Which means?

Which means that we have a substance in our bodies, or an energy, that responds to magnetic force and can be changed by magnets.

What?!

It sounds weird to me too, but the thing is that the treatment he developed actually worked. He treated mentally disturbed patients and women who suffered from hysteria or depression, and cured them.

What do you mean, treated?

He had a kind of bathtub full of magnetised water. Iron

rods stuck out of the tub in every direction and Mesmer showed his patients how to put the tip of the rod on the area that hurt them.

And it worked?

Looks like it. Or people convinced themselves that it worked. When I was little and my mother used to take me to the clinic, to Dr Shneidshter, I felt better straight away.

My mother didn't believe in medicine at all. She had her own medicine for every sickness. And we were never sick for more than a day or two, not me and not my sister Mirit.

That mother of yours sounds interesting, but still, if we can just finish the story about Mesmer . . . He kept getting more and more patients, and people used to wait months for an appointment with him. Finally, he founded an organisation and a school where he taught people how to use his method of treatment and they attracted more and more patients –

Until . . .

How did you know there was an until?

There's always an until in this kind of story.

Until the medical establishment in Paris got sick and tired of him stealing away their patients and they formed a special committee to check out his methods and the committee decided that the magnets had no therapeutic value and ordered him to stop using them.

Did he?

Yes. But his students kept on using them. Secretly. And the book says there are rumours to this day, two hundred years later, that Mesmer's followers meet secretly in the forests of Europe and treat each other with those magnetic rods.

Wow, that's interesting. You told that really well. Seriously, you made me want to go back to college.

So go back.

Don't rub salt in my wounds. But I think you're well prepared for the exam.

Not really, but it's fun to study like this. Do you want to hear about Breuer too?

Sima looked at her watch and her face tensed in alarm: shit! I have to pick up Liron from kindergarten in two minutes. He hates me to be late. He starts breaking toys if I'm not there on time.

She took Lilach into her arms and got up from the rug. I got up too. Now that we were standing, I noticed how small she was. I could peek down her neckline and see that she was wearing a black bra today.

Thanks for the cutlets, I said.

You're welcome, she said. We stood like that, facing each other, embarrassed, and suddenly I had the weirdest feeling in the world, that a kiss had to come now. I can't explain it, but it was like a date, like the end of a date when two people feel there's a kind of magic between them. You can't photograph that feeling or break it down into parts. It's just there, in the night air, and suddenly, in the middle of the day, out of the blue, it was there between Sima and me. My eyes were drawn to her full, dim sum lips, and I leaned forward . . .

And kissed Lilach.

*

Moshe Zakian has been coming home earlier than usual this week. And before he can get his jacket off, Sima's caressing him so passionately that he can hardly speak. I hope you're in shape, she whispers to him, her voice hoarse. And he says, of course. His prick is already hard and his voice is thick. After they put the children to bed, she grabs his shirt and says: come on. Quick. But he likes to play with her a bit. Moving back a little, he says: but you always tell me that without a shower, there's no way. She digs a nail into his right shoulder and says: it's OK, baby, it's OK. She drags him into the bedroom, climbs on top of him and has her way. Her skin is electric. Her body's on fire, trembling with wave after wave of desire. He puts his hand on her mouth when she begins to shake, and whispers, shh, Sima, you don't want to keep the whole neighbourhood awake. When they had finished sucking out all the sweetness of their lovemaking, she lies next to him, temporarily relieved of her aching. He says, wow. And she says, I know. What's happened to you? he asks. I don't know, maybe it's my hormones, she replies and sighs. And he thinks, hormones, huh? Don't I have eyes? She thinks I don't know it's because of that student next door. But I know the score. I hear her say his name in her sleep. I hear that little-girl excitement in her voice when she talks about him to Mirit. What are you thinking about? Sima asks, and for a minute he's tempted to tell her, but he decides to retreat. What's the point? She'll deny it, he'll get upset and they'll be at war. That I'm crazy about you, he says at last. That you're too wonderful to be true. She puts her warm hand on his thigh and says, I'm crazy about you too. Then she falls asleep at his side. He remembers her moaning and tries in vain to fall asleep: OK (he holds a conversation with the wall), let her dream about that guy. Outside in the street, doesn't he undress women with his eyes when he sees them walking by? As long as it stays only in her mind – and it will, because he knows that Sima is not that kind – then it's not something he should dwell upon.

In bed he says out loud to himself, trying in vain to subdue his fear: don't be right. Be Don Juan.

*

I'm sorry. I can't seem to fall in love with this city. All that Bauhaus doesn't do it for me. The view of a valley or a mountain doesn't leave me breathless, because there aren't any. There's no Upper and Lower Tel Aviv, there's just Tel Aviv. And there's no street called Valley of the Giants like there is in Jerusalem. There's just Bograshov and Rokach. And no one here is hiding behind a wall that's thousands of years old. At best, they're hiding behind this morning's façade. And you won't see any Arabs here, or poor people or bereaved parents or kids Yotam's age.

How different my first few days in Jerusalem were. I'd felt like it was Purim. Everyone looked as if they were in costume: the ultra-orthodox men with their penguin suits; the ultra-orthodox women, whose femininity burst through their buttoned-up dresses; the young Americans who flood the high street in the summer with their T-shirts that have English writing on them and legs that are too white; the Cinematheque nerds in their checked shirts and that serious look of theirs that just can't be real; the tough guys with their gelled hair; the Border Guards with their tight uniforms; the old Yemenite from the Yemenite falafal stand.

And here – it's all so homogeneous that you could die of boredom. Everyone tries to be special, but somehow they all come out looking the same. As if there's a hidden code they're adhering to. As if city inspectors will fine you if your clothes are a bit *passé*. And it isn't just your clothes. Everywhere you go, you hear the same music coming from the same radio station. In the cafés, people talk about things they've read in the local papers and ask each other, 'Did you hear that . . . ?' instead of 'Did you read that . . . ?' Then the waitress – they all have the same look in their eyes – brings a menu and people concentrate so hard on it that you'd think it was a book of poetry. Then they order exactly what they ordered last time. And they're all gay, or into their bisexuality. And left-wingers, of course. As if there were no other possibility. As if a political opinion were just another piece of clothing, another trend you had to get in step with and not something personal. (Amir would say now: as if your political opinions are so different.) True. There's something comfortable about it. Like marrying your first love. No one here threatens you too much. Everything's familiar and predictable. No one will throw a stone at you if you drive on Saturday or claim that the Oslo Accords were a gamble, and chances are that you won't see any real Arabs, unless you insist on looking for them in Jaffa. But even then, they'll sell you *sambusek* politely and would never even think about breaking into a Jew's house in the middle of the day and making holes in his wall like Madmoni's worker did.

It's safe here in Tel Aviv. Safe. And fuzzy. And flat. I've been walking around the streets with my camera for a week already looking for something that'll give me that yellow pepper feeling. And nothing.

(Amir would say now: maybe you're not looking in the right places.)

Yesterday, coming back from one of my unproductive walks, I met the guy from the balcony at the entrance to the building.

Well, hello there, he said in a kind of sarcastic tone. And I thought: he barely knows me and he's already using that tone?

Hi, I said, and to my amazement, my tone sounded just like his.

Did you take any pictures today? he asked, pointing to my camera.

No, I didn't find anything interesting, I admitted and turned to go.

Do you have a flash? he suddenly asked in a different, nicer voice.

Sure. Why?

If you do, I could show you an interesting place tonight.

Ah . . . look . . . I was about to make up an excuse, but then I thought: why not? Maybe all I need to help me tune in to this city is a good guide. And the guy from the balcony looked pretty nice in the daylight. There was something about his shoulders that made you think you could trust him. I wasn't attracted to him, because he was too short, which was great. And anyway how long could I sit in Aunt Ruthie's apartment and look at albums?

OK, I said. What time?

I'll call you from the balcony at around one.

One in the morning?

What do you think, in the afternoon? What planet are you from?

The planet Castel, I wanted to say. But didn't.

*

Sima has stopped coming over since our almost-kiss. It scared her. And that wasn't Yotam's soft knock. So maybe it's Noa, I thought. I put on a pair of trousers and a shirt, and a pounding heart, and opened the door. A teenage girl was standing there holding a pot. Are you Amir? she asked, shooting looks to the sides. Yes, I said. My mother made this for you, the girl said, handing me the pot. Your mother? I asked. Who ... Who exactly is your mother? Ahuva Amadi, the girl said, shifting her weight from one leg to the other. We live at 43 HaGibor HaAlmoni Street. One house before the turn. You don't want it? It's *kubeh metfunia*. It's very good. My mother will be insulted if you don't take it. Yes, sure, thanks, I stammered and took the pot from her. The handles were still hot. Why are you standing outside? I asked, come in. She walked in and stood in the middle of the living room. She had the expression of someone who'd heard about this apartment, and now was comparing what she saw to the expectations she had. Why did your mother send this? I asked after coming back from the kitchen. The girl blushed and smiled, as if my question was funny. We thought, she started talking after she realised that I was waiting for an answer, I mean, my mother thought that you probably didn't have much food now that ... Now that what? I asked her, and the demon's tail was already wagging inside me. Now that ... the girl said, looking up at the ceiling, now that there's no woman in the house, she finally said and sat down on the sofa with a sigh of relief.

The next day, another girl appeared at my door. With a different kind of *kubeh*. Who spread the rumours about my being alone? I wondered. Sima? Moshe? It wasn't clear. In any case, I gradually learned that there were a lot more kinds of *kubeh* than I had thought. Red *kubeh metfunia*, with tomato paste, okra, parsley and sour lemon. Yellow *kubeh mesluha* with turmeric and marrow. Sour-green *kubeh hamusta*, which comes in soup with beet leaves, turnips and marrow. *Kubeh hemo*, which is shaped like a flying saucer and comes in soup with onion and hummus. And the most delicious, at least for me: *kubeh nabelsia*, which is fried with onions and chopped meat. You eat five or six pieces and you're still not tired of it.

The *kubeh* always came with a girl as a side dish, and it was always 'her mother' who sent her. It took me a while to realise that this was actually a parade of candidates to replace Noa. It was all done very delicately, tacitly. None of the girls actually offered herself, but they were all dressed too well for a short walk in the neighbourhood. Most of them wore make-up, and one or two had been daring enough to spray perfume on themselves. Girls' perfume. Two or three days after they brought me the full pot, they would come back to get the empty pot. There were so many pots that I was getting confused, and they had to come into the kitchen and pick theirs out of the pile. Then they'd sit in the living room, give brief answers to my questions, check out the walls curiously and run away after two or three minutes, not longer.

I was able to get into a proper conversation with only one of them. She was a soldier on leave who had sincere eyes. A random question about what it's like serving on a base she couldn't leave every day pressed the right button. It turned out that on her base there was a group of girls who always laughed together, and she didn't understand what was funny. It seems that she was always getting the worst shifts because she wasn't one of the in-group. Not that she minded about the shifts. She minded that the other girls knew they could step on her because she was alone.

And she minded that she didn't have anyone she could borrow shampoo from when she ran out. And she minded that when she came home, no one cared that she was tired and her mother made her do laundry and clean and cook.

. . . and bring food to people you don't know, I continued.

Yes! she agreed enthusiastically, then immediately caught herself and laughed: no, that's something I don't mind doing.

She took off one shoe, then the other, which – Modi taught me this once – is a sure sign that the girl intends to stay, and maybe remove other articles of clothing.

*

People were sitting at the bar with large spaces between them. The guy from the balcony gave me a quick, cold goodbye and went to sit at the far end, on a brown armchair. Pictures of naked body parts glittered on the walls. You couldn't always tell if they were male or female. Bottles filled with golden liquid stood on long shelves. Air conditioner pipes were stuck on the ceiling like magnets on a horizontal refrigerator door. The light was dim, very dim. Even with a flash, pictures would come out dark here, I thought. But maybe that's good. You don't have to do anything, the guy from the balcony had told me before we came in, they'll come to you.

In the background, the female singer of Portishead was singing 'Nobody loves me', and I thought it was a little cruel to play a song like that here. I sat down on a high stool and ordered a Guinness from the barman with a Popeye tattoo on his shoulder. I knew I needed a little alcohol to get through this night. The Guinness arrived with a man. May I? he asked and pointed to the empty stool next to me. I nodded. I asked the barman if I could bring your order, he said and smoothed his hair. Is that OK? Fine, I said and took a sip. I haven't seen you here before, he said, and stroked his cheek. Is this your first time? Yes, I admitted. Do you want to go somewhere

325

quieter? he asked, putting out his cigarette. Already? I said in surprise, maybe we could just talk a bit first. Usually a few seconds are enough to know whether it's yes or no, he said. I didn't know that, I said. So now you do. Great. So what do you say, he asked, rubbing a long finger around the rim of his glass, yes or no? Do I have to decide now? Yes. Or no.

There were others after him. Men on a platter. One was a wise guy. One was a shy guy. One smelt good. And another had the name of a street in my old neighbourhood. One couldn't look me in the eye. Another tried to put his hand on my thigh. I have no idea why I'm saying this in rhyme. Maybe because I was drunk. Maybe because everything seemed a little fake, kind of glittery, like an Alterman poem. In the background, Portishead was repeating itself in metallic loops and the sound seemed to be getting louder and louder all the time. Couples walked past me on their way home. The girls actually looked nice. Like students. One of them probably went to school with Amir. Why can't I be like them? I asked myself. Wham bam thank you ma'am. Why not? Because of the camera. No. Because of Amir. Wait. What's that all about? How did Amir get into my thoughts twice in one minute? And where's the guy from the balcony who brought me here? Has he gone? And left me here alone? How will I get home by myself?

Hi, he said, surprising me from the direction of the bathroom as if he'd picked up on my anxiety.

Hi, I said, as glad to see him as if we'd known each other for years.

You drink a lot, he said, pointing to my half-empty glass.

Yes, maybe we should really go.

Don't you want to take pictures?

Not today.

So come on.

After we left, he said, we could hop over to the supermarket on Ben Yehuda.

The supermarket? Now?

Not to shop, silly. To hunt.

I think that bar was enough for me, I said, swallowing the bile that had risen into my throat.

There's a new place that opened not far from here, with a DJ who only plays film soundtracks. Maybe you'd like that better.

Forget it. Let's go home.

The air outside was dripping. I was slightly dizzy, but I didn't want to lean on the guy from the balcony in case he got any ideas. A short female parking attendant was putting tickets on cars parked in no-parking zones. At this time of night? I asked. Any time, he said. They get a percentage. I didn't know, I said and he said, be careful, pointing at the dog shit lying in wait on the pavement. I walked around it at the last moment and almost lost my balance.

You were really doing great there, in the bar, he said and grabbed my arm to steady me.

Yes, I admitted, wriggling gently out of his grasp. But they all had such cold eyes. And they were curt. It was like . . .

Like what? he demanded.

Like none of them believed in love any more, I said. And regretted it right away. Why am I dumping these perceptions on him in the middle of the night?

It's not that they don't believe in love, he said, and judging from how offended his voice sounded, it was clear that the 'they' could easily have been 'I'.

So what is it? I asked, looking at him as we walked. He was quiet for a while, as if he were about to say something crucial and his words had to be precise. I started to feel the bile rising in my throat again, but I also felt that there was a real moment in the air and I shouldn't miss it, so I took a deep breath and leaned against a tree.

It's not that they don't believe in love, he repeated. It's just that sometimes love is too much of an effort.

327

Wait a second, I said. And went to vomit in the front yard of a building.

*

I didn't want to make that girl soldier my own. The one and only desire I felt was to make her feel better. So I told her about my basic training, how I'd been so lonely that I didn't sleep for nights on end. How everyone around me snored peacefully and I'd lie there in my bed with my eyes open, thinking what's-wrong-with-me, why-is-everyone-adjusted-but-me, how-will-I-survive-two-or-three-years-of-this?

She nodded in surprise and said, 'You mean there's someone else in this world who felt like I do?'

Yes, I continued, encouraged by her nodding, but you know what? The fact is that everyone there was scared. Everyone burned their fingers when they vacuum-packed their kit, and no one believed you could run to the weapons depot and back in ten seconds or run a circle around the entire base. But I walked with my head down so much that I couldn't see it. The people in the platoon seemed like a big, threatening block that functioned in perfect harmony, and I was the one who ruined it. I was wrong. It wasn't a block. It was just a collection of confused people making a huge effort to hide their confusion from each other.

So what should I do? she asked and gave me a look that said, you're smart, you know.

First of all, lift your head up, I said. When do you go back? Sunday? Good. Go like a queen. Smile at everyone. Ask how they spent their time off. Don't be afraid. And every time that lonely feeling starts to come back, look at them and say to yourself: they feel this way sometimes too. It's not just me.

I don't know . . . she said, drawing out the words as if she wasn't sure that what I suggested was doable, but she liked the idea.

Try it, I said. The worst that can happen is that it won't work. How much more time do you have?

Eight months.

That's nothing. If you take away Saturdays and holidays and sick days and real dentist days and fake dentist days, and two or three family affairs, how much is left? Four months, tops. And you have to subtract your discharge holiday leave, and right before that, no one will even notice you any more, so you can go back to the base on Monday instead of Sunday and leave on Wednesday instead of Thursday. And on Monday, there'll be a day of fun in Eilat and you'll take a sick day on Tuesday because you'll get sunstroke. Which easily takes off another two, three months. In short, tomorrow or the day after, tops, you'll be discharged, young lady. So what's your problem?

She laughed and looked pleased with the way I'd juggled her time left in the army. For a minute, I could imagine how, after the army, she'd let her hair grow and be attractive. Very attractive, even. And someone else – not me – would run two fingers slowly along her naked arm, climb to her shoulder and then to the back of her sweet, white neck. Someone else. Not me. Sorry. I have to go back to studying now. I have an exam. What am I studying? Psychology. Interesting. Yes. Even though it can be a pain sometimes. Why a pain? Some other time. Tell your mother I said thanks, OK? And come over again. Don't be shy.

Before she left, she surprised me with a kiss on the cheek. Thank you, she said. I didn't ask what for because I was tired of pretending. I watched her through the window till she disappeared at the end of the block, and then I paced around the apartment for a few minutes feeling like I always do after I do a good deed and someone thanks me. It's hard to explain the feeling. I'd say that maybe it's a little bit like *kubeh metfunia*. It has a core of soft happiness wrapped in a sour feeling of guilt – who am I to give other people advice – and on the side, there's a red sauce made of emptiness. And okra.

I lay down on the bed. The smell of Noa still lingered on

the sheets even though I'd changed them three times since she left. She'd understand, I thought. She'd understand how a feeling can be like *kubeh metfunia*, and how doing something good for another person can actually make you sad.

She'd say: it's the law of connected vessels of feelings.

And say: it's easier for you to give than to get. So you give, and then you feel like you've missed out on something because look, you haven't got anything this time either.

And say: who's that knocking on the door now, in the middle of our conversation? Maybe you won't answer it?

The knocking continued, persistent. Stop it, I really am in the middle of a conversation with Noa, I thought, but I went to the door anyway. Ever since I hadn't opened the door for Yotam and he disappeared, I don't dare not open it.

Standing in the doorway was a young guy wearing black. With the scraggly beginnings of a moustache.

Ahalan, brother, he said.

Ahalan, I said, returning the greeting, not understanding where he was hiding the pot of *kubeh*.

Would you be interested in an amulet from Rabbi Kaduri? he asked, pulling out a yellow box. We have all kinds of amulets in all shapes and sizes.

Ah . . . look . . . I started to say, but he'd already opened the box.

This, he said, pulling out a medallion, is a pendant with a portrait of Rabbi Kaduri, also inscribed with letters that have special power in the Cabbala. You probably know what they are.

I nodded as if I did.

And here, he went on, I have cards with the Rabbi's blessings on them for all occasions. This card has a blessing for success in business, this one for health and a happy life, and this card is for marital reconciliation – all signed in the Rabbi's own hand.

And what's that? I asked, pointing to the candles sticking out of the box.

Those, he explained, slightly embarrassed, are oil candles. You have to light them while you say the prayer that's written here, on the side, and that will guarantee our success in the elections next month. Would you like a candle?

No, thank you.

Maybe a pendant? Some cards? You can also send letters to Rabbi Ovadia Yosef and get a personal reply from him.

I think I'll pass.

That's a shame, brother, because it's all free. Maybe you'll take something anyway? A card? Come on, just one card.

OK, I said. Give me the card for marital reconciliation.

He handed me a card excitedly, patted me on the shoulder and asked if I wanted to buy a cassette of religious songs by Benny Elbaz, ten shekels, all of it for charity.

No thanks, I said, rubbing the card nervously.

No problem, he said, patted me on the shoulder again and announced to the empty lot and the cats, we're on the way back to our former glory! and skipped quickly down the tiled path.

I closed the door and threw the card into the rubbish bin. A second later, I regretted it, took it out and hung it on the noticeboard above a bill.

I went back to bed, got under the covers and put the pillow behind my neck. Tiny fragments danced in my eyes. For a minute, I wasn't sure if that quick visit of my long-lost brother had really happened or whether I'd imagined it. I thought that if Noa were here with me, I'd tell her everything and that would make it real for me. An invisible fly buzzed in the room and kept bumping into the window. Suddenly, I missed her terribly.

*

And then, one night after I came home from the bar, it appeared. All at once, like those fans at the games Amir watches who burst naked on to the football pitch and steal all the attention.

Suddenly I knew. I knew. What. I wanted. To do. For. My final. Project.

I was so excited that my hands started to shake, actually to shake, but I didn't try to steady them, I let the idea – which at that minute contained only one word, LONGING – spread through my mind and send associations in every direction. It all happened with lightning speed. As if that project had been incubating deep inside me, just waiting for the right moment to hatch. Come here, my little beauty, come here, I coaxed it. I took a pile of white paper out of the drawer and started drawing sketches that I taped to the wall. In the centre, I hung an illustration of myself holding a phone, and then I started surrounding myself with more and more longing. My mother was there, with a scarf she knitted for her first boyfriend, who died in the Yom Kippur war and she never talks about him. Saddiq, the worker who came into Avram and Gina's house was there with his grandmother's gold chain around his neck. And there was a new immigrant from Argentina who I called Franka, and a cinema usher who caught my eye in Jerusalem a year ago and seemed to fit now. And there was a guy I'd never met, but I could see him, I could imagine him down to the smallest detail, and I knew that there would be no objects in his frame, just the text of what he says about longing for something since he was a child, but not for anything specific, just in general. I drew him and stuck the drawing on the wall. I drew other figures with and without objects and wrote all kinds of words that came into my head, like toy, boy, joy, and the whole time I had the feeling in my throat that I was about to cry, the feeling I get whenever I'm creating from the right place. Suddenly, I didn't care about what my instructors would say. When I have an idea that really makes me shiver, no one can put me down, no one! And if they dare to make a peep, I'll just add them to

332

the list of the people I'm photographing because they must be longing for something too. Maybe for the time when they really did create and didn't just criticise. Yes! That's it! Fantastic! I'll photograph Yishai Levy at the door to a gallery. Standing there, but not going inside.

I was so excited that I couldn't sleep all night. I wanted it to be morning so I could start setting up appointments with all the people I wanted to photograph. I wanted to call Amir and tell him that I finally had an idea for my project. I thought about the fact that I shouldn't call him, because it would ruin everything. I thought about the fact that I didn't want to be an artist because you use so much of your emotions as raw material for creating that you lose the ability to just feel. I thought about the fact that I didn't know how to do anything but take pictures, so I had no choice, I had to be an artist and pay the price. I thought about the fact that I was hungry. And that's a kind of longing too. I got up to make a grilled cheese sandwich, and when I was separating the slices of cheese from the paper, I thought: will they miss each other? I thought I was an idiot, but talented. A talented idiot. I ate the grilled cheese in the kitchen and picked up the crumbs with the tip of my finger. Then I sat on my bed and waited for the first light to flicker between the slats of the blinds.

*

They sat on my bed and talked. Really talked. I squeezed my eyes shut so they'd keep on thinking I was asleep. Dad sat on the right, and every once in while, I felt his knee touch my leg. Mum sat on the left and I could smell her perfume, which she hasn't used since Gidi, and then this week, all of a sudden she did.

Mum said: It ended OK this time, but it could have ended badly.

And Dad said: Yes.

And Mum said: We should have paid more attention to him . . . I don't know . . . Tried harder.

And Dad said (I couldn't believe he agreed with my mother two times in a row): Yes.

And Mum said: You should have told me about the business, Reuven.

And Dad said: I should have done a lot of things. But what's the point of talking about what's over? What good will it do?

And Mum said (I could already feel them start to fight): Look, you're doing it again. You're not willing to talk about anything.

Dad took a deep breath (I felt the bed go up and down with it) – and didn't answer her.

Mum didn't say anything either. I felt how – very slowly – the fight that was hovering right over my bed went out of the room.

After a while, Dad said: You know, he's right. We really have to try and go back to the things we used to do. Then he cleared his throat and said: Like going out on trips. Or dancing.

Mum sighed and said: I can't. Every place reminds me of him. Tel Aviv because of the sea, and the Dead Sea because of the time he opened his eyes in the water, and the Carmel because of the pitta and *labaneh*, remember?

And Dad said: He ate the whole thing in three bites.

And Mum said: So how? How can I go there? I'll choke the minute we pass Zichron Ya'acov. If I manage to keep breathing till we get to Zichron, then there's that military cemetery at the entrance to Haifa, and on the way to the mountain there are three or four monuments in memory of children killed in road accidents or terrorist attacks. It's like that everywhere in this country. Everything's full of death, of things that remind you.

Yes, Dad said and sighed. Then they were both quiet. My neck itched, but I forced myself not to scratch it, so they wouldn't know I was awake.

So let's leave, Dad finally said, and the bed squeaked on his side.

I knew right away what he meant, and I think Mum did too, but she still asked: What do you mean?

And Dad said: We'll leave the country. I'll sell my part of the business. We'll sell the house. And go.

And Mum said: What? To another country? To live? Are you mad? Just what country did you have in mind?

The bed squeaked again on Dad's side. He said: I don't know. There are all kinds of possibilities. I haven't thought it out yet. Maybe we could go to your sister in Australia.

And Mum said in a too-loud voice: My sister? What are you talking about? She didn't say anything else. The bed squeaked on my mother's side now. And a few seconds later, in a voice that was both surprised and angry, she said: Have you been walking around a long time with this idea in your head?

And Dad said: A week, two. And I'm not 'walking around with this idea.' It just crossed my mind a few times.

And Mum said: But why didn't you say anything to me?

And Dad said: I'm telling you that I myself didn't . . . That it's just . . . And besides, I was afraid you'd get upset. I was afraid you'd say that I want to run away, that I *am* running away.

And Mum said: I would never say such a thing. Besides, when did you become such a coward?

And Dad said: It's not that . . . But . . .

And they were both quiet.

Then Mum said, quietly: It's too bad you didn't tell me, Reuven. It's too bad you always keep everything to yourself.

And Dad said: So now I've told you.

Mum shifted a little on the bed and said: Yes, now (and from the way she said it, it was clear that now wasn't good enough any more). Then she was quiet again. A few seconds later, she said: What are you talking about. Absolutely not. Did you stop to think that it means dragging Yotam to a foreign country? And it's not like everything will disappear if we get up and go, Reuven. It's not that the minute we land in Australia, everything will be fine. Because if that's what you think will happen, then forget it. With me, that lump is inside. Do you understand? Inside my body.

And Dad said: It's in mine too, but . . . Then he gave a little cough, the kind that comes before an attack.

And Mum said. I don't know, and gave the mattress a small smack. I don't think it'll work. That kind of hocus pocus. Australia. What will we do in Australia? And we have to talk to Miriam too. Did you even think about that? Who says they're ready for this?

I wanted to say: Don't you think that before you talk to Miriam, you should talk to *me*?! Maybe *I* don't want to go? Maybe *I'm* not ready for this? But I couldn't just include myself in the conversation after pretending to be asleep the whole time. So I just let out a kind of croak, like a nervous dog.

And Mum said: We're disturbing his sleep.

And Dad said: Yes. Maybe we should go to the living room.

Mum leaned over – I could smell her breath – and gave me a kiss on the forehead.

Then there were steps. Four feet walking. The door creaked, then closed. I waited a few more seconds, just to be sure, and opened my eyes in the dark.

*

I saw him in the street, slipping a ticket under a windscreen wiper and then typing something on the machine hanging around his neck. What grabbed me, I think, was the hair. Lovely, soft white hair, the kind old people have, even though he was young. Excuse me, I said, going up to him, and he, used to people attacking him, started defending himself right away: I'm sorry, miss, I can't do anything now. After the machine prints out a ticket, you can't cancel it. Write a letter to the council if you want, maybe they'll cancel it for you. But that's not my car, I said, and he looked me in the eye for the first time and said in surprise, not your car? So what ... What do you want from me? I wanted – I said and delayed the rest of the sentence, enjoying his suspense, and my own – I wanted to ask if I could take a picture of you. Of me?! he said, and smoothed down his white hair with a quick, almost invisible movement. Yes, of you. I'm sorry, he said, looking at my camera with interest, we're not allowed to have our pictures in the newspaper. There's an order from the unit manager saying we can't have our pictures taken for the newspaper or TV without permission. But it's not for a newspaper, I explained. Then what is it for? It's a project that I'm doing for college, and I thought I'd take your picture as part of the project. My picture? Why mine?! I don't know, it's hard to explain. I just have a feeling it would fit. What are you studying? Photography. Is that a profession, photography? I thought it was a hobby. Not exactly. Some people actually make their living from it. Ah, he said, a new light flashing in his eyes, you get paid money for this project? No, it's a project I have to hand in. I get a grade for it, not money. No money?! he said, his shoulders drooping in disappointment, so why should I let you take my picture? Look, I said, taking a quick look at the ticket sitting on the windscreen behind him, they say that if a person does one good deed a day, it makes up for ten bad deeds. Is that what they say?! he said, half surprised and half jesting, and looked at the ticket too. Yes, I said. And it would really help me if you let me take your picture. He studied my face for a few seconds, then said, you know what? OK. That's great, I said happily, thank you very much. You're welcome, he said, tucked his shirt into his trousers and leaned on the car, posing like a model. Just a second, I said. Before we take the picture, I have to ask you a few questions. Go ahead, he said, hooking his thumbs in his belt.

What's your name?

Kobi, Kobi Goldman.

How old are you?

Thirty-nine.

How long have you been a parking attendant?

Six months. Ever since I got fired from Tevel, the cable TV company. I worked in the stockroom there.

Do you miss working at Tevel?

Miss it? I wouldn't say that. Did you ever work in a stockroom? You know what it's like not to see the light of day from seven in the morning until seven in the evening?

So what do you miss?

In the stockroom, or in general?

In general.

Is this question connected to your project?

Yeah, it is. It's all connected to the project.

So what can I tell you. In general, I'm a person who tries to look ahead in life. Not back. How will missing things help? You can't change what happened.

But even so?

Kobi the parking attendant scratched his chin, then stroked his cheek with one finger, as if there were stubble on it, even though there wasn't, and finally put his hand on his chest the way you put your hand on the Bible in court and swear to tell the truth, the whole truth and nothing but the truth.

So? I said, urging him a little.

I once had a dog, he said.

What was its name?

Snow, he said, pronouncing the name gently, as if the dog were right beside him, and the first signs of longing began to appear on his face: swollen cheeks, moist eyes.

I called her Snow because she was completely white. She was the most beautiful dog you've ever seen in your life. The kind of dog they put in ads. And she was so good-natured. If I came home from the stockroom feeling down, she'd sense it and start to lick my face.

What happened to her? I asked, and Kobi showed another sign of longing: his shoulders drooped.

We lost her, he said quietly, and his right hand clenched into a fist. My wife went out to walk her in the grove of trees near the house and came back without her.

From his tone, I could tell that he thought if he'd gone out to walk her, it wouldn't have happened.

We did everything to find her, he went on. We put notices on trees. We went looking for her at night. I even called that woman who has that all-night radio programme and asked her to announce that we'd give a reward to the finder.

And nothing helped?

Nothing. Someone must have dragged her into his van and sold her for a lot of money. She was pedigree, with papers.

And you didn't want another dog?

Are you crazy?! Kobi said angrily, as if I'd parked in a handicapped spot and would have to pay a huge fine. How could we, after such a thing happened?

You're right, I agreed quickly, so he wouldn't get really angry and walk off. And . . . Tell me, do you have anything left of Snow's, a memento?

I have a few pictures at home, he said, pulling a bunch of keys out of his pocket. And I have her tag.

He separated the tag from the rest of the keys and handed it to me. It had the Tel Aviv/Jaffa logo on it, along with a small drawing of a dog and a serial number. If it had been a little larger, it would have been perfect. But the way it was, I'd have to close the frame to get him and the tag in it. And a closed frame wouldn't be right for the feeling.

A tall guy with a short dog turned into the street. Ordinarily, I wouldn't have had the nerve to walk up to a total stranger, but when I take pictures, I become shameless. Wait a second, I asked the parking attendant. I don't have all day, miss, he protested, but his tone was more complaining than angry. I ran over to the tall guy, ignored his dog's barking, smiled my number two smile and asked if I could borrow his leash just for a minute. With the leash in my hand, I ran back to the parking attendant and asked him to hold it. How, like I'm walking a dog? he asked, and I grabbed my camera and said, however you want. Hold it any way you feel like. He moved to the right a little and wound the leash around his neck, like a scarf.

Is that what you used to do with the leash when you walked Snow? I asked.

Yes, he said, and gave a small, nostalgic smile.

I clicked the shutter. That was exactly the smile I'd been hoping for.

*

I hope you realise that this will influence the reference I give you, Nava said. You can't just disappear for a month and expect it to go unnoticed.

I never thought it would, I replied, looking at the picture on the calendar hanging behind her – two tiger cubs fighting playfully.

Do you have other people to give you references? she asked, and before I could answer, she continued: because if you do, you should probably go to them instead of coming to me.

It's OK, I reassured her: for the time being, I'm not planning to register for a Master's.

You're not?!! she cried, as if such a thing – someone who wasn't dying to be a psychologist – were impossible.

No, I repeated, stretching my legs comfortably. That was the first time I'd spoken my decision out loud, and I liked the sound of it.

But why, Nava said, surprising me by removing the black ponytail band that held her hair, why, if I may ask?

Lots of reasons.

It would be a shame if it's because of what happened in your crossword puzzle group. Things like that happen, and with time and experience, we learn how to handle them. How to set limits.

I raised an inner eyebrow – am I imagining it, or did this woman just show some real caring for me? I looked at her and thought that with her hair loose, she actually looked nice. She felt my eyes on her and pulled her hair back into a ponytail again. That's just it, I said. I don't think I can set limits. How can I explain it to you . . . Did you ever have a talk with Shmuel?

Nava nodded.

He probably told you that he didn't have a protective layer of skin, I said, and that's why he feels everyone's unhappiness penetrating his body, and when he told you that, you obviously thought he was crazy, that he was talking nonsense. But here's the thing: I'm just like him. I feel other people, especially their inner pain, at full volume. And I'm not sure I want to turn that into a profession. It makes my personal life complicated enough as it is.

I understand, Nava said, and unlike the hundreds of time she'd said 'I understand' before, this time it felt real. So I raised the barrier and told her some even more secret things: that I was sick of the sensitive psychologist image I'd been selling to the public for so long that I'd forgotten it was just an image; that I wanted to talk, not just to listen; that since the time I was a child, I've always listened, taken an interest, learned how everyone behaved, and then I talked, and I was sick of that, sick of trying to make myself fit in because I was the new kid in the building, in the neighbourhood, at school; I was sick of keeping all my thoughts to myself because it was too dangerous to expose my true, ugly, jealous, nervous self, the one only my family knew, the one Noa had begun scratching the silver coating off and maybe that's why, that's why . . .

That's why what? Nava asked.

Never mind, I said. And thought: enough. You've opened up too much already.

So what you're really saying, Nava said, is that you want to remove yourself from playing the role of a psychologist and keep yourself out of it permanently.

Yes, I admitted. Even though I hate it when people mirror me.

Are you sure that's the real reason you don't want to continue studying?

You know, I shot back at her, that's exactly what annoys me, your thinking that there's another, truer reason and you have to guide me to it. I'm not sure that there are absolute reasons for things. For me, the lines between right and wrong are very thin. Sometimes, only an asterisk separates them. And the really important things that happen between people are hidden and can't be broken down into words. So how can I pretend to tell people what's good and what's bad?

That's not exactly what psychologists do, Nava said, and the muscle in her cheek trembled slightly, a sign that she wanted to say even harsher things. But let's leave that for a minute. There's something else I don't understand: why is it so important to you to come back to the club if you don't plan to stay in the field anyway?

Why? I said, feeling my anger spray her with the most naked words I had inside me. Why?! Because for once in my life, I want to say goodbye the right way. You don't know me. I'm one of those people you're about to end a phone conversation with and before you can say bye, they've already hung up. Enough. I want to stop being like that. I have unfinished business here and I want to finish it slowly, gently.

OK, I have to think about it, Nava said, stealing a quick glance at the pile of papers on her desk. A very crooked paper clip sat on top of the pile.

Will you let me know? I asked, clutching the edges of the chair.

Yes, she said, writing something on a piece of coloured

notepaper, probably my name. Then, just when I expected her to look pointedly at her watch or shift restlessly in her chair, she leaned back and spread her arms to the sides as if she had all the time in the world, as if now conditions were ripe for a simple conversation between two ordinary people who didn't have the threat of a reference hanging between them, a conversation on a subject not related to the club or to psychology, let's say a conversation about the mating habits of tigers, or the kind of music she likes. I almost asked her, but in the end I didn't say anything and let the waves of loneliness she was suddenly emitting break on my skin, and her eyes roam the wall behind me. I have to tell Noa about this moment, I thought, I have to describe every little detail of it to her. Including the colour of the ponytail band, because Noa was the only person who'd been with me through all my previous Nava moments and she was the only one in the world who could understand what's so weird here, so absurd.

A few days later, Nava called and told me that it was frowned upon, but OK, if it was so important to me, and I went down the stairs to the shelter with a new rolled-up crossword puzzle under my arm. My heart was pounding and I kept rubbing my cheeks to make sure I'd shaved. For the last few days, I'd envisioned the scene dozens of times, with a new scenario each time. But the only thing that never appeared in any of them was the possibility that no one would pay attention to me when I came in.

The draughts players kept looking at their boards. Mordechai kept showing his football album to some woman I didn't know. Ronen and Chanit were sitting very close together, as if they were about to kiss. And Shmuel, my Shmuel, was staring at the wall.

I went over to the coffee corner and made myself some tea. It was too hot for tea, but I wanted to look busy. When I finished stirring the sugar, someone tapped me on the back. I turned around. Amatzia the vacillator was standing in front of me. He wanted to say something, but the words didn't come out. I waited. Tell me, he finally said, scratching his chin, aren't you the student with the crossword puzzles? Of course not, he answered himself before I could say anything, you can't be. That one was ... But maybe you are. That one looked pretty much like you, but a little taller. No, he was actually the same height. Almost.

That's enough, Amatzia, don't make him crazy, Joe said, coming up to us and extending his hand to me. How are you, Amir? You disappeared on us. We were starting to get worried that the Security Services had kidnapped you. No, don't be silly, I said, shaking hands with him and Malka and Mordechai and Haim and Ronen and Chanit. Suddenly the whole club was gathered around me, as if they'd been waiting for Amatzia to take the first step. Malka asked, where have you been for so long? I was ill, I said, and Joe said, it's too bad you didn't consult us. We're experts when it comes to medicines, and everyone laughed, including Nava, who was standing off to the side observing. Then Amatzia said, so did you bring us a new puzzle? quickly adding, we're tired of puzzles. Actually, we did miss them a little, but what's the point, what good does it do us to solve crossword puzzles? Even though it's fun, it's really fun, even though it's a bit stupid. I said, yes, Amatzia, I brought a whole new puzzle and we'll start working on it together in a few minutes. Everyone's invited, even the ones who weren't part of the crossword puzzle group before, I said loudly, looking over at Shmuel in the hope that he'd get the hint. But all he did was take off his glasses and start cleaning them.

After the puzzle was solved and all the members of the group applauded and made me promise not to be ill again, because they're crazy about crossword puzzles, I took it off the wall, put a rubber band around it and stood it on its side. Then, empty-handed, I went over to Shmuel.

Hello, I said, sitting down next to him.

He didn't answer.

Shmuel, I said, trying again. It's me, Amir. Don't you remember me?

He didn't answer.

Shmuel, come on, I said, sounding as if I were pleading, don't you remember that we used to talk? You told me about your theories. About how the world is divided into three colours . . .

Red, white and transparent, Shmuel continued my sentence and I breathed a sigh of relief without breathing. The red, he said, always wants to go to the extremes, to eat a red apple from the tree of knowledge or a white apple from the tree of life. And God won't allow that. God is transparent. God is the middle road.

He kept talking, telling me about the three junctions of pain at which God revealed himself to him, and I nodded attentively, even though I'd already heard it all, in exactly the same words. A sweet sense of submission seeped into me with every word he spoke. He didn't remember that he'd already told me. He probably didn't even remember who I was. What's the point of talking to him if he doesn't remember anything afterwards? What's the point of this whole club if it doesn't improve the members' conditions by a single millimetre?

Shmuel had reached the second junction, at which God had appeared to him as a dog, and I leaned back in my chair and looked around at what was going on in the room. Joe was playing draughts with Malka. And winning, as usual. His eyes darted in all directions, as usual, to make sure no one had come to kidnap him. Amatzia started to climb the steps to go outside, then stopped and came back down. And went up again. And came down. Mordechai was showing his football album to Nava, who had undoubtedly seen it a thousand times, but still she smiled, occasionally pointing to a picture and asking about it. And he answered. His voice mingled with hers, and with Shmuel's, and they mingled with the cigarette smoke and the steam coming from the kettle, with the drawings that dripped from the walls, and very slowly I began to feel how the line that separated me from them and had disappeared so that I'd thought it didn't exist, took shape inside me again. It was long and thick, and the fear that had seized me the last time I was here, the fear that I'd go back to the bad, shaky times of basic training, slowly faded and almost vanished.

Shmuel went on to the third junction and started telling me how he'd stood in front of the picture of the girl in that museum in Herzliya and felt God appear before him from a spot in the middle of her forehead. Feeling a pleasant tiredness spread through my body, I closed my eyes and thought: there's something about all this that makes a person feel sane.

And then I thought: where is Noa now? And what will I do with all these thoughts I'm so used to sharing with her?

*

How often I imagined this moment. How much I wished for it and prayed for it and ached for it, and here they finally are, all the prints, hanging next to each other on the wall in Aunt Ruthie's apartment: my mother in the centre, holding the letter from her beloved (in the end, I decided that was more interesting than a scarf), and on the right, the guy from the balcony wearing a shirt showing the dates of Nirvana's last performances, which never took place. On the left is Suzanna, the new immigrant I found through the Association of Argentinian Immigrants, sitting in a white plastic chair on the promenade. A row below them is Kobi Goldman, the parking attendant and Orna Gad, the archaeologist, and Akram Marnayeh, an Arab I posed standing in front of a gate to a house in Jaffa holding a big, rusty key. And in the third and last row, three people who aren't holding anything. One is a young poet, Lior Sternberg, who I saw give a reading of his poems on television and thought he had a longing face. The second one is the singer Etti Ankri taken from the back so you can't see who she is. And the third one is me standing next to Aunt Ruthie's painting, 'Girl'.

I move closer to the wall, then back. I walk to the right and then to the left. It looks perfect from every angle. Everything is perfect. The composition of each picture separately. The way the pictures converse with one another. Especially the ones of me and my mother. The lighting. The background. The variety of backgrounds. Even the light-coloured frames I'd chosen, and at first thought were a mistake, looked right now.

So why doesn't it do anything to me? I think, flopping on to the sofa. Why do I feel so dried up? Why can't I think about anything but the fact that Amir hasn't seen the project?

*

So Yotam, is this how you hide things from me? Amir asked, moving his bishop, and I thought: how does he know? Then he said, after all we've been through together, I have to hear from Doga that you're moving away? He smiled to show that he wasn't really cross. I moved my king back one square and said, you're right. Every time I planned to tell you, it just never came out. Don't worry, Amir said and moved his castle one square forward. The main thing is, how do you feel about it? Do you want to move to another country? And when is it actually going to happen? Really soon, I said, answering the easiest question, and blocked his castle with one of my pawns. My mum and I are going to Aunt Miriam's in Sydney in two weeks to look for a school for me, and Dad is staying here a while longer to close down his business, sell the house and put the furniture in storage. And . . .? Amir said, jumping his knight forward, do you want to go? Are you happy about it? What difference does it make, I said, moving my king back one square to get away, no one ever asks me anyway. My mother and father sat down in the living room, turned off the TV while I was in the middle of watching *Star Trek* and told me they'd been thinking about it a lot and that it would be best for all of us. I told them they didn't know what was best for me, but they said I was too young to decide and I had to trust them. So I asked how I was supposed to talk to the kids there, because I don't know English, and they just laughed and said that was silly because I'm such a fast learner that I'd know the whole dictionary in a month. Well, they're right about that, Amir said and captured my knight with his bishop. How do you know, I said, and captured his bishop with my pawn (why all these exchanges, I thought. What's he planning?). First of all, Amir said, moving his castle one square to the right, you really are a fast learner. Look at how quickly you learned chess. And secondly, my parents also took me to Australia when I was a kid and I remember that it didn't take me long to learn the language. You were in Australia too? I said, surprised, and captured his castle with mine. I had the feeling that he was setting a trap for me, but I captured it anyway. Yes, Australia too, Amir said, laughing and moving his queen, who'd been waiting quietly until that moment, to the far corner of the board and said, check. From that minute on, we stopped talking. My king was in danger and I had to protect him, no matter what. Amir attacked and attacked, and I found a way of rebuffing his pieces every time: I sacrificed a bishop and a castle and even four pawns so my king wouldn't fall. I kept waiting for him to make a stupid mistake that would turn the game around, but he didn't make even one. In the end, after my queen went, I had no choice and I surrendered. I hate losing, most of all in chess, but Amir didn't leave me with the bitter taste of defeat for too long. He went to the kitchen and came back with two glasses of lemonade and said, nice of you to let me win before you go off to Australia. And I said, what are you talking about, I never let you win. I know, he said, of course.

All I have to do is see how you sweat during the game to know that. I took a big gulp of lemonade and asked, so how was it in Australia? Very nice, Amir said. It's a calm, quiet country. The people are nice, much nicer than the Americans. No terrorist attacks. No wars. Lots of nature. But they have all the mod cons: fast motorways, giant shopping centres, computer games. Wow, I said. It sounds cool. Yes, Amir said, I've been to a lot of countries, and it's one of the best.

So maybe you'll come with us? I said suddenly. I hadn't planned to say it. I hadn't built it, move by move, the way you build a trap in chess. The words just flew out of my mouth, but the minute they reached my ears, I thought: what a great idea! Amir doesn't go to the club any more anyway. He'll be finished with his exams soon. And how long can he sit here and wait for Noa? Yes, I thought excitedly, he should come with us. I was already picturing us walking together in the streets of Sydney, and suddenly that city didn't seem so scary any more.

I'd love to go with you, Amir said, but . . .

But what?! Why not?! I blurted out, picturing us sitting next to each other on the plane, going together to games of the Australian football league . . .

First of all, Amir said in the voice of someone who couldn't be persuaded, I think you and your parents have a lot of lost time to make up for, and I don't think anyone should stick himself in the middle.

But you wouldn't be doing that! I yelled, and inside, I felt just like I did before, when we were playing: that no matter what I did now, my king would fall in the end.

And anyway, Amir said, I've done enough wandering. I'm tired of it. I promised myself that this time I'd stay and wait for Noa.

What if she doesn't come back? I asked.

If she doesn't, Amir said, then she doesn't. But whatever happens, you and I won't stop being friends.

And just how will we do that? I asked. Amir was quiet for a minute, the way grown-ups are quiet after they promise a kid something just to shut him up, and the kid picks up on it.

*

I can imagine Amir walking in front of the pictures, his hands behind his back, quiet at first, smiling at my mother's picture – which really did come out a little funny – recognising Etti Ankri right away (he adores her), wondering where I dug up that parking attendant, lingering a while in front of my portrait, then turning around and saying: horrible.

Really? I ask him in my imagination, and he answers, are you joking, Noa? It's huge. It's the strongest work you've ever done. The most perfect. You can see in every frame that you spent hours on it. That's true, I say, straightening my shoulders, I really did invest time, but it can't be that you don't have any comments. Listen, he says, looking at everything again, if you force yourself to look for it, you can always find something. What? I press him, knowing that's his code for 'I have some criticisms.' The arrangement, he says, hitting my G-spot of fears right on the nose. That matrix, three by three, is more suitable for a TV game show than for a project about longing. Why, I ask, arguing with him in my mind, defending my arrangement with my life, but knowing very well that he's right and that very soon, my claims will die.

God. I'd like him to be here for real. Not just in my imagination. I'd like him to see the corrected arrangement. To hug me. To kiss me on the neck. On the mouth.

But what if he doesn't want to?

I remember that American writer, the one who said in an interview that he finds it difficult to write when his wife is in the house, so he goes off to the woods by himself for three months every year. Later on in the interview, which appeared at the end of the supplement along with the continuations of other interviews, the journalist asked who he gives the manuscript to when he's finished, who is actually his first reader. My wife, he answered without hesitation, and I thought then, when I read the interview, it can't be. Why does she agree? After he left her alone with the kids for three months, how could she bring herself to sit with his pile of papers and read with an open heart, as if she weren't angry?

*

Angry with her? Of course I'm angry with her, I said to David. OK, I understand that she had to breathe, so did I, and the truth is, I was pretty glad to have a break. But what's the big drama about picking up a phone? Why does everything with her have to be so dramatic? So extreme?

And what would you do if she called you now? David asked.

I have no idea, I said.

So there you go, David said, taking his guitar out of its case and starting to tune it. Every conversation with him reaches the point where words get tired and let music take over.

A new Licorice song? I asked.

No, he said. An instrumental segment. We're thinking about opening the album with it. Tell me what you think.

I closed my eyes. The first sounds began. I leaned back into the sofa and let my thoughts drop away, drop away, until only pure emotion was left in my body. I couldn't give the emotion a name. And I didn't want to. All I wanted was to ride on it for as long as it continued. The sounds twisted along like a narrow path that goes up and down a mountain, in and out of houses, through people, and every time you think it's ending, it starts all over again. I rode on that path, I rode with my eyes closed and my hands spread to the sides. Rustling branches caressed me and birds landed on my shoulders. Leaves kept falling, falling, falling, tickling my ears. The wind whistled around me and spiralled me up towards the sheep-shaped clouds, setting me down gently, gently on the roof of an unfamiliar house.

You're the king, David, I said when the last sounds finally broke away from the air.

Really? You liked it? he asked. Those artists – leaves in the wind.

Very much, I said.

We still don't have a name for it, David said, putting down his guitar. Got any ideas?

You could call it . . . osmosis, I suggested.

Too heavy, he said, rejecting the suggestion out of hand.

*

The yellow peppers arrived in Tel Aviv. Late, of course. After I'd finished my project, of course. But it doesn't matter. Today, I came back from the beach via Neveh Tzedek and on the corner of Piness and Shabazi I felt tingles of excitement creeping up my spine. Finally. The right combination of ugliness and beauty. Of happiness and pain. Of old and older. I strolled through the narrow streets, went into a different shop each time – jewellery, posters, beads, handbags. I didn't have my camera with me, so I didn't take any pictures, but it turns out that sometimes, unsatisfied desire is more intense. A FOR RENT sign on a house that had only columns, no walls and no roof. A click in my head. Luxury hotels rising up over a Yemenite synagogue. Click. A big fridge parked in a red-and-white no-parking zone. A flower sprouting from an iron gate. A sink on the street for washing your hands. A sign on a metal door, 'We Mend Angels' Broken Wings'. Click. Click. Click.

OK, sure you love Neveh Tzedek, it looks like Jerusalem, Amir said, scoffing at me in my mind. And I said to him, no, that's not true. But I knew he was a little bit right.

And he said, when are you coming back? The day before yesterday was three weeks.

And I said, I love you.

352

And he said, what does that have to do with it?

Meanwhile, without my noticing it, I'd walked out of the neighbourhood and was standing at the foot of the Shalom Tower.

I wonder if the tower sways when there's a strong wind, I thought, looking up until the sun blinded me. Then I thought, maybe on a clear day you can see Amir from the roof. Maybe you can follow his movements in the apartment. Going into the kitchen. The bedroom. Tidying up the living room. No. He doesn't actually tidy up the living room, because I'm not there so it doesn't need tidying up. But wait a minute. Who said he's alone? Who said he's waiting patiently for me. I wouldn't even give him my phone number. So why should he wait? Maybe now he feels the relief I felt the first few days and he thinks he'd be better off with someone else who won't be such a burden. Wait a second. Let's have a close-up. No. My pictures are still on the wall. He didn't take them down. When he goes over to the noticeboard he still sees the poem about the forbidden chocolate. Zoom out to the door. The sign with our names and the fish drawing is still there. Without being aware of it, we had suddenly made a home. Only now, during these last few weeks, did I realise how much of a home it was.

I always thought I was free as a bird. That a house was just four walls. And that because I was an artist, walls put limits on me. That when I was travelling in the East, I didn't miss my parents' house for even a minute. Just the opposite. Going away from them was always a little like escaping from prison. Like running in the fields after digging a tunnel under the barbed-wire fence. But now, suddenly, I want to go back. Suddenly there are millions of little things I miss. Say, watching Yotam and Amir play chess. Talking to Sima and feeling her energy fill me up. Watching *The X-Files* with Amir, both of us in the same armchair, hugging each other on Zakian's steps, having sex with him, burning in the sparks of his eyes, coming. Leaving the house with the smell of him on me. Coming home and hearing the squeak of his chair when he gets up to hug me. Talking to him before falling asleep, with only the words to light up the dark. Telling him that I heard noises and knowing that he'll get up to investigate. Ending his unfinished sentences. And making mistakes. Deliberately leaving a hairband on the rug and seeing it drive him crazy. Putting my finger on his lower lip and watching his twitch go away. Hearing a new Jeremy Kaplan song on the radio and arguing with him about whether it's good or bad. Asking him for a slice of his orange, then another slice, until he gives up and hands me the whole thing. Laughing at the words he makes up to describe people, like depressionistic about someone at school, or nymphulterous, about the girlfriend he had before me. Being sad or weak in front of him without being ashamed, or not wearing make-up in front of him without being ashamed. Talking to him in the middle of the day and feeling completely understood. Seeing myself through his eyes. Seeing him bent over his books. Hearing his little stories. Fighting with him, being jealous, making up. Feeling something.

And what about the poison? A man in a suit walking past me on the street bumped into me and brought me back to the world. Watch where you're going, I yelled after him, but he disappeared into the entrance of an office building. I started walking towards Nahalat Binyamin Street, making my way through the doubts. The minute you go back to him, the poison will start bubbling again. He hasn't turned into someone else in three weeks. He won't suddenly be crystalline and tough and happy. So why, damn it, should anything change? I don't know, I don't know, I answered myself and turned into Mazeh Street.

Pieces of white cloth with political slogans on them hung from a few balconies. All of them for the same candidate. Amazing, I thought. If you walk around Tel Aviv, you're sure that the Labour Party will win with a twenty-vote margin, and if you walk around Jerusalem, you think the Labour Party won't even get the minimum they need to be a real party. It's funny, I thought as I walked. Funny that there are elections now. Only six months ago, Rabin was still Prime Minister. Six months? That means that we moved to the Castel seven months ago. Seven months ago, we looked for an apartment and stumbled into the *shivah* for Yotam's brother by accident. It's incredible how many things were crammed into that short period of time. As if it were a story, not reality. The work I handed in, my tutors' put-downs, Yotam. Sima. Moshe. And Amir and me, getting so involved with each other without realising it, so involved that now it's so hard to be apart. Like conjoined twins who share a nerve, and if you separate them surgically, neither one will survive.

That's it, I thought, and looked up.

A group of people was gathering at the end of the block next to the nut and candy stand. They're probably watching a football match, I thought. But when I came closer, I saw a totally different kind of tension on their faces. What happened? I asked, and a man with a red peaked cap shushed me and pointed to the TV hanging from the ceiling of the store. In the middle of the screen was a map of central Jerusalem, and a yellow star shone at the junction of Jaffa and King George Streets.

Oh no.

I started running through the streets looking for a payphone. I have to know, I have to know that he's OK. I ran around trees, between couples. I skipped over holes, crossed a red light, fell down, got up, asked, ran in a different direction. There was no phone there. I choked, suffocated, ran past another group of people, another nut and candy stand. A hound of Baskerville barked, scaring me very badly, but I had no choice, I kept running. Please don't let anything happen to him now, please, please, not now. Finally I spotted a payphone on the corner of Carlebach and Hashmonaim Streets. I slowed down to a fast walk, got some air back into myself, took my phone card out of my bag and stuck it in the slot. Suddenly, because of all the pressure, I couldn't remember our number. I pictured the payphone at work, my fingers dialling the apartment. Six three nine five nine five. The call was disconnected. Idiot. You have to dial zero-two before the number. I dialled the whole number, saying to myself: I'll just hear his voice, just hear that nothing happened to him, and hang up.

*

I wanted to say thank you, Yotam's mother said and remained standing in the doorway.

Please come in, I said. She came in and stood in the middle of the living room. Are you in a hurry to go somewhere? I asked.

No, she apologised and sat down. It's just that there are so many things to take care of before we go.

It was all pretty sudden, wasn't it? I asked, lowering the volume of the CD player. Elvis Costello was probably not her cup of tea.

Yes, she said with a sigh. I don't know if we're doing the right thing. Maybe we'll feel worse there. But we can't stay here any more.

I understand.

Sometimes you make a change just to make a change, don't you?

Yes, I agreed, thinking about Noa in Tel Aviv, making a change. Tell me, I said, barely dragging myself away from my thoughts about Noa, have you found a school for Yotam yet?

No, she said. That's why we're leaving a week early. The school year starts in June. Because everything's upside down there, all the seasons. Yotam and I are leaving at the beginning of next week and Reuven will stay here another week or two to close his business and empty the house.

You mean you have buyers already?

Yes, a young couple with two children. Very nice people. He's an engineer and she's a teacher. I think you'll both get along with them very well.

I thought: who's 'both?' Do you see any 'both' here? And I said: so how's Yotam taking the whole thing?

He runs hot and cold. Sometimes he gets up in the morning and says he's not going with us and he doesn't care what happens. And sometimes, he asks me little questions, things he's curious about. As if we're just taking a trip. This whole year, he's been wanting to go on a trip.

Yes, I said, thinking that she still doesn't know I didn't open the door that Saturday.

And, she went on, he told me that he talked to you and you told him that Australia was a fun place.

Yes.

So that's why I came. To say thank you.

You're welcome, I said, moving uncomfortably on the sofa. Maybe some day I'll have the courage to stand with my chest exposed and let the compliments in. Meanwhile, I have a tendency to evade them, the way cowboys in films dodge bullets.

Really, Amir, thank you for everything, Yotam's mother said. You have no idea how important you were to him. He didn't stop talking about you all year. Amir this, Amir that. And last week, he had the idea that you'd come with us to Australia.

Yes, I heard about that idea, I said, smiling.

He loves you very much, you know.

I love him too, I said. And stopped for a second to celebrate that word, which is not spoken every day. He's a wonderful boy, I said. Sensitive. Full of ideas and imagination.

Yes, he is, his mother's nods said.

Besides, I said, trying out different words in my mouth before I found the least hurtful phrasing, I understand what it's like to be at home and feel alone.

You know, Yotam's mother said, ignoring my last remark, I think you'll be a really good psychologist.

Maybe, I said, again evading the compliment shot at me, but there's a good chance I won't be a psychologist at all.

Why not?

Oh, don't worry, it's complicated.

She didn't say anything and looked at the wall. Her eyes travelled around for a few seconds, then stuck on Noa's photographs from the East.

And what about . . . your girlfriend? she asked and immediately blushed. It's all right if I ask, isn't it?

Yes, I said. Of course it's all right. But I don't really have an answer. I hope she'll come back. I think she has to come back. But I'm not at all sure if and when it'll happen.

Tell me, Yotam's mother said, averting her eyes, did the girls I sent come here?

What girls?

With the food.

Aha, I said and laughed. Now the mystery is solved. You sent them.

Yes, she said, looking at me again. I thought you'd probably be hungry. I would have cooked for you myself, but I only started cooking again this week. I didn't have the strength before, you know.

Of course.

Was the food good?

Very good. I'm already addicted to *kubeh*.

And how were the girls?

The girls? I flashed up in my mind the parade of girls who'd been in the apartment during the last month. The girls were lovely. But you know, I'm still waiting for Noa.

Of course, yes, Yotam's mother said and smiled – unbelievably – a mischievous smile. It's amazing how a smile changes a person's face. A different woman suddenly showed through.

OK, she said, looking at her watch. I have to go back to packing.

I walked her to the door and before she left, we hugged. On both cheeks! she scolded me after I'd made do with only one kiss. Yotam will probably come to say goodbye himself, she said. I asked him to come with me, but he said he wanted to come alone.

He's right, I said, and she nodded and turned to go. I watched her until she disappeared past Moshe and Sima's house, and then I went back inside.

I paced around the house for a while, hands behind my back, like a professor who's finding it hard to solve a mathematical mystery. In a few more days, Yotam and his mother will leave, I thought. And Sima has been avoiding me ever since that almost-kiss of ours. The delicate threads that bound me to this neighbourhood are coming undone one by one. And I'm left unravelled. If Noa were here – I turned and started walking in the opposite direction – it wouldn't bother me. If Noa were with me, I'd even be ready to live in a neighbourhood of meditators. But the way it is now, I feel like the new kid in class.

Funny, I thought. I've looked at that picture a million times and always thought it's a bed in a hotel room in another country and that the man is looking out at the moon, feeling homesick. Now a different story suddenly popped into my head: the man is sitting in his own house. The house that *used* to be his. He's looking out with the hope that the woman who left him will return and give him back that feeling, because without her, that bed is just a bed like any hotel room bed. And the sheet is wrinkled from tiredness, not from lovemaking. And the four walls are just four walls, nothing more, and the door is a hole in the wall filled up with wood, and the roof is pitch black, and the armchair, the table, the chairs – they're all cold, dead pieces of furniture.

Only the phone is alive. A sudden ring. Filling the space with a strident sound. I pulled myself away from the picture and went over to it. I'm sick and tired of hoping it's Noa, I thought, and picked up the receiver.

*

Hi.

Hi.

Are you OK?

What happened?

A terrorist attack. On the number fourteen bus.

You know I don't take buses.

Still, I wanted to know that you're OK.

Wait, I'll turn on the TV.

Horrible, isn't it?

Yes, it is. But what's even more horrible is that it doesn't affect me any more.

Well, how much can a person take.

Yes, but what's happening to all that pain we don't let in? It doesn't really disappear.

Maybe it spills into the sea.

Like sewage?

Exactly.

Great. Only three weeks, and you already have a head full of Tel Aviv images.

I wish. I haven't found myself here.

So come back.

Will you take me back?

Eight dead. Of course I'll take you back. I wouldn't have said it otherwise.

Do you miss me?

No.

No?

Maybe a little. Did you know that Yotam and his parents are going to live in Australia?

What? When?

There's a story behind it. He ran away from home and they found him in some ruined shack in the wadi. To cut a long story short, they decided just like that to go to Australia. Yotam and his mother are leaving on Sunday. The father a little while later.

Wow. So if I want to say goodbye to him . . .

You should start packing.

Can you say that again?

Say what?

You should start packing.

Why?

Because I love your voice, Amir.

What else do you love about me? It's nine dead now, by the way.

That's a lot. Yesterday, I dreamed we were fucking in the Israel Museum.

The Israel Museum?

Yes. In the archaeology department. Where all the brown pottery is.

Interesting. I was sure you'd want to do it at your photography exhibition.

I didn't choose it, it was a dream. By the way, I finished the project.

What? So quickly?

I always knew that when the idea came, it would be finished in a week.

That's great. I'm really happy for you.

It's weird, I know. I was sure I'd be happy, but all I feel now is emptiness, maybe because you still haven't seen it.

I don't think that's it.

No, really. I have this strange feeling that things don't count until you see them.

So come.

But . . .

But what?

I read in some American self-help book I found in my aunt's library that missing someone is not a good enough reason to go back to them.

What do you mean? If missing them isn't enough, then what is?

The book says something like this – 'Longing is sweet. But if you don't want the going back to turn into the beginning of the next parting, there has to be a real change in the pattern of the relationship.'

That book is for Americans, right?

Come on, Amir, be serious.

I'm completely serious. I have a lot of new thoughts, but they're not for the phone.

What if I come back now, and in two weeks we both feel suffocated?

If we're true to ourselves, we won't feel suffocated. If each one of us dumps the fantasy he had about the other before we started living together, we have a chance. Besides, we're in the first-draft stage. We're allowed to make mistakes and fix them a lot more times.

You and your beautiful words.

I really feel that way. And besides, Yotam will be very happy if you come back. He kept complaining that it's no fun being with me since you left. And Sima is always asking about you.

I can't believe you're doing this to me. I swore to myself that I'd only call to hear if you're OK and then I'd hang up.

And I swore to myself that if you called, I'd be awful to you.

So what happened?

This thing between us must be very strong.

And maybe it's too strong? Maybe we can only do it from a distance?

Maybe. When are you coming?

Oof!

Why oof?

Soon.

Tell me when so I can mess up the house. So you'll feel comfortable.

Very funny.

It's time to hang up. I have to go out to sit on Sima and Moshe's steps.

The steps? Why, are you waiting for some girl?

*

When I heard Noa's quick steps, I smiled to myself in the dark and said, I knew it. I really hate people who say, I knew it, after everything's over, because how clever do you have to be to do that? But this time I really did know, I swear. Before Noa left, I only knew Amir through stories and dreams. And you can't really know anyone that way. Like Doron, Mirit's husband, before she brought him home, she told us the most amazing stories about him. How smart and responsible he is, and how you could always depend on him. But meeting him once was enough for me to see that he was one of those men who always needs a new girl to fall all over him or else he shrivels up. So what I'm saying is, it wasn't till I got to know Amir up close, after we went looking for Yotam together and he taught me about magnets, that I realised something about him and Noa: they're alike. I mean, not on the outside – even though they are a bit – but on the inside, as if they come from the same town. No, the same country, and they're the only two people who are citizens there. When I talked to him, there were times when I thought I was talking to her. It's not the words they use. It's the melody. Like their speech has the same melody. Take Moshe and me, we have the most different melodies in the world. Mine is happy and bouncy and a little nervous. His is slow and pleasant, like a ballad. I don't know if this melody example is a good one. But anyway, when Noa walked up the steps I caught my breath and tried to figure out what was happening from the noises I heard: were they hugging now? A long hug or a short one? And what about the kiss? A polite little one on the cheek or a long one with all the trimmings? They started walking down the path and I thought: he's probably leading her the way you lead a guest. And she's keeping her distance, so as not to bump into him. Now I hear them laughing. She must have bumped into him anyway.

I can't say I wasn't jealous when I heard their door open. And close right away.

I can't say I didn't imagine how embarrassed they'd be with each other at first, sitting down with a little distance between them on the sofa. Then she touches him while they're talking, and he touches her.

I can't say I didn't think I'd like to be in her place in another few minutes when he carries her piggyback into the bedroom.

But I didn't get up to listen through the hole in the wall. It wasn't burning inside me any more. It didn't give me a sour taste in my mouth. Those two, I thought, they're better off together than apart. Apart, each one gets lost. And besides, I thought, turning towards Moshe, I have my teddy bear. I stroked his cheek, and that stopped his snoring for a few seconds.

Maybe he snores, I thought, stroking his forehead. Maybe his religious brothers have too much influence over him. Maybe there are a lot of subjects you can't talk to him about. But I'm a big enough talker for both of us. And most of the time, I actually like him to be that way, kind of heavy, because it makes me feel light. And he's mad about me. He thinks I'm the cleverest, most beautiful woman in the world. When you're with someone who thinks that about you long enough, you start to believe it's true. And the children worship him. He has a lot more patience with them than I do. They can pester him and cry so their noses run all over him, and he couldn't care less. And there's something else: he would never leave them like my father left us. He can drive his bus to Eilat – but at the end of the day, I know I'll hear the brakes squealing, the beeping when he backs up, the sound of the doors closing, his heavy steps scraping the pavement, and then his leather bag dropping on to the floor, and the turn of his key in the lock, twice, and the little cough he always gives before he says – in a voice that sounds a little tired and a little excited – Simkush, I'm home.

*

Before I reached the door, I knew that Noa was back. Her shoes weren't outside and there were no girls' knickers hanging on the line, but I heard happy music coming from their house and I knew that Amir wouldn't play music like that if she hadn't come back because lately, he always put on heavy music, in English, and wouldn't change it even when I asked him to.

I knocked on the door and combed my hair back with my fingers, in her honour.

She opened the door, and before I could say hello, she pulled me over for a hug and right after that, she shook me by the shoulders and said, you came just in time. We're having a party. She made the music louder, tossed her hair from side to side, then grabbed my hand and twirled me around so that I passed under the bridge that our hands made. Amir danced alongside us, and I said to myself, if he's brave enough to dance like that, moving like a camel, then why shouldn't I, and I started dancing. At class parties, I'm always a wallflower and after Gidi died, I stopped going to those parties altogether; I mean, at first, I really did stop going and then later on I wanted to start going again, but they stopped inviting me and I'd started to think, that's it, I'll never learn how to dance. I had hoped that in Australia kids my age didn't have parties, but now, in Amir and Noa's apartment, with all the furniture pushed to the sides so it wouldn't get in the way, I suddenly felt I was a good dancer. The floor shook under our feet like a heart beating, and I waved my arms and danced the number eight around Noa and the number five around Amir for no real reason, just because I felt like it. I passed under the bridges they built and went through imaginary tunnels, all to the rhythm of the music, which was a kind of long song without words that never ended, never ended, never ended. Until it did.

You're going to break a lot of hearts, Yotam, Noa said after we flopped on to the sofa.

Yes, Yotam. You're terrific, Amir said.

I put on a modest expression, but inside I felt really puffed up.

You know, I'm very jealous of you, Noa said.

About what?

I always wanted to go to Australia.

Everyone who hears we're going says that. My English teacher. Dor's brother. I don't get it, what's so great about Australia, the kangaroos?

Maybe it's because Australia is as far away from here as can be, Amir said, and sighed the way you sigh when you drink a lot of water.

What's so bad about here? I wanted to ask, but I knew that was the kind of question grown-ups make a when-you-grow-up-you'll-understand face after you ask it, so I didn't.

So when are you leaving tomorrow? In the morning? The afternoon? Noa asked.

The flight's at eight-thirty in the morning. And we have to be there two and a half hours before. So we'll probably leave at five.

That means . . . we won't see you tomorrow, Amir said, and all of a sudden there was this kind of sad silence, like the silence there used to be before Noa left and came back.

Well, then . . . Amir said, bent over and pulled a football out from under the sofa, this is the time to give you your going-away present.

He threw me the ball.

I caught it.

And couldn't believe it.

On the white squares were the autographs of all the Beitar players. All of them. Ohana. Abucsis. Harazi. Kornfein. All of them.

How did you get this? I yelled. Noa laughed.

Beit Vegan, you know it? Amir said and gave a little smile.

Course I do! Our practice field!!

Avraham Levy, you know him?

Course I do, the Beitar manager.

That's the whole story, Amir said, his smile getting wider. I went there yesterday, told him a bit about you and asked him to get all his players to sign the ball.

I don't believe it, I said, running my fingers carefully over the ball. I was afraid I'd erase Ohana's autograph with my fingers.

Believe it, Amir said, then touched the ball and said: this is so you won't forget Jerusalem, even when you're on the other side of the world.

And this is so you won't forget us, Noa said and handed me a picture in a frame. It was a picture of me and Amir playing chess, with the empty lot in the background. At the bottom was written: To Yotam, our best friend in the Castel, from Noa and Amir.

Wow, this is great, I said and kissed Noa on the cheek, even though the truth was that, at that moment, I was more excited about the ball.

Then we all ate some Bamba peanut snacks from a huge bag and Amir and I played a last game of chess that ended in a stalemate. Then we put all the pieces back into the box, the black separately and the white separately. We did it really slowly to make it last longer, but finally all the pieces were inside and there was no choice, so I got up to go. They said, you can stay longer, and I said, no, I promised my mother to help her pack. I hugged and kissed and high-fived them goodbye at the door. Noa started crying and Amir put his arm around her shoulder. I said one last bye and walked away without looking back. But a few seconds later, I came back and knocked on the door again to take the framed picture I'd forgotten in all the excitement. They gave it to me and Amir laughed and said, go quickly before she starts crying again. He gave me one last hug, a man's hug, and closed the door again.

The sun was starting to set and I'd promised Mum I'd be home before it got dark, but I had one more thing to do. I walked slowly through the lot until I got to the monument. I put the framed picture down next to it and shoved a stone under the ball so it wouldn't roll down.

This is the last time I'll be visiting you here, I said to Gidi. Maybe I'll build a monument in Australia too. It depends on whether there's an empty lot there. I hope you're not cross with me for leaving, I said, and added three more stones to the monument. Two of them fell down and one stayed. Because I'm not cross with you any more and I'm not waiting any longer for you to surprise me and come back some day, or answer me when I talk to you. I know you can't. Anyway, Gidi, I hope you'll keep watching me from up there even when I'm in Australia. From heaven, it's the same distance, right?

The stones didn't move, and I got up. And picked up the picture. Then the ball. And I said goodbye to Gidi because 'see you later' didn't seem right, and then –

At first, I thought I was imagining it. Then I closed my eyes and opened them again.

A giant kangaroo was jumping around the lot, between the rocks, over the piles of rubbish. It wasn't a dog or a cat, but a real kangaroo, just like in the pictures Amir showed me in his album, with a long tail, enormous ears and a pouch. Sitting in the pouch was someone I didn't recognise at first because the kangaroo was too far away from me, but when it cleared the monument in one jump and came closer, I saw that it was my brother Gidi. Wearing a uniform that was almost the same colour as the kangaroo. Hi, I said, holding out my hand. Hi, he said, holding out his hand to me too and smiling with his eyes. But before we could do our regular handshake, with our fingers and everything, he and the kangaroo gave one more jump and moved away from me. I ran after them, but I didn't have a chance. They jumped all the way to the bottom of the lot, crossed the road and over Madmoni's brand new house in two springy jumps. I looked around to see if anyone else was watching, but the street was completely empty. They started jumping down in the direction of the wadi and I ran up to the highest spot in the empty lot, climbed up the pile of boards and from there I could see them jumping, hippity-hop, straight to the sun. I put my hand on my forehead to shade my eyes and watched them for another few minutes, jumping over bushes and huge rocks, getting smaller and smaller, smaller and smaller, until they disappeared, and so did the sun.

I went home and Mum was angry with me for being late, so I didn't tell her about the kangaroo because I didn't want her to think it was an excuse. Then we had to find a place in one of the suitcases for my new football and decide what to do with the old one, and the next day, we drove to the airport and then there was another kind of excitement.

*

It's a hot night in Maoz Ziyon. The air is still and it's hard to sleep in bed. Yotam's father is lying on the living room floor with a pillow under his head. Yotam and his mother flew to Australia on Sunday. He's the one left behind to turn off the lights before he goes on his way. He had a few ends to tie up at work. You know how those things are. And someone had to advertise and sell the car.

He'll put all the furniture on the street. A friend is supposed to come with a van and pick it up. Meanwhile, he'll wait there. Sit down on an armchair. Nibble at a pear. A neighbour will wash his car, a hose in his hand. He'll remember that when he was Yotam's age he used to watch the streams of water running off the cars to see which would be the first to land.

A woman whose bags he once carried from the shops will make her way between the sofas and smile at him as if she had something to say.

Another woman will stumble against the cabinet and grumble: you're blocking the way.

*

Madmoni has been blocking the pavement since yesterday. Trucks unloaded furniture for the new house – a table, a sofa, a sideboard. It's all sitting there on the street. And now he's trying to fall asleep, but can't because of the heat. And it's all so new. He hasn't got used to it yet, and the smell of paint is making him feel sick. His thoughts float in the space of the bedroom, wandering to and fro. And he suddenly remembers a picture taken many years ago. He found it today, in the garden in a hole in the ground. One of the Romanian workers must have left it behind, and now it had been found. It was a picture of a woman who was neither young nor old. Something between a girl-friend and a mother. Or maybe she was his sister and he was her brother. He looked at the picture for a while, then put it away in a drawer. But now, suddenly, the picture was keeping him from sleeping, and he couldn't ignore it any more. Maybe he should look for that Romanian and give the picture back. What did he need it for?

*

Angrily, Saddiq remembers the house he was building in el-Castel. Those bastards cut me off in the middle of my work and put me in a prison cell. I'm interested how the second floor came out, he says to Mustafa A'alem, who is teaching him Hebrew. Mustafa corrects him: *Curious*, not 'interested', is the right word, son. Then he pats Saddiq on the back and says: *Ili·fat, mat.* What's done is done. It's better to think of what the future will bring. Think about going back to el-Castel with the commandos to capture the land, the houses, everything. *Mazbut*, you're right, Saddiq says, because he can't think of anything better to say. But in his heart he's tired of the old man, of the prison, of hearing those speeches every day. Most of all, he misses his wife, Nehila. And he worries about his mother. And his children. At night he dreams about his grandmother Shadia's gold chain escaping from one of the brown bags in the confiscated goods department, passing by the guards, getting through the fence, floating above his head. Then it lands on his neck, caressing, choking, till he wakes up and sees that there is no chain in his bed.

Avram thinks about Saddiq every now and then, but he doesn't tell Gina so she won't worry that he's ill again. But she's known him for fifty years. When he gets out of bed and stands where Saddiq pulled the stone out of the wall, she knows he's thinking about Nissan and his heart is as bitter as gall. She tries to sweeten it with cheesecake she serves him on a gleaming white plate. He eats every last crumb, goes back to bed and says, *kapparokh*, Gina, that's the best cheesecake I've ever eaten.

Sima and Moshe aren't alone at night in their bed. First Liron crawls in, saying there's a mosquito in his room, buzzing round his head. Then Lilach finds her way into their bed too, but for her, that's nothing new. And now they're like a multi-limbed octopus: all the arms and legs of a mother, a father, a son and a daughter. Every once in a while, Sima gets up and brings a glass of water. Moshe drinks. She drinks. Even Liron puts the glass to his lips and takes a few sips. When everyone's finished, she slips under the cover and thinks: you have everything you ever wanted in life: you have a home full of love, you're a mother and a wife. So don't be a fool, Sima, what else do you need? Moshe strokes her hair and says to himself: thank God.

For a few weeks, he'd felt that it was only Sima's body he had, that her thoughts were elsewhere and it was all a façade. He'd begun to fear that she wanted to leave him for a man who was thinner and knew how to talk a lot. But he tried to be patient, telling himself, you don't want to lose what you've got. And in the end, his restraint paid off. She's finally back, this time with her whole heart. Or so it seems.

For Amir and Noa, the homecoming celebrations are over. And the daily, crushing march up the path of love has begun. They try to argue more and gloss over less. And every time the buzzing between them starts, they talk or dance to relieve the stress. There are nights, like this one, when restlessness seeps into the heart. And each on his own side of the bed is hatching a plot that will let them live apart. Are you sleeping? Noa asks, breaking the silence, and Amir admits that he hasn't shut an eye. So why don't you read me a story to make the time go by? OK, he says, getting up and going into the living room. He comes back with Modi's last letter, and she asks, are you sure it's OK? He wrote that letter to you. It's perfectly OK, Amir says, spreading the pages out on the bed. And Noa rubs her foot on his and reaches out to stroke his head. A minute before he begins to read, Amir gives her a kiss and she puts her hand between his legs, caressing and kneading. He turns the page over and says, sorry, but if you do that, I can't do any reading.

And someone looking at them now would say, in a year or two, they'll be married and having kids, you can bet on it. And someone else looking at them now would say, in a month or so those two will have definitely split.

*

Bro,

I'm going to use you. I'm telling you this right off so you won't get pissed off and wonder why the next few pages don't mention you or Noa or ask any questions about what's happening there. Forget it. The chances are that this letter won't get to you until after. In five hours, I'm taking a taxi to the San Juan airport, and in less than a day, I'll be in Tel Aviv. It'll be Friday there, if I'm not mistaken. And I promise that on Saturday, Sunday at the latest, I'll be at your place in the Castel with all the pictures and stories and bullshit of someone back from a long trip. But meanwhile, I need you to be my witness. To read all the promises I made to myself on this trip so that later it'll be harder for me to back out of them. I'm tired of making great decisions on trips and then when I'm home, feeling them slip through my fingers. This time I want all my resolutions to be documented in writing and I want you to read them and remember and hit me if you see me starting to squirm out of them.

Is that OK with you?

So let's get to it.

I want to start swimming. Don't laugh. I'm serious. Tennis is nice, but (a) there are more babes in the university swimming pool than on the tennis court, and (b) there's something about swimming that leaves you with more room in your soul. That gives you the natural rhythm of things. Besides, why am I apologising? A pool. Once a week. Write it down and shut up.

I also want to be less cynical. I've spent the last year with people from all over the world, and I'm telling you for a fact that the Israelis are the most cynical of all. And I'm sick and tired of it. I'm sick and tired of pretending that nothing turns me on just so I don't look pathetic. I'm sick and tired of shooting poisoned arrows at other people just because I'm afraid they'll hurt me. I want to come to people with an open heart. What's the worst that can happen?

I want to eat big breakfasts. Like on a holiday. With scrambled eggs and avocado salad and vegetable salad and black bread. I want to start the morning with an enormous breakfast and eat it leisurely, no stressing out.

I'm sick of being stressed out. I want to take my time so I can make my time. I want to work hard, but not like a maniac. The Europeans I met here work four days a week, go home at six and don't think there's anything wrong with that.

I want to watch less TV. I haven't watched any for six months, I don't miss it at all.

I want to live in nature. And if that's too complicated, then I want to at least leave Tel Aviv at weekends. I want to stand on the edge of something and see far into the distance, over the rainbow.

I want to get turned on by little things. Walking barefoot on the sand. Eating the cone after the ice-cream's gone. Colourful graffiti on a dirty wall. New music I never heard before. Not shaving. Shaving after a long time of not shaving and running my hand over my smooth cheek. I want to get turned on by all those little things. Not to let them pass me by without noticing them.

I want love. For too long now, I've been using my split from Adi as an excuse and now, after those two weeks with Nina, I know that I don't have to settle for kiss-fuck-we'll-talk-tomorrow-bye.

I want to read more. Ride my bike more. Get on better with my sister. I want to look people in the eye more. Speak the truth more.

And, besides, I want to go home.

The HEBREW LITERATURE SERIES at Dalkey Archive Press makes available major works of Hebrew-language literature in English translation. Featuring exceptional authors at the forefront of Hebrew letters, the series aims to introduce the rich intellectual and aesthetic diversity of contemporary Hebrew writing and culture to English-language readers.

This series is published in collaboration with the Institute for the Translation of Hebrew Literature, at www.ithl.org.il. Thanks are also due to the Office of Cultural Affairs at the Consulate General of Israel, NY, for their support.

ESHKOL NEVO was born in Jerusalem in 1971. He teaches creative writing at the Sam Spiegel Film and Television School, Tel Aviv University, Sapir College, and the Open University. He has published a collection of short stories, a book of nonfiction, and two novels, both of which have been bestsellers in Israel. In 2008, Nevo received the French Raymond Wallier Award.

SONDRA SILVERSTON has lived in Israel since 1970. Among her other translations is fiction by contemporary Israeli authors Etgar Keret, Savyon Liebrecht, and Aharon Megged.

PETROS ABATZOGLOU, *What Does Mrs. Freeman Want?*
MICHAL AJVAZ, *The Golden Age.*
The Other City.
PIERRE ALBERT-BIROT, *Grabinoulor.*
YUZ ALESHKOVSKY, *Kangaroo.*
FELIPE ALFAU, *Chromos.*
Locos.
IVAN ÂNGELO, *The Celebration.*
The Tower of Glass.
DAVID ANTIN, *Talking.*
ANTÓNIO LOBO ANTUNES, *Knowledge of Hell.*
ALAIN ARIAS-MISSON, *Theatre of Incest.*
JOHN ASHBERY AND JAMES SCHUYLER, *A Nest of Ninnies.*
HEIMRAD BÄCKER, *transcript.*
DJUNA BARNES, *Ladies Almanack.*
Ryder.
JOHN BARTH, *LETTERS.*
Sabbatical.
DONALD BARTHELME, *The King.*
Paradise.
SVETISLAV BASARA, *Chinese Letter.*
MARK BINELLI, *Sacco and Vanzetti Must Die!*
ANDREI BITOV, *Pushkin House.*
LOUIS PAUL BOON, *Chapel Road.*
My Little War.
Summer in Termuren.
ROGER BOYLAN, *Killoyle.*
IGNÁCIO DE LOYOLA BRANDÃO, *Anonymous Celebrity.*
Teeth under the Sun.
Zero.
BONNIE BREMSER, *Troia: Mexican Memoirs.*
CHRISTINE BROOKE-ROSE, *Amalgamemnon.*
BRIGID BROPHY, *In Transit.*
MEREDITH BROSNAN, *Mr. Dynamite.*
GERALD L. BRUNS, *Modern Poetry and the Idea of Language.*
EVGENY BUNIMOVICH AND J. KATES, EDS., *Contemporary Russian Poetry: An Anthology.*
GABRIELLE BURTON, *Heartbreak Hotel.*
MICHEL BUTOR, *Degrees.*
Mobile.
Portrait of the Artist as a Young Ape.
G. CABRERA INFANTE, *Infante's Inferno.*
Three Trapped Tigers.
JULIETA CAMPOS, *The Fear of Losing Eurydice.*
ANNE CARSON, *Eros the Bittersweet.*
CAMILO JOSÉ CELA, *Christ versus Arizona.*
The Family of Pascual Duarte.
The Hive.
LOUIS-FERDINAND CÉLINE, *Castle to Castle.*
Conversations with Professor Y.
London Bridge.
Normance.
North.
Rigadoon.
HUGO CHARTERIS, *The Tide Is Right.*
JEROME CHARYN, *The Tar Baby.*
MARC CHOLODENKO, *Mordechai Schamz.*

JOSHUA COHEN, *Witz.*
EMILY HOLMES COLEMAN, *The Shutter of Snow.*
ROBERT COOVER, *A Night at the Movies.*
STANLEY CRAWFORD, *Log of the S.S. The Mrs Unguentine.*
Some Instructions to My Wife.
ROBERT CREELEY, *Collected Prose.*
RENÉ CREVEL, *Putting My Foot in It.*
RALPH CUSACK, *Cadenza.*
SUSAN DAITCH, *L.C.*
Storytown.
NICHOLAS DELBANCO, *The Count of Concord.*
NIGEL DENNIS, *Cards of Identity.*
PETER DIMOCK, *A Short Rhetoric for Leaving the Family.*
ARIEL DORFMAN, *Konfidenz.*
COLEMAN DOWELL, *The Houses of Children.*
Island People.
Too Much Flesh and Jabez.
ARKADII DRAGOMOSHCHENKO, *Dust.*
RIKKI DUCORNET, *The Complete Butcher's Tales.*
The Fountains of Neptune.
The Jade Cabinet.
The One Marvelous Thing.
Phosphor in Dreamland.
The Stain.
The Word "Desire."
WILLIAM EASTLAKE, *The Bamboo Bed.*
Castle Keep.
Lyric of the Circle Heart.
JEAN ECHENOZ, *Chopin's Move.*
STANLEY ELKIN, *A Bad Man.*
Boswell: A Modern Comedy.
Criers and Kibitzers, Kibitzers and Criers.
The Dick Gibson Show.
The Franchiser.
George Mills.
The Living End.
The MacGuffin.
The Magic Kingdom.
Mrs. Ted Bliss.
The Rabbi of Lud.
Van Gogh's Room at Arles.
ANNIE ERNAUX, *Cleaned Out.*
LAUREN FAIRBANKS, *Muzzle Thyself.*
Sister Carrie.
LESLIE A. FIEDLER, *Love and Death in the American Novel.*
JUAN FILLOY, *Op Oloop.*
GUSTAVE FLAUBERT, *Bouvard and Pécuchet.*
KASS FLEISHER, *Talking out of School.*
FORD MADOX FORD, *The March of Literature.*
JON FOSSE, *Melancholy.*
MAX FRISCH, *I'm Not Stiller.*
Man in the Holocene.
CARLOS FUENTES, *Christopher Unborn.*
Distant Relations.
Terra Nostra.
Where the Air Is Clear.

SELECTED DALKEY ARCHIVE PAPERBACKS

STEVEN MILLHAUSER,
The Barnum Museum.
In the Penny Arcade.
RALPH J. MILLS, JR.,
Essays on Poetry.
MOMUS, *The Book of Jokes.*
CHRISTINE MONTALBETTI, *Western.*
OLIVE MOORE, *Spleen.*
NICHOLAS MOSLEY, *Accident.*
Assassins.
Catastrophe Practice.
Children of Darkness and Light.
Experience and Religion.
God's Hazard.
The Hesperides Tree.
Hopeful Monsters.
Imago Bird.
Impossible Object.
Inventing God.
Judith.
Look at the Dark.
Natalie Natalia.
Paradoxes of Peace.
Serpent.
Time at War.
The Uses of Slime Mould:
Essays of Four Decades.
WARREN MOTTE,
Fables of the Novel: French Fiction
since 1990.
Fiction Now: The French Novel in
the 21st Century.
Oulipo: A Primer of Potential
Literature.
YVES NAVARRE, *Our Share of Time.*
Sweet Tooth.
DOROTHY NELSON, *In Night's City.*
Tar and Feathers.
ESHKOL NEVO, *Homesick.*
WILFRIDO D. NOLLEDO,
But for the Lovers.
FLANN O'BRIEN,
At Swim-Two-Birds.
At War.
The Best of Myles.
The Dalkey Archive.
Further Cuttings.
The Hard Life.
The Poor Mouth.
The Third Policeman.
CLAUDE OLLIER, *The Mise-en-Scène.*
PATRIK OUŘEDNÍK, *Europeana.*
FERNANDO DEL PASO,
News from the Empire.
Palinuro of Mexico.
ROBERT PINGET, *The Inquisitory.*
Mahu or The Material.
Trio.
MANUEL PUIG,
Betrayed by Rita Hayworth.
The Buenos Aires Affair.
Heartbreak Tango.
RAYMOND QUENEAU, *The Last Days.*
Odile.
Pierrot Mon Ami.
Saint Glinglin.

ANN QUIN, *Berg.*
Passages.
Three.
Tripticks.
ISHMAEL REED,
The Free-Lance Pallbearers.
The Last Days of Louisiana Red.
Ishmael Reed: The Plays.
Reckless Eyeballing.
The Terrible Threes.
The Terrible Twos.
Yellow Back Radio Broke-Down.
JEAN RICARDOU, *Place Names.*
RAINER MARIA RILKE,
The Notebooks of Malte Laurids
Brigge.
JULIÁN RÍOS, *Larva: A Midsummer*
Night's Babel.
Poundemonium.
AUGUSTO ROA BASTOS, *I the Supreme.*
OLIVIER ROLIN, *Hotel Crystal.*
ALIX CLEO ROUBAUD, *Alix's Journal.*
JACQUES ROUBAUD, *The Form of a*
City Changes Faster, Alas, Than
the Human Heart.
The Great Fire of London.
Hortense in Exile.
Hortense Is Abducted.
The Loop.
The Plurality of Worlds of Lewis.
The Princess Hoppy.
Some Thing Black.
LEON S. ROUDIEZ,
French Fiction Revisited.
VEDRANA RUDAN, *Night.*
STIG SÆTERBAKKEN, *Siamese.*
LYDIE SALVAYRE, *The Company of Ghosts.*
Everyday Life.
The Lecture.
Portrait of the Writer as a
Domesticated Animal.
The Power of Flies.
LUIS RAFAEL SÁNCHEZ,
Macho Camacho's Beat.
SEVERO SARDUY, *Cobra & Maitreya.*
NATHALIE SARRAUTE,
Do You Hear Them?
Martereau.
The Planetarium.
ARNO SCHMIDT, *Collected Stories.*
Nobodaddy's Children.
CHRISTINE SCHUTT, *Nightwork.*
GAIL SCOTT, *My Paris.*
DAMION SEARLS, *What We Were Doing*
and Where We Were Going.
JUNE AKERS SEESE,
Is This What Other Women Feel Too?
What Waiting Really Means.
BERNARD SHARE, *Inish.*
Transit.
AURELIE SHEEHAN,
Jack Kerouac Is Pregnant.
VIKTOR SHKLOVSKY, *Knight's Move.*
A Sentimental Journey:
Memoirs 1917–1922.
Energy of Delusion: A Book on Plot.

SELECTED DALKEY ARCHIVE PAPERBACKS

Literature and Cinematography.
Theory of Prose.
Third Factory.
Zoo, or Letters Not about Love.
CLAUDE SIMON, *The Invitation.*
PIERRE SINIAC, *The Collaborators.*
JOSEF ŠKVORECKÝ, *The Engineer of Human Souls.*
GILBERT SORRENTINO,
  Aberration of Starlight.
  Blue Pastoral.
  Crystal Vision.
  Imaginative Qualities of Actual Things.
  Mulligan Stew.
  Pack of Lies.
  Red the Fiend.
  The Sky Changes.
  Something Said.
  Splendide-Hôtel.
  Steelwork.
  Under the Shadow.
W. M. SPACKMAN,
  The Complete Fiction.
ANDRZEJ STASIUK, *Fado.*
GERTRUDE STEIN,
  Lucy Church Amiably.
  The Making of Americans.
  A Novel of Thank You.
LARS SVENDSEN, *A Philosophy of Evil.*
PIOTR SZEWC, *Annihilation.*
GONÇALO M. TAVARES, *Jerusalem.*
LUCIAN DAN TEODOROVICI,
  Our Circus Presents . . .
STEFAN THEMERSON, *Hobson's Island.*
  The Mystery of the Sardine.
  Tom Harris.
JEAN-PHILIPPE TOUSSAINT,
  The Bathroom.
  Camera.
  Monsieur.
  Running Away.
  Self-Portrait Abroad.
  Television.
DUMITRU TSEPENEAG,
  The Necessary Marriage.
  Pigeon Post.
  Vain Art of the Fugue.
ESTHER TUSQUETS, *Stranded.*
DUBRAVKA UGRESIC,
  Lend Me Your Character.
  Thank You for Not Reading.
MATI UNT, *Brecht at Night*
  Diary of a Blood Donor.
  Things in the Night.
ÁLVARO URIBE AND OLIVIA SEARS, EDS.,
  Best of Contemporary Mexican Fiction.
ELOY URROZ, *The Obstacles.*
LUISA VALENZUELA, *He Who Searches.*
MARJA-LIISA VARTIO,
  The Parson's Widow.
PAUL VERHAEGHEN, *Omega Minor.*
BORIS VIAN, *Heartsnatcher.*
ORNELA VORPSI, *The Country Where No One Ever Dies.*
AUSTRYN WAINHOUSE, *Hedyphagetica.*

PAUL WEST,
  Words for a Deaf Daughter & Gala.
CURTIS WHITE,
  America's Magic Mountain.
  The Idea of Home.
  Memories of My Father Watching TV.
  Monstrous Possibility: An Invitation to Literary Politics.
  Requiem.
DIANE WILLIAMS, *Excitability: Selected Stories.*
  Romancer Erector.
DOUGLAS WOOLF, *Wall to Wall.*
  Ya! & John-Juan.
JAY WRIGHT, *Polynomials and Pollen.*
  The Presentable Art of Reading Absence.
PHILIP WYLIE, *Generation of Vipers.*
MARGUERITE YOUNG,
  Angel in the Forest.
  Miss MacIntosh, My Darling.
REYOUNG, *Unbabbling.*
ZORAN ŽIVKOVIĆ, *Hidden Camera.*
LOUIS ZUKOFSKY, *Collected Fiction.*
SCOTT ZWIREN, *God Head.*

FOR A FULL LIST OF PUBLICATIONS, VISIT:
www.dalkeyarchive.com